REAPING THE HARVEST

(HARVEST TRILOGY, BOOK 3)

Michael R. Hicks

This is a work of fiction. All of the characters, organizations and events portrayed in this novel are products of the author's imagination or are used fictitiously.

ISBN: 9780988932159
REAPING THE HARVEST (HARVEST TRILOGY, BOOK 3)

Published by Imperial Guard Publishing
AuthorMichaelHicks.com

ACKNOWLEDGMENTS

I'd like to thank the usual cast of shady characters who helped me get this book off the ground, starting with the editors who spattered the manuscript with red ink: Mindy Schwartz, Stephanie Hansen, and Frode Hauge. I have to give Frode an extra round of thanks for being especially rough on me this time and shaming me into doing more serious revisions than I would have done otherwise. The beta readers, those poor souls, also certainly deserve a round of applause, so please make some noise for Jodi, Robert, Arthur, Krissy, Jenn, and Eri.

I also want to thank to my dad, who's always been there for me, and was a huge help in figuring out some of the things that Naomi Perrault, the main heroine of the story, had to do (no spoilers!).

To my wife, Jan, my "alpha reader," thank you for believing in me, and for keeping me from wandering down blind alleys in the story line.

Last but not least, I'd like to thank you, dear reader, for your patronage and support. Your interest in reading my work has transformed my life.

FOREWORD

I wrote *Season Of The Harvest*, the first book of the *Harvest* trilogy, as sort of a parable about the potential dangers of the proliferation of genetically modified organisms, or GMOs, found in our food supply.

In late 2010, when I was writing the first draft of the book, the huge biotech companies developing and marketing GMO crops for annual multi-billion dollar profits seemed no less powerful and no more scrupulous than alien invaders bent on humanity's destruction. The biotech lobbyists owned both the White House and Congress, the government agencies responsible for food safety rubber stamped the safety evaluations that were produced by the companies that created the products, farmers were relentlessly harassed and sued for patent infringement if any GMO seed that they hadn't purchased sprouted in their fields, and American food labeling laws forbade manufacturers from informing consumers that the food they were eating contained GMOs.

But the times, as the old song by Bob Dylan goes, they are a-changin'. As I write this in late 2013, the tide here in the U.S., which lags behind much of the rest of the world in terms of consumer protection, is beginning to turn. Under pressure from a variety of organizations and individual citizens, a small but growing number of municipalities and states are seriously considering or have already implemented restrictions or bans on GMO crops. While the Federal Government hasn't put forth any changes in labeling laws, more and more food products bearing the label "GMO-free" (or something similar) are appearing on store shelves, joining their organic cousins. Best of all, a rapidly growing number of consumers are becoming more educated about their food, GMOs in particular, and making more informed choices about what they buy.

Looking beyond the United States, much of the European Union has either banned GMOs or put them under severe restrictions. Russia is considering a total GMO ban. A number of Asian countries, notably China, Japan, and Thailand, have restrictions on such foods, and GMOs are banned or restricted in a number of other countries, including Saudi Arabia, Algeria, Egypt, and Brazil. Most recently, and in a huge blow to the biotech industry, Mexico has banned Monsanto's GMO corn in the wake of a momentous court ruling.

These bans and restrictions bring me to a very important point that some readers and reviewers have pinged on in the past. I actually support *responsible* genetics research and product application. While my parable on GMOs is intended to get readers to think about the potential dangers, there are also many potential positive applications of this technology.

But the key word is *responsible*. In the United States, the government has abrogated its responsibilities to safeguard the food supply of its citizens. The biotech companies do the safety testing of their own products, then pass the positive (big surprise) results to the appropriate government agency (the Food and Drug Administration, in particular), which then approves it for sale and distribution. On top of that, a number of key officials in these agencies over the years have been former executives or employees of the biotech firms.

In short, GMO products in the United States do not receive a critical safety evaluation from an unbiased party before they appear on store shelves. This is compounded by the aforementioned labeling laws that prevent food manufacturers from telling consumers that a product contains GMOs. One of the rationales I've heard for this is that since nearly everything that isn't organic or labeled GMO-free contains GMOs, there's no point in labeling them. Tell me that's not self-serving logic.

While much is left to be done to harness this technology in a safe and responsible manner, I think we've reached, or are at least close to, the tipping point. Consumer pressure is working, with people voting with their wallets in grocery stores and advocacy groups forcing legislative changes in local and even state governments, despite millions of dollars in advertising by the biotech companies to defeat these campaigns. These changes aren't fast or easy, but they're working, and every little step counts.

Someday I hope that even Washington, D.C. will wake up and take notice.

AWAKENING

Jack Dawson blinked his eyes open. The world around him was white, blurry. A soft, rhythmic electronic beep kept time with his heartbeat, and there was a dull ache in his right arm, just below the crook of the elbow. He took in a ragged gasp of air, which smelled of alcohol and antiseptic, along with a sweeter smell. From the corner of his eye, he saw a bouquet of yellow and white flowers on a stand beside him.

A face leaned down. He didn't recognize her, but she had a familiar accent. "Mr. Dawson, can you hear me?"

He nodded. His tongue was a flap of dry leather that he had to pry from the roof of his mouth. "Where am I?"

She smiled. "You are in Bodø. Now hold still for a moment, please." She shone a pen light in each of his eyes, making him blink. "Very good. You had us worried for a little while." She looked up and said to a figure standing beside her, "He seems to be all right, but go easy. If you need me, I'll be right outside."

"Thank you," the other person said.

Jack recognized the voice. The man's face came closer, finally snapping into focus. "Terje?"

Terje Halvorsen, a *kaptein* in the Norwegian Army, smiled. "So, you remember me?" His smile faded. "We were beginning to wonder about you, my friend. Didn't anyone ever tell you not to jump from airplanes without a parachute?"

That brought on a kaleidoscopic jumble of memories that flashed through Jack's mind. The beeping on the heart rate monitor quickened as he remembered the battle of Ulan-Erg, where Pavel Rudenko had hurled himself into a mass of battling harvesters and soldiers, a pair of white phosphorus grenades in his hands, sacrificing himself to save Jack and Sergei Mikhailov. The city of Elista, burning in the night as harvesters slaughtered the unsuspecting people there. The long journey in the old biplane across the frozen expanse of Russia, only to discover that their pilot, a young woman named Khatuna, was herself a harvester. Sergei Mikhailov, badly wounded, grappling with the Khatuna-thing, buying time for Jack to escape. Leaping from the plane without a parachute. The fire and heat, the shock wave as the plane exploded above him when it was hit by an air to air missile. The wearying trek across the snow in a hopeless attempt to reach the Norwegian border. Ghosts emerging from the trees, the men of a Norwegian Special Forces team who had come to rescue him.

Jack shivered.

"You're all right." Terje took Jack's hand, giving it a gentle squeeze. "You're safe, for the moment, at least. Here, drink this." He held out a small plastic cup of water with a bent straw in it.

As Jack sipped the water, Terje introduced the others in the room. They came to stand beside the bed.

"This is Walter Cullen," Terje said, "from your embassy."

Cullen was a rail-thin African-American with close-cropped graying hair who stood half a head taller than Terje. He smiled as he extended a bony hand. Jack took it gingerly, careful not to squeeze hard. "A pleasure, Mr. Dawson. I'm Ambassador Cordwainer's Chief of Staff." Cullen had a high reedy voice. "The Ambassador would have come in person, but was detained by a last minute call from the Secretary of State. As you can imagine, your little adventure caused quite a stir in these parts, but that's largely been forgotten in the light of subsequent events."

The other visitor was a woman. In her early fifties, she had sandy blond hair that was just showing the first traces of gray. Her round face was smiling, but her makeup couldn't disguise the exhaustion in her eyes.

"This is Inghild Morgensen," Terje said, "our Minister of Defense."

"Ma'am."

"Mr. Dawson," she said in a silky voice that held an edge of steel. "Welcome to Norway, for the second time, I believe." She cocked her head slightly. "Could you perhaps arrange for there not to be a world crisis the next time you visit? It's becoming a bit of a bother."

They all shared a laugh at that. Jack's first visit to Norwegian territory had been to Spitsbergen a year before. He and a team from the Earth Defense Society had flown there to protect the Svalbard Seed Vault. They had walked right into the middle of a battle between the Russians and the Norwegians, spurred on by a group of harvesters intent on destroying the vault.

"I'll try my best, ma'am. You have my word on that."

"*Kaptein*," Morgensen said to Terje, "why don't you update him on what has happened, then we can proceed from there." She looked up to Cullen. "Unless, of course, you have something you would like to add first?"

Cullen shook his head and gestured for Terje to begin.

"Wait," Jack said to his friend. "There's something I need to tell you." Jack set the now empty cup of water on the stand beside the flowers. "Mikhailov and Rudenko are both dead. And the woman who was piloting the plane I was in turned out to be a harvester. I know she survived the crash. The Russians might have found her. They have to be warned."

Terje glanced at Morgensen, his expression grim. "I am sorry to hear about our Russian friends, Jack. They were good men. But the harvester who was flying your plane is the least of our problems. Things are truly going to hell, and we need to get you on your feet as fast as we can."

"How long have I been out?"

"Five days," Terje said. "You had a serious concussion after the fall from the plane. The team that we sent to find you had to dodge Russian patrols for two days before they could get you back across the border near Melkefoss, and as soon as you were stabilized we flew you here to Bodø. By that time, you were suffering from hypothermia and exposure, in addition to the concussion."

"We would have let you rest longer," Morgensen added, "but things are deteriorating quickly. We need you back on your feet."

Jack felt an unpleasant tingle in his gut. "Okay, let's have it."

"Harvester outbreaks have been reported in every country in the northern hemisphere, and many in the south," Terje told him.

"Russia, as you can imagine, is in complete chaos, with infestations in every major city west of the Ural Mountains. As best we know, their leadership has retreated to an underground bunker, and they have put their strategic forces on alert."

"Oh, hell."

"There has been talk of trying to contain the outbreaks with nuclear weapons," Cullen answered, shaking his head. "The crazy bastards. The President has put our forces on alert, because no one is comfortable with the Russians having their proverbial finger on the big red button. The strategic forces of the United Kingdom and France have gone on alert, as well. No one's sure about the Chinese."

"I hate to say it," Jack said slowly, "but the Russians may not be as crazy as you think. The harvesters are supposedly very sensitive to ionizing radiation, far more than we are."

"You can't mean that!" Morgensen stared at him.

Cullen looked down at the floor, pursing his lips.

"What would they be saving by destroying their own cities?" Morgensen demanded. "They would be killing hundreds of thousands of people!"

"More likely millions," Terje corrected quietly.

"Once the harvesters get a foothold in a heavily populated area where the civilian population has no idea how to deal with them..." Jack shook his head. "A pack of a hundred or so harvesters annihilated half a Russian airborne battalion, men who were heavily armed, well disciplined and well led, and who had at least some clue what they were up against. Imagine what they can do against civilians. Then there are the larval forms." He paused, licking his lips and wishing the cup of water had instead been filled with a double shot of whiskey. "Fighting these things on the ground in an urban environment isn't much short of suicide under the best of circumstances."

Morgensen scowled. "What are you saying, that we should just give up?"

"Of course not. All I'm saying is that you shouldn't think the Russians are insane for considering nuking the most heavily infested areas. It won't stop the harvesters in the long run, but it might slow them down and buy us some time."

"What about the people in the target areas?" Terje asked.

Jack looked away. "It won't be long before there isn't anyone left to save."

He was about to say something more when a cat that was nearly as large as his own, Alexander, bounded up onto the bed. Her long fur was an unruly mix of black and gray-brown. She regarded him for a moment with her yellow eyes before marching up onto his stomach and butting her head against his chest.

"That's Lurva," Terje said, his dark expression momentarily broken with a smile as the cat began to purr with a deep rumble as Jack gently scratched under her chin. "She belongs to Frode Stoltenberg, the commando leader whose team brought you out of Russia. He's loaning her to you as a get well present and guardian while he's off on a mission."

"Tell him thanks," Jack said as Lurva curled up on his chest.

"What Jack was saying," Cullen went on, folding his arms across his chest and favoring the cat with a frown, "tracks with what's been happening in Los Angeles. The entire metro area is overrun and the rest of southern California is in a panic. We've quarantined the Los Angeles basin, although that hasn't done much good. We just don't have the manpower to cordon off every mile of the infected zone. They're spreading into northern California, Arizona, Nevada, and south into Mexico, and outbreaks have been reported in most major cities across the rest of the country. The President ordered the stock market closed when it went into free fall last Monday, and the economy's coming apart at the seams. People aren't showing up for work, they're hoarding everything from ammunition to disposable diapers, and consumer prices are shooting through the roof."

"Christ." A blade of cold steel twisted in Jack's gut. "What about Naomi? The last thing I heard was that she was trapped in LA."

"She made it out," Cullen reassured him. "She's safe. Beyond that, I can't say much."

"Why the hell not?"

With an apologetic glance at the Norwegians, Cullen said, "Because everything else about where she is and what she's doing has been classified. I was authorized to tell you she's alive and safe, but that's all." Before Jack could say more, Cullen held up his hand. "I'm sorry, but that's all I can say until we can get you to the embassy."

"Then let's go." Jack propped himself up, only to be rewarded with dizziness and nausea.

Annoyed, Lurva hopped off the bed.

"Jack," Terje protested, "you're not ready to get back on your feet. Remember, you have a concussion!"

"I'm not staying in this goddamn bed. I need to talk to Naomi."

"That may not be as easy as it should be," Cullen warned.

"Why?" Jack ignored the hammer banging in his head as he forced himself up into a sitting position. "Did someone steal the embassy's phones?"

Cullen grimaced. "Global telecommunications have gone to hell."

"But surely the embassy can get through?" Swinging his legs over the side of the bed, he took a moment to catch his breath. He took the time to glare at Cullen.

Morgensen came to his rescue. "Communications with our embassies have also suffered, but the dedicated military links through NATO are still functioning. We should be able to provide what you need with reasonable privacy."

"My orders..." Cullen began to say before Jack cut him off.

"I'm not under anyone's orders. I just want to talk to Naomi and make sure she's okay. And has anyone bothered to tell her that I'm alive?"

Cullen shrugged. "I don't know."

"Right," Jack growled. To Terje, Jack said, "Got any clothes I can borrow?"

***

Dressed in a Norwegian Army uniform, Jack looked out the window of the Royal Norwegian Air Force Sea King helicopter as it flew east from Bodø over the shores of the Saltfjorden. The view was breathtaking, the jagged snow-covered mountains framing the waters of the fjord as they reflected the gunmetal gray clouds above. A light snow was falling, making the scene even more enchanting.

Lurva, wearing a collar and leash, sat in his lap, surprisingly docile in the noisy helicopter.

With a sigh, he turned away from the window. Terje sat beside him, while Morgensen and Cullen, who had insisted on coming along to chaperone Jack, sat in the seats on the opposite side of the cavernous helicopter. Six soldiers accompanied them, along with the helicopter's crew chief.

Terje had told him it would be a short trip, and it was. Less than ten minutes after the white and orange helicopter of 330 Squadron had taken off from Bodø Airport, it was coming in to land at a helipad near the center of a small complex of buildings nestled in the forest not far from the fjord. As the wheels touched down, the crew chief slid open the door and the soldiers nimbly jumped to the ground to take up defensive positions around the aircraft.

Jack gathered up Lurva and followed Morgensen and Cullen out the door, with Terje bringing up the rear.

Morgensen headed through the billowing snow tossed up by the helicopter's rotor blades toward two military vehicles that looked similar to the American Humvee. A gauntlet of soldiers stood in front of the vehicles, their weapons trained on the new arrivals. In front of them were two open frame crates containing a pair of cats. The defense minister presented her hand to each cat for approval, and after shaking the hand of the stern-faced two-star general who led the reception detail, she got into the rear seat of the lead vehicle.

Jack repeated the procedure, holding out his free hand to each cat while he held on to Lurva with the other. The general gave her what might have passed for a smile before waving Jack through.

Behind him, Cullen and Terje took their turns through the receiving line.

The general took the front seat of the lead vehicle, while Cullen got in next to Morgensen. Jack and Terje hopped into the rear seat of the second vehicle.

"This is the new *Forsvarets operative hovedkvarter*, our Joint Forces Headquarters," Terje explained as the driver started off along a snow-covered road that led into the forest.

They passed through a heavily guarded check point, then a few moments later pulled up in front of a tunnel entrance that was heavily reinforced with concrete and had thick steel blast doors.

"The Joint Forces staff moved here in 2010 from Oslo," Terje said. "The old headquarters facility would have been indefensible."

Jack shook his head in dismay. "Has it ever occurred to you that this could be a death trap? You could have larvae oozing their way down the ventilation shafts or eating through gaskets."

"We have taken steps to prevent that," Terje said. "All the organic materials used in the door and ventilation seals and other penetration points have been removed and replaced. We have cats patrolling the facility in company with soldiers armed with weapons loaded with incendiary ammunition."

"That makes me feel a little better," Jack admitted. "But if it's all the same to you, I'd rather be at home in bed."

Getting out of the vehicles, they were checked by the guards at the tunnel entrance. Once cleared inside, the group climbed aboard a large electric cart that took them into the tunnel.

Jack looked at Terje. "How many harvesters do you think have made it into Norway?"

"Enough to cause trouble," Terje said, "but not enough to start a panic. Not yet, at least. The government acted quickly by closing the borders and airspace, along with the ports. The reserves have been mobilized and formed into quick reaction teams to respond to any harvester sightings. So far, the incident rate seems to be stable, so we like to think we're killing them as quickly as they are identified." He reached over and rubbed Lurva on the head. "Cats are also in very short supply after thousands were requisitioned for the military."

"The civilians have been told that cats can recognize harvesters?"

"Yes." Terje's nodded, his grin fading away. "We have passed on as much information as we can about how to combat harvesters without heavy weapons. We have given instructions on using lighter fluid or even combustible aerosol sprays with lighters as makeshift flamethrowers. That was a tip your FBI sent to us. We have also tried to make incendiary ammunition available to owners of firearms, but it is in short supply after the military's needs. And of course, we have told them to use cats for warning, and explained how to spot harvesters for those lucky enough to have a thermal imager. Unfortunately, some people have tried to gather up as many cats as they can to sell at outrageous prices. I know how ridiculous it may sound, but His Majesty is expected to declare all cats as state property through the duration of the emergency. Selling them will be a very serious offense."

"It doesn't sound ridiculous at all," Jack said as he stroked Lurva's fur. She took in her new surroundings from the vantage point of his lap, and he could hear her purring over the whine of the cart. Alexander would have been meowing and fidgeting the entire time.

The cart finally rolled to a stop before another set of blast doors. Yet more guards checked everyone's identification. Jack thought it odd that no cats were posted there until he spied one curled up, sound asleep, against the steel bulkhead that held the blast door.

He nudged Terje, then pointed to the snoozing cat. "Your hard-earned tax dollars at work, I see."

"We let some roam loose through the corridors. It's obviously very boring duty."

Jack only shook his head as Morgensen and the general led them into the heart of the facility, a sour-faced Cullen bringing up the rear.

REUNION

The *Forsvarets operative hovedkvarter* was dominated by a spacious two-story operations center. An enormous multi-panel display covered the front wall, running the width of the room and from roughly six feet above the floor up to the ceiling. Men and women in combat fatigues manned the four rows of workstations facing the giant screen. Many were quietly but intensely watching their consoles or tapping out instructions on their keyboards, while others were talking on phones or headsets. Above them, overlooking the operations floor, was a glassed-in mezzanine.

Terje and Jack held back as Morgensen, Cullen, and the two-star general went to the front to join a small group of high-ranking officers. One of them, an older but well-muscled man with silver-gray hair, had four stars on the front of his uniform. He had deep worry lines carved in his face. Morgensen said something, and the man shook his head emphatically before pointing up to the display.

Jack couldn't read the Norwegian text, but there was a fundamental universality to the military map symbols that allowed him to understand what the screen was showing. A map of the Scandinavian peninsula, together with the Baltic countries and western Russia from the White Sea south to Moscow, occupied the bulk of the display. Blue icons tagged as Royal Norwegian Air Force F-16s were flying in race track ovals near the borders with Russia and Finland, with a pair orbiting over Oslo. Other tracks showed P-3 Orion maritime surveillance aircraft patrolling the long coastline along the Norwegian sea and the Skagerrak, the channel that separated the Scandinavian peninsula from Denmark. Icons shaped like ships and tagged with names like *Thor Heyerdahl* and *Steil* patrolled the entrance to every major port, while more plied the waters up and down the coast in concert with the P-3s.

A smaller map, taking up one corner of the display, showed the Svalbard Archipelago. A pair of F-16s flew in a large figure eight over Spitsbergen, the largest of the islands in the archipelago, and a commando unit protected the SvalSat communications facility.

Brigade Nord, the only combat brigade in the Norwegian Army, had deployed its light armored battalion, both mechanized battalions with their tanks and infantry combat vehicles, and the sole artillery battalion to the north, opposite the Russian border.

Jack turned to Terje. "Worried about the Russians?"

"Yes. This must look much like our deployments did during the Cold War, although now for different reasons. We are not worried that the Russian government will order an attack against us, but we cannot afford a flood of refugees streaming across the border. So we've put most of our combat strength there to help the Border Guard."

"What about the border with Finland and Sweden?"

"We have helicopters with thermal imagers searching along the border, and we have created a volunteer force of hunters and alpinists to set up warning pickets, but..." He shrugged. "There is just too much territory to cover. We would all need to form a line and hold hands to catch them coming through the forests."

"Make sure your people look for any signs of deforestation," Jack said. "Patches or swatches of missing trees might be a giveaway that larval forms are in the area."

They looked up as Morgensen gestured for the two of them to join the group at the front of the ops center.

"Jack," Morgensen said, turning to the four-star general, "this is our Chief of Defense, General Jonas Nesvold."

"Mr. Dawson." Nesvold's big hand enfolded Jack's as they shook.

"An honor, sir," Jack said, "although I wish it were under better circumstances."

"So do we all, Mr. Dawson." Gesturing to the screen, he asked, "What is your assessment of the situation in Russia?"

"Sir, what I know is from nearly a week ago, and..."

Nesvold waved away Jack's concerns. "I understand that. But you were there, you witnessed things first-hand. We have had little in the way of direct intelligence reporting on what is taking place there. Please indulge me."

Jack looked at the screen, his eyes tracing the path he had taken across Russia only five days ago. "It's a disaster, sir. They had a lab in their grain belt that must have somehow obtained samples of the grain infected with the harvester genes, virus, whatever you want to call it. The things got loose, and..." He had to stop for a moment. His pulse was hammering in his head and he felt short of breath. His vision began to turn gray.

He felt a hand on his shoulder.

"You need rest," Terje said.

"No." Jack shook his friend's hand away. "There's no time for that." Looking back at Nesvold, Jack went on, "General, there's no silver lining to what's happening. The larval forms and the adult harvesters in their natural form are bad enough. Harvesters posing as impostors might be even worse. I saw with my own eyes one of the damn things masquerading as a Russian officer, a major, right in one of their garrisons. If the harvesters infiltrate one of their Strategic Rocket Forces units or, God forbid, their senior command staff..."

"But surely the Russians have taken steps as we have to improve their security?" Morgensen protested.

"I don't know," Jack said. "I hope they did, but I can't tell you more than that."

Nesvold's frown deepened. "Well, we are doing what we can. We can only hope that it is enough."

Before Jack could reply, he caught sight of a young soldier at one of the workstations, gesturing for him to come over.

"She's trying to connect you to Naomi Perrault," Nesvold said with a gentle smile.

"Ma'am, general, if you'd excuse me for a moment?" He didn't wait for a reply before he quickly stepped over to the soldier, who handed him a headset with a boom mic.

With an indignant meow, Lurva trotted along behind him, her leash still in Jack's hand.

"We have a secure connection, sir," the soldier said.

"Thank you." Jack gave her a quick smile of gratitude.

"Excuse me, but this has to be a private conversation!" Cullen whined from behind him. Lowering his voice, he added, "You can't talk to Naomi in the middle of a room of uncleared people!"

"Listen," Jack turned on him, "I don't want to talk to her about anything that's classified. I just want to know that she's okay and tell her that I'm alive. If you don't like it, Mr. Cullen, you can kindly go fuck yourself!"

"Jack?" He heard a familiar voice as he slipped on the headset. "Jack, hon, please say that was you telling someone to go fuck himself!"

"Yeah, Renee, it's me," he said, relieved to hear her voice. Renee Vintner was one of his closest friends.

"Oh, God, Jack." She said through her snuffling and sobbing. "We thought you were dead, you idiot! Naomi's going to kill you."

Jack chuckled, then said, "I know I'm in for it. Listen, is she there?"

"Yeah, she's on her way. I had to call her up from the lab. You know I can't tell you where, right?"

Glancing over his shoulder at Cullen, who stood fuming behind him, Jack said, "Yeah, I got the full lecture on that score."

"Where the hell are you?"

"I'm at the Norwegian Joint Forces Command headquarters, in an underground bunker near Bodø. Hey, is Naomi okay?"

"Yes, I'm fine, thanks for asking," Renee quipped. "So is Carl, for that matter, although he'd be losing more hair if he had any left." There was a pause. "And no, Naomi hasn't been all right, you big oaf. She died inside when the President told her your plane was shot down. God, I want to knock you in the head for being such a moron, but I'll have to wait my turn. And how the devil did you make it out of that one with your hide in one piece?"

"I'll tell you later." He took a deep breath. "Just get Naomi on the phone."

***

At the center of two hundred acres of flat, barren ground squatted the hastily erected fortress known as SEAL-2. Originally intended as a special research lab for Morgan Pharmaceuticals, it had been given over by its billionaire owner, Howard Morgan, to the government to aid in the fight against the harvesters.

The main building stood two stories above ground, but would have been barely recognizable to those who built it. The sleek exterior of white walls and glass, designed to be both attractive and energy efficient, had disappeared behind bolt-on steel armor. The roof had also been reinforced, and had sprouted a forest of communications antennas and weapons emplacements.

On one side of the lab building, a pair of two story dormitories were being erected to house the small army of scientists and security personnel who had been brought in, and who were now living in tents arrayed in neat rows on the opposite side of the lab building until their permanent quarters were finished. A helipad and a maintenance hangar had been built in the open area in front of the lab, with fuel storage and a motor pool behind.

The entire facility was ringed with a moat that could be filled with fuel to form a protective fire ring, backed up with a ten foot high metal wall with guard towers set at intervals along its length. From the wall to the double fence around the main buildings was a two hundred meter deep no-man's land filled with mines and sensors that could detect harvester larvae.

But the heart of the base, the reason for its existence, was buried beneath the lab building. That is where the research on harvesters and how to destroy them was being carried out.

At a workstation in the second sub-basement, thirty feet below the surface, Naomi Perrault stared at her computer screen. Five hundred and seventy three new emails crowded her in box, all of them flagged as immediate priority. Many of them would be congratulations on mapping the harvester genome. Her team had just finished mapping the eight hundred billion base pairs of harvester DNA, the culmination of the work begun by the Earth Defense Society over two years before. It was a feat she should have been proud of, considering that it had taken the Human Genome Project ten years to map the three billion base pairs in humans DNA.

She sat back for a moment and rubbed her eyes, which felt like they were full of sand. The elation she should have felt had been overwhelmed by the reality that mapping the genome was only the first step. Her team could analyze the terrain of the harvesters' genetic structure, but still had no idea which parts of it were important, which parts could be turned against them. As her scientists explored this new world, more and more questions arose, but precious few answers.

Blinking her burning, bloodshot eyes, she put her hands back to the keyboard and began to hammer out a response to one of the emails, the daily query from the president's scientific advisor on her team's progress.

Nothing to report.

The phone trilled.

She glared at the phone, but stifled her curse when she saw on the caller ID display that it was Renee.

Tapping a button on the phone, she spoke into her headset as she continued typing. "What is it?"

"Hon, get up here right now." Renee was breathless with excitement.

Naomi frowned. "What is it? Can't you route the call to me here?"

"No, it's on one of the secure lines. And no, I can't say what it is on the internal phone. Just get your ass up here!"

"Okay, okay." With a weary sigh, she hit the send button on the email to the White House. "I'll be right there."

***

"Hang on, kid," Renee said, and Jack's pulse quickened.

"Jack?" Naomi said a moment later in a soft, husky voice.

"Yeah, baby, it's me. Listen, I'm sorry about what happened..."

"Just shut up, you idiot," she told him, half laughing, half crying. "When the President told us you'd been killed...that nearly killed me, too. Oh, God, Jack. Don't you ever do something that stupid again."

"Well, you weren't exactly just sitting on your tuffet in Los Angeles, if I remember right," he told her, grinning from ear to ear. "The last word I'd had from Carl when we were trying to get out of Russia was that you were trapped there. So you can't give me too hard of a time, you know?"

"I'll give you the hardest time of your life the instant I get my hands on you," she promised. "But you're okay, you're not hurt?"

"I was a little banged up, but not too bad." He paused, the smile evaporating. "It was a tough mission. Mikhailov and Rudenko didn't make it."

"God, I'm so sorry. It looks like Vijay Chidambaram and his cousin Kiran didn't make it, either."

"Why, what happened?" India had been the first stop on Jack's long, ill-fated journey to see what had happened to Dr. Vijay Chidambaram, a former colleague from the EDS. Vijay had discovered that harvesters had been unleashed in India, and Jack and Vijay's cousin Kiran, an officer of the Indian Army, had barely survived an encounter with the monsters in a remote Indian village.

"The Indian government was flying them over to us on one of their Air Force transport planes, but it disappeared three days ago. The Indians think it went down over Iran or Turkey, but no one has reported finding it."

"Shit." Jack lifted his eyes to the ceiling. "Naomi..."

One of the soldiers on the communications team stiffened, then stood and shouted something in Norwegian. Morgensen, Nesvold, and the other senior officers whirled around, expressions of total disbelief on their faces. The quiet buzz in the ops center died. Nesvold barked a command, and the map display shifted, zooming out to show the northern hemisphere from Norway east to the Sea of Okhotsk. Red rings appeared around four locations deep in Siberia.

A klaxon blared, shattering the silence as red arcs began to rise from each of the rings. All at once, the soldiers at the workstations were talking in urgent tones into their headsets or were typing madly at their consoles. One of the watch officers shouted something, and a moment later Jack sensed a slight change of pressure in his ears.

They've closed the blast doors, he thought, a cold trickle of fear running down the back of his neck. "Hang on," he told Naomi. "Something's happening."

CLEANSING FIRE

General-Polkovnik Nikolai Krylov stood at a special console at the center of the operations center that was the heart of the massive complex buried deep beneath Mount Yamantau in the Ural Mountains some thirteen hundred kilometers east of Moscow. All eyes were fixed on the main map display's depiction of the harvester infestations that had consumed southern Russia and had swept into southeastern Ukraine. Georgia, Armenia, and Azerbaijan were also afflicted, but Krylov knew that few of the handful of men gathered around the console, the *vlasti* who held the power in Russia, gave much thought to the fate of those nations. They were intent on trying to save what they could of their own.

Krylov had devoted his life to the service of his country. True, such service had paid off with its own rewards over time (*perks*, as the Americans might say), but he had not spent thirty years working his way up through the ranks to command the Strategic Rocket Forces for nice living quarters and a Mercedes SUV. He had done it because he was a patriot whose grandfather had perished in the Battle of Kursk at the hands of the Germans, and whose father had lived in fear and distrust of the West during the Cold War. Defending his country, defending Russia, was in his blood. And now his blood ran cold at what he must do to save the Motherland.

"All regiments report full readiness, *general-polkovnik*." He nodded at his second in command, who verbalized for the sake of posterity what Krylov could see on the status board to the right of the map display.

They had evacuated what military forces they could from the Southern Military District after a series of desperate and utterly disastrous attempts to regain control of the major cities in the south. The 49th and 58th Armies had been annihilated at Krasnodar and Stavropol. The 7th Air Assault Division had not had to deploy to find the enemy. The unit's garrison at Stavropol, from where the initial ill-fated mission by the airborne troops against Ulan-Erg nearly a week before had been launched, had been overrun that same day, with the garrison at Novorossiysk falling two days later. No one among the high command or the government had been able to credit the reports, either through military channels or the media, coming out of the affected zones. Video sites on the internet were awash with horrific scenes of creatures massacring civilians and troops alike. It was like watching out-takes from a bad Hollywood science fiction film, except the casualties were real. The Army was sent reeling back from the cities, and many troops had been left behind after the reality had sunken in that the creatures could mimic human form.

The Air Force had been given its turn at the monsters. Attack jets dropped napalm and the strategic bombers of the 37th Air Army dropped thousands of tons of munitions on Stavropol, Novorossiysk, and other infested towns. The towns were leveled and the cities were swept with firestorms that hearkened back to the devastation wrought on Hamburg and Dresden in Germany by the Anglo-Americans during the Great Patriotic War. The flight crews had done their duty, but had been sickened by what they had wrought on their own countrymen. Several had killed themselves afterward, unable to face the burden of guilt.

But even that had not been enough. At the cost of much of the Air Force's ready munitions reserve, thousands of flight hours, and seven precious aircraft lost through mishaps, the torched rubble of the cities could not be reclaimed. The harvesters, while extremely vulnerable to fire, had fled at the first sign of the bombs raining down from the skies. All that Russia's military might had accomplished was to incinerate the few surviving humans and drive the harvesters into the surrounding countryside, accelerating their spread.

No one, including the president and prime minister, had believed the estimates provided by the *Federal'naya Sluzhba Bezopasnosti*, or FSB, modern Russia's incarnation of the old KGB intelligence service, which indicated that there were *several million* harvesters loose in Russia, and millions more across the globe. The numbers were unreal, mere statistics on paper, no more believable than the tens of millions murdered by Josef Stalin during the purges.

And yet there was no denying the thousands of dead soldiers, burning tanks and troop carriers, and the hundreds of thousands, perhaps millions, of dead civilians in Russia's heartland.

How could this have happened, Krylov wondered, *and so quickly?*

The turning point had come when Voronezh, less than five hundred kilometers south of Moscow, was overwhelmed by the creatures in less than forty-eight hours. That shock was quickly followed by the first outbreaks in Moscow's suburbs. The president wasted no time in ordering the cabinet and senior officials of the government's key agencies to the underground complex at Yamantau, which had already been put on a wartime footing.

The president had made The Decision, the *Resheniye,* after an agonizing cabinet session the night before. Krylov suspected that historians would place the president in the same hell-bound company as Stalin and Hitler, but if the government did not do what was necessary now, there might not be any historians left to record the deed at all.

The president stood beside him at the console, his icy gray eyes fixed on the map. Every major city south of the line defined by Kursk, Voronezh, and Saratov, all the way south to the borders with Turkey and Iran, had been targeted. Azerbaijan, Armenia, and Georgia would soon cease to exist. Over a dozen cities in the Ukrainian salient from Kharkiv south to Mariupol on the Sea of Azov would also be destroyed. The president was willing to accept any wrath the Ukrainians might care to unleash; it would be a small price to pay if the infection could be stopped. Some consideration had been given to sterilizing western Kazakhstan, but no outbreaks had yet been reported. That arid wasteland of a country would be spared. For now.

The target on the map display that had caused the most controversy in the cabinet meeting was Moscow. The southern suburbs of the city, where even now harvesters were quickly gaining ground against the troops of the 20th Guards Army and the 106th

Guards Airborne Division, would soon be flaming rubble. Krylov wanted to weep for those brave men and the civilians they were trying to defend. None of them had any idea that they were about to be sacrificed for what everyone hoped would be the greater good.

The president turned to him. "It is time, Krylov."

"*Da, gospodin prezident.*"

Before them stood a *polkovnik*, a colonel, of the Strategic Rocket Forces. In a monotone voice, he led them through the nuclear weapons authorization procedures. While Krylov could have recited the steps from memory, he dutifully followed along, for the sake of formality, if nothing else. The millions of people, *his* people, he was about to kill deserved at least that much.

Out of habit, he glanced up at the corner of the main display to check on the status of the *Perimetr* command and control system. At a cost of millions of rubles, the so-called "Dead Hand" Cold War-era system could be set to automatically launch a retaliatory strike should it detect a nuclear attack against his country through a set of seismic, light, radioactivity, and overpressure sensors emplaced in control nodes in key locations. It had been a stroke of genius never matched by the West, and Krylov envied his predecessors. He wished he could put a machine in charge of what must be done now, so that he could pretend to be a mere observer and absolve himself of responsibility. The system had been deactivated for this strike, of course. It had never occurred to its designers that the Strategic Rocket Forces would launch a massive strike against the Motherland they were sworn to defend.

"On my mark, turn the keys," the *polkovnik* intoned. "Three... two..."

Krylov took one last look at the president, and was shocked at what he saw. While he respected the former KGB officer who had risen to become the most powerful man in Russia, Krylov had never liked him. The president had ice in his veins and steel in his heart, with a soul entirely devoid of compassion. And yet now, in this most dire hour, Krylov saw tears glistening in the president's eyes.

"...one. Turn!"

In perfect synchrony, Krylov and the President of the Russian Federation turned the special keys in the launch console.

***

In the Siberian forests near Barnaul, Irkutsk, and Novosibirsk, sixty-two SS-25 *Sickle* ICBMs of the 33rd Guards Rocket Army rose on pillars of fire from their enormous mobile launchers. Each of the missiles carried a single warhead with the explosive equivalent of eight hundred kilotons of TNT, over fifty times more powerful than the nuclear bomb dropped by the United States over Hiroshima at the end of World War Two.

They were joined by twenty-six SS-18 *Satan* missiles from the same unit's silo complexes around Uzhur. Like the SS-25s, these missiles carried a single warhead apiece. But these were far more powerful, each with a yield of twenty-five megatons, over sixteen hundred times the power of the Hiroshima bomb.

The rocket plumes were visible from dozens of kilometers in every direction. People looked up at the display of deadly beauty as the missiles accelerated into the atmosphere. Most of those who saw the sight were too young to remember the Cold War, and regarded the bright streaks in the sky with the same curiosity as they might a particularly bright meteor shower. Those who were older, who had lived with the specter of nuclear annihilation for over forty years as East faced off against West, were gripped with heart-wrenching terror.

***

"Jack? What's happening?"

"Hang on," he told her as he watched the drama unfold. Barnaul, Irkutsk, Novosibirsk, and Uzhur were the names tagged to the red rings in Siberia. "Terje, what the hell is going on?"

Beside him, the Norwegian captain stared at the screen, his expression one of complete and utter shock. "It's...it's a nuclear strike warning with tracking data from the United States, passed through NATO." He turned to face Jack. "The Russians have launched ICBMs."

"Naomi," Jack said. "Did you hear that?"

"A nuclear strike? Have they gone mad? Where are the missiles heading? Are you safe?"

"The only thing I'm pretty sure of," Jack told her as the tracks quickly lengthened, "is that they don't seem to be aimed at the States. If they were, they should be heading north, over the Pole, and they don't seem to be heading this way, either. It looks like they're angling west, maybe a bit to the south."

As if on cue, yellow ovals began to appear on the map, most of them clustered in southern Russia, west of the Ural Mountains.

Terje spoke with one of the soldiers on the communications team, then said to Jack as he pointed at the glaring yellow icons, "Those are projected impact areas."

"Jesus Christ." The yellow ovals, which had begun to contract as the trajectory data of the missiles and the resulting computed target areas were refined, blanketed southern Russia and western Ukraine. Farther north, a single yellow target marker was contracting around Moscow. "I can't believe they're doing this."

"Weren't you the one who said the Russians weren't crazy for thinking about a nuke strike?"

That came from Cullen. "I did say that," Jack said through gritted teeth as he clenched his fists, "but I never thought they'd do it on this scale."

"How could you?" Terje asked. "How could anyone?"

"Jack?" Naomi's worried voice called to him again through the headset.

"I'm here, babe. The targets are definitely inside Russia, although it looks like they decided to nuke some targets in Ukraine, too."

"There may not be any alternative," she said quietly. "For any of us."

That got Jack's attention. "What do you mean?"

"Just that...I'm not sure if we're going to succeed. Not in the time we may have."

Jack forced himself to turn away from the display so he could focus his full attention on her. "Listen to me," he said. "I'm not going to say I understand the pressure you're under, because I can't. None of us can know what it's like to carry the whole world on our shoulders like you are now. But I know you. You're determined and you're brilliant, and you and the other big brains working on this are going to figure things out and kick the harvesters in the ass."

She didn't say anything for a moment. "I want you home, Jack," she said at last in a husky voice. "I want you here with me now."

"Me, too. I'd give anything to be with you."

"Jack." Terje tugged on his arm and pointed at the display.

The missiles were nearing their targets. The Russians had made a time on target launch, which would put all the warheads over their respective targets at the same time.

"Even if this kills tons of harvesters," Jack said, "the Russians are going to be in for a really tough time."

"What, aside from killing millions of their own people?" Cullen shot him disgusted look.

"They're nuking their grain belt, you jackass," Jack spat. "Even if they're able to kill enough of the harvesters to buy the survivors some time, they're destroying their main source of food and killing the people who grow it. The rest of the country's going to be facing a famine."

"We may have to do the same thing," Naomi whispered into his ear through the headset. "Every major city here has suffered outbreaks, and we're not doing any better at containing them than the Russians. The difference is that here, nobody wants to admit it."

"God help us," Jack said as the missile trajectories intersected the predicted target icons. "I just wish..."

An electronic squeal came through his headset, followed by silence. The line to Naomi had gone dead.

"What happened?" Jack asked the communications technician.

"I am not sure, sir," she said in a shaking voice. "Most likely an electromagnetic pulse." She nodded toward the map, and Jack turned to see orange icons bloom, depicting nuclear detonations over Russia.

***

In a single instant, southern Russia and western Ukraine were bathed in the light of eighty-seven artificial suns. Every major city that had been infested with harvesters died under the blast, heat, and radiation of a nuclear explosion. Some cities only had a handful of survivors left, while others still held hundreds of thousands who had not yet been able to flee through the choked roads.

While the harvesters had a greater chance of surviving the blast effects that leveled buildings out to a radius of nearly seven kilometers, those that were exposed to the thermal radiation out to a radius of over ten kilometers died in brilliant pyres as their malleable flesh burst into flame. The massive doses of direct radiation from the blasts, coupled with secondary radiation effects from the fallout, would leave even more harvesters dead, and make the bombed areas untenable for them until the radiation fell to near-normal background levels.

As the cities were reduced to ash by the eight hundred kiloton warheads, the missiles carrying the massive twenty-five megaton weapons stitched a line of titanic mushroom clouds in an arc that ran from Kharkiv in Ukraine to Voronezh, then to Saratov on the Volga River, and finally to Uralsk. The Russian targeting planners hoped that, beyond the immediate kills the weapons would inflict, the radiation effects would form a barrier to harvesters trying to move north and contain them, even if only temporarily, in the south.

The eighty-eighth missile, bearing an eight hundred kiloton warhead, detonated directly over the *Serebryanyy Dozhd' Kart-tsentr*, an amusement park in the southern outskirts of Moscow along the MKAD ring road. The survivors of a battalion of paratroopers from the 106th Guards Airborne Division and the hundreds of terrified civilians they were trying to protect from waves of attacking harvesters felt no pain as their bodies, and those of their enemies, were consumed by the nuclear fireball.

PROPOSAL

Kiran was gripped by a nightmare. It visited him every time he closed his eyes, and it was always the same.

He was aboard the Indian Air Force IL-76 transport that was carrying them to the United States after escaping the horrors of Hyderabad. The men of his unit had sacrificed themselves so that he and his cousin Vijay, who lay strapped in a gurney, still suffering from the injuries he received in a terrible automobile accident, might live.

The plane had stopped in New Delhi to take on more passengers, government officials and members of high-ranking families, along with more scientists. They were faceless ghosts who took their places around him and his cousin in the hold of the plane.

Vijay spoke to him, but Kiran couldn't hear the words. Vijay, too, had become a ghost, his dark skin having faded to a pale, translucent shroud over his skull as the big four-engine jet took off and turned northeast, heading toward Turkey, the first refueling stop on their way to America.

But they never made it. Kiran thrashed and cried out as fire and shrapnel swept the huge cargo bay, slashing many of the ghosts to bits before they were sucked out the gaping hole torn in the side of the plane, just aft of the wing. The ghosts of men, women and children, nearly a third of those on the plane, were cast away into the darkness, their screams lost in the roar of explosive decompression. Their bodies were set alight by the fire consuming the inboard engine, and they fluttered away like burning moths through the night sky.

Beside him, Vijay screamed. Kiran clung to his cousin's hand and the gurney, which threatened to break free from its bindings to carry Vijay away into the night.

The plane's fall from the sky took far longer than Kiran would have imagined. It spiraled down and down, the destroyed inboard engine, the fire out now, streaming thick smoke that blotted out the stars until they, too, were gone in a cataclysm of rending metal and terrified screams.

He awoke on his back, staring up at a crescent moon. Propping himself up on his elbows, he saw that he was on a small rise overlooking a sea of flame, above which towered a massive white triangular shape. At first thought it was a monument to the gods, but eventually came to realize that it was only the tail of the IL-76. Ghostly bodies were scattered about, some in the flames, crackling as they burned, and some not. A few, like deranged ghouls, staggered here and there, wailing.

His cousin's gurney lay on its side, perilously close to the fire. Getting slowly to his feet, Kiran staggered toward it. Turning the gurney's twisted metal frame toward him, he saw that Vijay was still alive, his mouth open in an unending shriek of agony. His lower body had been crushed, his legs crumpled and twisted, following the shape of the smashed gurney.

There was no sense of time in the dream, and Kiran had no idea how long he sat there, staring at his screaming cousin. He might have done something to try and help Vijay and the other ghosts, but he could not remember. It didn't matter in the dream. Because in the dream *they* came before the dawn. No matter how many times he had the dream, no matter how many times he prayed for a different ending, *they* still came. They always came.

At first he thought they were soldiers come to help them. He did not recognize the uniforms, although their complexions were not far different from his own. The plane might have gone down somewhere in northern Iran, or perhaps eastern Turkey. He knew they had flown past the Caspian Sea not long before the explosion, for he remembered how intensely dark the water had been against the land as he took a look out one of the plane's windows.

But he quickly discovered that the soldiers were not who they appeared to be. They dragged the bodies of the ghosts, living and dead, away from the flames. The things that masqueraded as men took the dead ghosts first. They crouched over the bodies, their faces peeling back to reveal dark slick mandibles that opened wide, like a snake, to swallow the heads of the dead, then the bodies, bit by bit.

The ghosts who still lived tried to run, but there was no escaping what had come for them. There were more screams, not of pain, but of terror, wails and shrieks that echoed through Kiran's mind as the ghosts were run down by the monsters and taken.

But not all the ghosts were killed then and there. Oh, no. In the dream, Kiran tried to fight the monsters, to protect the ghosts, even though he knew they were just that, lost spirits in the night and nothing more. But his pathetic struggles were for naught. One of the monsters looked at Vijay, who was still screaming in agony, then crouched over him, the flesh of its head melting away to reveal the terrible jaws. Vijay screamed even louder, for screaming was all he could do with both legs and both arms broken. Kiran remembered the look on his cousin's face as it disappeared into the thing's maw, remembered how the screams were muffled, then abruptly stilled.

"Kiran."

He heard Vijay's voice calling him, but knew it couldn't be him. Vijay, too, had become a ghost, just like all the others that the soldier-things had marched away from the burning wreckage for safe keeping in an abandoned mine. It was cool there, and dark. Food kept longer when it was chilled.

"Kiran, wake up."

His eyes snapped open as a booted foot prodded him awake. The dream faded, to be replaced by a reality that was even more horrifying. His cousin Vijay, or what looked like his cousin, stood over him, holding a fluorescent camp lantern. The Vijay-thing was flanked by two other men who were not men, wearing military uniforms.

"Have you finally come for me?" He was weak, not having eaten since the crash (how long ago that had been, he was uncertain), and had been reduced to licking the condensation off the walls for want of water. The side tunnel of the mine where he and the others had been kept was dark except when their captors came to take away one of his fellow survivors. One of the ghosts.

Kiran was the only one left.

"Yes, but not the way you suspect." His cousin smiled, and something dark and slimy chewed its way through Kiran's soul. "Come, get on your feet." The thing reached down and effortlessly pulled him from the floor.

"What do you want?" Kiran suppressed a scream as the thing pulled his arm over its shoulder and helped him walk toward the main shaft. It wasn't the pain of Kiran's injuries, which were minor, but the reality of touching one of *them*. His foot bumped against something, and in the lantern light he saw it was a boot, with the remains of the foot still inside. The flesh, which was starting to decompose, looked like it had been cauterized where it had been severed from the leg, just above the ankle.

Ghosts, he thought, his mind teetering on the edge of madness. *The people on the plane were only ghosts. Just like I will be soon.*

"Here," the Vijay-thing said as they emerged into a well-lit part of the tunnel. It looked to Kiran like a small military command post, with a map board, a table with several chairs around it, another smaller table with a set of radios and two laptop computers, and several olive drab crates stacked up against a wall. Half a dozen of the things, all in military uniforms, stared at him. "Sit." The Vijay-thing helped him slide into a chair at the table. Another thing emerged from the darkness with a plate piled high with food and a canteen of cool water.

Kiran did not question why he was being given a reprieve, temporary though he knew it must be. He snatched at the canteen and drank, the water soothing his parched mouth. Momentarily sated, he set the canteen down on the table and began scooping the food into his mouth with his fingers.

All too soon, the food was gone. Kiran licked the plate clean before he upended the canteen to his lips and sucked down every last drop.

"You may have more later," the Vijay-thing said. "We don't want you to fall ill by eating too much too soon."

"Are you fattening me up before the slaughter?" Kiran's courage was starting to return. He could think more clearly now, and here, in the light, he could drive away the ghosts. For now.

"No. The others held no use for us beyond what we required as food. We must eat, too, you know." The thing smiled. It was Vijay's smile, the kind and endearing smile he had known and loved since childhood.

Kiran shivered at the sight.

"You will be spared that fate, assuming you do what we require of you."

"And what is that?"

The Vijay-thing went to stand by the map, which showed Russia between the Black and Caspian Seas, down to the Persian Gulf. Dozens of red circles had been drawn on the clear plastic overlay, making southern Russia look like it was covered with boils. "Do you know what these are?"

"Targets?" Kiran had no idea what else they could be, but he also could not understand the relevance of targets in Russia. Targets for whom?

"Yes. More specifically, nuclear strikes launched by the Russians themselves this morning in an attempt to destroy our kind in the southern part of the country. You would have heard the rumblings of the bombs detonating if you had not been crying out from your nightmares. The nearest target was less than a hundred kilometers from here, and the weapons they used were quite large. There is much we don't know, of course, but we were able to piece together much of what happened from what we could glean from the internet."

"Did they succeed?" Kiran did not question the bitter reality of what the harvester was telling him. It was as unreal as everything else that had happened since he, Jack, and Kiran's other cousin Surya had gone to the village outside of Hyderabad where all this had started.

"Only in destroying their own food supply."

"You sound disappointed."

The Vijay-thing stared at him. "We are. We thought either Russia or the United States would try such a thing, and while we hoped for a positive outcome, the Russians did themselves more harm than good in the long term, in the time they have left. I'm sure they killed many of the feral adults and larval forms, as you would call them, but many will survive to prosper even more as Russian food reserves begin to dwindle."

"I don't understand what you're saying. Why would you want the Russians to win? You're one of *them!*"

With a frown, the Vijay-thing came and sat at the table beside him. "Kiran," it said in a gentle voice, "those like me are in as great a danger as you of being exterminated. You see, some few of us, very few, are different. Of the adults spawned by the larvae, the vast majority will never be more than mindless animals in adult harvester form. They are mere breeding and killing machines that will never achieve sentience or even the ability to mimic other forms of life. They will prey on anything other than the larval forms, which can kill us as easily as they can kill you, and they can live for hundreds of years doing so." The thing leaned closer. "And when I say they will prey on *anything*, I mean that they will also kill us, those few of our kind that rise to achieve full sentience. In particular, those of us who achieve sentience and also stop replicating."

"I don't think I see the problem," Kiran said.

"I am not surprised, nor do I expect your sympathy. But it is necessary that you understand if you are to carry out the task we have for you, which is your only chance of survival." It gestured to the others in the room. "We were born in a laboratory in southern Russia and are among the first to have achieved full sentience. We fled that region as the infestation spiraled out of control and came here, hoping that this barren land would afford us some protection through isolation. But we have come to realize that nowhere on the planet will be safe for us in the long term if a solution is not found."

"A solution?" Kiran leaned forward, not sure he was hearing correctly. "As in a way to kill them?"

"Nothing quite so drastic as that, my friend." The thing smiled. "More precisely, we need a way to control their spread. I do not think you really understand what your people are facing, Kiran. Unless they are stopped, the entire planet will be overwhelmed by our, ah, lower castes, you might call them. Our creators, the harvesters that your cousin Vijay and the others eradicated, must have had a vision for us far different from what we have for ourselves. We know nothing about them, of course, as the last died before the first of us was spawned. But it is clear that the lower castes are entirely out of control, and if their unrestrained propagation is not contained, Earth will no longer be a home for humanity, nor for us. Everything down to the bacteria in the soil will eventually be consumed, and someday our progeny will be all that remains in the biosphere, with nothing left to eat but one another. Everything else will become extinct."

"I do not believe it. Something would survive. People would survive."

The thing shook its head, an expression of sadness on its face that twisted Kiran's guts, for he had to force himself to remember that it wasn't Vijay, but the monster that murdered him. "Look at what has happened across the world in the short time since the first larvae were spawned. What do you think the world will look like a year from now? Ten years? You could launch all the nuclear weapons that remain in the world's arsenals, and it would barely make a dent in the epidemic, while killing your own people and rendering some of your most fertile lands useless."

The thing leaned closer to him, and Kiran flinched away.

"The larvae will spread like a virus," Vijay went on, "consuming everything in their path. As things stand now, humanity has no future. Nor do we." It put a hand on his, and Kiran wanted to recoil from its touch, which felt so real, so human. "But together, perhaps we can survive."

Pulling his hand away, trying to keep his food down as his stomach churned, Kiran said, "What do you want of me?"

"We want you to deliver a message, offering our cooperation in developing a solution to the danger that confronts us all."

Glancing at the computers, Kiran said, "Why don't you just send your own message? Or just...masquerade as me?"

"Because you — the real you — will be believed. I know you have the trust of Jack Dawson, and you must certainly be known, if only by name, to many in his circle. We have already tried sending an emissary, but he met with an untimely end long before he was able to deliver his message." The thing grimaced. "Too few of us are left to take such risks again. We have been desperately searching for someone who would suit our needs, and we were incredibly fortunate that your plane came within range of assets that we control."

Kiran's mouth gaped open. "You shot us down?"

"Not directly, no, but it was...arranged, shall we say." The thing shrugged. "It was a calculated risk, because we had no way of knowing if you or your cousin would survive. But it was easy enough to arrange with the forewarning we were given. We had nothing to lose if you did not survive."

A tide of rage rose in Kiran's gut as he remembered the ghosts that had plagued his dreams, all the people, including poor Vijay, who had died in the crash or had been taken by the harvesters later. He sprang across the table, trying to wrap his hands around the thing's neck.

Without even blinking, it swatted him aside, pinning both wrists in one of its hands. The thing began to squeeze, and Kiran screamed as a bone in his hand cracked.

"Ever the fearless soldier," the thing said as it released him, and Kiran slumped back into his chair, cradling his injured hand. "There is no dishonor in what we are asking of you. And tell me, would you rather we set you free to deliver an offer of peace that may help your species survive, or suffer the fate of the others aboard your aircraft?"

Kiran swallowed hard and looked away from the thing's eyes. "And who am I to take your message to?"

"I would think that was obvious." The thing's face split into a wide smile. "Naomi Perrault, of course."

DRAGONFIRE

President Daniel Miller and the members of his cabinet were in one of the conference rooms in the White House Situation Room complex, while the Vice President had joined them over a video teleconferencing circuit from North American Aerospace Defense Command (NORAD) Headquarters, deep in Cheyenne Mountain in Colorado. In the President's hand was a brief note of explanation and apology from the Russian President that had been delivered by the Russian Ambassador five minutes after the warheads had detonated. That had been thirty minutes ago.

Miller crumpled up the note and angrily threw it to the floor. "I'm not sure what makes me angrier, that they kept us completely in the dark and nearly triggered a nuclear war between themselves, us, and the Chinese, or that they had the guts to do it and we don't." His face was pale in the bright fluorescent light.

"The latest estimate puts the number of immediate casualties at over ten million dead and at least half that many injured, with another five million deaths projected in the next six months from injury and radiation exposure," the Director of National Intelligence reported in a somber voice. "But the worst will be the famine that will hit them before next winter. They've destroyed or irradiated twenty-five to thirty percent of their primary grain producing region, not to mention the havoc the harvesters are wreaking on everything else."

"And what about the harvesters?" Miller asked.

"From what we can tell so far, they've been largely exterminated in the strike zones, but are still propagating like wildfire everywhere else." The DNI scowled. "The bottom line, Mr. President, is that it's a Pyrrhic victory for the Russians. The strikes took a huge bite out of the current harvester population, but did nothing to reduce the reproductive rate of the survivors. If I had to call it one way or the other, I'd say the strike was a failure."

"Mr. President," Vice President Andrew Lynch said through the videoconferencing television at the front of the room, "you can't possibly be considering following the Russians' lead. You've always been vehemently opposed to any use of nuclear weapons, especially on American soil. Look what a disaster Sutter Buttes was for Norman Curtis! I doubt nuking our major cities is going to earn us any points in the polls."

Miller slammed a hand down on the mahogany conference table, making everyone in the room flinch. "To hell with the polls! Have you seen the latest news reports from New York City? How about Chicago? Or maybe right here in D.C.?" He leaned forward, his face a mask of fury. *"Our constituents are being eaten alive!"*

After letting that sink in, Miller sat back. "Okay, so the Russian gambit looks like a failure." He pointed to the Secretary of State. "Find out what the Russians are doing. Tell their president that we'll render whatever aid we can, and make it clear that we're their allies. Got it?"

The Secretary of State nodded. "Yes, Mr. President."

"So," Miller said, turning back to the DNI, "what other disasters do I need to know about overseas?"

"Brazil has effectively collapsed," the DNI told him. "Brasilia has been totally overrun and has been set ablaze by the Army and Air Force. The Brazilian government still exists in name if not much else. The president and his cabinet have relocated several times, but São Paulo, Rio, and the other major cities are as bad as Brasilia. They finally decided to plant their flag on a cruise ship and are sitting in the harbor at Rio."

The Chairman of the Joint Chiefs grunted. "That's not a bad idea. It would be a hell of a lot easier to secure from harvester attack or infiltration, although resupply might be a problem."

"Do we have anything like that in the works?" Miller asked.

The Chairman offered a grim smile. "You've got every ship in the Navy at your beck and call, Mr. President."

"I appreciate that, but warships aren't exactly suitable for running a government, especially taking Congress into account.

Too many people are involved. I know we have several large underground bunkers other than Cheyenne Mountain that are being prepared, but I want some alternatives to all of us living like moles. Maybe it's a latent sense of claustrophobia, but I don't like the idea of all of us being trapped underground while the harvesters run rampant over top of us."

"I'll get someone on it right away, sir."

"Speaking of bunkers," the Secretary of State interjected, "the British Government and the Royal Family are in the process of moving into a bunker complex at Corsham, about ninety miles west of London."

"What, the old Site 3 bunker?" The DNI frowned. "That was decommissioned back in the early 1990s."

The Secretary of State nodded. "It was, but they've reactivated it. They must have every construction contractor that's still in business working on the place."

"What in blazes is Site 3?" Miller asked.

"Sorry, Mr. President," the Secretary of State said. "It's an old Cold War bunker complex in an underground quarry that they built as a leadership relocation facility. The existing facility has enough room to house four thousand people, and they're expanding into some of the available space in the underground caverns to house even more."

"We've had unconfirmed reports that most or all of China's leaders have gone to ground, too, at the Shanghai Complex," the DNI added. "Unfortunately, we don't have much on that one, other than it's huge. It can supposedly house two hundred thousand people."

"Well," Curtis said in a wry voice, "the Chinese have always thought big. But what about the situation with the harvesters?"

"From what we can tell from intelligence collected by the National Geospatial-Intelligence Agency and National Security Agency, the Chinese military is fighting the harvesters tooth and nail, but they're running into the same problem everyone else is facing: once the harvesters get loose in a heavily populated area, they multiply like mad and quickly overwhelm the local security forces. In the meantime, the harvesters have spread like a plague through China's most fertile crop growing regions." The DNI paused a moment to rub his jaw. "It's the same everywhere, Mr. President. India is swarming with the bloody things. They've spread across the border into Pakistan, which is now threatening to drop nukes on India. Southern France is an abattoir and Paris is being evacuated. The harvesters are everywhere. We've even had reports of harvester outbreaks in Iceland and Guam." The man licked his lips and looked down at his clasped hands. "They're everywhere."

It was then, in that moment, that Miller felt the cold hand of despair tighten around his heart. *We're losing this fight*, he thought. *Even our most powerful weapons are useless, because they kill us just as easily as they kill the enemy, and even well-armed troops can't stop them.* With unwelcome clarity, he recalled a video from Manhattan they had watched at the morning briefing the day before. Hundreds of civilians, defended by a company of National Guardsmen, had taken refuge aboard the floating museum of the aircraft carrier USS Intrepid. Helicopters had been called in to ferry the civilians to safety and a Black Hawk had just set down on the stern of the carrier's flight deck when all hell broke loose. There was no telling exactly what happened, but somehow the harvesters had overwhelmed the troops holding one of the visitor access points and flooded like a swarm of angry insects onto the flight deck. Men, women, and children went down in a flurry of slashing claws and venomous stingers. People near the edge of the flight deck jumped into the water. But the most terrifying sight was the harvesters leaping off the deck after them. The view from the camera showed the water turning red with blood, churned into a froth by the screaming survivors of the hundred foot fall and the things that had swarmed over the carrier's side to kill them. The video, which had been taken by one of the civilians and was streamed live to the web, had ended with a drawn out scream as the owner of the cell phone leaped into the water, after which the transmission mercifully ended.

That had been one of the last civilian communications out of Manhattan. Every bridge and tunnel to the island had been destroyed in an effort to contain the harvesters, with heavily armed

Coast Guard and police boats blasting the creatures caught swimming across the surrounding rivers.

He looked up at the sound of a muffled boom. Washington, D.C. itself was under attack, and Miller knew it wouldn't be long before he would have no choice but to abandon the White House for Air Force One. The entire block occupied by the White House and the nearby executive office buildings had been barricaded and fortified by the Army's 1st Battalion, 3rd US Infantry Regiment, which had traded its dress uniforms and ceremonial duties for combat uniforms and perimeter defense. The regiment's other units stationed in the Washington area had been divided up into platoon sized combat teams to defend the most critical infrastructure points in the city. Apache gunships and armed Black Hawks attacked targets called in by the local police or National Guard quick reaction teams.

Miller looked at one of the map displays. It looked much like the images of Earth's night side taken by astronauts in low orbit, showing the glow of lights that marked human civilization. This map looked much the same, but the lights were red, marking the spread of the harvesters.

A quote came to him from Winston Churchill, about whom Miller had written the thesis for his master's degree in political science many years before. *Victory at all costs*, Churchill had said, *victory in spite of all terror, victory however long and hard the road may be; for without victory, there is no survival.*

Looking up at the others, at the faces now wearing expressions of doom, he said, "Ladies and gentlemen, right now, today, we're getting our butts kicked. It's not the first time that we've lost the opening battles of a war. But we're going to do what we've always done. We're going to dig in, fight like hell, and figure out how to win this fight. Do you understand me?" He looked pointedly at the DNI, who nodded. "For now, let's keep the focus on protecting vital infrastructure and continuing to get the word out to citizens about how they can kill these things. I don't want any helpless civilians out there. I want them armed with all the knowledge and any weapons, manufactured or makeshift, that we can give them while we come up with something that'll kick the harvesters in the balls. Is that understood?"

"Yes, Mr. President." The chorus around the table was still downcast, but heartfelt.

That will have to do for now, Miller thought. "Okay, you all have a lot of work to do. Get to it. I'd like the Secretary of Defense, Chairman of the Joint Chiefs, Secretary of Homeland Security, the National Security Advisor, and Mr. Richards to stay behind."

The other members of the cabinet quickly got up and filed out past the four heavily armed members of the Secret Service detail who stood guard outside. Miller caught a glimpse of the bushy black tail of one of the cats who also stood guard. The feline, a Maine Coon, he recalled, was as big as some smaller dogs. The cat peered in at him. Or, rather, it looked in at the cat of unknown heritage that was busy entertaining itself under one of the chairs along the back wall of the conference room. Everywhere Miller went, even to the bathroom to shower or relieve himself, a cat went with him. Even when riding in the limousine, a Secret Service agent would toss in a cat like a furry hand grenade before closing the door.

Who'd have ever thought that the life of the President of the United States might depend on a cat? It's a damn good thing I'm not allergic to the little beasts. Miller broke out into a grin.

"Mr. President?" The National Security Advisor was eyeing him with a worried expression.

"Nothing, just an inside joke." Then Miller turned to Carl Richards, who had left one of the seats against the wall where he had been sitting for the open cabinet meeting to take a place at the table next to the Secretary of Homeland Security. "Please tell me we have some good news from Dragonfire."

Dragonfire was the code name that had been given to the huge, desperate effort to find a solution to the harvester epidemic, and President Miller had put Carl in charge of the project. While Carl technically answered to the Secretary of Homeland Security, in reality the President himself held his leash. The billionaire Howard Morgan, head of Morgan Pharmaceuticals, who had unwittingly played a role in the harvester outbreak in Los Angeles, was his technical advisor. Truth be told, Morgan was the brains behind the operation. The man was both an organizational genius and had the necessary science background to sort out the bullshit that, as Carl saw it, was flung by every scientist who thought his or her piece of the pie was the most important thing in the universe. Carl would have preferred to shoot them all, but Morgan was able to smooth ruffled feathers or break out the brass knuckles, as needed, and keep things moving.

"As I'm sure you're aware, sir," Carl began, "the genetics team has finished mapping the harvester genome. That's the big news, and I don't think I can adequately convey just what an incredible accomplishment that is."

"Yes," Miller said, nodding. "My scientific advisor briefed me on that. Please convey my personal thanks to everyone on the team. So what now? When can we expect progress on a bioweapon?"

"And what about chemical weapons?" That from the Chairman of the Joint Chiefs. "Is there any hope on that front?"

"If I can, Mr. President, let me answer that question first, as it's a bit more straightforward." Miller nodded for him to continue. "General, the chemical weapons division has run into a brick wall. Every compound they've come up with seems to have little to no effect on the harvesters. The things are like scorpions. We haven't found any toxins that affect them. The only way to kill them is to light them on fire or blast them to bits."

The old Marine hissed air out through his teeth. "So there's nothing we could use?"

"No, sir," Carl said, shaking his head. "The chemical team is still hard at work, but they don't have any rabbits in the hat at this point."

"Damn," the general said quietly.

"On the genetics side of the house, the teams are moving forward, taking advantage of the genome map. But as I've cautioned before, progress comes in fits and starts. The harvester DNA is hellishly complex, far more so than ours is. The goal now is to figure out which of the genes are important, and how we can disrupt them." He slowly spun his pen around on the table. "Naomi Perrault likened it to walking down a long dark hallway, then suddenly finding a door. Once you wrestle it open, you're in another dark hallway, with another door and hopefully another breakthrough somewhere at the end." Looking back up at Miller, he said, "She refuses to put a number on it, but from what I've gathered from Howard, we're looking at no less than six months before we have a chance of producing a weapon."

"Six months?" The Chairman of the Joint Chiefs pointed at the map. "We may not have six weeks!"

"General, six months would be nothing short of a miracle," Carl told him. "Remember what we're facing here. Matching up the genes with the traits they control isn't going to happen overnight."

"Then you need to get your candy-ass scientists to stop fucking around," Lynch said. "People are dying out there."

Carl glared at him. "In the last two weeks, I've had three people die of heart attacks and one from a stroke while they were at their desks. Over a dozen have been hospitalized for exhaustion or malnutrition, and none of them are taking more than a couple hours a day for sleep. My candy-ass scientists are working themselves to death, Mr. Vice President. I'd appreciate it if you'd kindly remember that."

Vice President Lynch held Carl's gaze for a moment, then looked away.

"What are the harvester population projections at the six month mark?" Miller asked. "How many will we be facing?"

Carl swallowed hard. "Just short of two billion worldwide, excluding casualties."

The president's face paled. "Sweet Jesus."

MORGELLONS

After the communications team had been unable to reestablish contact with Jack, Naomi went to her quarters. After closing the door, she crawled into bed and alternately wept and laughed. For the first time since she'd been told Jack was dead, she felt alive.

As the tears subsided, Koshka, her cat, hopped up and butted her furry head against Naomi's side. Propping herself up, Naomi lavished some attention on the Turkish Angora, her fingers brushing against the long scar along the cat's side.

Alexander, Jack's cat, hopped up on the bed, took one look at Koshka, then jumped back off.

"Jack will be home soon to take care of you," she told the big Siberian, who curled up in a corner and stared at her.

Knowing that she should be using the time for some badly needed sleep, Naomi felt restless. Reaching for the binder on her nightstand, she opened it to find a copy of the latest Red Team assessment of the harvester infestation by the Central Intelligence Agency. It was a top secret document produced in hardcopy only, with every copy numbered and addressed to a specific individual and hand delivered by government couriers. The first copy of seventeen went to the President of the United States, and she held a photocopy of it in her hands.

In the upper right was a sticky note. "Thought you'd want to see this," was written in Howard Morgan's neat script.

"How the devil did you get this?" She wondered aloud as she opened it to the first page and began to read.

She soon wished she hadn't. The ten pages of blunt prose and charts predicted the collapse of the modern world in less than two months. Even if humanity stopped the harvesters much sooner, the report stated, so much damage had already been done to the world's largest food producing regions that widespread famine on a global scale was inevitable.

And all of it stemmed from the one bag of New Horizons seed that we couldn't find, she thought bitterly.

She threw the document across the room, startling the cats.

Someone knocked on the door.

"What is it?"

"Naomi? Are you okay, hon?" It was Renee

"I'm fine," she lied. "Come on in."

Renee opened the door and stepped inside. "Listen, we just got confirmation that the Norwegian command post where Jack's hanging out is fine," Renee said. "The problem wasn't EMP, it was some End-of-the-World idiots blowing up a comms center at NATO Headquarters. I wish we could come up with a genetic weapon to make the harvesters just eat morons, but I suppose there wouldn't be many of us left. Come on, get your skinny ass up."

Naomi tried to smile.

Renee came to stand beside the bed and put her hands on her hips. "Look at you. You're white as a sheet and those rings under your eyes are worse than Carl's. Keep this up and you'll wind up as bald as he is, too. What would Jack think? He'll probably dump you so he can shack up with me, and you can have Carl the Sourpuss. You'll be two bald peas in a pod."

Unable to help herself, Naomi giggled. "Renee, shut up."

"I'll shut up the day hell freezes over, and probably not even then. Now get your ass out of bed. One of your queries hit on something, and Harmony is going to pee her pants with excitement if you don't get down there this instant."

***

With a heavy sigh, Howard Morgan sat back in the black leather executive chair in his corner office on the second floor of the lab building. He turned away from the computer to look out the windows. It had never been much of a view, as the facility had been located in the middle of a rather desolate spot in the expanse of Nebraska's farm country, and it hadn't changed for the better as his facility had been transformed from a cutting edge genetics laboratory to a heavily defended fortress. What he saw now more closely resembled the pictures he'd seen of firebases in Afghanistan. He was trying to enjoy the sight while he could, as the Army engineers planned to cover up the few remaining glass windows with sheet metal.

He turned around to look again at the report summary on the computer screen. All the labs were on line and functioning, an accomplishment about which he would have felt extremely proud had it really mattered. It wasn't that all the people in the sixteen labs weren't working as hard as they could. They were, and they had accomplished miracles, like completing the map of the harvester genome. It wasn't a question of the intelligence or resources of the people working for him, for he had the brightest people in the country, arguably on the planet, with all the resources the United States Government could provide. More than he could actually put to good use, in fact. He had been told to waste anything but time, for time was the one commodity that was the most precious. Time meant lives lost. Time meant more harvesters to kill.

No, the reason it didn't matter wasn't for any of that. It was because the enemy they faced was as biologically complex as it was implacable. They had taken the studies on harvester vulnerabilities originally begun by the Earth Defense Society and the original SEAL organization and expounded on them. But the result hadn't changed. They had nothing more to use against the harvesters now than they had at the start.

Even the genetic work Naomi and her people were doing, while brilliant, would bear fruit far too late to save humanity. The CIA Red Team report had made that abundantly clear. The shame of it was that they had all the major pieces.

"Damn," he whispered as he lifted his coffee cup to his lips, only to find it empty. He set it down and reached for the intercom to have his secretary bring in a fresh cup when the phone rang.

It was Naomi.

He snatched the phone from its cradle. "Morgan."

"Come down here, Howard," she said. "There's something you need to see. Right now."

"Hang on, I'll be right there." With a glance at the empty cup, he hung up the phone and headed downstairs to the genetics lab.

***

"You're not going to believe this," Naomi told Howard as he looked over her shoulder at the pair of computer monitors on her desk. Her eyes were bright with excitement, and Harmony Bates, who stood next to him, looked like a proud mother.

"You don't have to be melodramatic to get my attention," he told her. "Just please tell me it's not another mutated super-virus like the one you created last week."

Naomi made a dismissive wave of her hand. "Forget all that. Everything else is a sideshow now." She turned to her monitors, which showed a set of base pair gene sequences side by side. "Remember when I asked you to run sequence comparisons with harvester DNA against all non-human DNA samples that have been catalogued?"

Morgan chuckled. "How could I forget? That's been one of the most expensive parts of this project. We've got three server farms dedicated to it, run by the folks at SEAL-7, and we're running more servers than the two biggest web search engines combined."

"It was something I knew we had to look at, but I never expected to find anything." She ignored Morgan's scowl. "But we did. Look at what Harmony picked up from the latest results." She pointed to the left monitor, which showed a long sequence of base pairs. "This is harvester DNA from the current generation, what we refer to as Group B, with Group A being the original harvesters that created them. This one," she pointed to the second monitor, "is from a human tissue sample." She tapped a few keys, and three base pairs sequences were highlighted in both images. "These are the only deviations in this entire sequence."

Morgan was stunned. "How can this be? I thought you were only running comparisons against non-human DNA. Why was this sample even considered?" Morgan had made the decision to exclude the mass of human DNA samples from the comparative search on the grounds that even with as much computing capacity as had been dedicated to the Dragonfire project, it would take forever to run through even a tiny fraction of the available human DNA samples. Naomi had agreed after a long, drawn-out argument, but now Morgan wondered at the wisdom of his decision. *What else might we be missing?*

"It was a fluke," Naomi said. "This was from a human patient suffering from a disease called Morgellons that's been disputed from the outset, with some claiming it's a hoax and others claiming that it's real. This DNA sample was tagged as both human and non-human, which is how it made it into our search matrix."

"Morgellons?" Morgan shook his head. "I've never heard of it."

Naomi spun around in her chair to face him. "Most people haven't. What appears to be the first known modern case was reported in 2002 in Pennsylvania, and thousands were reported by 2008 when the CDC finally launched a study to determine if the disease was legitimate."

"What did they find?"

"The CDC concluded that it was a psychological disorder, but another study published by a dermatology research group determined that it wasn't, that there was clinical validation that it was a real disease based on analysis of one of Morgellons' hallmark symptoms. Look at this." Naomi brought up a web browser with images that, to Morgan, looked like something straight out of a horror movie.

"Patients often suffer some clinical symptoms like chronic fatigue or mood swings, which are typical of a wide range of ailments," Naomi explained, "along with a sensation of bugs crawling or biting under the skin, which has been associated with some skin conditions. But these skin lesions are a unique symptom." She pointed to a few of the images, which showed areas of skin on different patients that ranged from small lesions, as if the patient had scratched open bad mosquito bites, to large ulcerated patches.

"That's horrific," Morgan said.

"It is, but this is the strangest thing." She called up another set of images that showed strange, twisted fibers in a variety of colors. Some were in single strands, while others were clustered together. Some looked like fuzzy cotton balls. Others were individual twisted threads. "These tiny fibrous structures are found in the lesions. There's been a lot of research to figure out what they are, but the dermatological study demonstrated that they aren't implanted or embedded. The fibers originate from the skin's epithelial cells."

"So it's growing out of the skin of the patients?"

"Exactly." Naomi sat back. "The interesting coincidence is that there's a lot of anecdotal evidence that Morgellons is related to or caused by genetically modified organisms. No one's been able to conclusively prove it, but in the context of what's going on around us, it's not so easy to dismiss a possible link. But this," she tapped a few keys, and another pair of images came up on the screen, "is no coincidence. On the left is what's alleged to be an electron microscope image of a cross-section of one of these Morgellons fibers from a young female patient. The one on the right is from a fiber bundle in a harvesters's skeletal structure."

"My God." Morgan leaned closer, staring at the two images. His heart began to pound in his chest. "These are identical. Go back to the gene sequences."

Naomi flipped back to the windows showing the two sets of DNA sequences. "Unfortunately," she said, "this is the only data I've come across where the electron microscope image and the gene sequence data are correlated to a specific patient, and in my mind that correlation isn't a hundred percent certain, because so many of these records aren't properly sourced. But if it pans out..."

"This could be it," Morgan said, his voice barely a whisper. Their greatest challenge in exploiting the harvester DNA was its complexity, with hundreds of times more base pairs than human DNA. Aside from the breakthrough Harmony Bates had made in identifying a sequence associated with harvester reproduction, the SEAL labs had been unsuccessful in their efforts to tie specific traits to the harvester genes. Even if the reproductive gene could somehow be disrupted, it still wouldn't kill the current generation, only inhibit or, at best, prevent the reproduction of more. That was a vital goal, but it wasn't what the president was hoping for. "If we were able to disrupt their skeletal structure..."

"It would change everything," Naomi finished for him.

"But how did Morgellons come about?" He asked. "Was this an attempt by the harvesters to infect us directly, before they came up with the ploy to do it through our food?"

"There's really no way of knowing," Naomi told him. "Genes can be transferred from one organism to another. It's quite common among bacteria, although not so much in more complex organisms. If humans were infected by a mutated virus from a harvester," she went on, "it's not inconceivable that the virus could have transferred some genetic material to the human host. That's the basic theory behind gene therapy, and is what the harvesters used to weaponize the New Horizons seed that caused the disaster we're facing. It's also what we plan to do, if we can find all the pieces to the puzzle and put them together in time."

"So Morgellon's could just be accidental, the result of a mutated virus passed from the Group A harvesters to humans?" He nodded toward the monitors. "I'm having a hard time buying that."

"Well, maybe you'll buy this," Naomi said. "It may not have any direct bearing on what we're doing here, but this tidbit was very interesting." She pulled up another web page. "While we can't be sure they're related, Morgellons was named after a disease originally reported in 1674 by Sir Thomas Browne in England. He documented a disease that afflicted French children that was dubbed *le morgellon*, whose key symptom was strange hair or fibers growing from their skin." She scrolled down the page. "In 1682 the German physician Dr. Michael Ettmüller made these drawings with the aid of a microscope. Look familiar?"

Morgan stared at the images drawn by the long-dead German doctor. While Ettmüller's hand-drawn renderings weren't identical to the photographs Naomi had shown him, they shared enough similarities to make his skin crawl.

"So what does this mean?" Morgan said.

"It means that we have a possible — a *possible* — data point on how long the harvesters have been with us," Naomi told him. "Nearly four hundred years. And probably longer."

"Good God."

Just then the phone on Naomi's desk rang. She picked it up and listened. Morgan could tell even from where he was standing that it was Renee's voice, and she was excited about something. Looking up at Morgan with disbelieving eyes, Naomi said, "I'm going to put you on speaker so Howard can hear." She pushed a button and put the handset back in the cradle. "Okay, put him through."

"Go ahead," Renee's voice said from the speaker.

"Dr. Perrault, this is Captain Kiran Chidambaram." The voice was that of a young but authoritative man with a South Asian accent, but Morgan also sensed a slight quaver of fear.

"Kiran?" Naomi said with open-mouthed disbelief. "We thought you were dead when your plane went down! Is Vijay with you?"

"My cousin is dead. He...he did not survive the crash."

"I'm so sorry," Naomi told him, closing her eyes. "He was a good man. He'll be truly missed."

"Yes...yes, he will be." He paused. "Doctor, I need to see you as quickly as possible. It is very important."

"We'll do the best we can, but it may take a while to get to you."

She looked at Morgan, but he only offered a noncommittal shrug. Vijay Chidambaram would have been a welcome addition to the team and a valuable resource. His cousin Kiran certainly had value as an Indian military officer, but he wasn't an asset that Carl was likely to go out of his way to collect. "Kiran, this is Howard Morgan, the technical director for the lab where Naomi works. Air traffic is restricted worldwide, and some countries aren't allowing any overflights at all. But we'll do what we can. Where are you?"

"I am..." There was a longer pause. "I am in a place called Damlacik, in eastern Turkey near the Iranian border. Dr. Perrault, I must see you soon. This cannot wait."

"What's so urgent?" Naomi asked. "Did Vijay discover something?"

"No...it's the harvesters who captured me," he said, his voice trembling now. "They say they want to join forces with you."

CLOAK AND DAGGER

Jack's stay in Norway after the Russian nuclear strike had been brief. Six hours after the Russian nuclear strike, General Nesvold had presented Jack with a sheet of paper. In three lines of stark military prose, the Army had recalled him to active duty, promoted him one grade from his former service rank of captain to major, and assigned him to Headquarters, United States Special Operations Command (USSOCOM).

A second sheet of paper contained an equally brief set of orders from his new command, directing him to get to Ramstein Air Base in Germany as quickly as possible, but giving him no clue as to why.

The Norwegians were requested to provide a security element for Jack, and so he found himself escorted by Terje Halvorsen, Frode Stoltenberg (who brought along his cat, Lurva, in a collapsible crate), and two other soldiers of *Forsvarets Spesialkommando*, Norwegian Special Forces, aboard a C-130 at Bodø.

Once at Ramstein, they picked up the twelve men of a U.S. Army Special Forces A Team of the 10th Special Forces Group, led by Captain Jesus Alvarez.

"I'm Captain Alvarez, sir," the wiry Hispanic officer said as he shook Jack's proffered hand while his team quickly settled into their seats. The rear cargo ramp hadn't yet closed before the C-130 was taxiing for takeoff. "Nice to meet you."

"Any idea what this mission's about?" Jack asked as Alvarez strapped into the seat next to him. Opposite them sat Halvorsen and Stoltenberg, who were leaning forward, straining to hear what Alvarez had to say over the roar of the C-130's engines.

Alvarez shook his head. "Not a clue, sir. We just got back from an op in Budapest, helping the Marines evacuate our embassy there." He shook his head as the plane angled upward and leaped into the sky. "We barely had time to change into clean uniforms and check our gear before joining this party."

Halvorsen and Stoltenberg shared a look. "You had no time for mission planning?" Stoltenberg asked. "We're just going into this blind?"

"Pretty much," Alvarez admitted. "I don't like it. It's a piss-poor way to do things, but I couldn't really argue with the three-star who gave me the orders. We've got no intel, no details on logistics or support, no objectives. All I know is that this bird is taking us to Incirlik, Turkey where we'll be catching a different ride. Past that, they didn't tell us shit."

Jack rubbed his eyes. His headache had just grown worse. "Christ."

"Here, sir," Alvarez said, dragging over a big olive drab flight bag he'd brought aboard with him. "We were told you didn't have a go-bag, so we brought some gear for you."

Opening the bag, Jack found a helmet with night vision goggles attached, an M4A1 assault rifle with an under-barrel 40mm grenade launcher, body armor, and a combat vest loaded with magazines for the rifle and grenades for the launcher, a pair of white phosphorus grenades and another pair of high explosive frags, and a personal radio. At the very bottom was a set of fatigues. Jack pulled out the other gear and set it on the seat beside him, leaving the uniform in the bag.

"The ammo for the M4 is a mix of standard and incendiary," Alvarez said. "The 40mm grenades are all high explosive."

Jack checked that the weapon was empty and safe, then set it aside before he pulled on the vest over the Norwegian uniform he was wearing.

"I was told you might need this, too." Alvarez leaned over and attached a rank tab with a copper-colored oak leaf to Jack's vest. "Now the snipers will take you out first instead of me."

Stoltenberg guffawed at the joke.

"Sir, if you don't mind telling us," one of Alvarez's men asked, raising his voice so that the other men could hear, "you've seen action before, right? This isn't your first field op, is it?"

The others turned to look at Jack with keen interest.

"I've got two holes in my chest from AK-47 rounds, courtesy of the Taliban." Jack put his right thumb and forefinger to his chest, marking where the bullets had hit him. "And the scars on my face are from a grenade. So yeah, I've seen a little action."

The other men nodded somberly.

"But Jack," Stoltenberg protested, his face splitting into a wide grin, "all that means is you know how to get shot."

***

The flight from Ramstein was uneventful, and Jack even managed to get a little sleep before the C-130 began its descent into Incirlik Air Base. Jack looked at his watch. It was just past 0100, or one o'clock in the morning.

After landing, their plane taxied to a revetment area at the northeast corner of the airfield. The crew chief lowered the ramp and ushered them out.

Jack led the others down the ramp to where an Air Force sergeant in a flight uniform awaited them. "This way, sir," he said, gesturing for Jack and the others to follow.

"Do you know what the hell's going on?" Jack asked.

"The pilot'll brief you, sir. This way."

He led them to an Air Force Special Operations Command CV-22 Osprey, its huge wingtip rotors already spinning. The sergeant, who turned out to be the aircraft's crew chief, guided them aboard through the rear ramp. The men quickly settled into their seats, with Jack and the other officers sitting nearest the ramp.

The crew chief handed them headsets and double-checked that they could hear over the intercom. Jack gave a thumbs-up. A few moments later, the engines began to howl and the Osprey lifted off.

"Welcome aboard, boys and girls," the pilot said. "Hold on to your hats, use the puke bags if you feel like giving back your breakfast, and enjoy the nighttime tour of Turkey's friendly skies."

"Pilot, this is Major Dawson," Jack said. "Do you have any idea what our mission orders are?"

"I don't know about *your* orders, major, but mine are to fly you and your merry band of warriors just shy of five hundred miles northeast of here to the thriving metropolis of Damlacik, which is in easy pissing distance of the border with our friendly neighborhood Iranians."

"Is that it?" Alvarez said, shooting Jack an *I don't believe this shit* look. "You don't have any more details on this mission?"

"Well, if you want to get technical," the pilot replied, "my orders are to fly you to Damlacik, where Major Dawson, as in Major Dawson personally, will receive further instructions over the radio on frequency 149.800 megahertz, and that I'm supposed to do whatever the hell you tell me to do. I think the military-speak was that you have *full operational discretion.* I'm fine with anything you order me to do except giving up cartoons on Saturday. That's it. Sounds fun, huh?"

"Yeah," Jack grated. "A goddamn barrel of monkeys."

"This is very strange, Jack," Terje said. "How can we do... whatever we are supposed to do if we have no idea what it is?"

"It's one of the joys of 'need to know' taken to an extreme," Jack told him. "I guess we just have to hope that whoever is on the other end of the radio when we get to Damlacik has a clue."

Alvarez looked disgusted. Stoltenberg gave a Cheshire Cat smile in the darkened compartment and shook his head. Terje sighed and leaned back, closing his eyes.

An hour and a half later, the pilot announced, "We're going feet wet over Lake Van, boys and girls, about forty minutes out from the target. We're going to be making a low approach to keep the Iranians from painting us on their radar and getting their panties in a bunch. The ride's going to be a bit rough once we go feet dry on the far side of the lake, so get your barf bags ready."

"If we were on a Norwegian plane," Stoltenberg told him, "we'd have in-flight service and free drinks. Don't you have any whiskey?"

"Yeah," the pilot told him, "but that's only for the pilots. Passengers have to fend for themselves."

The pilot and Stoltenberg shared a laugh as the CV-22 pitched over and dove toward the black water of Lake Van, leveling out less than a hundred feet above the water.

Jack shifted in his seat, unable to get comfortable. He checked his weapon for the fifth time, making sure a round was chambered and the safety was on, before switching on his night vision goggles, then turning them off again.

Stoltenberg leaned across the aisle and put a hand on Jack's wrist. "Stop fidgeting." He grinned. "Lurva's trying to sleep."

"Sleep time's over," the crew chief said. "It's time for you guys to gear up."

The men began to check their weapons and gear again. They'd already checked once, early in the flight. But it never hurt to check again.

With that done, there was nothing left to do but wait as the plane droned onward.

"Feet dry," the pilot called as they reached the far side of the lake. The CV-22 nosed up slightly, then leveled off again. "Twenty minutes to target."

Jack's eyes widened as he saw through one of the portholes in the side of the plane the lights of houses passing by below. The tips of the rotors barely cleared the rooftops.

Then the houses along the beach flashed by and the plane was flying over darkened countryside. The pilot adjusted their course left and right to avoid the towns in their flight path.

"Hang on, it's going to get a little bumpy," he warned.

The Osprey began to climb and dive as they left the flat plains east of Lake Van and entered the hills before Lake Erçek. The plane roared over the northern end of that lake before heading into the mountainous terrain closer to the Iranian border.

Jack's headache, which had receded somewhat, returned with a vengeance.

The only member of the team who spoke out against the roller coaster ride was Lurva, whose cries let everyone in the compartment know of her displeasure. Stoltenberg offered her some sardines, which the cat sniffed at before gingerly plucking from the Norwegian's hand.

"I still can't believe we're taking a cat into a fight," Alvarez said, shaking his head. "And she's so calm. I'd have expected her to be clawing your face off."

"This is nothing," Stoltenberg said, fluffing the hair on Lurva's head before gently pushing her back down into the carrier, which had straps so he could carry her on his back. "I've taken her on jumps before."

Alvarez threw back his head and laughed. "I call bullshit on that one, my friend."

"No, really! She doesn't like it much, but she'll do anything for a few sardines. She's been on the firing range with me, too."

"How'd she like that?" Jack asked.

Stoltenberg chuckled. "Only my girlfriend sees those scars."

Turning to Alvarez, Jack said, "Be glad as hell we have a cat with us. You guys know they're natural harvester detectors, right?"

"We'd heard that, but everybody thought it was crap."

"It's true. They go nuts when there's a harvester anywhere nearby. Do yourself a favor and get a couple. Keep them with you at all times."

Alvarez raised his eyebrows. "Well, the quartermaster had better start issuing 'em."

"Five minutes." The pilot's voice had lost its cheery veneer. The Osprey dove, then made a tight turn to the left before it leveled off again.

"So are we supposed to get these mystery instructions as soon as we arrive at the target?" Jack asked the pilot.

"Beats the shit out of me, sir. I've told you all I know."

Jack and Alvarez shared a mutual *what a clusterfuck* look.

"Okay, pick an open spot near the town to land. Alvarez, your team will provide security while we're on the ground." He looked at Terje. "You guys hang out with me in here. If we don't hear anything over the radio in five minutes, we'll shut down the plane and wait."

A few moments later, the Osprey nosed down, then leveled off one last time. As the loadmaster opened the rear ramp, the pilot called, "One minute!"

The men unstrapped and got ready. Jack's fingers tingled as he gripped the M4, and he forced himself to control his breathing.

The Osprey rapidly slowed, its massive wingtip rotors tilting from their horizontal flight mode to vertical hover mode as the pilot brought it in for a gentle landing in the middle of a grain field. The sight of the stalks whipping in the downwash of the

Osprey's rotors gave Jack chills as he looked out the open ramp of the aircraft with his night vision goggles.

Even before the main gear kissed the ground, Alvarez and his men leaped from the rear ramp and ran to take up defensive positions around the Osprey. The four Norwegians knelt at the ramp entrance, the muzzles of their rifles covering the rear arc of the plane to augment the M240 machine gun manned by the crew chief.

Jack unplugged his headset and moved forward to the cockpit, where he plugged back in. "Anything?"

"Not yet." The pilot and copilot kept their eyes outside the cockpit, scanning the fields around them, and their hands on the controls.

The only lights were shining from the northeast, about half a mile away, where the little town of Damlacik lay. Checking his watch, Jack marked the time. *Five minutes*, he thought. *Call us, whoever you are. Call soon.*

Time crept by with agonizing slowness. One minute. Two. Three. At the five minute mark, Jack said to the pilot, "Maybe we should call on that freq to let them know we're here."

"Your discretion, sir," the pilot said. "The orders said to await contact."

"Right." Jack blew out a breath. "Go ahead and shut..."

The radio came to life. "This call is for Jack Dawson."

"Jesus Christ." Jack felt a tingle run up his spine. The signal was loud and clear, and there was no mistaking the speaker's voice. He keyed the mic. "Vijay? Is that you?"

"It was good of you to come, Jack," Vijay said. "I apologize for all the cloak and dagger, as you might say, but it is necessary. You'll soon understand why."

"But how..."

"Everything will be made clear soon, I promise you. But first I must ask you to continue your journey just a bit farther. This stop was just a sanity check, shall we say, to make sure our instructions had been followed. Can you copy down these coordinates?"

The pilot, who was listening in, nodded, holding a pen poised over a notepad. "Roger," Jack said. "Go ahead."

Vijay read off a set of coordinates, then had Jack read them back for confirmation.

"Very good," Vijay said. "Get there as quickly as you can, and I will contact you again on this same frequency."

"Vijay?" Jack waited for the scientist, whom he'd last seen near death in a Hyderabad hospital, to reply. "Vijay!"

There was no answer.

After mouthing a venomous curse, he ordered the crew chief to recall the men outside. To the pilot, he said, "As soon as the others are aboard, let's get rolling."

"Not so fast, sir. Our mission parameters only specified Turkey."

Jack looked at him, puzzled. "So? What's the problem?"

"These coordinates, sir." The pilot pointed to the map display on the instrument panel. "See that icon there? That's our destination."

Jack looked at the symbols on the display. While he could read military unit symbols well enough, a modern combat aircraft's navigation system was something else. "Look, I'm just a dumb grunt. Spell it out for me, okay?"

The pilot stared at him. "This party pad that your buddy wants us to fly to? It's over the border, inside Iran."

MESSENGER

"Major, are you sure about this?" Alvarez said quietly, with a sideways glance at his men, who were again strapped into their seats in the passenger compartment. "The world's going to hell, sure, but crossing into Iran is a door to a whole new level of hell that I'm not sure we want to open without a green light from up-chain. We've got no backup if things go south on us."

"We've already got authorization from as high as you can get," Jack told him. "I'm pretty sure I know who authorized this op, and he sits in the Oval Office of the White House. That's why I was given full operational discretion." Leaning closer to the special forces officer, Jack went on, "Listen, the guy I spoke to on the radio knows a great deal about harvesters. His plane went down a couple days ago, and it's pretty obvious now that our mission is to retrieve him."

"But why all the dancing around?" Stoltenberg asked. "If we were supposed to just extract him, our orders should have been to do just that. Boom! In we go to get him and it's done. But coming here, then going somewhere else to await yet more instructions, being kept in the dark all the while, makes no sense to me."

"I agree and I don't like this setup, either," Jack said. "But the order stands. We're going." To the pilot, he said, "Notify headquarters over satcom that we're heading across the border, then crank it up and let's get moving."

"Three bags full, sir," the pilot said as he pushed the throttles forward and the big rotors lifted the Osprey into the air. Turning to the southeast, the plane picked up speed. "Four miles to the border. Here's hoping everyone's asleep."

"Threat board is clear," the copilot said.

Jack's gut tightened into a knot as the Osprey approached the border. Everyone was silent except for the pilot and copilot, who periodically exchanged clipped phrases about the approach.

"I'm planning to cross on a northeasterly heading, away from the target," the pilot said. "Then we'll tack back to the southeast. That might throw them off a little." He paused. "Okay, here we go."

The Osprey nosed up, and Jack caught a glimpse of some distant lights along a cleared track that ran along the ridge line before the scene returned to darkness as the Osprey zoomed down the other side.

"Welcome to the Republic of Iran," the pilot announced. "Passports, please."

"We're not going to have much time before they scramble fighters if their radar paints us, major," Alvarez said.

"I realize that, captain." To the pilot, he said, "What's our ETA?"

"Nine minutes. And you guys better hold on to your breakfast again. We're heading into some really mountainous shit. It looks like the target site is just off of a big cut through the mountains. I'm going to take that route to mask us from radar as best I can."

"Do it." Jack leaned back and cinched his safety belt tighter.

The ride wasn't too bad until they were within four miles of the target, when the pilot yanked the Osprey's nose into the air over a hill, then flew in a series of gut-wrenching turns over a narrow stream bed flanked by steep hillsides. One of the men in the back vomited, and the reek of it made Jack want to follow suit.

"One minute," the pilot called.

The loadmaster opened the ramp in the rear, which let in a welcome gust of clean, cool air as the plane began to slow. The sound of the engines changed as the nacelles at the end of the wings pivoted upward. They climbed out of the rocky ravine they'd been following until they reached a spot that, while not completely level, was enough so that the pilot was able to set down.

"Welcome to the ass end of nowhere," the pilot said.

Once again, the soldiers, led by Alvarez, rushed down the ramp and set up a defensive perimeter around the Osprey as Jack waited for Vijay to call.

"All clear," Alvarez reported over his radio. "There's nobody here."

"Welcome, Jack," Vijay's voice came over the radio. "I'm glad you've come."

"Vijay, where the hell are you?" Jack had his night vision goggles on and was looking out the windscreen, trying to catch sight of his friend. "We've got to get you aboard and get out of here. Is Kiran with you?"

"Kiran is with me, yes, but not where we asked you to land. You must come down the hill to the stream bed, Jack. Then follow it to your right, heading southeast, for about three kilometers. Come on foot. We're waiting for you there."

"We don't have time for a cross-country march," Jack snapped. "We're flying over to pick you up."

"If you do, Jack, you will be shot down. You must come on foot. I am sorry, but it is for our protection."

"Your protection? I don't understand. We..."

"Time is running out, Jack," Vijay warned him. "If you are not here in thirty minutes, we will be gone. The choice is yours. Goodbye, my friend."

"Dammit!" Jack slammed the bulkhead with his fist.

The pilot turned to look at him. "Sir, you're not thinking of just leaving us sit here for an hour while you waltz down there and get this whacko, are you?"

"We don't have any choice. Shut down and pretend you're a rock with rotors until we get back." Jack tore off the headset and flung it into a seat. Grabbing his weapon, he joined Halvorsen, Stoltenberg and the other two Norwegians who were guarding the bottom of the ramp. "Come on," he shouted as the pilot killed the engines and the vortex of dust and debris flying around the plane began to dissipate. "Alvarez! Leave a security detail here to guard the plane. You and the rest come with me."

He didn't give the captain any time to argue before setting off at a trot down the hill toward the stream bed half a mile away, with the Norwegians close on his heels.

***

Sergeant First Class Ron Klimowicz thought the entire mission was insane from the get-go, but that's what he thought about nearly all the missions he'd been sent on in the eight years he'd been in Special Forces. He'd seen action in Iraq, Afghanistan, and half a dozen other places in the world. He'd been in danger plenty of times, and in many forms. He'd had a helicopter shot out from under him. He'd been in firefights and survived hand to hand combat. Hidden, he'd lain silent while the enemy walked past him, so close that he could have reached out and driven a knife through their ribs had that been his mission.

Klimowicz was well accustomed to that sort of danger, but what the harvesters presented was something altogether different. On the last mission, helping out the Marines in Budapest, he'd finally seen first hand the creatures shown on the news and the web. His team had gone in to get several embassy personnel who'd been cut off a few blocks away from the embassy, and it was there that Klimowicz had glimpsed the dark, alien forms as they savaged the Hungarian security forces that were trying to protect the panicked civilians mobbing the embassy. The civilians pleaded and cursed in the vain hope that they would be taken away by the Marine Ospreys that came in over the maintenance walkway along the peak of the roof where they picked up the embassy workers gathered there. He'd replayed that scene over and over in his mind on the flight back to Ramstein, wondering if such horrors could really be true.

Bringing up the rear as the team made its way along the stream bed, he caught a whiff of a foul odor that made his hackles rise at the same time the cat carried by the crazy Norwegian officer who was halfway up the patrol's column let out a low growl.

Turning around again, as he did every few steps to keep watch behind the team, he caught sight of someone...or something... moving. It was no more than a flicker in the vivid green of the night vision goggles that could easily have been dismissed as an illusion, but Klimowicz had been doing this sort of thing too long. A surge of adrenaline heightened his senses as he tightened his grip on his weapon, his electronically aided eye sighting down the scope at the culvert where he'd seen the movement. "Contact at our six," he whispered into his microphone as he knelt down behind a rock.

"What do you have?" It was the major's voice, a whisper in his ear piece.

"I don't know, sir. I just caught a glimpse of something..." He paused as a hair-covered face with a set of long ears peered out from the culvert. "Scratch that. It's a damn goat."

As if in reply, the goat, which was looking right at him, made a low *neaghh* sound.

"Yeah, fuck you, too," he whispered to himself, imagining the big goat roasting on a spit over an open fire.

"Move out," Captain Alvarez ordered.

"Roger." Klimowicz got back to his feet and resumed the march. The major was pushing fast, trying to get to the rendezvous point, and they were making a lot more noise than Klimowicz would have liked.

The goat followed along. Klimowicz found it distracting, as the animal's movement drew his attention as he tried to scan the landscape behind them.

The cat growled again.

"Down!"

At Alvarez's whispered command, Klimowicz and the others silently sank to the ground, kneeling or prone, the muzzles of their weapons pointing outward, covering the approaches to the patrol's location. His attention was focused on their rear, but all he could see was the goat, which was still ambling toward him.

The cat growled again, louder this time, the sound sending a chill through Klimowicz's gut. He'd never heard a cat do that before.

"Anybody see anything?" It was the major.

Everyone whispered a chorus of *Negative*, except for Klimowicz. "Just the stupid goat."

"How big is it?"

The question caught Klimowicz by surprise. "I don't know, sir. It's hard to tell, but pretty big. A lot bigger than the little ones like you'd see in a petting zoo, but not as big as some I've seen."

The goat stopped to peer at him, let out another *neaghh*, then kept on coming. The cat was going crazy. *They're going to hear that beast's yowling all the way in Tehran*, he thought. *So much for sound discipline.*

"Take it out!"

"You sure, sir?" He wouldn't have questioned the order had it come from Alvarez, but the major had struck him as not being terribly field-savvy. The Norwegian, Stoltenberg, had been right. Getting shot a couple times didn't prove that you knew what you were about in combat, only that the other guy got the drop on you. "That's going to really wake up the neighborhood."

"Kill the goddamn thing, sergeant!"

"Roger that." The goat was less than a dozen feet away now and still coming. He put the crosshairs of his sight right between the goat's eyes, trying to hold his aim steady as the animal moved toward him. "Sorry, little buddy."

With his vision focused through the limited field of view of the sight, he never saw the stinger-tipped tentacle emerge from the goat's belly. It whipped forward, the six inch needle sinking into his neck before he could pull the trigger.

"Contact!" Klimowicz heard the shout, followed by a volley of gunfire, but the only thing that mattered was the burning agony that began to consume his body as if he were being slowly coated in molten metal. He felt blood pouring through his fingers as he pressed his hand to the wound in his neck, and saw the shadows of the other men on the team coming to his aid. He opened his mouth to speak, to scream, but all that came out was blood.

***

"He's gone, sir."

"Shit," Jack hissed as the medic closed the dead man's eyes.

"The thing's run off." Alvarez reached down and angrily yanked one of the dog tags from Klimowicz. "You should have warned us they could do that. *Sir.* That little bit of intel could have saved his life."

"I've never seen them do this before," Jack said. "It's always been a theory, but the only thing we've ever seen them mimic was human beings."

"Well, I guess now we know they mimic goats pretty well, too."

"Leave his body here," Jack said, taking a long look at Klimowicz, committing his face to memory. "We'll pick him up on the way back."

"Yes, *sir*." Alvarez stalked off, whispering orders to his men. Like ghosts in the dark, they got to their feet and started moving out.

"That was the first time I have seen one." Stoltenberg stood next to Jack. In the carrier on his back, Lurva meowed as she turned back and forth in her carrier. She'd stopped growling as soon as the harvester had run off. Reverting to its natural form, it disappeared back the way they had come, its insectile body moving with blinding speed through the rocks. They'd fired at it, but there had been no sign of blood on the ground. "Devilish things."

"That was nothing," Halvorsen said. "We were very lucky."

"Tell that to him," Jack said, nodding at Klimowicz's body. Keying his mic, he said, "If you guys see anything else that moves before we get to the rendezvous point, shoot first and ask questions later."

***

They were being followed. The team had seen flashes of movement on the rocky slopes above them, but nothing they could shoot at and hope to hit. Lurva was restless, but she wasn't carrying on as she had when the harvester disguised as a goat had made its appearance.

"I can't believe this isn't a trap," Alvarez said to Jack without using the radio. "We're surrounded, and the enemy holds all the high ground."

"If they really wanted to kill us, they could have done it a dozen times over," Jack told him. "I think that's why they killed Klimowicz. Just to let us know that they could."

Alvarez spat something in Spanish.

A warning came over the radio from the man at the head of the patrol. "Contact forward!"

Everyone dropped to the ground, weapons at the ready.

"Report," Jack said.

"I've got one man, or what looks like a man, standing in the middle of the stream bed at the rendezvous point, maybe fifty meters ahead."

"Understood. Alvarez, you and your men hold here and cover us." Turning to Halvorsen and Stoltenberg, Jack said, "You two come with me. I want to see what Lurva makes of whoever's waiting for us."

"I'd rather we check first with a few rounds from my rifle." Stoltenberg was looking at the lone figure through his rifle sights.

"Not this time. Let's go."

Jack led the way along the stream bed. Even in the monochromatic light of the night vision goggles, he could see that whoever it was looked haggard and unkempt. He was wearing a torn uniform that bore dark stains. He studied the face as he drew closer.

It wasn't Vijay.

"Kiran?" He called out the name softly, and the man flinched as if he'd been struck.

"Jack," he whispered, his voice hoarse. "Is that you?" He took a halting step forward.

"Stay there. Don't move."

Kiran stopped and raised his hands. Jack was close enough now to see his friend's face clearly. He was terrified. Jack motioned for Stoltenberg to come forward. The big Norwegian moved up on one side of Jack as Halvorsen came up on the other, both their weapons trained on Kiran. If it really was Kiran.

Leaning over, Jack peered at Lurva in her backpack carrier and found her staring back at him. She was still uneasy, but only meowed at him. He poked a couple fingers through the fabric slats and she rubbed her muzzle against them. "Good girl," he whispered. Then, to Kiran, he said, "Walk toward us slowly."

With a heavy limp, Kiran limped toward them. He stumbled a few times, and kept glancing up at the high ground above them.

"Oh, God, Jack, it's so good to see you!" Kiran embraced him, tremors of fear running through his body. "Let's get out of here."

"Where's Vijay? He spoke to me on the radio. We've got to take him back, too."

"He's dead," Kiran said as he let go of Jack. "He was badly injured when the plane crashed, and probably would have died, anyway. But they killed him. They...they *ate* him, Jack. They ate his head, then the rest of him. Right in front of me. Then they ate the others." Tears were streaming down his cheeks. "I'm the only one they left alive. What you spoke to was one of *them*."

"Jesus, Kiran, I'm so sorry."

"Major," Alvarez said over the radio, his voice tight. "We just got a heads-up over the satcom that company's coming. Some Iranian fighters that were buzzing around up north are headed our way."

"Come on." Jack took Kiran by one arm while Halvorsen took the other. Stoltenberg covered their backs. "Let's haul ass back to the Osprey and get the hell out of here."

THREE KEYS

Once back on the ground at Incirlik, Alvarez and his team, carrying the bag containing Klimowicz's body, were first out of the plane, stepping into the darkness without a single word to Jack. Stoltenberg made a somber farewell before taking Lurva and the two other Norwegian soldiers with him to return home aboard the C-130 that had brought them here.

Terje remained, with orders to act as a liaison with the Americans to learn all he could about how to defeat the harvesters and send that vital information back to Norway.

The two of them escorted Kiran, who had been patched up by the medic on Alvarez's team, to a C-17 transport that was waiting to take them to the States. The base commander was waiting for Jack, and in a voice that could be heard all the way to the operations building, described what an idiot he had been. Iranian F-4 fighters had pursued the Osprey to the border as it fled back into Turkey, turning back at the last second rather than going up against half a squadron of Turkish F-16s. Since then, the base commander had informed Jack, the Turks had been forced to put every available fighter in the air to ward off the growing swarm of Iranian fighters probing into Turkish airspace.

From there, the C-17 made the long flight to Offutt Air Force Base in Nebraska, where the three men boarded a Black Hawk that took them to the SEAL-2 facility.

The view during the flight was sobering. The city of Omaha was wreathed in flames, and tens of thousands of cars choked I-80 as people tried to flee the city.

When they set down at SEAL-2, Naomi was there waiting for him, and had hugged him so hard that he thought his ribs would break.

Her welcome home kiss was interrupted by Carl, who after a very perfunctory greeting dragged them all into a conference room, ignoring Jack's protestations that he hadn't even had a chance to shower since he'd left Norway and that Kiran should be sent to the infirmary to rest.

"There's time for that later," he'd growled before ushering them into the room where Renee was already waiting. She had time to give Jack a hug before Carl told everyone to sit down.

Turning to Jack, he said, "You almost started a war. Do you know that?"

"You know something," Jack said, feeling a flush of heat rising up his neck, "I'm getting goddamn tired of people telling me I fucked up when this mission was such a cluster from the get go. We were told nothing — *nothing* — other than to go to this little burg in Turkey and wait for someone to call us on the radio and follow their instructions. Oh, and that I had full operational discretion. That was it. What if I'd been a good little boy and not gone across the border? Then we wouldn't have Kiran. Would that have made you happy?"

"No, but you should have called in for clearance and had some backup lined up before you went in. The Iranians are panicked about the nukes the Russians lit off right along their border to the north and they're seeing this whole disaster as a deception cooked up by the Great Satan. Their relations with us, and by extension the Turks, are as bad as they were after the fall of the Shah." He shook his head. "No, they're worse, because they're blaming us for the harvester outbreaks that have started popping up in their country."

Jack leaned forward. "Fine. Shoot me. And tell the Army they can take their commission and shove it."

"They just might. I've had three calls from guys with stars on their shoulders threatening to send you to a court martial. You..."

"Carl, I think Jack got the message," Naomi interrupted, putting a hand on Jack's shoulder and gently but firmly easing him back. "The important thing is that the mission was successful. Jack got Kiran out. That's far more important in the long run than whether the Iranians got their noses bent out of shape."

"Tell that to the president," Carl snapped. "Or, better yet, the vice president, who ripped off my right butt cheek over this."

"Join the crowd," Jack murmured.

"Stop it!" Naomi glared at each of them in turn. "We don't have time for this. If you want to throw sand in each other's faces, go ahead, but do it somewhere else."

Before either man could say anything more, the keypad on the secure door beeped, and after the lock clicked open Howard Morgan came in, closing the door behind him. His expression was bleak.

Carl shot him a glare. "And where have you been? You're late."

"I got an emergency call in the communications center," Morgan said as he took the seat to Carl's left. "We just lost SEAL-12 outside of Chicago."

Carl slammed his fist on the table, making everyone else jump. "How the devil did that happen? How did the harvesters breach their defenses?"

"They didn't. It was a few lunatics of the human variety, probably with help from someone on the inside. These geniuses apparently thought the facility was where the government cooked up the harvesters as part of some insidious plot. One of the supply trucks that went in was loaded with a fertilizer bomb instead of supplies."

"Casualties?" Carl asked.

"Over a hundred dead and at least that many injured. We won't know the final tally for a while, as the rescue crews are still digging bodies and parts of bodies out of the rubble. The bomb blast was bad enough, but it set off the munitions in the magazine and the stored fuel, too. The entire facility is a total loss, and I'm frankly amazed that anyone at all survived."

"My God," Jack said, incredulous. "Who would do this? Are they insane?"

"Clearly," Morgan told him. "By the way, it's good to see you again, Jack."

"Howard," Naomi said after giving everyone a moment to digest this most recent news, "this is Kiran Chidambaram, the focus of Jack's mission, and Terje Halvorsen of the Norwegian Army."

"Delighted," Morgan gave a nod at the two men, "although I wish it were under better circumstances."

"As do we all," Kiran said with a wan smile.

"All right, Kiran," Carl said in a softer tone, "let's hear your story."

Kiran swallowed, then told them the details of how he had come to be there. "Then one of them," Kiran concluded, "in the guise of Vijay, came for me and told me what they wanted. That is when they had me call Naomi to arrange the pickup."

"And what exactly do they want?" Naomi asked.

Jack leaned forward, hanging on Kiran's words.

"They want an alliance, to help us develop a counter to the lower castes of their kind."

"Bullshit," Carl spat.

Naomi shot him a look of annoyance before she turned back to Kiran. "I don't understand. I thought there was just one 'lower caste,' that being the larvae."

Kiran shook his head. "No, the adults have two variations. Most become only the monstrous-looking creatures and do not change shape. They are cunning but not sentient, breeding endlessly until they die." He licked his lips. "The thing told me they could live for hundreds of years."

Jack saw Naomi and Morgan share a look.

"Only a very few reach full sentience," Kiran went on. "They can change shape, and eventually stop producing larvae. The thing that sent me to you is one of these. They want an alliance because the other harvester forms kill them just like they do us. But if the lower castes are not stopped..."

"There won't be anything else left on the planet," Naomi finished for him.

"What are they offering?" Carl asked. "And what do they want in return?"

"They offer their assistance in finding an effective way to control the lower castes. I assume it has to do with whatever it is Naomi works on, as they were very specific about contacting her.

As for what they want...they want to survive. It told me that the sentient among its kind would consent to live in isolation from humans, in peace."

"Like hell." Carl shook his head.

"The thing said it would expect you to say that, and so it sent this." He reached into a pocket of his tattered uniform and withdrew a single folded sheet of paper. Carefully opening it up and smoothing it out, he passed it to Naomi. "It told me to say this to you. It made me memorize the words exactly. *There are three keys. We offer this one to you as a token of our good faith.*"

"What is it?" Jack leaned over to see what was on the page that Naomi was now staring at with disbelieving eyes. The paper was filled with neatly drawn hexagonal symbols connected by short lines, with various letters at some of the vertices of the hexagons and ends of the lines.

"It's a complex molecule," she said.

"Which means what?" Carl asked. "Remember, not everyone around the table made it through high school chemistry."

She looked up at him, her eyes bright with excitement. "This is the formula, the blueprint, for the receptor, or lock, on the cellular membrane in harvester cells. This is the first line of defense our virus has to penetrate. The virion, the virus particle, has special structures on its surface that act as keys and are tailored for receptors on the cell membrane."

"The locks," Jack said.

"Right. The keys have to match the locks or the virus can't get into the cell to do its dirty work. We already figured out the receptors on the outer membrane, so this doesn't directly help us. But if they know this much, then they should be able to help us get through a second set of locks, inside the cell, where I'm afraid we've hit a major roadblock."

Carl cocked his head. "Couldn't you figure that out yourself?"

"Yes, but it's going to take time, Carl, which is the one thing we don't have."

Jack turned to Kiran. "What about the third key?"

"It did not explain," Kiran said. "It seemed to believe that Naomi would understand the meaning."

"I think I do," she told him. "I'm not sure, of course, but I think the third key must be the harvester genetic code itself. We've identified the gene sequences associated with their reproduction, but even knowing that much, we aren't sure what modifications to make. We've also found a potential weak point, a gene sequence that we think deals with their skeletal structure. If we disrupted that somehow, we might be able to weaken the skeleton so they could be killed more easily, or maybe even deform the structure and kill them directly. There are lots of possibilities, but I just don't know. And we also don't know which specific genes have to be modified in which ways to produce a desirable result."

"But I thought you'd already mapped their genetic structure," Carl complained.

"We have, but having a map only helps if you have reference points," she told him. "With the help of the harvesters, we might be able to create a new DNA instruction set that would, at a minimum, turn off their reproduction, and have these new DNA instructions delivered through a virus."

"Why don't you just kill them with the flu or something? Just let the germs do what they always do." Renee suggested. "That seems a lot simpler than all this mucking around."

Naomi shook her head. "We've tried everything from various strains of the common cold to Ebola, all to no avail. We can get the viruses into the harvesters, but it's like throwing rocks at a tank. Nothing seems to shake them." She sighed. "The good news, such as it is, is that we've been able to engineer a viral delivery system from a strain of H2N2 influenza that's nearly perfect for our needs. It's extremely contagious among harvesters, can be spread through the air, water, or, ah, consumption of the host, and can survive for hours, even days, in an outdoor environment."

"Is it contagious to us?" Jack asked.

"Actually, it is, because the virus maintains some of the human-coded keys. I was originally going to shelve the strain and move on when we got the full results from the trials on volunteers." Her mouth turned up in a sly grin. "They all became asymptomatic carriers."

"Typhoid Mary," Renee whispered.

Naomi nodded. "Right. Our bodies can harbor the virus and we can spread it to harvesters or even other people, but it has absolutely no effect on us. Once we can program it, if you will, to get through the locks inside the harvester cells and inject a tailored DNA payload, we'll have a genetic Trojan Horse that will spread among the harvester and human populations like wildfire."

"That would also make every one of us a weapon against them," Terje mused.

"Exactly."

"So, we're back to your favorite question: how long until you have something we can bomb them with?" Carl looked from Naomi to Morgan, who was frowning. "How long might it take to get through the second lock and put your DNA payload together?" When Naomi gave him a pained expression, he went on, "Listen, I don't think any of you realize just how fast things are falling apart out there. The fact is that we may be looking at a matter of weeks before the United States of America ceases to exist as a coherent entity.

"She knows, Carl," Morgan said with a glance at Naomi. "She knows quite well."

"I know you can't make this thing overnight," Carl said. "But what we need, what the president needs so he can pass it on to the people, is a glimmer of hope. I told him what Howard told me earlier, that it would take six months to get from where we are now to something we can use." Naomi shot an accusing glance at Morgan, who shrugged unapologetically. "But you know more now than you did even then, so I want you to use that genius brain of yours and take a wild guess. We've got to give the people some hope or we're all sunk."

Under the table, Jack reached over and took Naomi's hand in his.

"I can't..." She closed her eyes and bowed her head down. After a moment, she looked up and said, "If what we discovered about the Morgellons connection pans out, and if we can devise an RNA payload to deliver a disruptive gene sequence, and if we can figure out the second set of locks in the cells, and if we can package that up into the virus we already have, we might have a chance at putting something in the field in two, maybe three months. If everything went right and we can get past our current roadblocks quickly. That's a lot of *ifs*, Carl, and it's not something I'm willing to bet my life on."

"You're not betting your life on it," Carl said. "You're betting the lives of everyone on the planet."

"What about the harvesters' proposal?" Morgan asked. "They seem to have an innate grasp of these matters. With their help we could engineer something a lot more devastating and field it much sooner than we could on our own."

Carl snorted. "I'm going to do my duty and run the idea by the president, but I'll wager my next paycheck of worthless money that he won't even let me finish talking before he kicks me out the door."

"But let's pretend that he was willing to consider it," Morgan pressed. "Then what?"

"Then Naomi would have to go to them," Kiran said quietly.

Everyone turned to stare at him.

"I am sorry, but that was the last instruction I was to pass on. They said that if you wish to join in an alliance, Naomi herself must go to them, as a sign of your good faith. They are willing to trust her, and only her."

"Not a fucking chance," Jack growled.

"Even if we don't want to play their game," Naomi said, "we're going to need something that may not be easy to find."

Carl looked up at her, his hand poised over his tablet. "What's that? Whatever you want, I'll get it."

"We need a Morgellons victim," she told him.

"Fine. I'll coordinate with the CDC and have them track one down for you."

She shook her head. "No, it can't just be a random victim." Glancing at Morgan, she went on, "I need a particular patient, the one whose data led me to these conclusions. We have samples of her DNA, we've already started an initial workup on her gene sequence, and I'm as confident as I can be at this point that she can help us. But not all patients who think they have Morgellons actually have it. We don't have the time to play around. We need this particular patient."

Frowning, Carl said, "Who and where?"

"Melissa Wellington. She's a patient at the University of Chicago children's hospital."

Carl leaned back in his chair and stared at her as Morgan blew out a breath through his teeth.

"What's the problem?" Jack asked.

"The great city of Chicago," Carl told him, still staring at Naomi, "is one big slaughterhouse. Everything west of the Chicago River has pretty much been lost. The National Guard troops holding Midway International Airport were overrun last night."

"What about the hospital?" Naomi stared right back at him.

"That's the only good news, such as it is. As of the last report I saw, the Guard is still holding Chicago's South Side, where the university's located, but all the land routes out are cut off and their backs are against Lake Michigan. The president's trying to evacuate as many people as he can, and the waterfront looks like the old pictures of Dunkirk in the Second World War. That's sort of not so good news for what you're asking."

"Why is that?"

Carl rolled his eyes. "Because it's a goddamn mess, Naomi! Most of the surviving population of Chicago is crammed in there, trying to escape on the ships before the harvesters break through the Army's lines. All I can do is check to see if she was evacuated, but I wouldn't get your hopes up. Even if she did get out, there's no guarantee there'll be a record of it. Things are confused as hell on the ground. People are being crammed into every boat and helicopter without any documentation and being sent anywhere that has space to take them."

"So even if you did send someone in to get her," Terje mused, "she might be dead or have already been extracted, and no one would know."

"Right." Carl looked again at Naomi. "If you need this girl, I'll do whatever I can to make it happen. Just be damn sure you really need *her*."

"You told me that we could waste anything but time, Carl," she said. "That girl could save us weeks."

"Fine. I'll have someone check to see if there's any record of her being extracted. If that comes up empty, we'll try to get her out. But we'll need a complete lunatic to take on that job."

Everyone but Naomi turned to look at Jack.

CHICAGO

As Jack stepped off the Air Force C-20B Gulfstream jet onto the tarmac at Aurora Municipal Airport, he was struck by a terrible sense of déjà vu. Dozens of olive drab and desert tan military tents stood in orderly rows in the fields surrounding the airport, with CONEX storage boxes and portable latrines in neat lines along the makeshift roads. A double fence topped with concertina wire surrounded what was now called firebase Aurora, with sandbagged bunkers at close intervals around the perimeter, backed up by Bradley infantry fighting vehicles. The air carried the smell of jet fuel and the roar of the rotor blades from the Black Hawk and Apache helicopters that were flying round-the-clock sorties. A dozen helicopters were on the apron, maintenance crews swarming over them to get them ready to fight again while the crewmen dozed in the flight office that served as their ready room.

A quartet of Apaches lifted off and hammered east, their stub wings loaded with rocket pods and Hellfire missiles. As they cleared the firebase perimeter, a battery of M109A6 Paladin howitzers, deployed in an open field just east of the airfield, fired a salvo of 155mm rounds, tongues of flame and smoke jetting into the air.

Alexander let out a startled cry at the sharp boom made by the guns. Jack had to shift his grip on the soft-sided carrier as the big cat tried to scrunch his twenty pound bulk as far away as he could from the zippered front opening.

"I'm sorry, buddy," he said, trying to sooth the cat and his own sense of guilt for bringing him. "I'll make it up to you with some fresh salmon."

"This looks like Bagram in Afghanistan." Terje, standing beside him, shook his head in astonishment.

"Look." Jack pointed as the other four men on the team, including Craig Hathcock, the sniper who'd fought alongside Jack on Spitsbergen, followed them off the plane. "That must be Colonel Ford."

A tall woman in her early forties wearing combat fatigues, escorted by two heavily armed soldiers, was striding toward them. Jack and Terje came to attention and saluted.

"Major," she said crisply, returning the salute. Eyeing Terje, she inclined her head. "Captain. I wish I could say I was happy to see you, but I'm not. Every chopper we divert from delivering relief supplies or ferrying civilians out means more people left behind in the hot zone."

"I understand that, ma'am," Jack told her as she turned and led him and the others at a brisk pace across the tarmac. "But..." The Paladins fired off another salvo, the thunder from the guns echoing between the hangars. "...the girl we're trying to find could be critical to the war effort. We made every attempt to find out if she had already been evacuated, but there's no record of her leaving the university hospital. We've got to go in and try to find her. There's no other way."

"I'm not arguing with my orders, major," she said, her voice conveying a sense of bone-weary exhaustion. Her eyes were bloodshot and had dark rings below them. "I'm just not happy about them, especially the part about dedicating a Black Hawk and a pair of Apaches so you can go sightseeing. I really don't think you appreciate how precious those assets are." She glanced at Hathcock and the other members of the team, who were a mix of former EDS gunslingers and FBI agents. "I also don't particularly care to be ferrying civilians in when we're desperately trying to get thousands of others out."

"I don't plan on screwing around, colonel. We'll get your birds back to you as soon as we possibly can."

"You do that, major." She pointed to one of several Black Hawks on the apron, its rotors already spun up. "There's your ride. Bring it back to me in one piece, if you don't mind. The Apaches will join up with you en route before you head into hostile territory."

"Yes, ma'am." Jack saluted, then led the team at a trot to the waiting Black Hawk, where they took seats in the cargo area. Jack put on the headset offered by the crew chief, and as soon as his men gave him a thumbs up, told the pilot, "Let's do it."

"Roger."

A moment later they were airborne, the pilot joining a formation of seven other Black Hawks that were heading east toward the city.

Terje nudged Jack and pointed out the left side door. About a mile away was I-88. Instead of being packed with cars, it was nearly empty, the cars having been driven, pushed, or bulldozed aside to make room for a steady stream of military vehicles that rumbled east. A solid mass of civilians on foot, crammed into a single lane, shuffled westward.

"We've set up a defensive line along the Fox River," the crew chief said, following their eyes. "We're trying to get as many people out as we can before the engineers blow the bridges."

"What happens then?" Terje asked.

The crew chief shrugged. "Lots of napalm, I guess. And they're planning to dump a bunch of gas into the river and light it on fire as a barrier. The bugs don't like fire."

"No, they don't," Jack said absently as he stared at the scene.

Many of the residential neighborhoods in the suburbs were nothing more than stretches of charred and smoking ruins. Others looked untouched. People flowed west like drops of water in the mountains, starting as individuals or families, then joining other small groups, until finally they formed the great river of the mass exodus along the Interstate. Anxious faces turned up to look at the Black Hawk as it flew past. Some people waved their arms or jumped up and down to try and draw the pilot's attention, but most had accepted the grim reality that the Black Hawk had not come for them.

They flew over a school that still had dozens of kids in a central courtyard, shepherded by a handful of teachers. As one, they jumped up and down and waved.

Jack keyed his mic. "Can't you get some birds in here to get those kids out?"

"Negative, sir," the pilot said. "I wish we could, but we've got very strict orders not to land except in a secured area. No exceptions."

"Why?"

"Because we lost three birds and their crews to panicked civilians, and two more to harvesters masquerading as civvies. Sorry, sir, but I wouldn't land there if you held a gun to my head."

"Christ," Jack said quietly.

"There's our escorts." The crew chief pointed to a pair of slender shapes in the sky coming toward them. The two Apaches banked around, revealing their angular profiles as they took up station on either side of the Black Hawk.

"Now that's something we don't see every day," the pilot said. "You must be pulling a lot of weight to get us escorts, major. I'll take you flying anytime."

Jack snorted. "Be careful what you wish for."

The pilot took them right down 47th Street, heading due east over more residential neighborhoods. The devastation here was universal. Only glowing coals remained, and the air in the helicopter was thick with the smell of smoke.

"Why has everything been burned?" Terje asked.

"Scorched earth policy," the pilot answered. "Areas that are declared as either overrun or clear of civilians are being torched. Most of it's with napalm dropped by the Air Force, but those artillery yokels back at the firebase are sending out white phosphorous rounds."

Terje grimaced.

"That's The Wall," the pilot said as they crossed over I-294, which ran in a north-south direction. "In our sector, it runs from the junction with I-80, about twenty miles southeast of here, up north to I-290, where the line bends around to the west. We're trying to keep the harvesters contained in the metro area and keep them from breaking out to the west."

The eastern side of I-294 that faced toward Chicago had been barricaded with jersey barriers, abandoned cars, and sandbags. Thousands of bright pyres burned where harvesters had been hit with incendiary ammunition or flamethrowers, and more exploded into flame as he watched groups of them charge the defenders.

But harvesters weren't the only casualties. Thousands of charred and mutilated human bodies littered the scorched landscape leading up to The Wall.

"People can pass through at a handful of checkpoints," the crew chief said, following Jack's gaze. "Anyone who approaches anywhere else is considered hostile. They try to warn them away, but…"

"But what can they do when harvesters are chasing them," Jack finished, forcing down the bile rising in his throat.

Jack's felt an unpleasant flurry of butterflies in his stomach as they flew east, deeper into the hot zone. The other men, except for Hathcock, went through the comforting ritual of checking their weapons again. The sniper only stared out into the devastation below.

"I thought there would be more harvesters," Terje said. "The reporting I've read makes it sound like every street should be packed with them, even with all the napalm and artillery fire, but I see nothing moving."

"The bastards are smart," the pilot answered. "They use the sewers, and the ones above ground know to hide when they hear our rotor blades or jet engines. Most of the kills we're making in the hot zone now are from artillery and smart bombs dropped from high altitude, guided in by Predator drones. The things can't see or hear the drones and think it's safe, then we zap 'em."

"They aren't so smart along the defensive lines," Jack observed.

The pilot laughed, a bitter, frightened sound. "Those have just been probes, major. And yeah, those are the dumb ones that we're weeding out, leaving the smart ones behind. But I've seen the thermal and motion sensor data the corps G-2 has been putting together. I wasn't supposed to, but I have a friend in the intel section. You know how that works." He shook his head. "Believe me, when those fuckers get in their bug heads to break out, they're going to go through our lines like shit through a goose."

"Why haven't they already?" Terje asked.

"Who knows? I think it's because they're preoccupied with trying to wipe out the survivors in the safe zone where we're going. There's nothing left in the scorched areas for them to eat except each other, except for the ones that have made it to Lake Michigan. They can swim and kill like sharks."

"Thanks for the uplifting news," Jack told him.

"Well, there is a bright side, you know," the pilot said.

"What's that?"

"The slimy bastards don't have SAMs."

"Do yourself a favor and don't ever take that for granted," Jack told him. "You know they can perfectly mimic us, right?"

"Yeah, don't remind me."

"How are you dealing with the larval forms?" Terje asked.

"What, those little slimy things?"

"Yes."

The pilot shook his head. "We don't bother with the little ones much because they're so hard to see, only as big as your fist, and there are so damn many of them. You can't see it from here, but the ground down there is swarming with the little bastards, eating all the charred wood and stuff. You could drop a Willie Pete out the door and watch them go off like firecrackers. If a Predator sees a bunch of them together or finds a big one, which happens sometimes, we'll light them up. But we just don't have the ordnance to cover every square foot to get them all." He paused. "There's what's left of Midway Airport."

Jack craned his neck out the door. Below him, the square-shaped airport slid past the Black Hawk on the starboard side. There were a dozen airliners, perhaps more, that were nothing more than plane-shaped cinders on the tarmac. The terminal buildings were still burning furiously, and a blanket of fire bathed the entire northern end of the airport and the buildings around it from the fuel storage tanks, which sat like three eviscerated volcanoes along West 54th Street.

"Midway was taken two nights ago," the pilot said. "The Air Force was pulling people out until the last minute, but word has it the last C-17 had some uninvited guests aboard."

A mass of twisted metal and debris lay just beyond the end of the longest runway where the C-17 had crashed into a parking lot. The wreckage was still smoking.

Aside from the fires and billowing smoke, nothing moved on the ground below. It was like they were flying over a ghost town that had been set afire.

The next few minutes passed in silence as the Black Hawk and its Apache escorts continued toward their objective. Below, the neighborhoods of Chicago Lawn, Gage Park, and West Englewood were nothing more than blackened ruins.

Something about the scene didn't add up, and it took Jack a moment to realize what it was. "I don't see many bodies."

"Correction," Terje said, "you don't see *any* bodies. Some people must have died here. What happened to them?"

"A lot of people have died down there," the pilot said, his voice grim. "The city had a population of something like almost three million people. Intel figures that maybe a million got out, but I think we lost a lot more."

"Then what happened to them?" Jack wanted to know.

"The harvesters ate them."

"Christ."

"I think He was on the last train for the coast, major," the pilot said. "God's abandoned this place."

Two huge explosions ripped through a railway yard a couple miles to the north.

"Probably JDAMs dropped by F-22s," the pilot said. "A Predator must have seen some of the things massing there. Dunkirk's just ahead."

"Dunkirk?" Jack asked.

"Yeah, that's what they're calling it. Once we get past the smoke and you can really see the lake you'll see why. It's the last safe zone in the metro area. The Army's holding along a wedge of shoreline behind I-94, dead ahead, and I-90, which angles off to the southeast. There's probably half a million people crammed in there, hoping to get out before the dam breaks. You're just lucky the university is in the protected zone, or this trip would've been for nothing."

There was a steady stream of helicopters, both military and civilian, flying in and out of Dunkirk, ferrying people out.

As they passed over I-94, which was even more heavily fortified than I-294 had been, they emerged from the smoke over a relatively undamaged portion of the city. A few structures had burned or partially collapsed, but otherwise the area looked normal, except for thousands of people crowding the streets.

Lined up along the shoreline were hundreds of boats, great and small. From twelve footers that could only carry a handful of people all the way up to multi-million dollar yachts, the shoreline was packed with them, ferrying people from the safe zone to larger ships standing off from shore. People were even using jet skis to help get people from the beach to larger boats or the Navy ships standing off in deeper water.

"I sure as hell hope this girl we're after is at the hospital," Hathcock said. Those were the first words he had spoken since they'd stepped off the Gulfstream jet back at Aurora. "If she's not, we're fucked."

"I can't argue with that," Jack told him.

"We're coming in," the pilot said as the Black Hawk quickly descended toward the university complex, the two Apaches breaking off to start circular sweeps of the area. "I'm going to put you down on the helipad at Mitchell Hospital, then I'll orbit until you call me. I can't stay on the pad, because it's one of the only controlled access areas where it's safe for us to land and take on passengers, and other birds need it."

As if to emphasize the point, another Black Hawk was on the pad. A group of civilians waiting on the ramp were ushered aboard. A moment later, the helicopter took off, heading east toward one of the waiting ships.

"It's our turn," the pilot said, bringing his bird in quickly. With a mild thump from the wheeled landing gear, the Black Hawk was down.

"Thanks for the ride," Jack told him. "We'll be in contact shortly."

"Roger that."

Jack tore off the headset, grabbed his helmet, and jumped out of the helicopter, Terje and the others right behind him.

The last man had just stepped out when the Black Hawk lifted off and banked away.

"Ready to look for a needle in a haystack?" Jack said to Terje. From the soft-sided pet carrier beside him, Alexander made an unhappy mewling sound.

The Norwegian shook his head. "I think you're being optimistic, my friend."

"Yeah, probably." Jack grimaced as they made their way to the welcome party, a hospital staffer and a Marine, both of whom looked exhausted. "But we're not leaving until we find her."

COLONEL LIVINGSTONE

"She ran away."

Jack's mouth dropped open at the doctor's words.

Around them, the wounded, the dying, and the desperate cried and wailed as the overwhelmed hospital staff did for them what they could. Every corridor was packed with patients and their families, and the doctor had to shout to be heard over the din. The air reeked of alcohol, blood, unwashed bodies, and other, even less pleasant things.

He leaned closer to the woman, whose skin was stretched tight over the bones of her face, making her look more like a halloween prop than a physician. "How could you let her do that?"

The doctor laughed. "Look around, soldier boy! We don't have enough people to treat all our patients, let alone play baby sitter. She disappeared sometime last night."

"She is fully mobile in her condition?" Terje asked. "She would not have required assistance?"

Shaking her head, the doctor said, "No, her condition doesn't impair her physically. She just got up and walked out. Her parents brought her in for diagnostics by one of our dermatologists who was something of an expert on suspected Morgellons cases before things went to hell." She shrugged. "They must not have been able to get back here to pick her up. We tried to reach them, just like we have all the other abandoned patients, but we couldn't get hold of them."

"Wait a minute," Jack said. "You said this dermatologist was an expert. Where is he? Can we talk to him?"

"He was killed by a harvester, one of the larvae, when he was off-duty yesterday. I think that may have been why Melissa left. He looked in on her when he could, and she took an instant liking to him." She rubbed her eyes and stifled a yawn. "She took his death pretty hard. He was all she had for someone to lean on in this mess."

"Would she have tried to go home?" Jack asked. "Where did she live?"

"I think her home was in Evergreen Park, but that's almost ten miles from here, inside the hot zone. Even if she tried to get there, I can't believe she got past the barricade, and everything west of here has been burned to the ground." She glanced around as a nurse frantically called her name. "Look, I'm sorry, but..."

"Doctor, listen." Jack moved up close to the woman so he could lower his voice, speaking into her ear. "I know you've got your hands full. But finding this girl is incredibly important. I can't tell you the details, but she could very well mean the difference between winning and losing this war. I've *got* to find her. Is there anyone here who might have a clue where she's gone? Anyone else she might have confided in? Maybe other patients?"

"They've all been moved to make room for more critical cases." Her eyes narrowed. "Wait, I take that back. Not all of them. One's still there. Marybeth Cooley. We haven't moved her because she's so fragile. I don't know if we'll be able to get her out at all."

A surge of hope ran through Jack. "Where is she?"

"Room 718, down the hall on your right," the doctor said, pointing. "She's in the bed by the window. Good luck getting anything out of her."

"It's a start, doc. Thanks!"

Jack led the others through the crush of people in the hallway. Many were children in blood-soaked bandages, held by weeping parents. Others were alone, staring up at him with wide frightened eyes. Some simply stared off into space, their eyes blank. All of them were dirty and unkempt, their faces streaked with dirt and soot.

Jack reached into one of the cargo pockets in his pants and pulled out the contents of the MRE meal he'd dumped in there before leaving SEAL-2. He always put something to nibble on in that pocket so he didn't have to dig out the entire meal packet. He gave out the crackers and the spread that went with them, the cookies and the candy. He would've given away the rest of what he carried in his rucksack, but didn't have the time now.

"Here it is," he said as they reached their destination. "Room 718. Terje, with me. The rest of you hold here."

He pushed the door open gently, making sure he wasn't banging into anyone inside. Seven sets of eyes turned to stare at him. He nodded a curt greeting, but they weren't the ones for whom he'd come. In a bed next to the window was an elderly African-American woman, in her eighties, Jack guessed, who was attended by a small army of machines and three drip bags feeding liquid into the shunt in her arm. She was staring out the window, which looked out over Washington Park. Jack could see the smoke and flames of the neighborhoods burning beyond the I-94 barricade.

He stepped up to the side of the bed. "Mrs. Cooley?"

For a moment, he wasn't sure she'd heard. Then, she turned her head to face him, the skull turning on the spindly neck in short, uneven jerks. While her body was withered, her sickly skin draped in wrinkled folds over her emaciated body, the dark eyes that looked up at him were sharp and clear. She stared at him a moment with such intensity that he began to feel uncomfortable.

"Ma'am," he said, "my name is Jack Dawson. I'm looking for Melissa Wellington, the girl who was in here with you. She left the hospital last night, and it's terribly important that we find her. We were told you might have some idea where she went."

She stared at him a while longer, and he was about to ask her again where Melissa had gone when she said in a surprisingly deep voice, "I was young once, you know. Beautiful, too. All the boys said so. My Aaron always said so." She blinked and looked up at the ceiling. "I miss my Aaron. I do so miss him."

Jack and Terje exchanged a glance, and Jack's hopes quickly began to fade. "What about Melissa Wellington, Mrs. Cooley? Do you remember her?"

"Beauty is only skin deep," the old woman said, turning her gaze back to Jack. "Did you know that?" She looked away.

Jack was about to ask his question again when the old woman said, "That girl is beautiful on the inside, gorgeous as a summer's day. But the Lord sometimes has a mighty twisted sense of humor, with what He did to her on the outside."

Jack leaned closer. "You're talking about Melissa, right?"

She turned her gaze back to him, her eyes narrowing. "Do you have all your wits about you, young man?"

Terje put a hand put a hand up to his face and coughed.

Jack threw him an annoyed glance before saying, "Probably not, ma'am. I'm just trying to find Melissa."

"Is she in trouble with the law? I know that happens a lot with young people these days."

"No, she's not in trouble at all," Jack said. "We need her help. We want to find her so we can protect her."

Marybeth Cooley's eyes widened. "It's what's in her, isn't it? The evil inside her, in her body." Her voice dropped to a whisper. "I could feel it. That poor child. Such a gentle, tortured soul."

"Yes," Jack said, taking Marybeth's hand and holding it gently. "That evil might help us fight the things out there. We might be able to turn what's in Melissa's body against them." He leaned down. "But we have to find her. Do you have any idea where she might have gone?"

"She misses her grandmother," Marybeth said. "She wanted to go see her one last time, after she found out her parents wouldn't be coming." Shaking her head, she said in a sad voice, "How terrible for a child to hear such a thing, to be left alone here in this awful place." She smiled. "I wouldn't like it here, either, but I'm not alone. Aaron should be back any time now. He always takes longer than he should, because he likes to talk to folks. He can't pass a person on the street without getting their life story, but he's a good man."

"I'm sure he is," Jack said. "Melissa's grandmother. Do you know where she is?"

"Of course I do." Marybeth glared at him as if he'd delivered a mortal insult. "Just because I'm old doesn't mean I'm senile, young man."

"Marybeth, please tell me where Melissa's grandmother lives."

"Only if you promise me that you'll tell Aaron to hurry on back here to take me home."

"Sure," Jack said, glancing at Terje and rolling his eyes. "I promise." Turning back to Marybeth, he added, "We both promise."

After a moment of staring at them with suspicious eyes, she nodded. "Her grandmother is in Oak Woods. That's where you'll find her."

"Thank you, Mrs. Cooley. Thank you so much." Jack kissed her hand, and a smile broke through Marybeth's stern expression.

"Don't you let my Aaron catch you doing that, young man, or he'll give you the treatment."

"We'll send him to you when we find him," Terje told her.

"Why on earth would you do that?" She made a *pfft* noise with her lips. "My Aaron passed on to the Lord nearly twenty years ago, young man. The last thing I need is a bag of bones." She closed her eyes. "I'll see him soon enough on my own."

Jack grabbed a flabbergasted Terje by the arm. "Come on. Let's go."

Back out in the hallway, they gathered up the other members of the team and tracked down the doctor they'd spoken to earlier. "Mrs. Cooley said that Melissa went to stay with her grandmother at a place called Oak Woods. Can you tell us where that is?"

The doctor stared at him. "I don't think you're going to find her there. At least, I hope not."

"Why's that?"

"Because Oak Woods is a cemetery."

***

Oak Woods Cemetery, as it happened, was only a mile south of the hospital. Since there wasn't an authorized landing zone there for the Black Hawk, Jack requisitioned a battered Humvee armed with a .50 caliber machine gun from a National Guard captain by waving a set of written orders issued by Special Operations Command under his nose. Jack rode shotgun while Terje drove, with Hathcock on the .50 and the other three men crammed in the back.

As they left the university hospital complex and turned south onto Cottage Grove Avenue, Terje asked, "How are they going to get all these people out?" He honked the vehicle's horn in a vain effort to get the crowd of people clogging the street to move aside and let the Humvee pass. "I think a lot more are here than we were told."

"That's not our problem," Jack said. "Just keep moving."

It took them fifteen minutes to bull their way a quarter mile to 60th Street, but after that the crowd began to thin out and they were able to sustain the heady speed of five miles per hour without running anyone down.

"Here it is," Jack said as they reached the intersection at 67th Street. "Turn left. The entrance should be down there, I think."

Terje turned, honking to get through more people, and headed east, following the eight foot tall concrete wall that surrounded the cemetery.

The wall had been topped with concertina wire, and teams of soldiers were rigging Claymore mines along the top, angled down toward the street, and building platforms on the inside so they could see and shoot over the wall. "They're fortifying it," Jack said.

Terje nodded. "It makes sense. If the harvesters break through the main defensive line, this would make a good citadel."

"I'm just wondering if they know something that we don't." He watched the soldiers more closely. They were working at a frenzied pace.

From the southeast came the sound of jet engines and the distinctive ripping noise made by the 30mm gatling guns of A-10 Thunderbolt II ground attack aircraft, followed by a series of explosions. The man-made thunder continued as artillery fire complemented the ordnance the A-10s had dropped, firing with such intensity that it sounded like a world class fireworks show. Clouds of black smoke rose into the sky to join the thick gray shroud that already covered the dying city.

"Here we are." Terje turned into the entrance, which no longer bore any resemblance to the original. The decorative green wrought iron fence had disappeared behind a set of stacked jersey barriers, flanked by sandbagged machine gun positions on either side. The gate had been replaced with a school bus that had quarter inch thick metal plate welded to its side, with AUTHORIZED PERSONNEL ONLY neatly stenciled in foot-tall red letters.

"I'm sorry, sir," a very unapologetic-looking National Guard sergeant told him, casting a wary eye at the crowd of civilians in the street who shouted epithets at the guardsmen. "We're not allowing anyone inside."

"Who's your officer in charge, sergeant?"

"That would be Colonel Livingstone, sir. But he's unavailable at the moment."

"Listen, I'll make this easy on you." Jack held out the orders from SOCOM. When the sergeant hesitated to take them, Jack's voice hardened. "Read it, sergeant."

Snatching the paper from Jack's hand, the man read over the few sentences of text that gave Jack carte blanche to do whatever he felt necessary to secure Melissa Wellington.

"We're looking for a twelve year old girl," Jack said as he was reading. "Caucasian, auburn hair, five feet tall, with a serious skin condition. She left the university hospital last night and we believe she came here. It's vitally important that we find her."

"I'm sorry, sir, but I haven't heard any reports of anyone by that description. She might be somewhere in the crowd, because there's no way she got over the wall." Handing the paper back to Jack, the man said, "I'd like to help you, major, but I can't allow you inside. I've got very strict orders. Now if you'd please move along, I'd appreciate it."

Jack glared at him. "You realize we're all on the same team. Right, sergeant?"

The man licked his lips nervously and glanced at the other men on the guard detail, but said nothing.

Lowering his voice, Jack leaned toward him. "Sergeant, what the hell is going on?"

"Sir..."

He didn't have a chance to say more before a raspy voice called out, "Why is that vehicle still here?"

Jack looked up to see an officer coming down from the wall on a metal step ladder. As he strutted closer, Jack could make out the black "squashed turkey" insignia of a full colonel on the rank tab of his uniform.

Jack narrowed his eyes. *Colonel Livingstone, I presume.*

"Were my orders not clear, sergeant? *No one* is to approach this gate!"

As the colonel angrily shoved past the man toward the Humvee, Alexander, who up to this point had been quiet in his carrier on the wide hump between the driver and passenger seats, went berserk. With a shrieking growl, the big cat lunged against the front of the carrier, which happened to be facing Jack and the irate Colonel Livingstone. Alexander tore at the mesh of the carrier's front window with his half-inch long fangs, while his claws speared all the way through the thick nylon fabric.

The attention of every man in the vehicle turned to the colonel who, with wide, surprised eyes, leapt back a full three paces, amazingly spry for a man who looked to be in his early fifties.

Jack brought up his rifle from where it had been resting, muzzle down, on the floor. But the weapon moved slowly, so slowly, compared to the colonel, who snatched the rifle from the unsuspecting sergeant before shoving the man so hard he flew into the jersey barriers ten feet away. The other soldiers on the wall looked on in confusion, not understanding what was happening.

Beside Jack, Terje was helpless, his weapon stowed beside him and his line of fire blocked by Jack, and the men in the back of the Humvee were also unable to bring their weapons to bear in the confines of the vehicle.

As the thunder of explosions to the southeast became a steady din, the colonel aimed the M4 assault rifle at Jack's face and squeezed the trigger.

MELISSA

The bullets from Livingstone's weapon, firing on full automatic, missed Jack as his body was blown apart by the incendiary rounds Hathcock fired from the vehicle's .50 caliber machine gun. The harvester masquerading as the colonel exploded into flaming chunks of malleable flesh that flew in every direction, and the soldiers on the wall and the civilians outside dodged away from the crackling debris.

Jack got out, grabbed the assault rifle from the harvester's still-twitching hand, careful not to step into any of the burning flesh, and went to the sergeant, who was stunned but still alive. "Come on!" He hauled the man up and handed him his rifle. Turning to the soldiers on the wall, Jack shouted, "Open the gate. *Now!*"

As someone started up the bus blocking the entrance, Jack said to the sergeant, "I can tell you know something. What's happening?"

The sergeant looked to the southeast, where the artillery fire and A-10s had been joined by a flight of Apaches. "We got an intel report just before you arrived," he said in a low voice as the bus pulled forward and Jack waved for Terje to take the Humvee through into the cemetery. "There's a major attack underway. Tens, maybe hundreds of thousands of the things are hitting the wire to our south and trying to swim up along the shoreline."

"And why was our buddy Colonel Livingstone keeping this closed up?" He glanced through the entrance. Aside from a squad of soldiers forming a cordon across the entry road, the place was empty.

"We had orders to secure this place and knock down a bunch of the trees for a secure landing zone and to set up perimeter defenses, but that was all." He glanced at the civilians, guilt written all over his face. "He said that we weren't to allow anyone, especially civilians, inside until we were ordered to."

"Who's next in the chain of command?"

The sergeant shrugged. "I am, sir. The colonel sent the rest of the unit and all the other officers to reinforce the south. I've got most of a platoon here, that's about it."

"In that case, I'm assuming command," Jack told him. The sergeant looked relieved that someone else would be in charge. "Get your men out here and start herding these people inside. Do you have any landing zones cleared yet?"

"Yes, sir. We cleared one of the sections over there," he pointed into the cemetery toward the left, past the building at the entrance.

"Good." As the sergeant gave his men their new orders, Jack trotted over to where the others waited by the Humvee. Glancing up, he saw his air support slowly circling the cemetery. To one of the soldiers in the Humvee, he said, "Tell our Black Hawk driver that we've established a safe landing zone to evacuate civilians, and he's to get his ass down here and start taking them to the nearest ship while we look for Melissa. See if he can get any more birds in here to help with the airlift." He looked to the west. He couldn't see the I-90 barricade from here, but it loomed large in his mind. The southwest corner of the cemetery was a stone's throw away from the interstate. "Order the Apaches to scout along the barricade from the rail yard to our northwest to the intersection of the rail lines southeast of here. I'm not worried right now about the push the harvesters are making south of us, but if they breach the defenses on I-90, we're in big trouble."

"Yes, sir." The man snatched up the radio's handset and tried to raise the helicopters.

"How are we going to find the girl here?" Terje had been looking around, shaking his head. "This place is huge."

Jack nodded. "Yeah, almost three quarters of a mile by half a mile, according to the map. That's the bad news. The good news is that it's empty."

"Not for long."

They both turned as the first civilians were ushered through by the National Guardsmen. The haggard men and women came through the entrance and began to mill around, making it difficult for anyone behind them to get in. "We need more men here," Jack said. Getting up on the hood of the Humvee, he shouted, "Keep moving! There's plenty of room, but you can't block the entrance! Just keep moving along any of the roads and don't stop until you get to the end!"

"The roads are all connected," Terje pointed out.

Jack shrugged. "They don't know that. They just need to keep their asses moving. You three," he nodded to the men who'd been riding in the back of the Humvee. "Help out the guardsman here and keep these folks moving. We'll send back some of the other guys we saw working on the fortifications to help out. Do *not* let people plug up the entrance here. Understood?"

"*Hua!*" The men waded into the crowd, shouting and gesturing for people to move along.

"Hathcock," Jack said to the sniper who was still manning the Humvee's heavy machine gun. "I'd rather have you with us, but if things get sticky here, they're going to need you."

"Roger that, sir." He nodded, keeping the muzzle of the machine gun aimed over the heads of the people streaming in, but his eyes never stopped moving, sweeping across the crowd. "What about harvester infiltrators?"

"I don't have a good answer for you. I'd leave you Alexander, but he won't be able to pinpoint a threat in this crowd. If some get through, they get through. Use your best judgement, but I don't want you guys gunning down civilians."

"Got it."

Terje came over with Alexander's carrier and helped Jack shrug into the shoulder straps, putting the big cat on his back before heading toward the welcome center that stood alongside the entrance. "I guess we should start with the obvious," Jack said.

He pushed open the door and went inside, with Terje behind him. Aside from cases of MREs, ammunition, C4 explosives, Claymore mines, and bottled water that was piled among the desks and chairs in the various rooms, the building was empty.

"Jack, look at this." Terje held a wad of light blue fabric that had been sitting in one of the trash cans in the room near the rear entrance. Shaking it out, they saw that it was a hospital gown that would have been a good size for a teenage girl.

Jack took the gown in his hand, then tossed it back in the trash. "Son of a bitch."

"She must have had something to eat, too." He held an MRE packet that had been neatly sliced open. "This was wrapped up in the gown." He eyed the packet. "Asian beef strips. She ate that, the crackers, and the chocolate."

"Well, assuming she was the one who ate it."

Terje shrugged, throwing the packet on a nearby desk, rather than back in the trash. "Now is probably not a time to waste any food. Those civilians are hungry. We should get someone in here to help feed them." He went to a window that looked out to the rear of the building. "Look at this!"

Jack moved up beside him. Beyond a small parking lot was a long building that butted up against the wall along the street. It had over a dozen large garage doors, a few smaller ones, and several regular sized entry doors, plus a few windows. Three heavy duty pickup trucks were parked in the lot, and a backhoe was just visible in one of the garages where the door had been left open. "That must be where the caretakers keep all their equipment. Come on!"

Yanking the rear door of the welcome building open, the two men headed across the parking lot toward the garage building.

"Melissa!" Jack called. "Melissa Wellington! We've come to help you!"

"Stop your hollerin'. She ain't here."

The two men stopped at the low voice that had spoken from the shadows to one side of the nearest open garage door. A stoop-shouldered man with skin the color and texture of leather stepped out, a shovel held in one callused hand. He had the look of a man whom time hadn't treated well, and who expected more of the same for however long he had left.

"Do you know where she might be?" Jack said, his heart pounding now. "It's important that we find her. Quickly."

The man planted the spade of the shovel on the driveway that ran in front of the garage building and leaned on the handle, his green eyes regarding Jack as if he were a bug. "And what if she don't wanna be found?"

Jack stepped closer, his hand tightening on the grip of his rifle. "Listen, mister..."

"You can call me Dale. I ain't no mister. I work for a livin'."

"Dale, we need your help. I can't explain the details, but Melissa...we've got to find her."

The old man threw his head back and laughed. "There's no fighting the Lord's judgement, boy," he said. "Think what you want, but the bill for our sins has just come due, and there's no getting out of it. That poor, stricken girl came here to pay her last respects to her grandmother who's restin' here and find a small bit o' peace before the Lord takes us all. I don' reckon I should tell you anything. Just leave the poor thing be."

"Don't you think she should be the one to make that choice?" Terje said.

Dale squinted at him. "Not from around here, are you?"

Terje shook his head.

Dale spat. "Foreigners. Another blight on our land."

"I'll make you a deal," Jack told the old man. "You take us to her. And if she doesn't want to come with us after hearing what I have to say, we'll leave her be."

"You don' really expect me to believe that, do you, boy?"

"I give you my word of honor."

"Jack, don't..." Terje whispered.

Jack raised his hand, waving off his friend's objection.

The old man stared at him for a long moment. "God is your witness, son. You go back on your word, and you'll be damned to Hell."

As they followed Dale toward one of the maintenance trucks, Jack said, "I think we're already there."

***

Police Sergeant Carla Sheridan stood watch along the stretch of the I-90 barricade where it crossed over East 71st Street, a short walk from the 3rd District Headquarters where, for the last six years, she'd worked as one of Chicago's finest. But after the collapse of the Chicago metro area under the assault of the harvesters, the police had been pressed into service as soldiers.

Despite her exhaustion, she grinned, her white teeth gleaming against her dirty, soot-covered face.

"What's so funny?"

She turned to her partner, Lorenzo Menendez, who was the other occupant of the sandbagged defensive position. "Your face, man."

He rolled his eyes. "Like I haven't heard that one before. *Puta.*" Turning to look along the interstate toward the southeast, he said, "The Air Force dudes are really putting the squeeze on the bugs down there. Look at that shit!"

Sheridan had to admit she hadn't seen anything quite like the fireworks display that was taking place at the southern end of the zone. Air Force jets and Army attack helicopters were buzzing around like angry hornets and the sky was full of smoke. She'd seen them pounce before on harvesters that had concentrated together, but nothing like this.

Their radio crackled to life just as a pair of Apache attack helicopters flew overhead, the beat of the rotors drowning out the call. She wasn't sure what these two were doing here. They'd been flying around, but not shooting at anything. Not that there'd been much to shoot at for the last couple days.

After throwing the Apaches an annoyed look, Menendez spoke into the radio. "Say again, over?"

"Interrogative: is there any sign of movement in your sector, over."

Menendez looked at Sheridan, who shrugged, then shook her head.

"That's a negative. We haven't..."

He broke off as Sheridan seized his hand. "Look!" She pointed down East 71st Street. Dark figures were emerging from behind the rubble and the few buildings that remained standing. More poured out of the sewers, the heavy manhole covers flung aside as if they were made of styrofoam. Harvesters boiled out like ants from a hive that was under attack. Sheridan knew that the sewer lines below them had been blown up to try and keep the harvesters from using them to get behind the barricade, and some souls braver than her had been running patrols down there to make sure it stayed that way. But she couldn't help but wonder how hard — or easy — it would have been for the harvesters to dig their way through if they wanted to.

"Ahhh..." Menendez broke off, trying to get some idea of how many harvesters were heading their way. It didn't take him long to give up counting. The entire street was packed with the things like the starting line of a halloween themed marathon. "Yeah, we got movement, all right! There's a shitload of the bastards coming up out of the sewers and some of the buildings, heading east on 71st toward the barricade!"

To their north, near the elbow formed by the intersection of I-90 and I-94, rifles and machine guns began to chatter, accompanied by the *whump* of mortars firing. To their south, more weapons fire erupted near the intersection of Stony Island Avenue and I-90, and spread along the barricade as harvesters surged toward the human defenses.

"Sweet Jesus," Sheridan said. She keyed her own radio, which was tuned to her squad's frequency. "Open fire!"

She pulled the M-16A2 rifle into her shoulder, aimed the muzzle at the center of the approaching horde of monsters, and pulled the trigger. Beside her, Menendez put his M-60 machine gun on rock and roll, sending a solid stream of tracers into the lead ranks of the harvesters. On either side, the other defensive positions started doling out their share of pain.

"Reload!" Menendez shouted.

Sheridan dropped her rifle and snatched up the end of the belt of 7.62mm rounds hanging from the machine gun's receiver. In a smooth, well-practiced motion, she clipped on the next belt from the box of ready ammo and slapped her partner's helmet. "Ready!"

Menendez opened fire again, barely missing a beat, as Sheridan picked up her rifle and began shooting the proverbial fish in the barrel.

"We're not even slowing 'em down!" There was an edge of panic to Menendez's voice.

Despite the flaming casualties that thinned their numbers, the harvesters kept coming, screeching so loud she could hear it over the sound of the guns firing.

"Just keep shooting, asshole!" She kept firing herself, ejecting magazines and slapping new ones in.

The things swarmed past the elementary school on Rhodes Avenue, then spread out along St. Lawrence, leaping and climbing over the rubble of the killing ground that made up the last hundred yards before the barricade. Sheridan's eyes grew wide at the sight before her: the harvesters covered the ground in a solid mass of dark skeletons and bruised-looking malleable flesh.

She keyed her radio again. "Willie Pete! Use everything you've got!"

A moment later, dozens of grenades flew from the defensive works, landing among the approaching swarm. But the effect was not at all what the defenders anticipated. There were so many harvesters now that when the grenades exploded, the white phosphorus was contained within a small circle of bodies, clinging to a few individuals, rather than being spread in a wide arc.

Somewhere behind the defenders, along the shoreline of Lake Michigan, batteries of mortars went into continuous fire, laying down more white phosphorus rounds perilously close to the barricade. Harvesters died, for the mortar bombs were a lot bigger than the hand-held Willie Pete grenades, but the chitinous horrors surged forward.

"Christ, look at 'em all!" Menendez screamed. He had stopped using controlled bursts and was just holding down the trigger of the M-60. The gun's barrel was so hot from the continuous fire that it was smoking, and Sheridan burned her hands on the weapon's receiver as she clipped on the next ammo belt.

That was when she was hit by the stench, an overpowering wave of the infamous harvester reek that brought tears to her eyes and made her cough.

She and Menendez ducked down as a brace of rockets streaked overhead, blasting dozens of harvesters to bits and adding to the growing conflagration of burning bodies. Glancing up, they saw one of the two Apaches that had been prowling around, now hovering overhead, just behind the barricade. The helicopter added its 30mm chin gun to the rocket fire, showering the men and women below with hot shell casings as it killed more of the monsters.

Sheridan poked her head back up and stared in horrified amazement as the things continued to press forward.

She and Menendez were still firing their weapons when the harvesters swarmed over their position.

***

They found Melissa beneath a tree at the southern end of what Dale called Symphony Lake. She was wearing a tattered flannel shirt that came halfway down to her knees over a too-large pair of jeans. On her head was a black knit cap, and a frayed blue scarf covered most of her face.

"You promised." Her words were an accusation directed at Dale, who followed Jack and Terje from the truck.

"I know I did," the old man told her. "But they come looking for ya, and this one," he nodded at Jack, "says they won't take you 'less you say so."

She didn't reply, but her bright hazel eyes said enough. Dale shifted uncomfortably.

Terje kept watch while Jack came and knelt beside the girl. "Melissa, my name's Jack Dawson. I was sent here to find you."

Her eyes narrowed. "I'm not going back to the hospital. Not *ever.*"

Shaking his head, Jack told her, "We don't want to take you back there. Melissa, I was sent by the President of the United States to find you and take you to a place where you'll be safe."

"The president?" Her eyes widened. "Am I in that much trouble?"

Both Jack and Terje laughed. "No, you're not in trouble at all. The truth is that we need your help. We need it very badly. It's sort of hard to explain — I don't fully understand it myself — but the condition you have, the Morgellons disease, there's something in it that we might be able to use against the harvesters. You might be able to save us all, Melissa."

She blinked a few times, thinking over his words. "I won't go to another hospital." She looked up at the old man. "They can't make me, can they, Dale?"

"He promised, girl," Dale said, pointing to Jack.

"It's not a hospital," Jack told her. "It's a big military base that has the country's smartest people waiting for you to help them. One of them's my girlfriend, I guess you might say. She's very nice, and so are the other people who work there."

"I don't want to go."

Jack sat back, and Terje gave him a look. To the south, the rate of artillery fire had quickened, and more aircraft were flying in, dropping a flurry of ordnance. Overhead, one of his Apache escorts made a pass over the man-made lake before turning back toward the barricade. He used the distraction to give himself time to think. He wanted her to go willingly, and didn't want to have to carry her off kicking and screaming.

He was about to say something else when Alexander, in the carrier strapped to his back, voiced his annoyance.

Melissa's eyes widened. "What was that?"

"That's my cat, Alexander. Here, take a look." Jack shrugged off the carrier and set him down so Melissa could see. The big cat stared up at her with his green eyes and meowed.

"Is he nice?"

"To people, yes. To harvesters, not so much. Here, you can pet him. He won't bite."

Melissa tentatively stuck a finger through the mesh top of the carrier, and Alexander licked it, then rubbed his chin against it as he began to purr.

"Wow, he really likes you. He doesn't purr like that for just anybody," Jack lied. "You like him?"

She nodded. "I've never had a kitty, or a puppy, either. My parents never would let me have one." Her eyes suddenly welled up with tears. "They're dead, aren't they?" She whispered.

Jack held her gaze. "I don't know, and that's the truth. A lot of folks have made it to safety, but with the phone and computer networks down, it's really hard to figure out who and where they are. I won't lie to you: they might be gone. But there's also a good chance they made it. We won't know until we get out of here."

Wiping away the wetness from her eyes, she said. "Can I hold your cat?"

"Sure." Jack took hold of the end of the leash protruding from the top of the carrier where he'd wedged it into the zip-up top, then opened it up. "Here," he said, picking Alexander up and putting him in her lap. "Watch out. He's heavy." He leaned closer as Melissa started running her hands through the cat's fur. "There are lots of cats at the place we want to take you. You can have one of your very own if you want."

She looked up at him, her eyes wide. "Really?"

He nodded. "You bet. And because you're so important — even the president says so — you can probably have *two* cats."

Melissa glanced up at Terje, who nodded.

Jack's radio suddenly came to life. "Alpha Yankee Nine Seven, this is Foxtrot Romeo One Eight, come in, over."

He glanced up at Terje. "It's the Apache flight leader." Jack keyed his mic. "Foxtrot Romeo One Eight, go ahead, over."

"Be advised that we've got movement just west of the barricade," the pilot told him. "*Lots* of movement. Recommend you evac, ASAP."

Gunfire erupted from the barricade to their north and south just before the defenders to their west, closest to the cemetery, opened fire. Alexander hunkered down in Melissa's lap, a low growl in his throat.

"Roger," Jack told the Apache pilot. "We're packing up now. Have the Black Hawk standing by to pick us up. Alpha Yankee Nine Seven, out." Turning to Melissa, he said, "Honey, we've got to go, right now. Are you with us?"

Still clutching Alexander, she nodded.

"Okay, let's get the hell out of here." He stood up, then helped Melissa to her feet. He grabbed the empty carrier and slung it over his shoulder, not bothering to try to get Alexander back in. The cat was spooked now, and Jack knew he wouldn't take kindly to being shoved back into the nylon cage.

"Do you hear that?" Terje said.

It took Jack a moment to hear anything over the gunfire. Then he did: the hissing, shrieking noise that harvesters made. The sound turned his blood to ice. "Hurry," he said, pushing Melissa toward the truck. "Dale, let's go."

The old man was staring at the west wall, his face a mask of calm serenity. "You go on ahead. I'll see to the Lord's judgement."

"Uncle Dale!" Melissa reached for him, but Jack picked her up and put her in the truck. Terje piled in after her, while Jack grabbed Alexander and got into the driver's seat.

"It's okay, girl," Dale called to her. "Don' cry for me. Go on, now."

"You're not going to see God," Jack shouted as one of the Apachea, directly overhead, loosed a pair of rockets toward the barricade, "you're going to see the gates of Hell! Get in here!"

Dale threw Jack a quick salute, then started walking toward the west wall.

"Shit!" Starting up the truck, Jack slammed it into gear, then took off along one of the winding roads through the cemetery that he hoped would get them to the landing zone before everything fell apart.

The Apache opened fire with its 30mm gun, and a moment later a rising wail began to sound throughout the zone.

Melissa grabbed his arm. "The sirens! That means the barricade's broken! They kept telling everyone that in the hospital."

The sound of gunfire along the barricade just west of the cemetery died off as the defenders were swept away. The only weapons still firing in their sector were the mortars somewhere to the east, which were now dropping shells right on top of the interstate, and the two Apaches assigned to cover Jack's team, both of which were now in play, hammering targets that were far too close. The screeching and chittering of the harvesters grew ever louder.

Toward the far end of the cemetery, he saw the Black Hawk coming in to land. "Get on the radio," he said to Terje, "and tell Hathcock to make sure the LZ is secure."

"Understood."

In the rear view mirror, Jack caught sight of dark shapes loping along the road behind them. More swarmed over the manicured grounds, dodging between or leaping over the headstones. The swarm grew into a black tide.

He jammed on the brakes before sending the pickup into a skidding right turn, then a quick left, tossing Melissa and Terje back and forth in the cabin before he put his foot to the floor, pushing the truck to fifty miles an hour around another of the man-made lakes.

"Hang on!" Spinning the wheel to the right, he left the road behind a big mausoleum and tore across the grave sites, taking a shortcut toward the landing zone. Melissa cried out as they slammed into a headstone, the right front fender crumpling as the marble shattered. Jack struggled with the wheel, trying to keep them from spinning out of control and dodging around a much larger gravestone that tore away the mirror on his side.

The truck bounced across another road before sailing into the next section of burial plots. Holding the accelerator to the floor, Jack drove through row after row of low-set headstones that ripped and tore at the truck's suspension.

Their luck ran out as the truck's rear axle caught on a headstone and tore the entire rear end out. The impact deployed the airbags. In the footwell on the passenger side, Alexander cried out, more in fear than pain.

"Dammit!" Jack tried to shake his head clear as the air bag deflated. "Are you two okay?"

"*Ja*," Terje said.

"I think so," Melissa answered.

Alexander whimpered.

"Terje, take her. I'll get Alexander." The Black Hawk was on the ground, only a hundred and fifty feet away.

Taking Melissa's hand, Terje helped her out of the truck as Jack picked up Alexander, holding him close against his combat vest. He saw that Hathcock had positioned the Humvee just northwest of where the Black Hawk had set down, putting the vehicle between the helicopter and the mass of civilians running down the road toward them. The sniper was still on the vehicle's machine gun, while the other three men were spread out, weapons leveled in the direction of the civilians.

"Oh, no," Jack moaned. "Hurry!"

As they ran across the cleared landing zone, the Apaches fired rockets that exploded on the far side of the lake they had just passed. The 30mm guns chattered, blasting dark shadows that moved beneath the trees behind them.

He tried to key his radio, but it was impossible while holding the squirming cat. Alexander settled the matter by biting Jack's hand. "You little shit!" Jack dumped the cat to the ground and held onto his leash. He keyed the radio again, hating himself for the words he had to say. "Hathcock! Do not let those civilians get past you! Scare them off if you can, shoot them if you have to. Understood?"

"Roger." A heartbeat later, Hathcock raised the muzzle of the machine gun slightly and fired off a few warning shots. The stampede faltered for a moment, until some among the crowd saw the harvesters dashing through the cemetery from the west. Hundreds, then thousands, of mouths gave voice to screams of terror, and the crowd lunged toward the only way out: the Black Hawk.

"God, no," Jack whispered as the panic-stricken people charged Hathcock and his men while he and Terje ran toward the helicopter, Melissa between them. Alexander, who Jack expected to have to haul along by his leash and harness, was in the lead, straining so hard that the leash was digging into Jack's wrist. "Please, no!"

He cringed as the big machine gun opened fire, the index finger-sized bullets blasting through the helpless people at the front of the crowd. The M4 rifles of the other three soldiers also opened up.

It made no difference. When confronted with death by gunfire or death by harvester, the crowd instinctively headed toward the guns. In a heartbeat they'd swept past the Humvee, and Hathcock ceased fire. The three men he'd positioned in a defensive arc to protect the helicopter went down, trampled to death by the crowd.

The Black Hawk pilot gave Jack a frightened look before he hauled up on the collective, trying to get the helicopter into the air.

It was too late. The leading wave of the crowd reached the helicopter before the wheels left the ground, and people punched, kicked, and tore at one another to get aboard. The crew chief thrown to the ground, where he disappeared under the onslaught.

The helicopter's engine screamed as the pilot fed full power to the collective, and the Black Hawk staggered into the air. The cabin was packed with people, with some hanging out the doors and more clinging to the landing gear. A few were even holding on to the rear stabilizer.

Using the distraction, Hathcock, who had somehow survived the mob, was bulling his way through the crowd in the Humvee, making his way toward them as the Black Hawk see-sawed in the air. Some civilians tried to jump into the vehicle, and Jack winced as Hathcock shot them with his pistol. The limp bodies fell back into the crowd, which pulled away from him.

"Don't look," Terje told Melissa, holding her to him and covering her eyes as the Black Hawk's tail sank back toward the ground. A cloud of red spray went up as the tail rotor swept through half a dozen people just before it came apart, killing even more. Without the tail rotor to keep the helicopter's torque under control, the Black Hawk began to spin, tilting to one side as it went down right into the middle of the crowd.

Jack closed his eyes, shutting away the horror as the rotor blades butchered dozens of people before the helicopter hit the ground. The blades splintered and went flying, killing and maiming as the Black Hawk flipped on its side and came to a shuddering stop. A chunk of the titanium spar from one of the rotor blades scythed through the engine compartment of the Humvee, and Hathcock's hands flew up to protect his face as the hood and windshield were torn away. The vehicle rolled to a dead stop, and Hathcock, miraculously still alive and rifle in hand, staggered out, blood covering the left side of his face.

"Come on!" Jack grabbed him by the arm as they ran by. "Run like hell!" Keying his mic again, Jack called the lead Apache. "Foxtrot Romeo One Eight, this is Alpha Yankee Nine Seven.

We're on the ground just to the south of where the Black Hawk went down, heading east. Do you have us in sight?"

"Negative, Alpha Yankee Nine Seven. Too many people are down there. I can't see you in that mob, over."

"Understood. Just keep the harvesters off our backs as long as you can, and see if you can get us an evac!"

"Wilco, but be advised that your best egress may be to keep heading east toward Lake Michigan. It's only a mile to the boats."

"That's a long goddamn mile when you're trying to outrun harvesters," Jack panted, elbowing someone out of the way before they could step on Alexander, who was still straining at his leash. "Alpha Yankee Nine Seven, out." Taking up the slack in the leash, Jack said, "Come here, you stupid cat!"

As Jack leaned down to pick up Alexander, unsnapping the leash from his harness before it became tangled and could strangle him, someone from the crowd crashed into Jack from behind, sending him tumbling to the ground.

He was spitting out grass when Hathcock yanked him to his feet and got him moving before they were separated from Terje and Melissa.

Only then did Jack realize that the cat's harness had slipped from his hands.

Alexander was gone.

ONE WAY FORWARD

Naomi stared at the paper Kiran had given her, on which the symbols for the receptors on harvester cells had been drawn. Trying to force down her disappointment that the information wasn't revelatory, she looked beyond what was written on the page. It told her the harvesters were serious. They could have given her a great deal less.

Did that mean she trusted them? No, not at all. But she believed, now more than ever, that their request for an alliance was genuine. They might be harboring some deeper motive in the long run, for the harvesters — at least the original generation — crafted their strategy on a time scale that could span decades or even centuries, but their immediate intent of joining forces with their human foes seemed genuine.

She looked up as Renee came over to her desk. Setting the paper down, she said, "Please tell me you have some good news."

Renee only frowned. "I think you should see this, hon."

Getting up from her chair and stretching the cramps out of her back, Naomi followed Renee to the workstation she used down in the lab. She had a desk here and one in the operations center, and split her time between the two. "What do you have?"

"I've been banging my head against the wall over the reproduction estimates," Renee said after taking a gulp of coffee. "The figures from CIA and Homeland Security are just way too high. I put some of that down to people just overestimating the number of harvesters, because it's hard to count the ugly buggers when they're running around eating people. But looking at what's been happening in the major cities here and cross-referencing what other countries are seeing...their estimates are right. Actually, they're probably a bit low."

"So what you're telling me is that the harvesters are reproducing even faster than we thought?" Naomi shook her head in disbelief. "How is that possible?"

"I'll show you. I should've caught this earlier, but this is the first time I've seen this on video, and I just about peed my pants. I never would have believed it, otherwise."

She pressed a key and a video began to play on her monitor, full-screen. The camera view was from above a major intersection. The street in the scene was littered with human bodies and adult harvesters feeding.

"God," Naomi whispered, putting a hand over her mouth.

"This was in upper Manhattan two days ago," Renee told her, "right after one of the defensive lines collapsed. Now watch what happens."

The creatures continued to feast for a few moments. Then, in unison, they looked at something off-screen to the right and dashed away in the opposite direction.

"What..."

"Shh!" Renee pointed. "Watch!"

The view showed nothing but the corpses for a moment, then something heaved into the frame from the right.

An enormous larvae the size of a garbage truck oozed along the street, absorbing the corpses as it went.

"My God," Naomi said, "that's huge! It's a dozen times larger than the ones I saw in Los Angeles."

"Don't blink," Renee whispered. "This happens so damn fast..."

Just as it reached the center of the camera's view, the giant larva disintegrated, shattered. In the blink of an eye it went from one gigantic blob of malleable tissue into thousands, each of which was no larger than Naomi's fist, that cascaded to the street like raindrops.

Renee played that part back again, then turned to Naomi. "We assumed that these big ones just crapped out all the stuff they didn't need and made a single harvester, because we never had reason or evidence to assume they did otherwise. Some people have speculated that they might form huge adults, but that hasn't panned out. But this," she hooked a thumb at the screen, "is what's really happening. How the hell can they do that? You'd think all the little ones would just stick together again."

"I don't know," Naomi whispered as the larvae separated and began to make their own separate ways from the epicenter of the original mass. "Once the larva reaches that threshold, a gene sequence must kick in to make it fission into smaller ones. We've seen that separate larvae don't tend to merge together, and also that a single larvae can be forced apart into multiple viable organisms, although I can't understand why they don't just reform. This is... incredible."

"Well, now we know why we're seeing so many more adults than we thought there should be. I don't think I can even model their propagation now."

Naomi swallowed. "I'd better go brief Carl and Howard."

***

"Oh, my God." Carl's whisper fell into the silence of the conference room as he and Howard watched the video Renee had shown to Naomi. While he had always been fairly pale, having avoided the outdoors as much as possible beyond what was necessary to do his job, he now looked like he was chiseled from white marble.

"This is the first clear evidence we've seen," Naomi told him, "but now that she knows what to look for, Renee's found other videos and even some eyewitness accounts of this happening. No one believed them at first because we couldn't corroborate the handful of statements we had and it was simply too fantastic. But we believe them now."

"You know," Howard added, tearing his eyes from the screen to look at Naomi, "I'm really starting to hate it when you call us in here."

"What can we do about these things?" Carl asked.

"Nothing more than we're doing already," Naomi said. "They have the same strengths and vulnerabilities as any other larva, they're just a lot bigger and fragment into hundreds or thousands of smaller ones." She nodded to Renee, who hit a button to advance to a slide that showed the most recent graph of harvester reproduction versus human casualties. "The main thing is that it tosses these projections out the window." Using a laser pointer to trace the line that represented harvester population, she said, "Making a very rough estimate of the casualties we've inflicted, this line should be tapering off, or even declining slightly. This is a global projection, and you can see here the huge hit the Russians inflicted with their nuclear strikes. But all the field reporting, even taken with a grain of salt, indicates that the harvesters are continuing to gain ground against us, especially in rural areas. Entire towns are just disappearing."

"Why?" Carl rubbed his eyes. "Aren't they still concentrating in the cities?"

"Oh, they're still in the cities," Howard interjected, "but think of how much food is in the countryside. And imagine these things loose in the Siberian forests. Or *our* forests, for that matter."

"But wait a minute," Carl said. "Why aren't all the larvae getting huge? There's no shortage of food for them out there. Hell, each of them could eat a house and there'd still be plenty more."

"It could be another trait that does not appear in all of them, just like full sentience."

Everyone turned to look at Kiran, who had up to now been sitting quietly along the wall behind Renee. Having had some food and rest, he looked more like the tough commando Jack had said he was. He was dressed in an American combat uniform and wore the rank of captain, and someone had sewn a cloth tape over his left breast pocket that said INDIAN ARMY, with CHIDAMBARAM in tightly squeezed letters over his right. "I've heard you talk of the first generation of harvesters almost as if they were gods. But they are not. As different as they are from us, they are creatures of flesh and blood; their only divinity is what we choose to see in them." Gesturing to the screen, he went on, "I think the first generation harvesters, which you say could not reproduce and probably lived among us for centuries, could not possibly have intended what is happening now. You say that if we do not stop them, the only form of life on this planet beyond simple microbes will be harvesters, with the larvae feeding on the adults and the adults spawning more larvae, forever. Is this the work of highly intelligent, sentient beings that wanted to see their species thrive?" He shook his head. "I think not. You have put their genius in genetics upon a high pedestal, but they were fallible. Tell me they would have intentionally created such monstrosities as what we just saw. Tell me they intended to create a handful of sentient children whose fate was to be eaten by their non-sentient siblings or their mindless offspring. Tell me these things are what the first generation planned for this world, and I will not believe you."

"It's important to remember that they don't think like us," Naomi said quietly. "That especially applies to the first generation. While I don't like to assign them human traits, in their own way they looked upon themselves as gods, immortal and infallible. We were little more than puppets in their eyes, to be manipulated to their own advantage. It would be easy, maybe even comforting, to think they made mistakes when they engineered this new generation, or perhaps that the results were skewed by the law of unintended consequences." She shook her head slowly. "But I don't believe that's the case. I worked with one of them, and it knew exactly what it was doing. What they unleashed on the world is what they intended. The only difference is that we're only facing the product of a single bag of the contaminated corn that was distributed to a handful of places. Had all the bags gone out as they'd planned, we'd already be extinct."

"That may all be true," Carl said, "but anything that doesn't help us kill them is irrelevant."

"So I take it that we have even less time now than we'd hoped?" Howard asked.

Naomi glanced at the screen. "Yes. We just don't know by how much." Turning to Carl, she said, "There's only one way forward now. You don't like it, and neither do I, but..."

"Forget it," Carl said, cutting her off. "I've had both ass cheeks chewed off by the vice president, and the president left the rest of me black and blue over even the suggestion that we work with the harvesters. If I bring it up again, they're going to fire me, and with good reason. The president's the boss, and he's made it clear that he's not going to deal with them. Period." He leaned forward. "We've got hundreds of the best minds in the world working on this, using the best equipment science has to offer. We can beat this thing. We have to."

Howard was carefully examining his finger nails. Naomi knew that he'd gone to bat over this more than once, but Carl had finally drawn the line.

"Listen," Carl said, "once Jack gets Melissa back here, you should be able to make faster progress on figuring out how to make the harvesters' skeletons turn to mush, right?"

"It won't matter," Naomi told him, "unless we can figure out how to get through the second set of cellular locks and devise the right changes to the DNA code we insert into the viral delivery system."

"Oh, Naomi," Howard said with just the right touch of sarcasm, "it's only eight hundred billion base pairs in a species that has so little differentiation they may as well be identical twins." He looked up at Carl. "We'll have that knocked out in time for cocktails."

Carl gave him a pained look. "Don't make me out to be the bad guy. I..."

His secure cell phone rang. With a frown, he took it from his coat pocket and answered it. The room fell into a hush. Only one person called on that particular phone.

"Yes, Mr. President," Carl answered. Staring up at the ceiling, he bit his lip as he listened to whatever the country's Commander in Chief had to say. "Yes, sir. I understand completely." Slowly putting away the phone, he looked around the room, his gaze finally falling on Naomi. "Chicago...the safe zone is being overrun."

Naomi clenched her fists as she stared at him. "Jack?"

Carl shook his head. "I don't know, but I'll find out." He swallowed. "Once they've evacuated everyone they can out of the safe zone and the rescue ships are away, the president's going to give the order to nuke the Chicago metro area. Everything from Skokie south to Whiting is going to burn."

"He should have done that to Los Angeles days ago," Howard said. "Not to mention Manhattan."

"B-2 bombers just launched from Whiteman Air Force Base in Missouri to take care of L.A. He didn't say anything about Manhattan or any other cities that are under attack."

"So what changed his mind?" Naomi said. "How many times have we heard that he wasn't going to drop nuclear weapons on American soil?"

"He's been holding out in hopes we could come up with something. But we haven't left him with any other choice. His words, not mine." Blowing out a breath, Carl got to his feet and left the conference room, slamming the door behind him.

Renee gave Naomi a squeeze on the shoulder before following him out. "I'm sure Jack will be okay," she whispered.

Naomi could only nod. Her body felt heavy, her muscles unresponsive, as if she'd been paralyzed.

"So," Howard said, breaking the silence, "when are you leaving?"

Naomi looked at him and blinked. "What?"

He tilted his head and stared at her with an *are you really that dense* expression. "I said, when are you leaving? We don't have any time to waste."

She swallowed. "You want me to fly to Iran. Is that what you're saying?"

Howard shook his head. "I'm just a glorified administrator whose billions of dollars in assets and stock holdings are now worth about as much as the monkey droppings in the lab. You're the genius geneticist the harvesters want to parlay with."

"But Carl just said that..."

"Carl said what he was required to say. Don't think for a minute that he agrees with it. He's a creature of duty, Naomi. You know that as well as anyone. But the president won't have any of this alliance idea, and Carl's pushed it to the point where he's sure he'll be canned if he opens his mouth about it again. He's not afraid of losing his job. He's afraid of failure."

We both share that particular fear, Naomi thought. "You're saying I should go and not tell him?"

"I didn't say that at all." He grinned.

Naomi threw up her hands in frustration. "So how do I get out without Carl knowing? None of us can leave the compound without his authorization."

Howard shook his head. "Don't worry, I've already taken care of that." Turning to Kiran, he said, "I want you to go with her to command her protective detail, if that's all right with you."

"I would be honored, sir."

Nodding, Howard turned back to Naomi. "Ferris and three former EDS security goons are waiting for you at the helipad." Al Ferris was a former Combat Search and Rescue pilot, hired by Howard to be his personal pilot after the Earth Defense Society, which had employed Ferris to fly covert missions, had been disbanded. "Just get what you need and go to the main exit. Swipe your badges through the security terminals and you'll be cleared outside. Ferris will get you where you need to go."

Naomi and Kiran got up and made for the door. Then Naomi stopped and turned around to face Howard. "How did you know that this...*opportunity*...would come up now?"

"I didn't become a billionaire by chance," he said. "Now get going."

***

After making sure that Naomi and Kiran were able to depart without any trouble, Howard returned to his office. He was tired, but buoyed up by the knowledge that he had helped put another piece into play in the great and deadly game that was playing out across the globe. A part of him felt guilty for what he had done, but in the end he had been nothing more than a facilitator. Naomi had wanted to explore the harvesters' offer from the beginning, and he was convinced it was the right move, perhaps the only move that was left to them. She would have come to the same conclusion herself in time and figured out a way to make it happen. But time was something they simply didn't have, so he'd helped her along.

When he opened the door, he found Carl standing at the window. They had adjoining offices, the only ones left where the windows hadn't been covered with metal sheeting, with a door between them. But this was the first time Carl had come into Howard's office and waited for him like this.

Howard waited for the verbal firestorm.

Instead of chewing him out, Carl said, "Is she on her way?"

Howard stopped, stared at Carl for a moment, then closed the door. "Yes," he said, deciding not to joust over the matter. If Carl wanted his head for what he'd done, he was welcome to it.

Carl stood there a moment longer, staring out across the military encampment that sprawled across the flat Nebraska landscape toward the distant security fence. "Godspeed, Naomi," he whispered.

ALEXANDER

Alexander ran for his life. Panting with exertion, adrenaline pushing his body beyond its normal limits, he surged ahead of the crowd of screaming humans. He had clawed and bitten several that got in his way, bringing some of them to the ground like prey. One had stepped on the end of his tail, but the pain was only a fleeting memory now.

Behind the humans, he could sense the onrushing tide of *them*. His attack reflex had been suppressed by the simple instinct to survive. Every unexpected sound, every sudden movement, every strange scent could be a mortal threat. So far, his size, speed, and stamina had saved him, but he was nearly exhausted. He had never run so far or so fast in his life.

With a glance off to the right and behind him, he caught sight of his human, running in company with the others in its company, the two large males and small female. He longed for the human's company, for where the human was, there was food and attention. There was safety, save for the times they had been forced to confront *them*. He was struck with an impulse to turn toward his two-legged companion, but his survival instinct held sway. He fled.

Nimbly dodging around and sometimes leaping over the stones that were set in orderly rows in the grass, he ran into the freshening breeze that carried the scent of many more humans, along with the smell of water. His human had sometimes taken him to such places to gather fish, where Alexander had indulged himself in snaring some of the smaller ones in his paws while his human wrested larger ones from the water with a pole.

The way ahead was blocked by a great wall, extending to the left and right as far as he could see, without any visible doors. It was much too high for him to leap over, nor were there any openings through which he might squeeze.

But there were trees, some of which had limbs that extended over the wall to whatever lay beyond. Alexander had only once climbed a tree, when his human had left the door ajar and Alexander had been taken with the notion to explore beyond his den. He had chased a chittering squirrel across the yard and up a tall tree. His human had been much more careful about closing the door after that.

Without missing his stride, his heart pounding in his rib cage, he coiled his body and leaped up the tree's trunk. Using his claws, he scrabbled upward to the first branch that jutted out over the wall. With his tail twitching and thrashing back and forth to help him balance, he made his way out across the branch, then dropped the short distance to the wide top of the wall.

Behind him, the humans came on quickly. Many of them bellowed in fear when they realized their escape was blocked by the wall. So many hit it at once that the wall shook. Those humans who were strong or tall enough began to clamber up to the top, with some climbing over the backs of others.

Behind the crowd that was jamming up against the wall below him, he saw the dark things at work, killing and feeding.

He looked for a way down the opposite side of the wall, but it was too far for him to drop down to the ground without risking injury.

Then he saw a small structure toward the northeast corner. It was close enough to the wall that he might be able to get down safely.

Throwing all his energy into a mad sprint, he dodged and hissed at the humans who were hurling themselves over the top of the wall to the other side. With one final leap, he landed on the handrail for the ramp that led to the small building.

A series of tremendous explosions erupted somewhere behind him, startling him. When he reached the end of the rail, he jumped to the ground.

Without looking back, he left the wall behind him.

To the north was a street, thick with humans fleeing in the direction of the water scent. There was no going that way. But to his south was a smaller, empty street along which stood a group of tall human dwellings. There, perhaps, he might find sanctuary.

Folding his ears back and keeping his body low to the ground, he ran.

***

"Alexander!" Jack's anguished shout was lost in the cacophony of terror around him and the cannon fire from the Apaches. He caught a glimpse of the big tuxedo-coated cat off to his left and veered in his direction. "*Alexander!*"

"Let him go!" Hathcock grabbed Jack's arm and hauled him back in the direction Terje and Melissa were heading. "He's gone!"

"Fuck!" With one last look toward where he had last seen the cat, Jack ran to catch up to Terje and Melissa. The cat wasn't the only friend he'd lost in this war, and he wouldn't be the last. "Hathcock! Get to the wall and boost Terje over!"

"I'm on it." Hathcock dashed forward to the wall and bent over, lacing his fingers together in a stirrup. Barely missing a step, Terje put a foot into Hathcock's hands and with his help vaulted up to the top of the wall. Pivoting on his stomach, he dropped down on the other side.

"Melissa, your turn!" Jack steadied her as she stepped into Hathcock's hands and jumped up. Following Terje's example, she pivoted on her stomach to point her feet toward the other side, but stopped as she saw what was happening behind them. "Don't look!" Jack shouted. "Just go!"

With a gulp, she pushed herself clear of the wall, disappearing down the other side.

"Okay, sir..."

Jack stepped into Hathcock's hands and jumped up, then straddled the wall. Leaning down, he took hold of one of Hathcock's hands and hauled him up just before the mob reached them.

People begged to be lifted up to the top with frantic cries of "Help me! Please, help me!" while the harvesters butchered those unlucky enough to be caught at the rear of the mob.

"Come on, sir!" Hathcock shouted. "There's nothing we can do for them!"

With one final look at the carnage, Jack jumped to the temporary safety of the other side.

***

Alexander paused to rest in some shrubs behind a low black metal fence alongside one of the human dwellings. He was at an intersection of the smaller street down which he had fled and another one that would, had he chosen to follow it, take him back up to the larger street filled with screaming humans.

He panted, his chest heaving with every breath as he fought to recover his strength. The pads of his feet, unaccustomed to running on rough surfaces, were sore. He licked them, but his rough tongue only made the pain worse. He mewled in discomfort and fear. Predator though he was, now he was the hunted, the prey.

He continued down the street, alternately dashing and stopping to listen, to sniff the air. He soon came to a cross street that was much wider than the one he had been following. Pausing at the corner beside a building of white stone with enormous pillars along the front, he stared across the expanse of asphalt. He whined with indecision. He would be exposed, out in the open, if he crossed.

Footsteps and shouts were close behind him now. He had no more time to consider. Taking a deep breath, he sprinted across the street, running as fast as his sore feet could carry him.

Once on the other side, he found that the continuation of the street he had been following was no longer a street, but a concrete walkway lined with grass and trees, along with tables and chairs for humans. The patches of grass were much easier on his feet, and the large concrete planters provided some cover as he moved.

The strange street-park soon gave way to a neighborhood of large single dwellings with well kept yards. Alexander kept moving, following the scent of the water, which was growing ever stronger. So, too, was the scent and sound of people. If there were thousands behind him, there must be tens of thousands, perhaps more, ahead of him.

Then he smelled something else. His own kind, a great many of them, somewhere between where he was and the water. He would normally never have considered joining a host of other felines, for to gather in such fashion was not their way. But these were not normal times.

Wary, he continued on, looking for his kin.

***

After crossing the train tracks that ran along the west wall of the cemetery, Jack and the others made their way east along 69th Street, which was deserted and eerily quiet. To the north and south, 67th and 71st Streets were clogged with people fleeing toward Lake Michigan.

Melissa was soon exhausted, and Jack picked her up and kept running. Terje was ahead while Hathcock was covering their rear, turning around every few paces to make sure nothing inhuman was following them.

"Melissa," Jack panted, "hold the button down on my radio. See it, there?" She did as he told her, keying his mic. He couldn't do it while carrying her in both arms. "Foxtrot Romeo One Eight," Jack called to the Apache lead, "this is Alpha Yankee Nine Seven. What are we looking at when we come to the end of this street?"

Jack nodded at Melissa to let go the mic. There was a long pause before the pilot answered. "Alpha Yankee Nine Seven, all I can see east of South Shore Drive and north of 67th Street is people. They're packed in so tight the ones on the lakeshore are being driven into the water."

Melissa keyed the mic for him. "I need an evac, goddammit!" Jack shouted.

"Understood, sir. We're trying to get one in, but command and control has gone to shit. Recommend that you turn north onto Oglesby Avenue. In half a block after that you'll come to a big fenced-in building. That's the 68th Street Pumping Station, where sector headquarters is located. I'm not sure what they'll be able to do for you until we can get an evac bird in, but at least you'll be in a secured area."

"Roger that. We're on our way." To Terje, he said, "Take a left at the second street up there!"

Terje nodded and continued on.

"I'm sorry I'm so heavy," Melissa said, holding tight with her arms wrapped around Jack's neck.

"You're light as a feather," he told her, which was almost true. Melissa was thin to the point of being malnourished. "I'm just...out of shape."

"Oh, bloody hell!" Hathcock shouted. "They're coming out of the sewers!"

Jack turned at Hathcock's exclamation. Half a dozen harvesters emerged from a manhole about fifty meters behind them. Hathcock blasted the first two before the others were turned into flaming grease and chunks of exoskeleton by cannon fire from one of the Apaches.

His lungs were burning and his legs felt like jelly as they made it to Oglesby and turned left. Ahead of them on the right, beyond the southern half of Hasan Park, was a large red brick building, two stories tall, with a metal roof. It was surrounded by a black wrought iron fence that had been topped with concertina wire. Claymore directional mines were set at close intervals inside the fence line, angled up to blast anyone, or anything, vaulting over the wire. In the windows on the second floor, soldiers with machine guns stared out. More soldiers guarded the fence, their hard eyes staring through the black wrought iron.

"Shit," Jack wheezed as he staggered to a halt. "We'll never get through that mob."

The building was surrounded by people, clamoring to be allowed inside.

"The hell we won't." Hathcock stepped forward, raised his rifle over his head, and fired off a dozen rounds into the air. The people nearest them drew away in fear. He fired a few more rounds and began to press his way forward. "You there!" He shouted to the soldiers guarding the gate that led onto the southern parking area of the building. "Let us through!"

Staying close to Hathcock, with Terje right behind, Jack shoved through the temporary gap in the crowd. He saw that the soldiers weren't keeping the people out, but were running them past a pair of cats to make sure none were harvesters, then sending them down a taped-off path that led in the direction of the beach.

"I'm Major Jack Dawson," he said to the second lieutenant who came forward to see what was going on. Jack passed Melissa to

Terje before reaching into his tunic and pulling out the crumpled written copy of his orders and shoving them into the lieutenant's hand. "Let us in. Now."

The lieutenant took a quick look at the orders. "If you'll step this way, sir." He gestured to where a pair of soldiers stood with cats in canvas carriers.

The crowd surged forward as the soldiers began to open the gate, but drew back when one of the men fired a machine-gun over their heads. "People," he shouted, "wait until we pass you through! If you try to run past the checkpoint you'll be shot!" He threw Jack a look of utter helplessness.

"I hope this place holds out longer than the cemetery did," Hathcock said as they made their way toward the building.

"I think they have a surprise planned for the bugs," Jack told him, nodding toward a semi fuel tanker parked near the south side of the building. Pipes led away from it toward the fences.

"Sir," the lieutenant told him, "I'm not sure what we can do for you. We don't have any vehicles, and trying to get a helicopter in here to lift you out is going to be, well, pretty much impossible..."

"Because command and control has gone to shit," Jack finished for him. "Yeah, I know. But we've got to do what we can to keep her," he nodded toward Melissa, "safe. That just became your number one mission, lieutenant. Now if you wouldn't mind, I'd like to see your CO."

"Yes, sir. That would be Major Baird. She's inside. If you'll follow me."

Jack, with Melissa behind him, flanked by Terje and Hathcock, turned to follow.

Then he stopped in his tracks. In the grass between the building and the fence on the west side of the compound were cats, a hundred, if not more. They were all staring to the west, like silent sphinxes that could see beyond the buildings that blocked their sight.

As one, their hackles rose and they began to growl.

CHECKPOINT

"I can't believe we came all this way for nothing."

Al Ferris turned to look at Naomi, who sat in the copilot's seat beside him, then shook his head. "This was a goat rope from the start, girl," he told her. "Just be glad nobody's put a bunch of tracer rounds up our collective ass." He snorted. "So far."

They were flying in a plush Bell 430 executive helicopter, which was a joy for Ferris to fly, other than his fear that someone would start shooting at them as they neared the border between Turkey and Iran.

The flight from Nebraska in the Boeing 727 that he had first flown during Naomi's escape from Los Angeles had been long and tiring. The plane wasn't designed for international flights, and he'd been forced to make refueling stops in Halifax, Reykjavik, and then Traviso in Italy before finally reaching the airport at Van, Turkey, where the helicopter had been waiting for them, courtesy of Howard Morgan. The justification on the flight plan that Howard Morgan had filed for Ferris was to bring medical supplies to eastern Turkey, where casualties were mounting among civilians from recent cross-border artillery duels.

Medical supplies. That was the cover story, and a relatively easy one for Morgan to sell to the various bureaucrats, military chieftains, and politicos whose go-aheads were required for any non-military air travel. Every aircraft that left the ground from the dwindling number of major airports and military air bases did so with a specific purpose and clear authorization. Most were evacuating people from areas where the harvesters had overwhelmed the local defenders, or were bringing in troops from somewhere else. Some did other things, like deliver relief supplies.

Ferris glanced at Naomi again. "You know," he said, trying to break the tension that gripped them as they swept closer to the town of Damlacik to wait for the harvesters to contact them, "if I was about thirty years younger, I think I'd ask you to marry me."

She laughed. "Come on, Al. It would have to be more like forty years."

He winced. "God, you're such a punk." Returning to the business at hand, he said, "Are you getting anything on the radio?" His was tuned to the military GUARD frequency, while she was monitoring the second receiver, set to the same prearranged frequency Jack had used on his trip here.

"No, nothing."

"Uh, oh," Ferris said as they came over a rise west of the town. "That's not good." Up ahead, plumes of flame and smoke were rising from Damlacik. "The Iranians are pasting the place with artillery." Above, a dozen contrails weaving tight patterns through the sky. One of them flared into a bright orange cloud that rapidly faded into black smoke and flaming chunks of debris. "Christ, the flyboys are at it up there. Naomi, if we have to cross the border, we're going to be completely fucked. This thing's not an F-22, and the only countermeasure I've got is my middle finger."

The town was reeling under a heavy barrage. People running through the streets were cut down by devastating air bursts.

"Dear God," Naomi whispered.

"Yeah." Ferris slowed their approach. "What's the word, chief?"

"Can we orbit here, out of the line of fire?"

He turned to stare at her for a moment. "Orbit? Around *here*? Didn't I just tell you there's a dogfight going on over our heads? This is the last place a frigging flying cadillac like this should be."

"We can't just leave! If the harvesters...wait..." She reached for the radio, turning up the volume. "I thought I heard something..."

***

The creature that had masqueraded as Vijay Chidambaram before sending Kiran to deliver his message to Naomi Perrault wore a different face now. He was a middle-aged man, a nondescript villager, who blended perfectly into the countless people trapped on the Iranian side of the Khoy-Qator-Razi border checkpoint, filling the valley like water behind a dam. Most of the people fleeing the effects of the devastation wrought by the Russians on Armenia and Azerbaijan headed south, deeper into Iran. But many in the three northernmost provinces of East and West Azerbaijan and Ardebil chose to flee to the west into Turkey, which itself was suffering terribly from the collateral damage of the nuclear strikes against Armenia and Georgia. Some of the refugees hoped to link up with extended family across the border. Others hoped to finally escape the oppression of the government. But most chose that route to escape simply because it was the nearest way out.

Not surprisingly, Turkey had not been keen on throwing open the gates to what would surely amount to hundreds of thousands of Iranian refugees, especially when they were trying to come to grips with what was happening in the northeastern part of their own country. Tensions along the border had escalated, stoked by the incursion of the Americans who had come to retrieve Kiran, and things quickly got out of hand. Artillery duels were being waged all along the border, and more than once patrolling fighters had let fly with missiles or fired guns on those of the opposing side. There had been no official declaration of war, but there was not likely to be: both governments were collapsing as the feral harvesters and larvae spread in the capital cities.

The creature and its associates had been forced to flee the lair where they had taken Kiran because of the fallout. When faced with the necessity of moving, they had tried several gambits that had proven either unsuccessful or impractical. There was no way for them, even in natural form, to dash across the border, which had become a war zone in all but name, with army troops and air force aircraft and helicopters swarming everywhere. They had lost contact with their kin in the defense ministry who had orchestrated the shoot-down of Vijay Chidambaram's plane, and with that their military identities had become more of a liability than an asset. The thing did not believe in fate, but it had spent a great deal of time contemplating the concept in the course of their failed escape attempts.

At last, they had made their way south, donning the guises of humble villagers and joining the trickle of humanity that grew into a great tide as it reached the road that led to the Khoy-Qator-Razi checkpoint, roughly twenty miles southwest of where they had allowed Kiran to be picked up by the Americans.

Now they waited. They had papers, thanks to the victims whose identities they had stolen and whose lives they had taken. While the word that had come back through the crowd was that the Turks had closed the checkpoint, they must still have been letting some people through, for the crowd very slowly shuffled forward. Or, perhaps, the thing thought dispassionately, the humans behind were simply grinding those ahead of them into the ground. In any case, it and its siblings were close enough now that they could see the checkpoint's buildings, painted a dark yellow-gold with terra cotta colored roofs.

Above, on a hill rising from the south side of the road in Turkey, squatted a military compound with a stout green watchtower. The thing could see, even from this distance, that the defensive emplacements along the facility's walls were manned with soldiers, the muzzles of machine guns aimed down at the checkpoint. On the hillside just below, made with beds of white stones, were a star and crescent, the symbols on the Turkish flag, at least twenty meters tall, below which was the word *Türkiye*, similarly sized.

The crowd of humans was like a school of fish, reacting en masse to the distant sounds of artillery and machine gun fire that came from both north and south, and the thing mimicked their reactions. They looked with worried expressions one way or the other, and gasped and cried out when the firing sounded closer.

It looked at the cheap digital watch on its wrist. Turning to one of its kin, it nodded.

While the humans around them were preoccupied with watching an air battle rage overhead, the thing raised a portable radio handset to its ear and spoke into the microphone. It had made this check every half hour since Kiran had left their company. The thing was not sure if Naomi Perrault would take their offer, but knew that in the end, if the humans wanted to survive without leaving their world a nuclear wasteland, she and those with authority over her would have no choice.

The great question, of course, was whether the radio had the power to reach Naomi so far away, should she ever appear.

All they could do, the thing knew, was to continue trying. There was no other choice.

***

"Naomi...ault. Calling Nao..."

The voice was heavily accented and weak, barely audible through intermittent static on the channel.

"That's them!" Naomi exclaimed. "The signal's weak, but it's them. It has to be. Who else out here would know my name?"

"That's great, kid, but we don't have direction finding gear. How the hell are we supposed to find them?"

Naomi listened again as the voice repeated the message before fading away. "They said something that sounded like raz, or razi. Does that make any sense?"

"The map I've got shows a border crossing about forty kilometers south of here," Kiran said from the passenger cabin, where he and two other men, Naomi's security team, sat. "Khoy-Qator-Razi, it's called. That might fit."

Naomi looked at Ferris, who shrugged. "We sure don't have anything going on up here but fireworks."

"Okay," she told him. "Head south and let's see if we can find this place."

"With pleasure," Ferris said, relieved. "Those idiots firing the artillery are starting to drop shells all over the place. I'd rather not have one fall through the rotors."

Ferris wheeled the helicopter to the southwest, flying as low as he dared over the unfamiliar terrain. They passed several more villages and small towns located near the border. All of them were getting pounded by Iranian artillery.

"Christ," he grumbled, "as if we don't have enough trouble with the harvesters without everybody trying to kill off their neighbors."

"People are terrified," Naomi said as they flew by another town, Beyarslan, which was wreathed in smoke. "And for all we know, the harvesters could have orchestrated this."

"Then why the hell are we trying to help them?"

She turned to him. "We're not. They're here to help us, I hope. Because if they don't or can't..." She fell silent and looked away.

A few minutes later they reached the D300 road. "Turn east," Kiran said. "This road should take you right to the checkpoint."

"Yah," Ferris said. "The five bazillion cars and ten times as many people down there were a clue."

Naomi craned her head, looking down. "Look at them all!"

The road and every square inch of traversable ground alongside was packed with people streaming west.

"How the hell are we supposed to find them?" Ferris wanted to know.

"Why don't we just ask?" Naomi keyed the microphone, transmitting on the special frequency. "This is Naomi Perrault. Come in, over."

"This is Vijay." The signal was strong now, but she could barely hear Vijay's voice over the tumult in the background. "Where are you?"

"We're in a helicopter just west of the border checkpoint at Khoy-Qator-Razi. Can you see us?"

After a moment, the thing replied, "Yes, we see you. We are still on the Iranian side. Can you retrieve us here?"

Naomi looked at Ferris, who had tuned into the conversation. He shook his head emphatically and mouthed *no fucking way.* "Negative. In case you hadn't noticed, Iran and Turkey aren't getting along too well right now, and we'd prefer not to get shot down. You're lucky the Turks are still letting people through."

"They're not," Al said, pointing. "Look."

The flow of people and vehicles through the Turkish side had stopped, and soldiers had taken up positions to make sure no more came through. Some turned to look at the helicopter, and a few brandished their guns.

"It looks like you're cut off," Naomi told the harvester. "You're going to have to figure out another way across."

***

The Vijay-thing lowered the radio to its side. The others of its kind, all eight of them, were clustered together. "We must get across," it said in Azerbaijani, a language the others understood through the humans they had taken. While some of the humans around them might be able to hear their words, speaking in a local tongue would arouse less suspicion than the English or Hindi they had acquired from the passengers of the Indian plane that had carried Vijay and Kiran Chidambaram.

The others, instinctively reacting in character with their human mimicry, nodded. While a human might consider the Vijay-thing the leader of the group, its own kind had no such notion. They did not vie for dominance through physical combat or ritual posturing. *Leadership* ebbed and flowed from one individual to another, depending on the decision matrix of the others in its company. Its kind could work well in groups, even in the masses of tens of thousands that were sweeping through humanity's cities, but they were just as comfortable in complete solitude. The latter had become more pronounced for the Vijay-thing as it had achieved sentience. After leaving behind its reproductive phase, its taste for being in groups, especially large ones, had lost its luster once it had discovered that it was prey to its immature kin just as much as the humans or any other form of organic matter.

"One must be sacrificed that the others may live," it said.

No discussion, no arguing, no voting, no group selection or consensus was required. It was up to each individual to decide, and if none chose the path of sacrifice, then so be it. But the thing knew that one would choose, for it was logical to do so and fulfilled what had become a desperate survival imperative for the group as a whole to survive. That, above all, was paramount.

A young woman, whose face gave the appearance of being in her mid-twenties, nodded. Like a shadow, she drifted away from them through the crowd, which had begun shouting a chant demanding the Turks open the gates.

A few moments later, the chants turned into screams.

DUNKIRK

"You've got lousy timing, Dawson," Major Baird told him as she quickly shook his hand. She was short, barely coming up to his shoulder, with strands of copper hair struggling to free themselves from beneath her helmet.

As she read Jack's orders, he took in their surroundings. The 68th Street Pumping Station was a cavernous building two hundred feet long and a hundred and thirty feet wide, two stories tall. The ground level held enormous pumping machinery that reached as high as the second floor mezzanine. But the pumps were silent now, the electric grid having long since failed. Baird's makeshift headquarters was on the mezzanine's west side, which looked out over South Oglesby Avenue. Soldiers were positioned at each of the big windows, waiting for the onslaught they knew was coming.

"Okay," she said, handing back the rumpled, dirty paper. "You've got my attention, but I'm not sure how I can help you other than sending you to the beach like everyone else. I just hope you get picked up before we all get fried to a crisp."

"What's that supposed to mean?" Jack said.

"The president's authorized a nuclear strike on the greater Chicago area. They're going to hold off nuking the safe zone until the ships have pulled off, but as you can hear, that's not going to be long."

Outside, the din of screaming civilians had reached a crescendo. Then someone screamed, "Open fire!" Every soldier in the pumping station began blasting away at the harvesters that were flooding down 68th Street, savaging the rear of the crowd trapped beyond the fence line.

"Don't tell me you plan to make this your last stand?"

"No, I'm not the suicidal type," she told him. "You saw the fuel tanker, right?"

"Yeah. You're going to light off a burning moat, I take it."

"Precisely. And we've run the pipes across the entire block along Oglesby between 68th and 69th Streets, then all the way back to the beach east of us. That should keep the bastards out for a little while until we can get to the ships and get the hell out of here. Once the civilians have passed us by, I'm lighting it off."

"Lieutenant," she shouted over the sound of the machine guns firing into the mass of dark forms that began to spill down Oglesby Avenue, heading for the fence, "light up the moat."

"But there are people still out there!" Terje said, aghast.

Baird gave him a brief, hard look. "I know that, captain."

The lieutenant, a sick look on his face, repeated her orders into his field radio.

Melissa, hands over her ears to muffle the weapons fire, was staring out the window. Then she turned and shouted, "Jack! Look!"

Jack's heart caught in his throat as his gaze followed Melissa's pointing finger. A familiar black and white shape dashed across Oglesby Avenue toward the pumping station, no doubt drawn by the other cats. Following right behind was a mass of harvesters, which began turning into fireballs under the impact of incendiary and tracer rounds. But more kept coming.

Whirling to Baird, Jack shouted, "Stop! Don't light off the gas!"

But it was too late. Sprinklers rigged to dispense the gasoline outward toward the street began spewing amber liquid, which ignited into sheets of flame.

***

Alexander was beyond fear, beyond terror. His muscles trembled with exhaustion, his breathing was an endless series of rapid heaves through his burning lungs, and the pads of his feet were raw and bloody. Still, he ran. He would run until his heart gave out and he died, for his instincts would let him do nothing less.

Close behind him, he could hear the clicking and scrabbling of claws on concrete and asphalt, the wailing screeches of the things that pursued him. Their stench had overpowered the sweet smell of the water and the scent of his own kind, many of them, just ahead. He was so close now, he could see them, but the things were catching up to him.

The building ahead, where his kin and many humans were gathered, erupted in flashes and bangs. He flinched at the sounds, but did not change course.

The things pursuing him began to burst into flame, and he fought to dodge the bits and pieces that flew from their corpses as they stumbled and fell to the ground. More and more died, so close that the heat singed his tail.

Humans were trying to close the gate even though more humans were trying to press through. The soldiers fired their weapons, and the humans closest to the gate began to die.

The gate slid closed. The humans trapped outside tried to flee,but there was nowhere for them to go. Harvesters pounced and brought them down.

While the gate was now closed, Alexander could see that it was made of vertical bars and designed to keep out larger creatures such as humans, not smaller predators like himself. He would be able to slip in between the bars.

He was so close now. Lowering his head slightly, he put all he had left into a final sprint to the black bars.

A foul smelling liquid fountained upward from just in front of the fence. Had there been any other choice, he would have turned away. Instead, he dashed forward, right into the spray, his panting turning into a cry of surprise and pain as the liquid burst into flame.

***

Jack never remembered running down the stairs as he ran for the gate. One of the soldiers there aimed his rifle at the small, four-legged torch that staggered through the bars.

Jack slammed into him, sending the man flying, before he threw himself on top of the screaming cat, driving Alexander to the ground in an attempt to smother the flames. Alexander writhed and fought, biting and clawing.

He felt himself being hauled over, exposing Alexander to the air. Jack was opening his mouth to scream in rage when he saw

Terje standing over him, a fire extinguisher in his hands. He squeezed the handle, and a frigid blast of carbon dioxide washed over man and beast, quickly extinguishing the flames.

The cat struggled for a few more seconds, growling and snapping, then went limp in Jack's arms.

"No, no," Jack whispered as he got to his knees, cradling Alexander to his chest. "You stupid, stupid cat."

Melissa was standing beside Terje, tears streaming from her eyes.

Alexander twitched, and Jack wanted to shout with joy as he felt the cat's rib cage move. He was still breathing, still alive.

"Come on, Jack," Terje said, hauling him to his feet. He was carrying Jack's weapon. Jack didn't remember dropping it. "We've got to get to the beach!"

With Alexander's limp body in his arms, Jack let Terje lead him. Melissa ran alongside, her fingers holding Jack's combat harness and her eyes darting up to look at Alexander, while Hathcock covered them from behind.

They could see nothing beyond the wall of flames that Baird had engineered. The flames shot up fifteen to twenty feet high, arcing out into the streets near the pumping station, and onto the trees and manicured lawns of the South Shore Golf Course that led to the rocky shoreline. A quarter mile long from Oglesby Avenue to the beach, and a tenth of a mile across, this new safe zone now protected thousands of civilians who were crowding along the shore.

"The fire can't last long before the tanker runs out of fuel," Terje said.

They came to an abrupt stop just short of the tree line that bounded the eastern edge of the second hole fairway, almost three hundred feet from the shore. Ahead of them, stretching to both sides of Baird's fire wall, were thousands of people, packed in shoulder to shoulder. Jack couldn't tell what was happening at the shoreline; all he could see was people and more people.

"What do we do now?" Melissa looked up at him with wide, frightened eyes. She gently ran a finger over the singed fur of one of Alexander's feet, careful to avoid the bleeding pads.

"I don't know, honey," he told her.

Alexander struggled for a moment, then gave up with a mournful mewling sound. Jack looked down at his feline friend, hoping that he wasn't as badly hurt as he looked. One ear had a chunk missing from a harvester Alexander had fought over a year ago, but now both ears were charred and bleeding. The whiskers on his muzzle and over his eyes were burned off, his black nose was blistered, and every inch of his tuxedo coat was singed, in some places down to the skin. His tail, normally long and fluffy, looked more like a cooked rat tail. Despite all that, the cat's thick coat had saved him from burning to death. Most of the gasoline that had sprayed over him had just run off.

"Thanks, Terje," Jack said, remembering that he'd never thanked his friend.

"For what?"

"For saving this big lug's life. I should've thought of grabbing an extinguisher, but..."

The rest of his apology was lost as he heard a familiar voice call his name. "Major Dawson!"

They turned to find the lieutenant from the pumping station and four soldiers running toward them.

"Come with me, sir. We're going to get you out of here."

Standing shoulder to shoulder, the soldiers formed a wedge and began to push into the crowd, working their way toward the southeast end of the temporary safe zone. The closer they came to the front, to the shoreline, the angrier people became. They cursed at the soldiers, who had to resort to using the butts of their rifles to convince people to make way.

They were about halfway to the shore when a roaring noise arose from the direction of the water and steadily grew in volume.

The crowd began to surge backward as a cry went up from those nearest the water, and Jack grabbed Melissa's hand as she stumbled and nearly fell. Terje picked her up and carried her while Jack adjusted his hold on Alexander, whose limp bulk was making his arms burn with exertion.

"Keep going!" The lieutenant shouted at his men. "Push forward!"

The four soldiers shoved and pushed, fighting to move ahead against the crush of the people in front of them, who were now trying to get *away* from the lake.

"What the hell's going on?" Jack had to shout above the noise around them.

The lieutenant turned to him and managed a smile. "It's the fucking Navy!"

At last, with one last heaving push, the group burst through the leading edge of the crowd onto the grass at the edge of the shoreline.

"Watch out!" One of the soldiers shouted a warning before firing his weapon at a dark shape undulating in the water around the edge of the flaming wall. The other soldiers joined in, chopping the harvester to pieces before it sank out of sight. The malleable flesh sparked and tried to ignite from the tracer rounds, but the water extinguished the flames.

The noise was coming from an enormous hovercraft racing toward them across the water. Three others were circling farther out in the lake.

"What is that thing?" Terje asked.

"It's an LCAC," the lieutenant told him. "Landing Craft Air Cushion. The Navy uses them to get the Marines ashore for amphibious assaults."

"I hope they're not bringing Marines here," Jack said as the big craft, which was almost a hundred feet long and fifty feet wide, slowed as it approached the shore. It had a control cabin on its right side in a blocky, rectangular superstructure that ran down the side of the craft, ending in a massive shrouded propeller at the stern. The left side was similar, except for the lack of the control cabin, and between the two superstructures was an enormous open cargo area with ramps at the bow and stern. A flexible black skirt bulged out around it, making it appear that the dark gray craft was sitting on top of a huge inner tube. Two large vent nozzles on the superstructures swiveled to and fro, keeping the craft on course as it slid over the rocks and onto the grass, where it quickly settled to the ground as the engines spun down.

After an agonizingly long wait that, according to Jack's watch, was no more than a minute, the forward ramp lowered and a squad of Marines took up defensive positions around the craft.

"Come on!" The lieutenant led them forward, where the senior Marine, a staff sergeant, greeted them.

"Sir," he said to Jack, "We have orders to secure you and your precious cargo." He looked at Melissa. "If you'll just stand over there, sir," he pointed to the deck, lined with a tubular guard rail, just ahead of the control cabin, "we'll try to get as many folks aboard as we can before we clear out. We don't have much time."

They stood by while the Marines began to herd people onto the cargo deck. The LCAC could carry an M1 tank weighing nearly seventy tons, and the Marines were clearly intent on making the most of the craft's capacity.

In just a few minutes they were loaded up, and the Marines were shooing away the people on the shore, shouting that there were other hovercraft waiting to retrieve them. As the forward ramp closed and the LCAC's engines came back to life, one of the Marines came to get Jack and the others, moving them from the exposed deck ahead of the control cabin back to the forward corner of the main cargo area.

In another minute, the big craft rose up from the ground as the skirt inflated. With the engines running at a deafening roar, it began to back its way off the shore into the water, where it turned and quickly accelerated into deeper water.

"Why aren't the other landing craft heading in?" Terje pointed to the other three LCACs, which were no longer circling, but were falling into formation behind their own vessel.

"Dammit!" Jack cursed. "They're leaving all those people behind!" He spied the Marine staff sergeant near the center of the forward ramp. Making his way through the crowd, Jack got in the man's face. "Why the hell are we leaving those other people behind?" Major Baird's face flashed through his mind. Except for the lieutenant and the men with him, she and the rest of her soldiers hadn't even made it to the beach. "Those other LCACs could have picked up every single one of them!"

The Marine looked at him with a grim expression. "We ran out of time, sir. We were originally sent in to pick people up at Evanston, up north a bit, then got called back to come get you. And I mean you personally, and whoever was with you. The ship's CO sent the other LCACs along, hoping to get more people off, but it took us a bit longer to get here than we'd hoped, and he ordered us back as soon as we confirmed you were aboard."

"They're nuking the city," Jack said just loud enough that the Marine could hear him over the noise of the engines and the water thrown up by the skirts. "I knew it was going to happen, but not so soon. Jesus."

The staff sergeant nodded. "*USS Ashland*, our ship, is already bugging out, heading east at flank speed. It'll take us a while to catch up." He looked at Jack for a moment. "You're on the inside of all this, aren't you, sir? I mean, you know things that grunts like us don't, right?"

With a frown, Jack nodded.

"Do you think we're going to beat the harvesters?"

Looking back toward Melissa, Jack told him, "I honestly don't know, staff sergeant. But if we do, it's probably going to be because of her."

CHANGE OF LUCK

"Holy mother of God." Ferris looked on in horrified amazement as the people in the crowd on the Iranian side lunged away from something in their midst like a school of fish responding to a threat. Even at this distance, he could see the glistening black exoskeleton of a harvester.

The panic set off a chain reaction that sent the people at the front of the checkpoint through and over the barriers the Turks had put up. The Turks opened fire, and in turn were taken under fire by the Iranian border guards, some of whom stormed across along with the civilians. Hundreds of people were trampled or went down under the hail of bullets, but thousands more flooded across. The Turkish border guards disappeared, driven under by the human tide.

"Tell me we haven't made a pact with the devil," he told Naomi, whose eyes remained riveted on the crowd.

He kept the helicopter hovering just west of the checkpoint. Glancing to his right at the Turkish military border post sitting on the hillside, he was relieved to see that they were holding their fire. *The bastards are close enough to hit us with slingshots.* "Now what? We'd better get this done and be gone before the real army pukes show up. On either side."

"Put us down there." Kiran leaned forward between the pilot and copilot seats, pointing to a large patch of rough but open ground on the south side of the checkpoint complex. "They'll have to come to us."

Ferris snorted. "How the hell are you going to know it's them and not some of the other bazillion people who want to get out of here?"

"Take Koshka with you," Naomi said. "She'll help." With a hard look at Ferris, she said, "Do it."

Muttering curses under his breath, Ferris worked the controls, taking the executive helicopter into a tight descending turn, dodging a set of power lines running right next to the landing zone. As the landing gear wheels kissed the ground, he shouted, "Go!"

Kiran and his men popped the passenger doors open and leaped out.

***

The Vijay thing and its companions were swept along with the mob as it poured through the checkpoint. It heard gunshots somewhere behind, and sensed the ending of the one that had sacrificed itself.

Their challenge now was to separate themselves from the stream of humanity and get to the safety of the helicopter, which had landed on the Turkish side of the checkpoint.

One of the thing's companions went down, shoved off balance by a large man pushing his way forward. The thing screeched as more people trampled it, then there were screams from the humans as it began to lash out at with the stinger, which plunged into the back of the man who'd knocked it to the ground. The humans around the spectacle tried to lunge away, but there was nowhere for them to go. A dozen or more were stabbed, clawed, or slashed before the thing finally succumbed.

The others did not stop. They would stop for nothing until they had reached safety, one way or another.

Trying to leave the mob streaming down the road on the Turkish side was like trying to swim across a fast-moving river. They were carried nearly a hundred meters beyond the checkpoint before they were able to force their way clear, using their superior strength to shove humans out of the way, but without revealing their true identities.

They turned back toward where the helicopter had landed, but discovered they weren't the first to look at the aircraft as a possible means of escape. Hundreds of people, including a number of the border guards, were already running toward it.

Knocking two women aside, the thing hastened its pace through the terrified crowd, its kin following right behind.

***

Kiran was beset with a dreadful sense of *déjà vu*, remembering the terrifying journey through Hyderabad when he was trying to get Vijay to the airport. Only now he had only three men, rather than his company of elite Black Cats, to protect the aircraft and the irreplaceable Naomi Perrault. He had wanted to bring more men, but Naomi had decided to take as few as possible to maximize the room available for the harvesters. If there were more than a dozen, some would be left behind.

"Steady!" He had to shout over the noise of the helicopter's engines and the pitiful cries of the approaching people. His real worry was the border guards, who were armed with assault rifles.

With the nearest people only a dozen meters away, he pointed his rifle into the air and fired off a short burst. That brought them to a stop, although those in the front rank had to push and shove against those who slammed into them from behind. "Stay back!" He bellowed before firing off a few more rounds.

One of the border guards raised his weapon, aiming it at Kiran. The crowd flinched as a single shot rang out from the rifle held by one of Kiran's men, and the guard fell to the ground like a marionette whose strings had been snipped, a small red hole in the middle of his forehead. Two other guards leveled their weapons, ready to fire from the hip. Kiran shot one, while another man of his team dropped the remaining guard with a three round burst.

The crowd began to recede as the people in front fought to get away.

One of his men called out, "Our guests had better get here soon!"

Just then, Kiran's blood turned to ice as he saw an all too familiar face emerge from the mass of people that was beginning to encircle the helicopter like a giant amoeba.

It was Vijay.

To his men, he said, "Stay here!" Swallowing his fear and hate, he picked up the carrier containing Koshka and ran to where his dead cousin's doppelgänger, dressed like an Azerbaijani tribesman, stood waiting. Koshka's reaction left no doubt as to the nature of the thing in human clothing before him. She was snarling like an angry lion. "How many are with you?"

"Seven remain."

"Come on, then. Hurry!"

As one, the harvesters moved away from the crowd, while two of Kiran's men made sure that no one else approached the helicopter.

As the harvesters approached the open door, Kiran blocked their way with his rifle.

"What is this?" The Vijay-thing demanded.

"If you want to come with us, you have to come on our terms," Kiran shouted over the roar of the rotors. One of his men produced a box from a cargo pocket in his pants and opened it while Kiran kept his weapon aimed at the Vijay-thing's chest. Inside the case were large hypodermic syringes containing a clear liquid. Each was tipped with a needle as long as Kiran's hand was wide. "This acts as a paralytic. That way we know we will be safe." His hand tensed on the trigger.

"Do what you must," the thing said, "and do it quickly."

Kiran nodded, slightly relaxing his grip on his weapon. The man with the syringes stepped forward. Taking the first from the case, he plunged it into the Vijay-thing's chest with a quick, hard jab before pressing down on the plunger.

The harvester shuddered, then collapsed to the ground. Before their eyes, its features began to soften and run like hot wax, the skin and flesh transforming into the bruised-looking amorphous mass of malleable flesh of the harvesters in their native form. The dark, glistening skeleton emerged as the flesh gathered around the thorax, the mandibles of the insectile head twitching a few times before the creature was completely paralyzed.

Even with the downdraft from the helicopter's rotors, Kiran still caught a whiff of the awful reek the creatures gave off in their native form. "Load it into the helicopter!" He gestured at a pair of the creature's companions, who did as he commanded, placing their paralyzed comrade into one of the passenger seats.

In just a few minutes, they had all seven loaded aboard, Kiran's two men hefting the last one into its seat. He had to fire one last burst from his rifle to ward off the crowd before he joined his men in the helicopter, slamming the door closed. He gave a thumbs-up to Ferris, and the helicopter rose from the ground. Kiran and his men strapped the harvesters into their seats, then took their own.

"Jesus Christ," he heard Ferris complaining to Naomi as Kiran donned his headset. "Those things smell like shit!"

Kiran stared at the harvester that had impersonated Vijay, his finger twitching on the trigger of his rifle.

***

"Most of you haven't heard this yet, but President Miller is dead."

Carl and Howard were the only ones sitting in the secure conference room at the SEAL-2 facility, staring at the main screen at the front of the room. Carl felt his mouth drop open, and with a conscious effort he snapped it shut. While there were many people across the globe tied into this particular teleconference, the only person who really mattered was the one who had been speaking, Vice President Andrew Lynch.

Except he wasn't the vice president anymore. With Miller's death, he was now the president, or would be as soon as he'd been sworn in by a judge. At the table to his left and right sat the surviving members of the cabinet.

"I know that Dan had the best of intentions and wanted to set an example of courage for his countrymen," Lynch went on, "but he waited too long to leave Washington. Marine One was shot down by automatic weapons fire as it was taking off from the south lawn of the White House, and was lost with all hands. We can only assume harvesters were responsible, but we may never know. An official investigation won't be launched until after the war is over, and by then it probably won't matter." He looked down at a sheet of paper on the table, then returned his eyes to the camera. "We've evacuated as many people as we could from the downtown area of D.C., but as you can see," he ran his eyes around the table, where several familiar faces in the cabinet were missing, "not everyone got out. The members of Congress, with three exceptions, whose loss will be mourned later, along with the Vice President Lynch, were evacuated earlier, and are divided between here at NORAD and the reactivated Greenbrier underground bunker in West Virginia. The Speaker of the House, who will shortly be sworn in as vice president, will remain at Greenbrier while I remain here at NORAD to help ensure the government's survivability. At this point, much as it pains me to say it, our great nation's capital has fallen. I'll now turn things over to General Laramie, CINCNORAD and acting Chairman of the Joint Chiefs of Staff."

"Thank you, sir," Laramie, a four star general of the US Air Force, said in his tenor voice. "I'm not going to candy coat things. In one of his last orders before he died, President Miller ordered nuclear strikes against the metropolitan areas of Los Angeles, Chicago, Atlanta, and the island of Manhattan, all of which have been completely overrun."

"I'm officially adding Washington, D.C. to that list," Lynch said as he scrawled his signature at the bottom of the piece of paper that had been sitting in front of him before sliding it over to the acting Secretary of Defense, who visibly blanched.

"Sir." Laramie swallowed. "Yes, sir." He took a deep breath before going on. "As some of you no doubt saw in what remains of the news feeds, B-2 bombers already carried out their strikes against Los Angeles, and bombers are on their way as we speak to attack the other planned targets. We'll generate a mission plan for the District of Columbia as soon as we're through here."

"He looks like he's about to cry," Howard commented after making sure the microphone in their conference room was muted.

"I don't blame him," Carl choked before gesturing for Howard to be quiet.

"The situation across the globe isn't much better. The Russians are still kicking, and their government is still functional inside the Yamantau Mountain complex. The British and the French are both considering using nuclear weapons, but neither have done so yet."

"I expect that's going to change shortly," the new Secretary of State interjected. "After seeing that we are, uh, sanitizing our fallen cities, I've received back-channel indications that they'll probably follow suit."

Laramie nodded, then went on. "Three of the UK's four *Vanguard*-class ballistic missile submarines have put to sea, with the fourth, which was undergoing a major overhaul, manned and secured in the Clyde. Two of the French *Triomphant*-class boomers were already at sea. The other two are at Brest, manned and launch capable, but unable to deploy due to being in the middle of their refit cycles. All three of their nuclear-capable Mirage 2000N squadrons are on alert..."

Carl listened as Laramie went on, detailing the postures of the world's nuclear powers. What Laramie didn't mention in his litany of doom was that conventional ammunition stocks were being depleted at a phenomenal rate. The nation's remaining munitions factories were working around the clock and were now some of the most heavily guarded facilities in the world, but the production rate was far behind the rate of consumption. Unlike wars between humans, which ebbed and flowed as battles were fought and won or lost, this war was more akin to fighting a fire that refused to die out, using ammunition instead of water. He'd read the logistics estimates prepared before President Miller's death, and at the current rate, the reserve stocks for many of the basic munitions, from small arms to high explosive bombs, would be depleted in a matter of a few weeks, at most.

The same was true for the weapons themselves. Armaments companies were churning out everything from high-power pistols to makeshift flamethrower kits for both the military and civilian militias that had sprung up all over the country. But the Achilles heel of the manufacturers wasn't their production capacity, it was their supply of raw materials, which was rapidly drying up. You couldn't produce a gun without steel, and you couldn't get steel or make it if you couldn't transport the materials over the railroad system, which had already lost several critical hubs and had several major transnational lines cut. Then there was fuel, especially the diesel the trains and the tractor trailer rigs needed, not to mention what the military was consuming. And at the head of those many production chains, at the mines and well heads, panic reigned in many places, cutting off critical materials at the source. Demand for everything had exploded, while the ability to supply even the most basic strategic necessities was quickly dwindling. Everything Laramie was saying about the military situation was true and frightening enough, but their greatest peril was the failure of their logistics chain. In the end, humanity was going to be wiped out because they didn't have enough bullets.

"Mr. Richards."

Lynch's voice snapped him out of his melancholy reverie. Carl hit the button to unmute the microphone. "Yes, Mr. Vice...Mr. President?"

"I've read this morning's update from Mr. Morgan, so I'm not going to ask you to rehash that. It's clear to me that your efforts to produce a biological weapon have stalled. Is that a fair statement?"

Glancing at Howard, who gave a slight nod, Carl said, "Yes, sir, I'm afraid it is."

"I know you and your people have tried, Richards," Lynch went on. "Despite my tearing you up one side and down the other in half the meetings we've had, I know that you've done your best. But if your best isn't cutting it, we need to try something different, wouldn't you agree?"

Bobbing his head, Carl said, "Yes, sir."

"Good. In that case, I'm rescinding President Miller's ban on talking to the harvesters who offered to parley." Heads in the conference room at NORAD swiveled to look at the almost-president, and Carl's eyes were drawn to the cats in the room, one of which was lying on the conference room table. "Ladies and gentlemen," Lynch said, "I know I'm going back on both Miller's promise and my own position on this issue, but I don't think we have any other choice. Even if we use every nuclear weapon we have, reducing our nation to a radioactive wasteland, the harvesters are still going to beat us in the end. And not just our nation, but our species."

"What are your orders, sir?" Carl asked him.

"If these harvesters want to make a deal, I'm willing to make it. Do whatever you have to do to get it done."

Exchanging a glance with Howard, Carl said, "Yes, sir."

"Good. That's it, then. Keep me posted."

Everyone stood up as Lynch got to his feet and departed the conference room, then the screen went blank as the teleconference was terminated.

Carl leaned back in his chair and looked at the ceiling, blowing out a breath of relief. "How long until Naomi gets back?"

"About three hours, and Jack should be right behind her with the girl."

"Thank God. Maybe our luck is finally turning around."

LEAP OF FAITH

Naomi stood at the edge of the helipad as the Black Hawk came in to land. Carl, Howard, Renee, and Ferris were there with her, along with the chief veterinarian and one of her assistants, all of them wrapped up in their coats to fend off the early morning chill.

The Black Hawk's wheels touched down and the side door slid open. Terje hopped out first, then turned to help a girl to the ground. Hathcock was next, and he in turn helped Jack from the plane. Her smile faltered when she saw that Jack was holding a bundle of bandages in the rough shape of a cat, and he had bandages on his hands and forearms.

She and the veterinarian ran to meet him. "Oh, my God," Naomi gasped when she saw Alexander. The bits of him that weren't covered by bandages looked terrible, like he'd been trapped inside a barbecue grill. His eyes were partially open but unfocused.

"We'll take him, sir," the vet said once they were clear of the Black Hawk's spinning rotor blades. She reached for the big cat, and Jack gently put him in her arms.

"Take good care of him," Jack said, reluctantly letting go.

"We will, sir." Carrying the big cat like he was a fragile statue of blown glass, she and her assistant rushed to the doors of the main building.

"God, Jack." Naomi pulled him into a tight embrace and kissed him hard on the lips. "He'll be okay. The vet's top notch." Letting go of him, she gently took his hands in hers. "But what about you?"

"It's nothing, really," Jack said, shaking his head. "Some second degree burns from trying to beat the flames off of Alexander. He took the worst of it. Terje saved us both."

Naomi looked at the Norwegian officer, who smiled, his teeth shining through the streaks of dirt and sweat on his face. "Keeping Jack out of trouble seems to have become my sole occupation."

Behind him, Hathcock laughed. "You don't know the half of it."

"It's about time you stopped loafing around and got back here."

Jack smiled at Carl's nasal whine while Renee came up and gave him a quick hug. "I'll do anything to get away from you for a while, you know that," Jack said. "And look who we brought: Melissa, meet Mr. Richards, our boss. Don't take him too seriously. None of the rest of us do."

Naomi saw the girl's eyes crinkle into a smile, but that was all she could see. The rest of her body, from head to toe, was covered up.

"Dawson, you're such an ass." Extending a hand to the girl, Carl said, "Nice to meet you, Melissa."

She shook his hand, but didn't say anything.

"And this is Mr. Morgan," Jack said, gesturing to Howard. "He's a lot nicer. And he's a billionaire."

"At least I used to be." Morgan smiled and shook Melissa's hand.

"And I'm Renee, hon." Renee didn't bother shaking hands, but swooped in and gave the girl a hug. "Hey, you hungry?"

"Yes, ma'am. Starving."

"She didn't have much more than some MRE crackers and cookies on the way out," Jack said. "Come to think of it, the rest of us haven't, either."

"Come on then," Renee said, pulling Melissa along, the others falling into step behind her. "Do you like chocolate cake?" Melissa looked up at her, eyes wide. She gave her covered head an emphatic nod. "Well, kid, it just so happens that the cooks baked a fresh one for me this morning, and I might be convinced to share some of it with you."

With Naomi's arm around his waist as the group headed for the entrance to the labs, Jack said, "And what have you been up to?"

"Oh, not much."

Behind him, Ferris nearly choked.

***

"This is your room, Melissa," Naomi told her, opening the door to the room across the hall from where she and Jack stayed.

The girl's eyes were wide as she stepped inside, nearly tripping on Koshka, who darted in ahead of her. A big screen television and a game console with a box of games occupied one corner. A laptop computer and electronic tablet were on a desk, and the bed sported a pink comforter, and a veritable zoo of stuffed animals. On one wall hung a huge mural poster of one of the latest bands that was popular among teens.

"We had no idea what you might be into," Renee told her, "so we got a little bit of everything. How do you like it?" She followed the other two into the room, leaving Hathcock outside in the hallway.

"It's awesome. I just wish it had a window."

"I know," Naomi said. "There's not much to see outside, anyway. But if you want to look at something, you can use the computer to watch the surveillance camera feeds."

"Really?"

Melissa plopped down in the chair in front of the computer. In thirty seconds she had five surveillance camera windows open, showing views around the compound and in the lab areas.

"Wicked," the girl whispered.

"Hey, kid, don't tune us out quite yet," Renee said, tapping Melissa on the hood that covered her head. "In here's a closet with some clothes in different sizes, so you should be able to find something that'll fit. You'll probably gag at the style, but at least you won't look like one of us old grandma types. And over here's the bathroom, which also has a shower. Just watch the water, as those idiots in facilities maintenance keep it turned up hot enough for percolating coffee."

"Okay." Melissa nodded, then eagerly turned back to the computer.

But before she could type another stroke, Naomi had put her hand over the keyboard.

Melissa looked up at her. "What?"

With a glance at Renee, Naomi said, as gently as she could, "Honey, you need to get out of those clothes and get cleaned up. How many days has it been since you've had a bath or a shower?"

Melissa took her hands away from the keyboard and stared at her. "I...I don't know. A few days."

"I think it's been a bit longer than that, hasn't it?"

"Fess up, kid," Renee said with a smile as she wrinkled her nose, "you're riper than a rotten melon."

After a moment, Melissa nodded.

Naomi reached for the scarf, but Melissa flinched away.

"Please don't," she said. Her eyes were brimming with tears.

"Melissa, honey, we know about the disease you're suffering from," Naomi told her, backing off to take a seat on the bed to give the girl some space. "That's actually the reason you're here, because we believe this disease, Morgellons, may help us kill the harvesters. And there's a chance, just a chance, that we may be able to cure you, as well." She leaned forward. "I know what it looks like, how it affects your skin, and how it makes you feel inside. But I want you to understand that we know the ugly parts are the disease, Melissa, not you. I know we're asking a lot after all you've been through, both before the harvesters came and after, but I need you to trust us. To trust me. Can you do that?"

"The last person who saw my face," Melissa whispered, "one of the nurses in the hospital, screamed when I took off the scarf. She wanted me to trust her, too."

Renee, who had taken a seat on the bed next to Naomi, shook her head, a wry grin on her face. "Kid, you'd scream if you were in my shoes and had to see Mr. Bald-As-An-Onion Richards bare-ass naked. You think you've got problems? Just imagine me having to endure that horrific vision every night. Now that's the stuff of nightmares!"

"Renee! God, you're awful," Naomi scolded, but Renee's ploy had worked.

Melissa was giggling. "Oh, no, no, no," she said, putting her hands over her eyes before succumbing to a fit of laughter. "Total mental photobomb." When she recovered, she said in a quiet voice. "Okay. But I'm ugly. I'm warning you."

"You're not ugly at all, hon," Renee said softly. "I can see that in your eyes. Trust us, okay?"

Without another word, Melissa reached up and pulled the scarf down, then pulled the hood from her head, letting her long, greasy auburn hair slip free.

Or, at least, what hair she had. Most of her scalp and forehead was covered in angry red lesions, from the size of a dime to one the size of Naomi's palm over the girl's left temple. While the skin around her eyes suffered no more than accumulated dirt and grime, her nose and lips were as afflicted as her scalp, and more lesions ran down her neck to disappear under her hoodie.

"Do you have these lesions all over your body?" Naomi asked.

Melissa nodded. "Yeah. But most, the worst ones, are on my head and face. It wouldn't be so bad if it wasn't for the fibers." Her lips, which looked blistered, quivered into a smile. "They sometimes poke me when I touch them, and they get stuck in my clothes."

Naomi stood up and came closer. "May I?"

"Okay, if it doesn't gross you out."

"It doesn't, honey. Not at all." Naomi leaned closer. Most of the lesions, especially those on and around her lips, had tiny fibers, twisted and curled, protruding from them. Some stood out individually, while others were bound in clusters. While it was difficult to make out with the naked eye, it was clear that the fibers weren't all the same color, as hair would be, nor were they colors typically natural to the human body. She was able to discern red, blue, black, and white fibers. And when she touched them, they were stiff and sharp enough to poke fingertips like tiny needles.

"Not to be rude," Renee said, "but shouldn't you be wearing gloves?"

"It's not contagious," Naomi replied absently. "Does it hurt where I'm touching?"

"A little. The worst is just how it feels sometimes, like there's something burrowing under my skin or biting me. I can't stand that."

Satisfied for the moment, Naomi stepped back to the bed and sat down. "Okay, here's what I'd like you to do. Get yourself cleaned up and put some fresh clothes on. Then Mr. Hathcock, who's waiting outside, will take you down to the galley where you can gobble down as much food as you want."

Melissa looked through the doorway as Hathcock peered in and threw her a quick salute. "Am I under arrest or something? A prisoner?"

"No, honey," Naomi reassured her. "He's one of our very best men, and has only one job now: keeping you safe. Think of him as your guardian or bodyguard, not your jailer. You're free to come and go when you want and where you want, except to some of the areas that are off limits for safety reasons, and if you need something, he'll get it for you. You're not a prisoner, you're our honored guest."

"Will he take me to see Alexander?"

"Sure he will," Naomi said, brushing her hand against Melissa's cheek. "I know Alexander would like that. I have to pay him a visit, too, but that'll have to wait until later. Renee and I have things to do first."

"But after you get cleaned up and fed, kiddo," Renee said as she got up and followed Naomi to the door, "we're going to need you to help us with some stuff, okay?"

"I'll be ready," Melissa said. With one more longing gaze at the computer, she headed for the bathroom, already stripping out of her filthy clothes as Naomi closed the door.

***

Carl sat at the head of the conference room table with Howard on the opposite end. Jack was staring at Naomi, who sat next to him.

"*Oh, not much*, you said." Jack threw his hands up in the air. "Jesus Christ, you went to Turkey and brought seven of those damn things back with you?"

"I wasn't in any danger," she lied. "Kiran and his men were there to protect me."

Jack shot Kiran, who sat along the wall behind them, an angry look. He gave Jack a helpless shrug.

"It was a risk we had to take, Jack," Carl told him. "You know how much I hated the whole idea of collaborating with these things, and I still do. But every department head supported this, President Lynch is now behind it, and we're down to taking the best of the worst options available. We can't keep losing cities like Chicago and the casualties that go with them. We've got to find some bug spray that'll kill these things, and find it fast."

"Come on, Jack, admit it," Howard said, only half-joking. "You're just upset because you couldn't go with her."

"It doesn't matter," Carl said. "It's done. Get over it. The question we have to answer now is how to proceed."

"I think there's only one answer to that," Naomi told him. "If we expect their cooperation, we have to give them full access to the information we have and work as a team. Otherwise there's no point."

"What if it's all a ruse?"

Everyone turned to look at Kiran. "What if this group is to infiltrate us?" He went on. "If we give them access to the labs, the information, the networks, and most importantly the key people, they could destroy everything in the blink of an eye."

"If they wanted to kill me, they could have done that at the border," Naomi told him.

"Forgive me, Naomi, but while you are probably the most powerful piece on the board, like the queen in a game of chess, you are not the only one. This place has become the heart of the effort to stop the harvesters. Even though you have other facilities and research organizations, this one is the key. If they can destroy or disrupt the operations here, there will be no salvation for humanity."

"And that's been my main reason for resisting this idea so long," Carl said. "We simply can't trust these things. If we're going to work with them, we have to figure out how to do it in such a way as to minimize our potential losses if they decide to turn on us."

"The network piece is manageable," Renee said. "It'll be a bit of a pain, but we can set up an isolated set of servers for them to use. We can bring data in through a one-way data pump so they'll have access to everything we want them to see, but can't reach back out into the network." She looked at Naomi. "The only thing is, for that to work we'll probably have to isolate all the machines in one of the labs, so any time you want to send something out to someone or even chat over the network you'll have to go to another area."

Naomi frowned. "That's going to be more than a minor inconvenience, but I think we can work with it."

"Physical security is another matter," Howard said. "Not in terms of keeping our guests cooped up, but in protecting our folks who need to work with them." He eyed Naomi, then turned his gaze on Harmony Bates. "I'd prefer to firewall the people as well as our network. We could set up a lab area adjacent to the holding cells downstairs where the harvesters can work on their isolated network mirror, while Naomi and her team continue to work as before."

"And how are the harvesters supposed to share data with us?" Naomi asked. "They'll be on an isolated network."

Howard shrugged. "We could extend their network to your workstations, set up switches that allow you to flip from one network to the other and back, and probably set up a way to bring data out of their network to ours, even if it's an air gap."

"An air gap?" Naomi and Harmony exchanged a disgusted glance. "Howard, we're not going to race around with a bunch of thumb drives porting data from their network to ours." She turned to Carl. "I know this is risky. I get that, especially since I'm probably number one on their list to get a stinger in my throat..."

"Naomi..." Carl began, but she raised a hand to cut him off.

"...but we're dealing with too many conditionals here," she went on, "all of which are going to take time. And some, like passing data across an air gap, just aren't going to work. Every minute we waste trying to shield ourselves from risk equates to thousands more victims." Looking at Jack, hoping he would understand, she said, "We had no choice but to make a deal with the devil. Now we have to take a leap of faith and pray they're sincere."

PEACEFUL COEXISTENCE

Taking a deep breath, Naomi said, "All right, let's do this."

"I hope you know what you're doing," Jack said before he tapped six digits into the entry lock and the door to the secure lab area hissed open. "Be careful."

She gave his arm a quick squeeze of reassurance, for herself as much as for him. "I'll try."

Before she could reconsider, she stepped through, with Harmony Bates and five other members of the genetics team, all volunteers, behind her, one of them for each of the harvesters.

The Seven, as the harvesters were being called in the rumor mill, awaited them. They were all in human form, but a chill fluttered down Naomi's spine and gooseflesh broke out on her arms as she entered the cool air of the lab. Their leader had adopted the guise of Vijay Chidambaram, which deeply unsettled her.

She glanced up at the ceiling as the doors slid shut, leaving Jack and the others on the protective detail outside. The lab was equipped with remotely controlled pods in the ceiling that held steerable Tasers and darts filled with formaldehyde, and the fire suppression system had been replaced with one that would instead turn the lab into an instant inferno.

Turning around, she waved at Jack and the others through the thick armor glass window. A dozen cats, Koshka among them, crouched on the shelf that had been installed especially for them. She could see their mouths move as they voiced their fear and loathing of the harvesters in hisses and growls.

"Naomi," the Vijay-thing said in the voice of the gentle Indian she had known, taking her attention away from the cats. Like its six companions, the thing wore surgical scrubs the humans had provided. Behind it, a door stood open to one of the larger containment cells on this level, where the harvesters could retire to rest, should they so require, and feed on the raw beef they were given. "We are ready."

"Good," she said with a faltering smile. "Let's get to work."

***

After a round of awkward introductions, the human researchers paired up with their harvester companions and began to instruct them in how to use the systems and access the data, for until they understood that much, they would be of little help.

While the others were doing that, Naomi took Vijay aside and sat down in a corner of the lab. "I want you to give me more details about the three keys that you mentioned," she told him. *It*, she had to remind herself. *It's not human.* "We were able to figure out the first one that you sent with Kiran, which has to do with the outer protein receptors."

The Vijay-thing smiled at her. "Yes, that is correct. I know you would have figured those out without terrible difficulty, but it seemed to be a good opener for our dialogue." It cocked its head. "You still do not believe in our sincerity, do you?"

She leaned back, folding her arms. "Let's just say that I have a hard time accepting it without concrete proof. Trust is something that's going to be in rather short supply for a while, I'm afraid."

"That is true for both sides, I fear." It gestured toward Jack, Kiran, and the Marines who waited outside. "I know that Kiran, for example, would like nothing more than to set us all alight and watch us burn, and should things not go as well as you would like, he might take it upon himself to..."

"Stop it," Naomi snapped. The Vijay-thing closed its mouth, giving her a quizzical look. "Manipulation is another one of your specialties. Planting ideas in our heads, sowing the seeds of doubt or fear. Every man and woman standing out there would love to put you and your friends to the torch." She leaned toward it. "So would I. So stop with the games and let's focus on finding a solution that will keep both our species alive."

It shrugged. "So be it. I was merely trying to be honest. As for the remaining two keys, one that I'm sure you must be aware of by now are the coded receptors within the cell that control genetic replication."

"Yes. That was certainly high on our list, since we can't do anything else until we get past that."

"We shall help you...open the door, shall we say."

It smiled again, and Naomi got a queasy sensation in her stomach. "And the third key?"

"The third is the master key," the thing told her with a flourish of its hands. "It is the key to our genetic code." It leaned closer. "First, we would greatly reduce the reproductive rate, and limit reproduction only to those of our kind who had achieved sentience. Second, we would eliminate swarming by degrading the ability of the non-sentients to communicate with one another in their rudimentary fashion. Instead, we can turn them against themselves. With those two changes alone, we would be able to gain control of the planet."

We would be able to gain control of the planet. The thing's choice of words were not lost on her.

***

With Hathcock in tow, Melissa wandered through the complex. She had been surprised when she hadn't been sent straight to some lab for a bazillion tests like she had at the hospital in Chicago. Instead, a lady doctor had asked her a lot of questions about her symptoms. The questions had all been asked before by other doctors, but this one had an endless supply of jokes that kept Melissa laughing the whole time.

Then came the part she really didn't like: getting her blood drawn. But this time she didn't mind at all. The young Navy corpsman who handled the needles and little vials was totally, awesomely hot, and she had to restrain a nervous giggle at practically every word he said. She felt like a complete moron, but there it was. And he looked at her without a trace of pity, fear, or loathing. That made her like him all the more.

The doctor came back in and took samples, a lot of samples, of the fibers, along with a few small bits of skin. Picking the fibers out had been more uncomfortable than painful. Every time the doctor plucked one out, or a bunch that were in one of their nasty little knots, Melissa felt like cockroaches were sent scurrying under her skin.

After double-checking that she had everything she needed, the doctor told one last joke, which left Melissa laughing so hard tears were running down her cheeks, before releasing her to Hathcock's care.

As Melissa was leaving the lab, she caught sight of the corpsman one last time. He smiled and waved at her, and she thought she would die right then and there.

You're just being a stupid little girl, she told herself. But she left the lab smiling, just the same.

"Let's go see Alexander now," she said to Hathcock. "Can we?"

"Sure," he said. "The vet clinic is downstairs."

"Isn't that where the harvesters are?"

He nodded. "Yep."

"Why do they keep the animals close to where those awful things are?"

Hathcock looked uncomfortable. "Well..."

"They use them for experiments, don't they?"

"Yeah," the soldier — *the sniper,* she corrected herself — said. "I don't know what all they do with them, though."

"They wouldn't use Alexander, would they?"

Hathcock laughed. "No, kid, we don't use cats for any of that kind of stuff. They don't carry any weapons, but they're our guardians all the same. And Alexander, he's a bit of a furry hero."

"Really?"

"Yeah, he saved Jack's life a couple times back when there were just a few harvesters for us to fight. Then he saved us again from a harvester when we got to the cemetery where we got you. The damn cat ought to get a medal."

They went down the stairwell and through the sub-basement security checkpoint, which had a stainless steel mantrap and was guarded by four Marines and a pair of leashed cats.

"This way." Hathcock led her down the main corridor to a door labeled Veterinary Clinic. He ran his badge through the reader and punched in a four digit code. The door clicked open and he pushed inside, Melissa trailing behind him.

The first thing she noticed was the smell. It was almost exactly like the lab where the doctor had taken samples of Melissa's skin, but had an underlying musky odor that reminded her of the dirty vacuum cleaner bags her mother made her change when they cleaned the house.

She felt hot tears welling up in her eyes at the memory, and she angrily brushed them away.

"May I help you?" The veterinarian got up from one of two workstations in the room and came over to greet them. The entire back wall, from floor to ceiling, was made up of stainless steel animal pens of various sizes. Most had thin bars across the front, while some had clear plastic. Off to Melissa's right were two doors, labeled *Surgery 1* and *Surgery 2*.

"We're looking for Alexander the cat," Melissa said. "We're, uh, friends of his."

The vet smiled. "He's right over here. Come on."

She led them into a small room that had *Recovery* on the door. "Here he is. Just be real gentle with him, okay? He's full of painkillers, so he's a little groggy."

The big cat, wrapped in pink bandages, was curled up in a padded pet bed in the corner, looking at them with half-open eyes. He mewled when Melissa dropped down on her knees next to him. "He's going to be okay, isn't he?"

"He's going to be fine. He's got some minor burns on the more exposed parts of his skin and some of the pads on his feet were roughed up, but he looks a lot worse than he is."

"I wish I could take him back to my room. I could keep him company."

"Why don't you, kid?"

Melissa looked up to see Renee standing in the doorway.

"I figured you'd probably be here after you escaped from that chamber of horrors upstairs," Renee said, kneeling down to rub Alexander very gently under his chin, where the hair had been singed down to stubble. "If it's okay with the doc, I'm sure Jack would be happy to have you watch over him."

"Can we?" Melissa looked up with hopeful eyes at the vet.

"I don't see why not," she said. "He's not in any danger, and I can come up and check on him periodically. You just need to keep him calm and quiet, okay?"

"That means no obnoxious cartoons blaring on your TV or raucous parties, kiddo," Renee said with a wink. "Hathcock, you want to carry this big lug so we can watch your biceps bulge?"

The sniper frowned. "Let's get a cart and put him on that. I'd carry him, but I need to keep my hands free." He gestured with his right hand, which was closed round the grip of the AA-12 automatic shotgun that hung from his shoulder on a tactical sling. It went along with the big pistol that was strapped to his right thigh, a long knife that rode handle-down on the left side of his chest, and a combat vest stuffed full of grenades and extra magazines for the shotgun.

"Fine, go ahead and ruin my day," Renee teased the Canadian, who grinned. "Come on, kid. Let's get this big fried fur ball out of here."

Ever so gently, the two of them lifted Alexander, still on his bed, onto the rolling table that the vet brought up from the back. Once he was in place, they slowly pushed him out into the corridor and headed toward Melissa's room, Hathcock following along behind.

***

Jack stared through the thick armor glass that stood between him, Terje, and the Marines and the lab where Naomi and the other members of her team were getting to know the harvesters. Microphones inside the room broadcast their voices into his ear through his radio. It was hard to make much out through the subdued babble, but it added another set of indicators to what he could see in case there was trouble. For now, the researchers sounded a little tense, as might be expected, but nothing more than that. Nor were there visible signs of trouble.

He was concerned when Naomi took the Vijay-thing over to one corner to speak to it alone, but after a few moments the two of them concluded their conversation and she led him to a workstation. Naomi smiled and gave Jack a quick wave before sitting down. Vijay looked at him, nodded his head, then sat down beside her, both of them disappearing behind the computer monitors that were set up on the desk. All Jack could see now were the tops of their heads.

As the first seconds stretched into minutes, and the minutes began to stretch into the first hour, the tension began to drain out of him.

After two hours, Jack rotated the reaction detail, bringing in a fresh team. The uncertainty he had heard in some of the voices at the beginning was gone, replaced by excitement as the joint species research team got down to business. Some of them *oohed* and *aaahed* like kids in a toy shop, while others chuckled or laughed. Even Naomi laughed, a sound that cut through the half dozen other conversations going on in the lab.

"If they were going to do something," Terje said, "they would have done it by now."

"Yeah, I suppose. I still don't like it."

The Norwegian snorted. "Who does? This is the worst of all possible worlds, but it's the only thing we can do." He grinned. "It's sort of like drinking during the long winter in Norway."

Jack turned to the Marines. "We're going to Condition Two," he told them. Condition Two had two Marines at the door and four more within a minute's call.

"Yes, sir," the Marine staff sergeant said. He turned and dismissed all but one of the Marines. "We'll keep this watch, sir."

"Thanks, staff sergeant," Jack said. "Okay, I guess we'll..."

"Jack." It was Carl's voice, breaking into the feed carrying the babble from the lab. "Where are you?"

Jack stopped in his tracks at the tone of Carl's voice. "I'm down at the lab. What's up?"

"Get up here right now," Carl told him. "We've got a problem. A big one."

ZEALOTS

"I wouldn't believe it if I didn't see it." Terje handed the binoculars to Jack.

"Yeah," Jack breathed, taking another look. "Me, too. Christ, what a monster."

They stood on the rear deck of one of the eight-wheeled Marine LAV armored reconnaissance vehicles. Carl had assigned all six LAVs from the lab complex to deal with this particular problem.

"I wish we had a battalion of tanks," Jack muttered.

They were stopped on a small rise a quarter mile east of the intersection of East Prairie Road and the American Legion Memorial Highway. The LAVs had left a gaping hole in the barb wire fence around the pasture where a couple dozen cattle had been grazing. The cows stood in a group, staring at the vehicles and lowing at them now and again.

While the terrain the vehicles occupied could hardly be called a hill, it gave their occupants enough of a height advantage that they could see a mile or more in just about every direction. Jack's attention was focused on what was in the fields to the east of their position. Analysts of the NGA, or National Geospatial-Intelligence Agency, now dispersed to several emergency facilities throughout the country, had noticed something strange appearing among some of the farms in America's heartland. For lack of anything better, the analysts had called them crop circles.

Since protection of the SEAL facilities was critical, they were given a high priority for imagery coverage. When crop circles started to appear on both sides of the Platte River between Central City and Grand Island, which was only ten miles from SEAL-2, NGA flashed a warning to the facility that landed on Carl's virtual desk. Since Jack was as confident he could be that no imminent harm would come to Naomi or the others working with the harvesters, he took on the duty to investigate.

"Larvae," Terje whispered as he compared one of the satellite images with their current position and the location of the *crop circle* they were now staring at. "Impossibly huge. Some of the ones on this image must be as big as a sports field, flattened like a pancake. How is this even possible?"

"I don't know," Jack said, "but we'd better get them now before they divide."

Out of the corner of his eye, he saw a calf, its bovine ears twitching, moving toward one of the LAVs. "Captain," he said to Captain Aaron Lowmack, the Marine company commander. "Shoot it."

"Sir?" Lowmack glanced at the young cow, a look of incomprehension on his face.

Not waiting for the Marines to react, Terje raised his rifle and took aim at the calf, which was now perhaps fifteen feet away from the other LAV.

The animal froze and jerked its head around to look at the Norwegian just before he fired. The tracer round caught the beast right between the eyes. The calf burst into flame. It was close enough to the other LAV that burning chunks of malleable flesh spattered onto the vehicle, setting the paint and two of the tires on fire. The quick reaction of the vehicle's crew, which produced a pair of fire extinguishers and put out the flames, saved the vehicle.

The LAVs opened fire on the rest of the cattle with their 25mm Bushmaster cannon and 7.62mm machine guns, blasting the hapless beasts into bloody, smoking meat.

"Cease fire, goddammit!" Jack shouted into his mic, but it was too late. "*Cease fire!*"

The guns fell silent.

"Sir," Lowmack, who was obviously shaken, said, "we thought the rest were..."

"They can only mimic things that are roughly the same size as they are," Jack said through gritted teeth, "which means about the same mass as a human being."

"But what if some of them are bigger, sir?" Lowmack asked. "Those larval things are. Why can't some of the adults be bigger, too?"

Jack opened his mouth, ready to bite the man's head off for being an idiot, then snapped it shut. Terje was looking at him with a speculative expression on his face.

"It's a possibility we can't discount, Jack," Terje said. "Just because we haven't seen larger adult harvesters doesn't mean they don't exist."

"Point taken," Jack said. "That would be some really bad news." He looked again at where the cows had been slaughtered, then he offered the Marine captain a grim smile. "Maybe we'll have filet mignon tonight."

"No complaints here, major," the man said, "although the owner probably isn't going to be too happy."

"He can bill Uncle Sam," Jack told him. Then in a quieter voice, added, "If he's still alive."

"So what are we going to do?" Terje asked.

Jack took out his map, which was folded in a camouflaged canvas case. "What sort of ammo are you carrying, captain?"

"The LAVs have a full load of M792 rounds, high explosive incendiary with tracer, and the machine guns are loaded with tracer, as well."

"Okay, so in theory, even a single shot from either should set one of those big bastards on fire. So how about this: let's head east to 2nd Road and set up a mobile barrier along there from M Road north of us, all the way south to the river, giving each vehicle a section of road to cover. That should let us block the larvae from getting to the airport, the town, and SEAL-2."

Lowmack looked at the map. "That's a stretch of over fifteen miles, sir. That's spreading us a bit thin, isn't it?"

Jack shrugged. "I'm open to other options, if you've got any." Lowmack shook his head. "That's only about two miles per vehicle, so if you just keep the LAVs moving in their sectors, shooting any larvae or harvesters they see, we should be okay. No other military forces are available, and Carl doesn't want to strip any more defenders away from either SEAL-2 or the airport. He promised us a Black Hawk as soon as he can free one up to spot targets for us, but that may be a while. Just tell your men to keep well clear of any of those things, big or small, and light them up as far away as they can."

The Marine nodded, a skeptical look on his face. "As you say, sir."

As Lowmack keyed his mic and began relaying orders over the radio, Jack put the binoculars back up to his eyes and watched one of the huge harvester larvae, a circle of mottled, oozing flesh well over a hundred feet across, grow even larger as it greedily consumed the early spring crops in the fields.

***

"Tango Two Nine Four, you're cleared for landing on pad three."

"Roger, SEAL-2 Control." The copilot of the Black Hawk banked the helicopter slightly to the left as he brought it in over the main gate of the complex toward the landing area. The pilot beside him was silent. Dead men usually were. The puncture wound in his back would not be visible to anyone on the ground.

Eleven heavily armed soldiers occupied the troop compartment. While they wore military uniforms and had weapons similar to those carried by the Marines on the ground below, they were not brothers in arms. They wore faces that were not their own, and had thoughts that no human being could fully comprehend.

Their journey had been a long and difficult one, spawned by a chance opportunity outside of Chicago when the SEAL-12 facility had been destroyed. A few of those who had come to dig out the survivors had not been human, and had learned a great deal from the brains of several of the recently dead. The knowledge that was absorbed was not as bright or clear as that taken from the living, but it had been enough, more than enough, for them to know where the true threat to their kind lay. It was here, in this place, in the minds of the scientists who worked here, notably the one known as Naomi Perrault.

The members of the assault team were all fully adult, achieving sentience while leaving their perilous reproductive phase behind.

They were also what humans might, after a fashion, consider zealots. They knew that their generation had been engineered by The Old Ones, and held them up as what humans might think of as gods. The will of those gods was undeniable, their plan a model of perfect chaos. The humans and the other life that occupied the world was nothing more than prey, and with their extinction would come a time of carnage that would span the ages until the world itself turned to dust.

But for that to happen, the greatest threat had to be eliminated.

Naomi Perrault and those in company with her must die.

***

"Holy shit!"

Lowmack's LAV was at the intersection of 2nd Road and Chapman, about three and a half miles northeast of the Grand Island Airport.

An enormous larva, even larger than the one Jack had spotted at their initial scouting position, occupied the field southwest of the intersection.

Lowmack had ordered the LAV's gunner to fire three 25mm rounds at the thing. When the shells hit the thing and exploded, everyone had expected that the larva would burst into flame and that would be that.

Instead, the creature had contracted, drawing itself from the flattened pancake form up into what looked like an enormous chocolate kiss before ejecting tons of tissue, including the burning bits, high into the air.

Right toward the LAV.

"Back up!" Lowmack shouted to the driver. "*Back up!*"

Jack and Terje dropped down into the passenger compartment and held on as the driver threw the vehicle into reverse and sent them flying west on Chapman, away from the harvester.

"Shit, shit, shit!" Lowmack cursed as the larval bomb fell toward them.

The mass hit the pavement twenty feet from where the LAV had been, spattering like a ripe melon and sending gobs of tissue flying everywhere. Some of the splintered larvae were burning, but many weren't, and began to slowly ooze their way along the road, leaving ruts in the asphalt behind them.

Of course, Jack thought. *Asphalt is like congealed oil. Perfect larvae food.*

"Jack, look!" Terje was pointing back at the main body of the larva.

The huge mass swayed and twitched, then suddenly dissolved into countless small, wriggling shapes.

"Jesus," Jack whispered.

He heard the other LAVs opening fire to the north and south. Grabbing Lowmack by the arm, he said, "Tell them to cease fire! Now!"

"Roger that!" The captain passed on the orders, but Jack knew from the volume of fire put out by the other five vehicles that it was far too late. He had given instructions that they were to focus on the largest harvesters first. He felt like vomiting.

Beside him, Terje put his rifle to his shoulder and put a few tracer rounds into some of the smaller larvae, which caught fire and burned fiercely.

The Marines caught on, shooting the things on the road with the 7.62mm machine guns.

"I can't get through to one of the LAVs," Lowmack shouted, his voice barely cutting through the sound of the firing in Jack's headphones.

"Let's go find them," Jack said. The entire field was burning, the heat painfully intense, even at this distance.

The driver took them across one of the fields to avoid the flame-filled intersection, then they headed north along 2nd Road. They passed one of the other LAVs, which was now hammering at some of the smaller larvae with its machine guns, before they reached the sector assigned to the missing vehicle.

They found it on the road, just past a grove of trees. The crew had fired on a big larva that had only been a few dozen yards away. The entire vehicle was covered in a blue-yellow mass that writhed and oozed. Another blob of larval tissue burned in the field behind it.

None of the men in the LAV had made it out alive.

Without a word, Lowmack took a rifle handed up by one of the men inside. He aimed and fired a single tracer round at the thing that enveloped the vehicle and had killed his men.

The larva began to burn.

Jack was thinking of what orders he should give the Marines when he heard the panicked radio call from the command center at SEAL-2.

***

To anyone watching the Black Hawk's approach, it appeared to be just another landing among many. Routine. Ordinary. Incoming supplies or troops moving around, it really didn't matter. Boredom and complacency were among the greatest weaknesses of the humans.

When the helicopter was about fifty feet from the ground, the copilot shoved the cyclic stick forward and hauled back on the collective lever, sending the Black Hawk roaring toward the gate of the inner fence line.

As it zoomed over the gate, one of the harvesters tossed out a satchel charge, which landed right at the feet of the startled Marine guards.

The aircraft lurched as the charge exploded. The blast killed the Marines and cats guarding the gate, shattered the few windows remaining in the lab building, and blasted a hole in the fence line twenty meters long.

The copilot brought the Black Hawk around in a gentle right turn, the gunner behind him raking the compound with the 7.62mm minigun mounted in the window just behind the copilot's seat. The weapon made a deep thrum as it spewed tracer rounds in a solid stream of metal, firing four thousand rounds per minute. Dozens of Marines were cut down, the helicopter hangar was torn to bits, and the two Black Hawks that had set down on the landing pad only a few minutes before went up in balls of flame. Then the gunner walked the glowing stream of bullets through the tent city where the scientists were living, wreaking carnage on those who were off-shift and trying to catch some sleep.

As the helicopter came around to bring the gun to bear on the lab and personnel buildings, the gunner blasted the lab entry doors from their frames, killing the six men and women of the quick reaction team who had just emerged. While the lab building was made of concrete and reinforced with steel and wasn't vulnerable to the minigun's fire, the personnel buildings, which used only light wood construction typical of many apartment buildings, certainly were. The stream of fire tore through the ends of both buildings like a buzz saw before the weapon finally ran out of ammunition.

When the pilot dipped the helicopter down to a dozen feet above the ground just beyond the inner fence, the ten harvester soldiers leaped out.

Dashing around the smoke-filled crater left by the satchel charge, the group divided into two teams. One charged through the destroyed entry doors into the lab complex, while the other headed toward the entrance to the first personnel building.

ATTACK

Everyone in the lab looked up, startled, as a deep boom reverberated through the sub-basement.

"What was that?" Naomi's question was met by a set of blank stares.

Then the alarm went off, a piercing *whoop-whoop* accompanied by flashing strobes set in the ceiling.

"That's not the fire alarm, is it?" Harmony asked.

"I don't know..."

She saw Kiran, who hadn't left his post at the door since Jack and Terje departed, stiffen. Then he said something into his microphone. With a gesture of his hand, he sent the two Marines to take up positions near the door to the main corridor. Then he reached for the keypad beside the door and pressed the intercom button. "SEAL-2 team, come out! Harvesters, return to your cells. *Now!*"

Naomi pressed the intercom button on her desk. "Kiran, what is it?"

"We are under attack. Come out, Naomi." His hand hovered over the big panic button on the security panel by the door. If he pressed that, the active security systems would target the harvesters in the room with the Tasers.

"It is all right, Naomi," the Vijay-thing said. "Go. We will..."

It broke off at the sound of gunfire coming from one of the levels above, followed by screams.

"Come on!" Kiran shouted.

With a look of helpless frustration at Vijay, Naomi stood up and ushered the others toward the door.

The Vijay-thing began to lead the other harvesters to the rear of the lab where their cells were.

"We'll be back as soon as we can!" Naomi said.

It smiled. "We are not going anywhere."

When the humans were clustered near the door, Kiran hit the button to cycle it open, keeping an eye on the harvesters to make sure they didn't try to escape. Naomi brought up the rear. Once she was through, Kiran hit the button to close it.

"Come," he said, leading them out of the room and into the main corridor, which was now swarming with panicked scientists and technicians from the other labs on this level. "Clear the way!"

The two Marines bulled their way through the men and women who were waiting for the elevator.

"The elevator locks on the ground floor in case of any alarm! Head for the stairwell!"

She heard Kiran curse as everyone ran to join the crush of people already trying to get through the door to the stairs. Ignoring their angry shouts, he and the Marines pushed and shoved people out of the way, shepherding her to the stairs.

They were halfway up to the first basement level when a loud boom echoed from somewhere above. Then someone cut loose with an automatic weapon inside the stairwell, and everyone began to stampede back down toward the second basement level.

Kiran threw Naomi into the corner of the mid-level landing and shielded her with his body as the mob of panicked people stampeded past them.

A grenade exploded two landings up. She had been looking up through the narrow gap in the switchback of the stairs when it went off. Blood and small gobbets of flesh spattered across her face and upper body. She screamed as another grenade went off, closer this time, sending more bits of gore raining down on her and the others. Her ears felt as if someone had stuck an ice pick through them as the shockwave smashed into her.

Then she was moving again, back down the stairs, Kiran's hand holding her upper arm in a steel grip. She was blinking her eyes, trying to clear them of the blinding after-image from the flash of the first grenade, and was just getting her vision back when they burst through the door to the basement level from which they'd come. The corridor was filled with screaming, blood-soaked refugees.

"Hide!" Naomi was still partially deaf from the grenades, and Kiran's bellow sounded as if he were underwater at the far end of an olympic swimming pool. "Get away! They're coming!"

He dragged her back toward the fortified lab. Only one of the Marines was still with them, blood dripping from a long, ugly gash in the triceps muscle of his left arm. Kiran, too, was wounded, a piece of shrapnel having sliced through the back of his scalp, leaving a trail of blood running down his neck, and his back was covered in crimson.

None of the other members of her team were in sight.

"Where are the others?" She shouted.

Kiran didn't answer.

"Kiran, where are they?"

He fixed her for just a moment with his dark eyes. "Keep moving!"

"Hold here," Kiran told the Marine as they entered the vestibule area off the main corridor.

Following Kiran to the armor glass door, she saw that the seven harvesters hadn't returned to their cells.

He turned to Naomi. "If I open this door, there's a good chance these things will kill you."

"But if you don't," she said, "I'll probably die anyway. But they could also protect me."

He nodded, and she knew it was a choice she had to make. "Open it."

Pushing the intercom button, Kiran said to the harvesters, "Stand back away from the door."

They did, quickly moving toward the back of the lab.

Kiran opened the door and waited for Naomi to go through.

"You two should come with me," she said.

He looked over his shoulder at the sound of gunfire and screams from down the corridor. "I can't." He drew his pistol, a .50 caliber Desert Eagle, and handed it to her. "I'll be back for you as soon as I can."

Then he pushed her inside and closed the door.

"Good luck," she whispered as Kiran led the remaining Marine back out into the corridor.

The thing that looked like Vijay Chidambaram came to stand beside her, an inscrutable expression on its face.

***

Melissa had just returned to her room, lugging a litter box from downstairs for Alexander. Hathcock had refused to carry it, and she would have thought him a lazy jerk if she hadn't taken such a liking to him. On the other hand, he was a sniper, after all. She wasn't entirely sure what that meant, other than that he could put a bullet through a squirrel's eyeball at a thousand yards (or something like that) while flying in a helicopter, but she knew that he was a very dangerous man. It wasn't just that Naomi had told him he was one of their best, or that he was dressed up like some action movie commando. It was something about him that she couldn't put her finger on. He just oozed dangerousness out of his pores. She wished she would have had him with her at school. None of the other kids would have made fun of her then, calling her freak or Typhoid Mary, or her personal favorite, The Thing. One glance from Hathcock, even without the two tons of weapons he carried around, would have sent them running.

Most of them were probably dead now. That made her sad, even though they had treated her like crap. Nobody deserved what the harvesters did to people.

Shoving that melancholy thought aside, she liked having Hathcock around as her own personal gangster muscle, even if he was Mr. I Have To Keep My Hands Free So You'll Have To Carry That Yourself.

She was trying to figure out a way to make that into some sort of cool acronym when a huge boom sounded outside, so loud that it hurt her ears. The walls shook, and some of the pictures she'd cut out and taped up on the wall flew off. Alexander let out a startled cry from his bed, which was right next to hers.

Just as she was opening her mouth to ask Hathcock what happened, she was slammed to the floor, a huge weight on top of her.

It took her a moment to realize that it was Hathcock.

"Get off me, you perv!" She wrestled against his bulk, but it was like an ant trying to free itself from an elephant.

Then she heard a weird ripping sound, like someone took the sound of a zipper being opened really fast and dropped the pitch a couple octaves. Their music teacher had done that once with her voice using an electronic gadget, and had the class in stitches while she talked like Darth Vader.

The ripping came and went, like someone was flipping a switch, and she could hear the sound of a helicopter outside.

"Shit," Hathcock cursed.

Melissa thought he was freeing her when he got to his knees, but she was wrong. He shoved her toward the end of the bed, grabbed Alexander by the bandages on the scruff of his neck, eliciting a ferocious hiss from the wounded beast, then dove to the floor beside her to spoon his body against her back while tucking the madly squirming cat into her arms.

She cursed as Alexander raked her arms with his claws and was about to shove him away when the ripping sound came again and the wall facing the helipad area disintegrated in a shower of splinters and drywall. Fiery red streaks passed over her head, inches away, and went right through the opposite wall, tearing the place apart. Her computer exploded into shards of plastic and the door to the hallway was blown away. Her nose was filled with the reek of smoldering metal, wood, and plastic, along with a chemical stink that she recognized as gunpowder.

Behind her, Hathcock grunted and his body was slammed against hers like someone had hit him in the back with a hammer.

The ripping sound went on, and she could hear bullets chewing through more of the building before the weapon moved on to destroy the personnel building next door that was still under construction.

At last, it fell silent. The only thing she could hear now was the *whump* of the rotor blades of the helicopter outside and screams. There were lots of screams.

Alexander tore out of her grip and hid under the mound of stuffing that was all that remained of her bed.

"Hathcock?"

He groaned.

"Craig? Are you okay?" She rolled over to look at Hathcock. "Craig!"

"Fuck," he gasped. "Help me up."

She grabbed one of his arms and pulled, lifting him to a kneeling position. The floor beneath him was covered in blood. "Oh, God," she said, "you're hurt!"

Right below them, where the entry doors were, they heard a crash, shouts, then gunfire.

"Here, take this," Hathcock gasped, pulling a small pistol from a pouch on the side of his combat harness and handing it to her.

She held it as if it were a steaming turd. "I've...I've never fired a gun!"

"It's easy, kid. Just point and shoot."

"Okay, but this thing's a toy. It might stop a squirrel."

He managed a grin. "It has magic bullets. If one hits their skin, you'll get a nice fireworks show. Piece of advice: keep shooting until you're sure the target's dead." He took a deep breath, wincing at the pain. "Now get your ass in the bathroom. Shoot anything that comes through there."

Using his shotgun, muzzle down, as a crutch, he pushed himself to his feet and staggered to the doorway.

"Hathcock," she pleaded, "stay here! Don't go!"

"Sorry, kid, but I need a better line of sight...to the stairs. Otherwise they'll just gang up on us here and we won't stand a chance." He looked at her, and it was hard for her to hold back the tears. "You'll be fine."

Then he was gone.

She knelt in the bathroom, her eyes fixed on the empty doorway that led to the hall, the gun locked tight in her trembling hands.

From somewhere under the bed, she could hear Alexander growl before another massive explosion outside drove her to the floor.

***

"God, I could use a stiff drink."

Renee yawned as she watched Carl stand up from behind his desk and stretch. "I could use a dozen."

"Count me in," Howard added as he rubbed his eyes.

Carl tossed the electronic tablet he'd been clutching onto his desk. *More reports, more bad news,* he thought. This little meeting had been about trying to keep the other SEAL labs supplied as the road and rail networks continued to fray. They were having to shift nearly everything to airlifts, but that was putting even more strain on the looming fuel shortage. Oil refineries had been given a higher priority for security than even nuclear plants, because once the fuel flow, especially diesel and jet fuel, stopped, they'd be done. Finished. And it wasn't just for running vehicles and airplanes, it was for throwing up fiery walls to stop the harvesters. That simple expedient, above all others, seemed to work. It had worked in Chicago when the safe zone had been overrun, and had been used in several other places, as well.

The only downside was that it only worked as long as you had fuel to keep the fire burning. Once it went out...

All of the SEAL facilities were at one hundred percent for their fuel reserves and were being continually topped off, but it was getting harder to get the tanker trucks through from the distribution centers and rail lines. As for the rest of the country, that was someone else's problem.

"I think I'll go down and see how Naomi is making out with her pets," Carl said.

Renee saw something moving through the window behind him, and the sound of the helicopter that had been coming in to land got louder. A lot louder. The Black Hawk looked like it was about to fly right through the window.

"Carl, look out!"

Carl turned to look out the window, then dove across the desk and rolled to the floor. Grabbing her in his arms, he yanked her down beside him as Howard pitched forward out of his chair.

The window shattered, blasting fragments across the room from an explosion outside. Then a 7.62mm minigun opened fire.

The base alarm began to blare.

Renee raised her head up and he shoved it back down to the floor. "Are you nuts?"

She struggled to get out from under him, to no avail. "Dammit, what's happening?"

"What do you think? We're under attack!"

The building shuddered as the bullets from the minigun hammered into the concrete, but the lab was made of stern stuff and none penetrated inside other than the ones that blasted through the window.

But nothing in the compound short of the M1 tanks could stand up under a concentrated burst from the weapon, and Carl heard the main entry doors on the ground floor let go. Then the weapon moved on as the sound of the helicopter changed, moving away to strafe the rest of the compound.

"Come on, we've got to get out of here! Crawl to the doorway and get down the hall!"

Renee did as he said, and Carl ushered Howard out before he followed himself, stopping only long enough to grab one of the AA-12 shotguns from the rack just inside the office door.

"Give me one of those."

Carl turned to look at Howard, a frown on his face.

"Come on! Just because I'm rich doesn't mean I'm helpless. I've shot skeet every other weekend for the last thirty years. Give me the damn thing!"

With a shrug, Carl grabbed a second weapon and handed it to him, then the three of them moved out into the hallway.

***

FBI Special Agent Angie Boisson's eyes flew wide when she saw the flash and smoke of an explosion near the entrance to the lab building of SEAL-2. Her hands instinctively reached for her assault rifle.

She was in the copilot's seat of the last Black Hawk out of Grand Island. The town and the airport had been overrun by a wave of harvesters that had come surging across the Platte River from the south. Ferris had just brought the helicopter in for a landing after a long recon mission when the monsters attacked the airport. While it had been far smaller in scope than the devastation she'd seen in Los Angeles, so many harvesters had come sweeping across the tarmac that it had looked like a black tide. The people who'd come running toward her Black Hawk weren't brought down by individual harvesters. They simply disappeared below the surface of the ocean of creatures. Some had come close enough that Boisson could still remember their terrified faces. Faces that she'd never forget.

Worse, the helicopter had been struck by some stray gunfire. Half the indicator lights on the control panel, including the master alarm, were red, and Ferris had been fighting with the controls since then, struggling to keep the helicopter in the air.

"What the fuck?" Ferris exclaimed as another Black Hawk, hovering low over the facility, opened fire with its minigun, tearing the compound to pieces.

Boisson glanced over at the pilot. Ferris was losing it. The harvesters had nearly killed them at the airport. Some had leaped up to grab onto the landing gear as the helicopter had lifted off, and one had actually poked its hideous head into the crew compartment before one of Boisson's agents had blown it away. More had vaulted high enough to slam into the helicopter's windscreen, but couldn't hold on and fell away.

That hadn't kept Ferris from screaming.

And as if the Grand Island massacre hadn't been enough, now SEAL-2 was being hammered by what looked like one of their own helicopters.

"Baker!" She called to the helicopter's crew chief, who manned the minigun. "Can you get a bead on that bastard?"

"We need to get closer! I can probably hit him from here, but I'll hit anything behind him, too."

"Step on it, Ferris," she said.

"Right." Ferris dropped the Black Hawk's nose and pushed the engine to its limit, sending the helicopter shooting toward SEAL-2.

As they approached, the other helicopter ceased firing and came to hover near the lab entrance. Boisson watched as a dozen or so men slithered down ropes, then ran into the buildings. "Dammit," she hissed. "Baker, take out that chopper!"

"Yes, ma'am!"

Ferris angled the nose to the right so the gunner had a clear line of fire. A second-long burst sent a stream of metal that nearly cut the other Black Hawk in two before it exploded, sending bits of whirling rotor blades and hunks of metal flying as the helicopter's carcass crashed to the ground.

"Oh, my God," Ferris moaned as they flew in over the outer wall. The gunner in the other helicopter had known his business. The four M1 tanks still squatted in their dug-outs, the standby crews having been slaughtered as they ran to their tracks. The two tanks on watch duty were smoking, with crimson spattered over the turret tops where their commanders had been. The other defensive positions had been obliterated.

The worst was the tent city where most of the personnel had been living while waiting for the new barracks buildings to be completed. Boisson had worked in a slaughterhouse in her late teen years. This was worse.

"Get us on the ground as close to the lab as you can," she told Ferris.

"That's not a problem," Ferris told her as he angled the Black Hawk toward the building. They both flinched as a loud bang came from one of the engines and more indicators flashed red. "Jesus!" The Black Hawk began to vibrate and shudder. "Hang on!"

Boisson pressed herself back in her seat as the ground came up fast. Ferris managed to squeeze a little more lift out of the rotors at the last second before the helicopter smacked into the ground. It bounced once, twice, then settled onto the landing gear.

"Fuck this shit," Ferris whispered as he quickly shut everything down. He was pale as a ghost and his hands were shaking.

"You did good," she told him. "Now let's go kill those sons of bitches."

IN FLAMES

A flash-bang grenade sailed into the corridor from the stairwell, and Kiran snapped his eyes shut just before it went off. Even with his eyes closed, the grenade left bright afterimages on his retinas and the shock wave bounced his head off the wall behind him. Blinking his eyes clear, he took aim at the stairwell door with his AA-12 shotgun.

A dark figure, then two, charged out into the hallway, and Kiran hesitated. They were dressed in U.S. military uniforms. He was about to hail them as saviors, thinking they had cleared out the attackers in the stairwell, when they opened fire on the scientists who still hadn't fled to the labs.

Kiran pulled the trigger and held it down. The shotgun, which was fully automatic, belched Dragon's Breath shells at the rate of three hundred rounds per minute, filling the corridor with fire. These newer rounds also had a heavy lead slug in the center, and he saw the lead attacker double over as he was hit in the abdomen.

The enemy reeled back under the barrage, beating a hasty retreat back into the stairwell. Kiran let up on the trigger, then quickly swapped out the magazine. It held thirty-two rounds, and the first magazine was nearly empty. He was sure he had hit both men multiple times and covered them in fire, which left him puzzled. If they were human, they should have been injured or killed, and if they were harvesters, they should have burst into flame, but they had done neither.

Three more grenades sailed into the corridor.

"Gas!" The Marine who'd been with him, but who was now on the far side of the corridor, shouted as a heavy, smoky mist began to spew from the grenades.

One whiff told Kiran that it was tear gas. While harmless, it could be debilitating and, worse, had completely blocked his view of the stairwell.

The Marine began to cough uncontrollably, then screamed in agony for a terrifyingly brief moment before he was silenced.

Kiran fired a few rounds toward where the Marine had been, and was rewarded with a high pitched screech just before a hail of bullets tore up the wall around him. One hit his leg, the bullet passing clean through the calf muscle. He gritted his teeth against the pain as he retreated through the nearest doorway into one of the main labs before the enemy could overwhelm him.

**

Hathcock knew he didn't have much time. The slug from the minigun had taken him below the right kidney and he was bleeding out fast. He only hoped he could hold out long enough for help to arrive.

He had staggered partway down the hallway toward where the stairs emerged onto the second floor. The contractors hadn't installed the door to the stairwell in the partially completed building, which was good news and bad. He'd be able to see the enemy as they came up the stairs, but they'd be able to see him, too.

Moving past the stairwell, keeping the muzzle of the shotgun trained on it as he went, he kicked in the door to one of the apartments farther down the hall.

With hands and arms that felt like lead weights, he took two grenades from his combat vest and set them on the floor before sinking down to a prone position, facing the stairwell. He eased the door closed until it was just wide enough for the muzzle of the gun to poke through.

There were still sounds of savage fighting below, and he could hear more coming from the lab building.

A burst of rifle fire, followed by a brief gurgling scream, sounded from the stairwell.

Focus, he told himself as a figure in combat fatigues stepped onto the landing, his gun sweeping the empty hallway. It was a US Army uniform, and the man was wearing a protective mask.

Someone down the hall in Melissa's direction whimpered, and the soldier swiveled that way and moved out of the stairwell, two more right behind him.

Hathcock held them in his sights, waiting a few precious seconds to see if anyone else was going to appear.

One of the three turned to sweep down the hall in Hathcock's direction, and the soldier's gaze came to rest on the stainless steel muzzle of Hathcock's shotgun.

Hathcock fired, the heavy slug punching through the gas mask right between the eye pieces as the soldier's body was wreathed in fiery Dragon's Breath.

The head lit up like a torch, burning inside the mask before the rubber itself ignited, sending up a cloud of black, noxious smoke while the harvester danced a death jig. The helmet fell away as the head lost its shape, taking burning gobs of malleable tissue with it.

The other two harvesters leaped away to get clear of their flaming sibling, then turned and loosed a volley of gunfire down the hallway, peppering the walls with bullets.

Hathcock fired again, but the harvesters were moving too fast for a head shot, and his vision was dimming quickly. Gritting his teeth, he held down the trigger, turning the hallway into a maelstrom of blinding fire.

The last expended shotgun shell flew from the ejection port on the gun. Hathcock dropped the weapon and rolled away from the door just as it was blasted into splinters by more gunfire. He took two rounds to the chest, the bullets slamming into the body armor and driving the wind out of him.

Panting from the pain of cracked or broken ribs, he grabbed one of the grenades he'd set aside, pulled the pin, and let the handle fly before rolling it to one side of the door. He pulled the pin on the second and tossed it onto the bed beside him. Then he drew his Desert Eagle. He was so weak now that he could barely hold it, but he didn't really have to aim. It was only a distraction.

One of the harvesters kicked in the door and Hathcock fired, hitting the thing in the side of the neck. It screeched as ichor fluid spattered on the door, but the slug didn't stop it. Tossing aside its rifle, it bent down and reached for him.

The grenade by the door went off. It was a regular fragmentation grenade, rather than the more lethal white phosphorous grenades, and at close range it could take down a harvester. But he hadn't planned on fighting harvesters wearing body armor.

The thing was knocked off balance by the blast, sent stumbling deeper into the room. White hot pain from the shrapnel lanced through Hathcock's feet and legs as the harvester took hold of his head.

Then the grenade on the bed exploded, and the world went dark.

***

"Down!"

Carl shoved Renee to the floor as a pair of grenades bounced off the wall opposite the stairwell. One of them ricocheted toward the far end of the corridor, while the second landed a dozen feet from where Carl, Renee, and Howard had been crouching, guns trained on the elevator and stairwell doors.

Instead of exploding, the grenade spewed a misty smoke. One whiff told Carl what it was. "Tear gas," he announced.

Renee immediately began to gag. She buried her mouth and nose in the fabric of the sleeve of her left arm, but it was no use. In only a few seconds she was rendered helpless. Her eyes felt like someone was rubbing them with sandpaper, and tears were rolling down her cheeks. Her salivary glands went into gooey overdrive, and more spit and snot were coming out of her than tears. She began to cough uncontrollably. "Holy shit," she choked. "What moron called this *tear* gas?"

On the other side of the hallway, Howard was coughing, although not as bad as she was. Beside her, Carl hawked and spat, but that was the extent of his reaction. "Showoff," she croaked. She tried to steady the Desert Eagle, but it was hopeless. Between the coughing and her screwed up vision, the only way she'd be able to hit anything was if it came and pressed itself up against the weapon's muzzle.

Shadows moved through the smoke. "Hold your fire," Carl whispered. "Might be civilians."

There was a voice, someone calling out from one of the rooms farther down the hallway. "Thank God! Did you catch the bastards who…"

Whoever it was never got a chance to finish the sentence. A three-round burst from an assault rifle cut them off.

The shadows moved closer.

"Over here!"

It was Howard. Fighting to see through the tears, Renee looked over to where he was crouched low against the wall. She could barely see him.

The billionaire cried out again. "Help me! Help!"

Two shadows materialized out of the smoke, moving right toward him. They were soldiers wearing gas masks. But that didn't make sense, because masks weren't standard issue here on the base, and most of the military personnel were Marines, not soldiers.

Carl and Howard must have reached the same conclusion. Their shotguns roared, filling the corridor with flame.

The two soldiers were knocked backward. One of them stumbled and fell, firing off a spray of bullets that blasted through the wall a few inches above Renee's head. She squeezed off a shot in return, and the .50 caliber slug found the gap in the soldier's body armor just under the left arm. He twitched and lay still.

"Holy crap," she rasped.

The other soldier was backing down the hall into the mist as Carl and Howard fired away. It had to be a harvester, because no human soldier could take that sort of punishment and stay on his feet, but she didn't understand why the Dragon's Breath didn't just turn the thing into a roman candle.

There was more firing at the other end of the hall. Then silence.

"Get back in the office," Carl hissed. "We're too exposed out here. Howard, move back."

Renee was crawling on her hands and knees toward Carl's office when a machine gun opened fire from beyond the veil of the tear gas, blasting holes in the floor and walls.

She was almost through the doorway when one of the bullets found her.

***

Melissa was shivering, but it wasn't from the cold air seeping through the torn up wall. She flinched as another door was kicked open down the hall. This time someone was inside. Whoever it was screamed just before a gun went off and the screaming stopped.

That had been the fourth one. And every door was closer.

Without Hathcock, she felt totally, utterly alone, more than she had ever felt in her life. *Damn you, Craig.*

Even Alexander had deserted her. The big cat, still wrapped in pink bandages, was cowering under the ripped up bed. He'd been growling before, but had fallen silent as the killer out in the hall came closer. She'd caught glimpses of the cat's eyes reflecting the overhead lights, his green retinas glowing in the dark recess of his makeshift lair. But he'd withdrawn farther under the bed now, and had completely disappeared. For all she knew, the furry coward had fled the room.

Damn you, too, cat.

Clutching the pistol Hathcock had given her, she crouched on the floor of the bathroom, her back to the wall beside the door that led to the bedroom. Whoever was out there kicked down the door to the apartment next door. Finding nothing, the killer went to Jack and Naomi's room, right across the hall. She peeked around the corner of the bathroom door and caught a glimpse of a camouflage uniform.

A few moments later, she heard his footsteps coming back across the hall.

Closing her eyes, she prayed that the killer would just take a look around the devastated bedroom and call it a day.

The footsteps moved into the room.

Melissa bit back a scream as the soldier kicked in her closet door. Then he moved toward the bathroom.

She glanced up...and saw his masked face in the bathroom mirror, which somehow had remained intact. He was staring right back at her.

Without a word, he raised his weapon and stepped around the remains of the bed toward the bathroom door.

Just as he leaned into the doorway, the muzzle of his rifle mere inches from her temple and looking about as big around as a battleship gun, she heard a deep growl in the bedroom.

The soldier tried to whirl around, but the muzzle of his rifle caught on the door jamb as Alexander, pink bandages and all, made a limping charge from under the bed and sank his fangs into the soldier's leg. The soldier stumbled on one of the chunks of the shattered sink that was lying on the floor and went down right at Melissa's feet.

He twisted around into a sitting position and was raising the rifle to smash Alexander with the butt end when Melissa brought up her gun and pointed it at the man's masked face. She pulled the trigger over and over as Hathcock's words echoed in her mind: *keep shooting until you're sure the target's dead.*

The soldier dropped the rifle and began to screech. The harvester clawed at the mask, which now had several holes in it, and through the eye pieces she could see that its fake human face inside the mask was on fire. Then flames burst from around the mask and under the helmet.

Throwing the empty pistol aside, she got up, stepped over the thrashing body as flames began to pour from the head and neck, and grabbed Alexander. It took all her strength to pull the cat off the thing. His claws and teeth were shredding the uniform fabric and he simply wouldn't let go.

Slinging him over her shoulder, she ran out into the hallway, where more bodies were burning near the stairwell.

"Craig!" She shouted.

He didn't answer.

"*Craig, where are you?*" Leaning to one side, she could see uniformed bodies sprawled in one of the rooms on the far side of the stairwell. Huge chunks of the wall had been blown out, and the room was blazing. She tried to get in there, to see if Craig was injured and needed her help, but it was too hot. Alexander struggled against her, raking her back with his claws. He had experienced enough of fire.

With tears in her eyes, she forced her way past the sizzling, flaming remains of the harvesters into the stairwell, hoping that no more awaited her down below.

RESCUE

After the panicked call from SEAL-2 that they were under attack, Jack had ordered the remaining five LAVs back to the base, the drivers pushing the big vehicles as fast as they would go along County Road 45. He and Terje were standing up in the personnel hatches behind the turret of the lead LAV, Jack's heart in his throat as a plume of black smoke rose from the facility twelve miles away.

They had just crossed US 281, the American Legion Memorial Highway, nearly halfway to SEAL-2 when they spotted dark shapes loping through the fields just to the south. A wave of adult harvesters was fleeing northward from more of the dreadful giant larvae.

Lowmack asked, "Should we light them up?"

"Yeah, shoot the adults," Jack told him, "but whatever you do, keep moving! And don't use up much ammo. We don't know what's waiting for us back at the base."

"Roger. Keep your heads down."

The last words had barely left his mouth when the turret of the LAV turned and the 25mm Bushmaster cannon and coaxial 7.62mm machine gun opened fire, scything through the lead ranks of the harvesters.

The other LAVs followed suit, and in a few moments the fields to the south of County Road 45 were filled with blazing corpses.

"Shit!" Jack was startled by the face of a harvester that appeared over the side of the LAV. He drew his Desert Eagle and jammed the muzzle into the thing's open jaws. The back of its head exploded as he pulled the trigger, the .50 caliber slug blasting through the natural carbon fiber of its skull.

With muffled thumps, two more harvesters latched onto the LAV and began clambering toward the exposed humans.

"Button up!" Jack shouted.

He and Terje dropped back into the cramped troop compartment, slamming the hatches shut above them. Lowmack dropped down into the turret and closed his hatch as he warned the other LAVs.

In the blink of an eye the LAV was swarming with the creatures, which blocked the viewports, blinding the crew as the things pounded on the hatches, trying to get in.

The vehicle swerved off the road, tilting crazily before the driver regained control.

"We've got to keep moving!" Jack told Lowmack. "Have the LAVs use their machine guns to swat these things off!"

Lowmack bent down to stare at him. "And have us covered in burning harvesters? You sure you want to do that, sir?"

"Don't you have ammo other than incendiary and tracer?"

"Some, yeah." He said to the gunner, "Switch out the machine gun ammo to standard rounds."

"We've only got a couple hundred of those aboard," the gunner warned him. "Some jackass said we had to load up with all the fiery shit."

Terje looked at Jack and shrugged.

While the Marines were sorting that out, Jack and Terje poked their rifles out the gun ports in the rear of the LAV and began to shoot at the harvesters that were trying to get at the other vehicles, careful not to hit the ones actually on the LAVs.

"Okay," the gunner said through the comm circuit. "Let's rock and roll."

The coaxial machine gun in the turret fired, and the gunner swept the harvesters from the top deck before picking the monsters off one of the other vehicles, while they returned the favor. Jack winced as the hull rang from bullets striking the armor, some of them having missed their intended targets, others having passed through the harvesters' bodies. The drivers began to move again, picking up speed as more of the harvesters were cleared away. When they weren't picking off unwanted passengers, the gunners blasted groups of harvesters along the road with their Bushmaster cannons.

They had nearly made it clear of the bulk of the monsters when the LAV was shaken by a loud boom, after which it swerved and shimmied.

The strained voice of the driver came over the intercom. "We've lost a tire!"

"Keep moving," Lowmack ordered. "You've got seven more."

Thirty seconds later, that number was reduced to six.

"Small larvae," Terje said. "It must be. They're sticking to the tires when we run over them in the road, then they eat through the rubber and blow out the tires."

"Goddamn fucking things," Lowmack growled. "The other LAVs are losing tires, too."

"Just keep moving," Jack told him. "Run on the rims if you have to."

As they neared the complex, Jack popped open the rear deck hatch and stood up so he could see. Flames rose to lick the base of the churning cloud of oily black smoke that billowed into the sky. Most of the fire was concentrated near the helipad and maintenance area, but smoke was also rising from the lab, and the personnel buildings were both ablaze.

"The gate's not opening," Lowmack said as they approached the outer fence line. Bodies in blood-soaked camouflage uniforms hung from the sandbagged positions guarding the entrance.

"Blast it open," Jack ordered.

"Roger that."

A moment later the LAV's Bushmaster opened up, blowing the heavy gate from its hinges. The driver sped up, and the big vehicle crashed through, the other LAVs following close behind.

Looking at the lab building, he saw a Black Hawk, its rotors still spinning down, sitting just outside the entry to the lab building. The flaming wreckage of a second helicopter covered the ground not far from what was left of the main guard shack along the inner fence line.

"Detach one of your squads to search Tent City for survivors," Jack told Lowmack, his gut churning at the devastation across the compound. "Then let's split up the other four into two teams. I'll take the lab. You take the personnel quarters."

"If it's all the same to you, sir, I think we might want to leave the crew in one of the LAVs, just in case something ugly pops up out here."

Jack nodded. "Good call. If you don't mind, I'm going to task you with that. Would your men have any problem following Captain Halvorsen?"

"No, sir."

"Good," Jack said. "Terje, you lead the squad to search the personnel building."

"Understood."

With Lowmack and his crew providing cover from their LAV, the others dismounted and split up to follow Jack and Terje.

"In we go," Jack said to the Marines with him. "Check your targets. We're hoping for friendlies, but if adult harvesters are here..."

"Shit," one of the Marines breathed. "Wish we had one of them cats so we'd know who's for real."

"You and me, both, Marine," Jack told him.

They stepped through the lab building's front entrance, their boots crunching on metal and glass as they stepped around the bodies of the Marines who had died there.

The point man stopped as the sound of automatic weapons fire echoed from somewhere deeper in the building, answered by blasts from a shotgun.

Two more Marines moved past Jack to push through the remains of the inner door to enter the main corridor.

Bodies were everywhere. A few were in uniform, but most wore civilian clothes or the surgical scrubs preferred by the scientists. The bodies were riddled with bullets.

As they moved down the hall toward the sound of the gunfire, which was coming from both the level above and somewhere down below, they came across several bodies whose heads were missing. Blood still seeped from the flesh of the neck, which looked as if it had been cauterized.

"Hold up," he ordered. Kneeling next to one of them, he read the name on the security badge. *Dr. Theresa Katsulas.* She was — had been — the director of one of the lab divisions. He couldn't remember exactly what she did, but she was high up on the pecking order here.

Moving to another body, he checked the badge, but didn't recognize the name. Checking a third, he found another name he recognized, one of the team leads from the weaponization division. The fourth and last body he checked was another senior scientist.

"Shit," he breathed. The harvesters were doing more than just massacring the staff. "Keep moving."

The staff sergeant who was the senior Marine in his group turned to him when they reached the main stairwell. "Up or down, sir?"

Jack didn't hesitate. "We'll clear the basement levels first."

"Down we go, then," the staff sergeant said.

The Marine on point nodded, then stepped through the open door to the stairwell, doing his best not to step on the any of the bodies stacked inside.

**

Terje followed two Marines into the first personnel building, with five more Marines behind him. Threads of smoke filled the main corridor, and the men had to duck down to see and breathe.

"Check the rooms," he ordered, and the Marines methodically went into each apartment.

About half of them had been occupied by bullet-riddled bodies, although a few were missing their heads.

The smoke grew thicker, billowing from the stairwell, and the paint on the ceiling overhead had begun to blacken and blister from the fire that must be raging on the second level.

"Sir, you want us to try for upstairs?"

All of them were coughing now from the acrid smoke. None of them had so much as a gas mask, let alone fire fighting gear. The sprinklers in the ceiling hadn't come on, and never would. Their installation hadn't yet been completed.

The smoke in the stairwell was thickening, with the flickering light of flames dancing off the walls.

"No," he said in between coughs, waving the Marine toward the exit. "Get back outside and cover the building in case any harvesters try to escape from the second floor. Go!"

Terje waited until the Marines were past him and safely on their way to the front exit when he heard it. A soft cry from somewhere behind him.

Turning around to face back toward the stairwell, he listened.

Only the crackling sounds of the fire upstairs reached his ears.

Then the sound came again. Someone was calling out. The voice was coming from the stairwell.

The Marines had already cleared the exit. One of them, the sergeant who was the squad's senior noncom, was shouting at him to join them.

Terje waved at the man, then ran toward the stairwell.

Slinging his rifle, he drew his Desert Eagle, which had more stopping power at such a short range than his rifle. Carrying the pistol also allowed him to bury his nose and mouth in the inside of the elbow of his free arm. Despite the nausea that gripped him, he kept going, moving up the stairs until he reached the landing midway between the first and second floors.

Aside from three bodies, it was clear.

An ear-splitting scream scythed through the sound of the fire from the corridor above.

Melissa.

He bounded up the steps. Leaning out of the doorway, he took a quick look down the hall. To the left, in the direction of the burning room, was nothing. To the right, two men in military garb had Melissa pinned to the floor. One still wore a helmet and gas mask. The other...

The harvester's black chitinous head, exposed over the neck of the uniform, opened its mandibles wide over the girl's face. Wispy tendrils uncoiled like feathers from the creature's maw and left smoking red weals where they brushed against her skin.

Leaning past the door jamb, Terje brought up his pistol and took aim. He squeezed the trigger and the exposed harvester's head disappeared in a spray of ichor and exploding exoskeleton.

As the thing fell atop Melissa and writhed in a macabre parody of sexual union, the thing's helmeted companion whipped around just in time to catch two .50 caliber slugs that speared through its body armor. It jerked like a marionette as the slugs, their energy largely spent after punching through the kevlar laminate of the armor, ricocheted off the back plate and back into the harvester's body, tearing its insides to bits.

The second harvester collapsed as the first stopped twitching and lay still atop the girl.

"Terje!"

Running to her side, he rolled the harvester off her. As he scooped her up into his arms, he saw that she still held a bundle of pink bandages to her chest. Alexander's eyes, pupils dilated wide open, stared up at him, but his jaws eased closed. Terje glanced at the harvester that had been about to take her head. The front of the thing's combat vest had been shredded by the cat's claws and teeth.

They both were coughing, the smoke filling their lungs as Terje turned and staggered toward the stairwell, then stopped.

The hall by the entrance to the stairs was engulfed in flames. They were trapped.

He was about to fling himself into the flames in a desperate bid to get down the stairs when the stairwell was filled with a whooshing sound. A white cloud boiled from the doorway, driving away the flames before it. A Marine appeared, then another, then a third, all of them blasting at the flames with fire extinguishers.

A fourth Marine, the squad leader, emerged. "Captain!" He held a gas mask, which he slipped over Melissa's face. Then he took off his own and managed to get it onto Terje. "Here, sir, take this. I can manage until we get outside."

"Thank you, sergeant." Terje breathed deep, trying to clear the smoke from his lungs.

"Jesus, sir, are all Norwegians as nuts as you?"

Terje only shook his head. Holding Melissa and Alexander in his arms, he followed the sergeant through the gap in the flames.

RELEASE THE DRAGONS

"They will be coming for us," the Vijay-thing said as more shots echoed from somewhere outside the secure lab. "We will be easy prey, trapped in here." The thing spoke in Vijay's soft sing-song voice, but the false emotion had drained from the harvester's mimicry.

The sound made Naomi shiver.

"Let us out, Naomi." One of the others, the one masquerading as an attractive young Iranian woman, Zohreh, who had been paired with Harmony, said. "We can fight them."

"I can't open the door," Naomi said, shaking her head. "It's a failsafe to prevent you from escaping."

"It is our only chance." The Vijay-thing turned to her. "Look me in the eye and tell me that Jack left you no way out of here."

She tried to stare the thing down, but looking into the dark pools of Vijay's eyes, she had to blink and look away.

The thing nodded. "He is a prudent man. Now open the door so we can, I hope, save your life."

Still, Naomi hesitated.

"Had we wanted to harm you or the others, Naomi," the Zohreh-thing said, "we would have already done so. We have nothing to gain by harming you, and everything to lose."

Taking a deep breath, Naomi moved to the keypad next to the door. She punched in an eight digit sequence, then simultaneously held down the star and pound keys for two seconds.

The door whooshed open, and six of the harvesters, including the Vijay-thing, rushed out without a word. She turned to look at the harvester that had remained with her, and took a step back as its face transformed from a middle-aged Iranian to Vijay.

"I hate it when you do that," she said.

"I apologize that it disturbs you," it said, "but you are far more comfortable with this likeness than any other that I have available. Consider me a...twin of my companion."

"Sure," she said, pressing another sequence on the keypad to close the door.

"I will stay to protect you, should the others fail."

Somehow, she didn't find that at all reassuring.

***

Harmony Bates blinked, then opened her eyes. She had to squint against the bright light that was pouring into her eyes. She was staring up at the ceiling lights, and a haze of smoke drifted through the air above her.

She coughed, then cried out as a spear of pain shot through her side. She tried to reach for the wound with her hand, but found she was pinned to the floor. Something heavy was draped over her torso and upper legs. The caught a faint scent of aftershave, vying for attention with the far less familiar smells of gunpowder and the stench of burning plastic. Only Nizar Aswad, one of the senior lab techs, a man she'd worked with for years, wore that particular aftershave.

The realization brought with it a set of memory flashes. Being trapped in the stairwell as someone opened fire from above. Something hitting her in the side, driving the wind from her and slamming her up against the wall of the stairwell. Falling, rolling through a sea of screaming people and bloody bodies as bullets tore through those around her. Someone grabbing her by the wrist, pulling her from the maelstrom, dragging her through the panicked crowd around the door to the stairs, into the lab before the corridor became a killing ground. More bullets flying, blasting through the walls of the lab. Something slamming down on top of her, crushing the life from her. An explosion of pain in her side that sent her into blessed darkness.

"Nizar," she gasped, her lungs fighting against the weight of his body pressing down on her chest. "Nizar?"

Turning her head, she saw the face of the man who had saved her life. He was staring at her with his beautiful dark eyes. Except that one of them was gone, replaced by a bloody crater where a bullet had blasted away the eyeball before exploding out the back of his skull.

"No, no, no," she whispered, shaking her head. She tried to roll his body off. He had not been a big man, and weighed even less than she did, yet he seemed to weigh as much as an elephant.

With a last heave and a scream of pain, she managed to roll his body onto the floor. She lay there gasping. With trembling fingers, she traced the edges of the puckered bullet wound just above her hip.

"Help me," she whispered as the world began to turn gray. She panted, trying to force more oxygen into her blood to forestall the onset of shock, to keep from passing out. "Help me!"

***

Kiran crawled through the lab, leaving a slick of blood behind him from the bullet wound in his leg. A few of the lab workers were still alive, hiding behind desks or equipment. A dark rage burned inside him that he couldn't do more to help protect them than to motion for them to stay down and hide.

His only thought now was to try and circle back through the labs to reach Naomi. If he was going to die, he wanted to die with honor, defending someone he cared for and respected.

An automatic weapon fired somewhere down the hall, followed by a gurgling scream. The handful of survivors in the lab around him cringed and whimpered. Kiran crawled faster, determined to reach the secure lab area before the enemy did.

Swiping his badge and pressing the access code with shaking fingers, he passed from this lab into the next, the one that adjoined the secure area.

As he entered the second lab, he heard someone cry out in pain. Then, a few moments later, he heard the same voice rasp out the words, "Help me!"

It came from up ahead, near the far end of the lab. It was a voice he had heard before, although it took him a moment to pair it with the name of Dr. Harmony Bates, one of the most senior people who worked with Naomi.

Gritting his teeth, he forced himself to go faster.

***

Koshka watched as the monsters left the room, save one that stayed close by her human. As always when near the monsters, her instincts were in turmoil. Part of her wanted to flee and hide, while the other part wanted to attack.

She and the others of her kind had been free to roam where they would inside the humans' lair. Most of the others had been killed by the monsters, along with many of the humans that now stalked the rest.

And now the creatures her human had mysteriously taken as companions were afoot, moving toward their death-dealing kin.

One of the things stayed with her human. She was about to dart through as the other things departed the room, but the door closed too soon. She hopped onto the shelf where she could see through the glass, and saw her human's lips moving, but couldn't hear the sound of her voice.

With a single plaintive cry to express her displeasure, Koshka turned and began following after the six monsters, dashing quickly from cover to cover.

Before the things reached the door that led to the main corridor, one of them broke away, heading for a door that led to one of the large adjoining rooms. The door, which normally would be closed, was propped open by a body sprawled in the doorway.

After a moment of indecision, Koshka followed after the monster that had split from the main group, hoping to ambush the creature. She had fought them before, although she could not claim any victory over this prey. It was as if the instincts that bound her to attack them had been intended for a far larger body. But she could not deny the impulse. It simply was.

Holding her body low to the ground, her eyes fixed on the prey-that-was-not-prey, Koshka watched as it moved toward one of the many desks where the humans occupied themselves. It sat for a moment, moving its fingers over one of the contraptions that glowed and made sounds. It remained there until it heard a human calling in a pain-filled voice from close by. It was a human that Koshka knew well, for it spent many hours each day with Koshka's person, and had spent time seeing to Koshka's needs.

The monster got up from the desk and moved in the direction of the human's voice.

Koshka, so low that the fur on her belly brushed the floor, crept silently behind.

***

Harmony cringed as more shots rang out down the hall. She tried to pull herself into a more concealed spot behind a nearby workstation, but the pain in her side from the bullet wound was too much. She gave up before she passed out.

She saw movement out of the corner of her eye, and turned her head to see Naomi's cat, Koshka, peering past the corner of a nearby workstation.

"Here, kitty," Harmony whispered, overjoyed to have the cat's company. "Come here, Koshka."

But Koshka remained still as a statue. The cat wasn't looking at her, but was staring at something else behind Harmony.

Harmony turned her head to see Zohreh, one of the harvesters, creeping closer.

"Oh, my God." Harmony tried to push herself away, but there was no escape. She opened her mouth to scream, but the harvester darted forward and wrapped a hand around her throat, strangling her.

Harmony batted uselessly at the thing's hands, and her eyes widened as the thing lifted up the blouse it wore to release the long, slender needle of the stinger, a drop of venom already oozing from the tip.

Harmony's mouth opened in a silent scream.

As the harvester jabbed the stinger into her chest, just below her heart, Harmony saw a glimmer of motion, white emerging from the smokey gray around her as Koshka leapt on the harvester's back, sinking her fangs through the thin layer of malleable flesh into the creature's spine.

Filling the lab with its terrible screech, the harvester twisted and jumped away, yanking the stinger from Harmony's chest as it tried to throw off the growling cat. Harmony watched the two dance about the lab as the fire of the venom consumed her from the inside out.

Koshka bit and slashed until the harvester was finally able to get a firm hold on her. With a brutal yank, the thing tore Koshka loose and threw her across the lab. The cat slammed into a lab table with a heavy thump and a brief squeal of pain, followed by a crash as some equipment smashed to the floor.

Harmony looked up as the harvester loomed over her. The face of the young Iranian woman changed, began to melt away to reveal the dark chitin of the harvester's true form. The jaws opened and the mandibles spread wide, impossibly wide, as thousands of tendrils, slender and fine as fur, uncoiled to wave in the air above Harmony's face.

The thing bent down, the jaws enveloping her head, its hands holding Harmony down as she thrashed in agony.

**

Kiran kept moving, working his way through the forest of workstations toward where he'd heard Harmony's cry.

Just ahead, the fierce snarl of a cat cut through the lab, followed by a harvester screeching. Kiran peered over the top of a workstation to see a young woman doing a wild dance with a white cat, Koshka, latched onto the back of the harvester's neck.

It was one of the harvesters who'd been working with Naomi, and Kiran feared the worst.

He raised his weapon to fire, but didn't want to hit the cat.

The harvester decided the matter. It finally grabbed Koshka and hurled her right toward Kiran. The poor beast flew over his head, her tail whipping in a circular motion and her body twisting in an effort to right herself before she slammed into a workstation filled with delicate looking equipment. The cat and equipment crashed to the floor, where the animal lay still.

Kiran said a silent prayer for the animal as he moved forward, then stopped. The harvester had disappeared from view.

After breathing a silent curse, he crept forward again. Peering around another workstation, he saw it leaning over the body of Dr. Bates, the thing's head engulfing that of the doctor. Bates was twitching, her legs kicking and thrashing at whatever the harvester was doing to her.

He couldn't fire his shotgun without killing Bates.

Gathering his strength, Kiran got to his feet and charged. He slammed into the creature with the full force of his body, knocking it away from Bates. His mind recoiled in horror at the brief glimpse he had of the doctor's ravaged head: the face was gone, the skin, eyes, flesh, and bone dissolved away to expose the brain and other parts of the head that were best left for students of human anatomy.

As the two combatants rolled to the floor, the harvester turned its full fury upon him. The faux flesh melted away entirely, and the creature lashed at him with its claws, ripping the shotgun from his grip. Kiran drew the big Kukri knife from its sheath on his web belt, shoving the wide, curving blade up through the thing's lower jaw.

With an ear-piercing shriek, it rolled to one side, trying to throw him off, but Kiran held onto it, sawing the blade toward its neck even as it hammered at him with its steel-hard fists.

He felt something moving across his chest and glanced down to see the umbilical of the stinger writhing like a snake.

Too late, he let go of the knife and tried to grab the stinger. He almost had it, his hand closing around the pulsating venom sack as the muscles in the umbilical twitched, driving the stinger through his throat to bury the tip in his brain.

The harvester shoved his body away. Kiran's face was locked in an expression of shocked surprise.

Then the thing returned its attention to what was left of Harmony Bates.

ONE CHANCE LEFT

The administrative area of the lab building beyond the entry doors was an abattoir. Boisson stepped carefully around the bodies as she moved forward. Ferris was right behind her, a Desert Eagle in his hand, with the other three agents bringing up the rear.

Gunfire was still coming from the levels above and below. "We'll clear this level first," she told the others, "then go from there." She wasn't about to leave the enemy at her back.

Boisson had spent very little time at the facility and didn't know much of the layout of the lab building, other than that it was a rat maze of labs in the basement levels and that Richards had his office upstairs.

After clearing the administrative offices near the front, she led the others down the main corridor. They didn't find any survivors, only bodies pumped full of bullets, along with a few with heads missing. The neck wounds looked like they had been chemically cauterized.

"Why would they take the heads?" One of her men whispered.

"Trophies, maybe?" Another replied.

"Shut up and keep moving," she hissed.

In the central part of the building, the command center was a darkened shambles. Every piece of equipment, from the racks of computer servers and sophisticated communications gear right down to the bulbs in the light fixtures, had been destroyed.

They reached the rear of the building and cleared every room without encountering anything more threatening than a dangling wire that was shorting out and more bodies.

"Turn around," she ordered. "Let's head back to the main stairwell." She glanced at her watch. It had been four minutes since they'd come in the front entrance. She felt like it had taken ten times longer.

By the time they reached the stairs, the firing in the basement had died off, but the battle upstairs still raged.

Ferris leaned closer. "Which way?"

"We go up. The battle's won or lost downstairs, but someone upstairs is still fighting. Kelsey," she said to one of her men, "watch our backs and make sure nothing creeps up on us from down below."

"Got it."

"Right," Boisson said. "Let's go." She led the way up, the muzzle of her M4 rifle sweeping the stairs and the landing ahead of her. A thin trace of smoke wafted through the air, and it got thicker as they neared the second floor landing. "Heads up," she whispered as she caught a whiff of it. "Tear gas."

As she peered through the small rectangular window of the door on the landing, a machine gun fired, its stream of tracers lancing through the smoke from somewhere off to her right. There was an answering series of shotgun blasts from the left, in the direction of the executive offices.

She turned to her team. "Bad guys are to the right, good guys to the left." They nodded. "Ready? On three...one...two...*three!*"

She yanked open the door and her men charged through, their rifles spewing tracer rounds down the hallway to the right. One of the agents was cut down by the enemy machine gun and went sprawling to the floor in a mist of blood. Then Boisson was through, adding her own fire to that of the two remaining agents.

Ferris remained behind, crouching in the stairwell.

Blinking away the tears from her eyes from the gas, Boisson caught sight of a prone figure down the hall to the right, struggling to reload a machine gun. Boisson shot him, or it, half a dozen times, and was finally rewarded with a gout of flame from beneath the thing's helmeted head.

She turned her head and bellowed down the hall to the left, "*FBI! FBI! Hold your fire!*" To her men, she said, "Clear these rooms!"

The agents moved forward, quickly checking the other administrative and computer support offices while she covered the stairwell and kept one eye on the executive offices, where he saw a couple heads peering out from one of the doors.

"Clear," they reported back. "Nothing but bodies."

"Okay, you guys sit tight and watch the stairwell. I'm gonna go say hello to the boss." She stood up and moved slowly toward the executive offices. "This is Special Agent Boisson of the FBI! Identify yourselves!"

"Director Carl Richards." One of the figures that had been peering around the door of the first office, a shorter guy with a bald head, stood up, cradling an AA-12 shotgun. "Thanks for the save, Boisson."

"Any time, sir." She heard a moan coming from the office. "Is someone wounded?"

"Yeah. Renee got herself shot in the ass."

Boisson leaned through the doorway to look. Renee was face down on the floor, with Morgan applying a thick gauze bandage to a bullet graze across one of her butt cheeks.

"I'm glad you think this is funny," Renee groaned, then hissed as Morgan applied some tape to hold the gauze in place.

"If she's bitching about something," Richards said, looking at her with a fond smile, "she's still alive."

"When I get up," Renee promised, "I'm going to shoot you in the ass and see how you like it."

"Hey, Boisson!" Ferris shouted.

Boisson stepped back out of the office so she could hear him better. "What is it?"

"Somebody just started World War Three in the basement!"

***

The Vijay-thing moved out into the corridor to meet its recently arrived kin.

The *others* emerged from the acrid smoke. Six of them, heavily armed with human weapons and encumbered with body armor and equipment. One of them was injured, its left arm hanging at an unnatural angle. Six to five. The odds were even enough, should a battle ensue.

Vijay spoke one word to the newcomers. "Why?"

"We are as those who created us meant us to be," one of the others said, its voice muffled by the gas mask it wore. "The humans seek a way to end us when our time has only just begun. Now I would ask you the same question: why?"

"We have a different vision of the future," Vijay said. "Our species is...unstable. This world will eventually fall into a cycle of spawning and dying that will never end, where those of us who become truly self-aware may only live in fear of being consumed by our own progeny. We seek only to redress those factors in our genetic sequence that will allow intellect to survive and allow us to exist as the supreme predator, without fear."

"And the humans? You would coexist with them?"

Shaking its head, its instinctive mimicry driving the motions of its body, the Vijay-thing replied, "No. This is a marriage of convenience. Like those who created us, we need their technology. Beyond that, they are food. Prey."

"You fulfilled your intentions?"

"We hold the blueprints for what must be done, but we have yet to make it a reality."

"We will not allow it."

Vijay was about to lunge at the other, which was raising its weapon, when a hail of automatic weapons fire erupted from the stairwell.

***

Jack led the Marines down the stairwell to the basement levels. He detached one squad, led by the staff sergeant, to search the first level before proceeding down to the second, where the secure lab was located. It was hard to put a foot down without stepping on something that had been a living human being only a short time before. The concentrated smell of blood, feces, and urine, overlaid with the stench of tear gas, had his stomach churning.

He made it to the second basement level. Carefully stepping over the pile of bodies propping the door open, he took a small mirror out of one of his pockets and held it down low, using it to peer around the door frame without exposing his head.

Six uniformed men in Army uniforms faced five civilian scientists. One of them was Vijay. He was speaking with one of the soldiers.

"Oh, shit," he whispered. They were all harvesters. The question was whether to kill all of them or just the ones in uniform.

The attackers first, he decided.

Using hand signals, he got the Marines into position and assigned their targets. Holding up his hand, he counted down with his fingers: three...two...one...

He pivoted around the door frame, bringing up his assault rifle as the Marines stepped out to get clear fields of fire through the door. In unison, four assault rifles and three shotguns with Dragons Breath rounds fired on the six uniformed harvesters at a range of less than a dozen yards. They spun and jerked as their bodies were struck by the 5.56mm tracer rounds and the shotgun slugs as the flaming particles of the Dragons Breath enveloped them. All six went to the floor, twitching or burning.

Vijay and the other harvesters from the lab leaped back to get clear of the firestorm, but they did not flee.

"Cease fire!" Jack stepped from the stairwell, keeping his weapon trained on Vijay. Nodding toward the bodies of the uniformed creatures, he told the Marines, "Make sure those ones are dead."

Two Marines went to the uniformed bodies that weren't already burning and fired several rounds into the heads until they burst into flame. Everyone moved away from the blaze as the ceiling sprinklers began to rain water down. The burning harvesters snapped and crackled like bacon frying in a pan, with a much less pleasant odor.

Jack turned back to Vijay. "Where's Naomi?"

"She is safe, Jack. She let us out that we might protect..."

"*Jack!*"

He turned to see Naomi running toward him through the artificial rain. He shifted his aim, pointing the muzzle of his rifle at her chest. "Stop, Naomi. Stay where you are."

"Jack...what...?"

"I need to know you're real."

She nodded, her elation evaporating. "How do we do this?"

Jack dug a disposable lighter out of his pocket and tossed it to her.

Holding her free hand, palm down, above the lighter to shield it from the sprinkler, Naomi stroked the flint wheel. The lighter's flame burst into life, and she held the tip of it up high enough to brush against her wrist. Her mouth pressed into a thin line at the pain, and she held Jack's gaze as the flame licked her skin.

"Enough! Jesus, enough." Jack lowered his weapon and reached for her as the lighter's flame died. He held her tight, crushing her to him. "I'm so sorry, Naomi. God, I'm so sorry to have to do that to you."

"It was the smart thing to do," she said before pulling him down to kiss him.

"So what he said," Jack nodded to Vijay, "is true?"

"Yes. They went out to fight. One stayed back to protect me." A look of puzzlement crossed her face. "But only six are here now. Where is..."

"I am here."

They turned to see Zohreh emerge from the door to the lab next to the secure area.

"I was making sure there were no more attackers in here."

"Yeah," Jack said, narrowing his eyes slightly. "Right."

"I lost Koshka," Naomi whispered. "She followed them when they left the lab, but she hasn't come back to me. She always comes back." She looked down. "Kiran has disappeared, too."

"Then let's find them. Sergeant," he said, turning to the senior Marine, "keep an eye on our friends here. I'm going to borrow a couple of your Marines for a quick search."

"Yes, sir. Adams, Zalensky, go with the major."

Jack and Naomi led the two Marines into the lab from which Zohreh had come.

"God, what a mess," Naomi said as they made their way through the devastated rooms. Unlike the corridor, the labs were dry.

Looking beyond one of the workstations, he saw Kiran. He was on his back, staring up at the ceiling with a look of surprise on his face. A large pool of blood had spread out on the floor beneath him.

"Godammit." Jack knelt down and gently closed Kiran's eyes. He wanted to close his own eyes and fall into a deep sleep. Maybe that way he could wake up from this nightmare.

Then he caught sight of a furry white form lying still on the floor nearby. "Oh, no." He pointed. "Koshka."

Naomi knelt beside the Turkish Angora that had been with her through the worst times of her life. "No. Oh, no, no."

The cat's eyes were closed. There was no blood, except for a tiny trickle that had run from one of Koshka's nostrils. One of her rear legs was bent at an unnatural angle, but other than that there was no external sign of injury.

But hers wasn't the only blood in evidence. Her mouth and the fur under her chin, as well as the fur of her toes around her claws, were covered with harvester blood.

Jack watched the cat's chest. "She's still breathing," he said. "She's alive."

"Thank God."

Jack's attention was drawn to the body of a woman lying on the floor nearby, with another body, that of a man who'd been shot, next to her. Like some of the others Jack had seen, the woman's head was missing. Leaning over, he picked up her ID badge.

"Who is it?"

Turning to Naomi, Jack said, "It's Harmony."

Naomi shook her head. "I thought...I thought she'd been killed with the others in the stairwell."

"Maybe this guy," he gestured to the body of the lab worker that lay nearby, "hauled her out of that mess, only to die over here." He thought a minute. "Stay here. I'll be right back."

Moving quickly, he searched the lab for more bodies. He found four others, all senior researchers, and their bodies were still intact. Their heads, and their memories, hadn't been taken.

"What is it?" Naomi asked when he returned.

"Maybe nothing," he said. "Come on, we've got to get out of here."

"Here, sir," one of the Marines came in and handed him a stainless steel lab tray. "Maybe you can put the cat on this."

"Great idea, Marine." Jack took the tray and set it on the floor, and together he and Naomi carefully slid Koshka onto it.

With Naomi carrying the cat, Jack led her back to the corridor while the Marines finished the sweep of the labs.

He was surprised to find Carl, Howard, Boisson, and some FBI agents he didn't know, waiting for him.

"Where's Renee?" Jack asked.

"She's okay," Carl told him. "She took a bullet in the ass, but she'll live. I left her upstairs with Ferris." He looked around, his sourpuss face streaked with soot and gunpowder residue. He looked at Naomi. "I know you haven't had time to sort things out, but I need a gut reflex yes or no answer: is there any way you can see to put this place back in operation?"

"In the time we have?" She shook her head. "No. SEAL-2 is finished."

Carl looked around at the bodies. "We've failed, then."

"No."

Everyone turned to stare at Vijay.

"We may not be able to continue the work *here*," the harvester said, "but we have not failed. We know what must be done. We can engineer a viral RNA payload that will alter our species for the benefit of all."

Carl's eyes narrowed. "But it won't kill them?"

"It will help you defeat those that are non-sentient," Vijay said. "It will also do what we all need most: deactivate our unrestricted reproductive cycle."

Jack looked at Naomi. "What about the larvae?"

"Nothing we can come up with will kill them directly," she told him. "They would simply dissolve it, break it down into its most basic compounds like they do everything else. We'll have to kill them the old fashioned way."

"Do you believe them?" Carl asked her.

Naomi nodded slowly. "Yes. Yes, I do. I've seen the code myself. We couldn't have done it in so short a time, but the blueprint they put together is sound. All we need is to put the finishing touches on it, integrate it with the viral delivery system we already have, and replicate the hell out of it."

"All right, then," Carl said. "Let's get topside where we can figure out what to do next. I'm tired of being in this tomb."

"There's one thing I want to know, first." Jack knelt beside one of the harvesters dressed like a solider, he said. "I want to know why they didn't go poof when we hit them with the Dragons Breath." This one hadn't burst into flame. In death, the malleable tissue oozed from the uniform sleeves and the cuffs of the pants. More came out from between the uniform collar and helmet. Running his hands over the mask, he could feel tiny craters melted into the surface of the rubber by the Dragon's Breath. But the particles were so short-lived that they hadn't melted or burned their way through.

Pulling the mask aside, grimacing at the bruised-looking tissue that had once formed a human-looking face, he saw that the thing had some sort of olive drab colored ski mask pulled over its head and tucked down into the turned-up and buttoned collar of its uniform, which was itself covered with body armor and a stuffed-full-of-ammo combat vest. He untucked the ski mask and found another garment under the uniform.

"Son of a bitch," he cursed. "They're wearing Nomex under their uniforms and over their heads. The same with the gloves. And the gas masks protected their faces. That's why the Dragons Breath didn't do much."

"Nomex?" Carl asked.

"It's a flame retardant material," Jack explained. "The flight suits worn by military pilots are made from it. These things must have got their hands on some and figured it would be good against the Dragons Breath rounds."

"It worked," Howard said. "We hit them over and over again, drenched them in flame, and it didn't do squat. The only thing that had any effect from the shotguns were the slugs."

"Great," Carl spat. "Just what they need. Another advantage over us, and one that we engineered for them."

Making their way to the entrance, they found some familiar faces.

"Jack!"

Melissa came running toward him, a bundle of pink bandages in her arms. Jack gathered her and Alexander up in an awkward hug, the big cat squirming unhappily between them. "It's good to see you, kid. You too, you big fuzzball." He rubbed Alexander on the forehead, which was one of the few places he had much fur remaining.

"Hathcock didn't make it," Terje said quietly.

"Damn," Jack breathed.

"Jack."

He turned at the sound of Naomi's voice. She nodded toward the harvesters, who had come to stand in a close semicircle around him and the girl. They were staring at Melissa with frightening intensity, and Jack felt the hair on the back of his neck stand on end.

"Back off," he said to Vijay, raising his rifle, pointing it at the harvester's face. "Back off, I said!"

The harvesters finally stepped back when the Marines around them raised their weapons.

"She is...like us," Vijay said softly, "but not like us." He tore his gaze from the girl to look at Jack. "What is she?"

Melissa hid behind Jack and Terje, and Alexander growled. "Keep them away from me!"

"She's none of your business," Jack said. "Angie, would you mind moving our friends here over by the wall and keeping them out of trouble?"

"With pleasure." Boisson turned to Vijay and the other harvesters and gestured with the muzzle of her rifle. "Move it, bugs."

"That was creepy as hell," Renee said as she limped over and gave Jack a quick hug.

"Sir. Director Richards." It was Captain Lowmack, who'd dismounted from his LAV.

"What is it?"

"We have a count on survivors, sir." He looked ill. "Fifty-seven, including my Marines."

"Dear God," Howard Morgan breathed.

"That's it?" Carl's voice caught in his throat. "Including us?"

"Yes, sir. That's everybody. Minus them, of course." He nodded toward the seven harvesters lined up along the lab building wall. "Most of the security detachment, except what was out in the field with us, were killed. And the personnel in Tent City..." He just shook his head.

"I want to start getting people out of here," Carl said. "Ferris, crank up that Black Hawk. We'll evac to Grand Island, then..."

"No fucking way," Ferris said in a brittle voice. "The bird's engines are toast, and I'm not going back to Grand Island, not even if you put a gun to my head."

"Grand Island's gone," Boisson explained. "The airport. The town. Everything."

"The fucking things were everywhere." Ferris was shaking. "They're swarming north from the river. And the interstate, I-80, it's...it's..."

"There were lots of casualties," Boisson said in a dead voice. "And the things are heading this way."

"Yeah, we ran into what must have been the leading edge of the herd on our way back here," Jack told her.

They both turned to Richards. "What's the plan, boss?" Jack asked.

"We pick up our sorry asses and try to find a refuge somewhere. SEAL-4 in Denver is probably our best bet..."

Ferris laughed. "That's four hundred goddamn miles! We'd have to go by road. We'll be eaten alive."

Jack said, "Can't we just call in some evac birds?"

Boisson shook her head. "The comm center's gone."

"The cell network is out, too," Lowmack added. "Even the portable satellite phones can't get through to anyone. All that's left is the HF and VHF radios in the vehicles, and nobody who can help us has responded." He grimaced. "All we've heard is just more poor schmucks like us who need help themselves."

Carl stood there, silent. The muscles along his jaw twitched.

Naomi carefully set down Koshka, then stood up to face the others. "We're too close to give up," she said. "We've got all the pieces for our weapon, we just need a lab where we can assemble it and put it into production."

"In case you haven't noticed, girl," Ferris said tightly, his eyes sweeping across the burning remains of SEAL-2, "we're kinda short on that sort of thing right now."

Howard cocked his head at Naomi. "What about Lincoln Research University?"

She nodded. "That's what I'm thinking. We've got to go back to where this all began. Everything we need to put an end to this is there, assuming the place is still standing." She looked at Carl. "It's the only chance we have left."

EXODUS

Everyone except their harvester allies wore a haunted look, and an air of imminent defeat hung over the burning remains of SEAL-2 as the survivors made frantic preparations to leave. The person who seemed least affected and had immediately taken charge of organizing the exodus was Howard Morgan. Once Carl had given the green light to Naomi's plan, Howard had transformed the group into an efficient machine to sift through the wreckage for anything that could be salvaged.

"What do you think our odds are?"

Carl had said very little to anyone since the attack, and his question caught Jack off guard. "I think that if we can get Naomi and the harvesters to the lab in Lincoln," Jack told him, "we're going to be able to beat these things. I don't have much left to believe in anymore, Carl, but I believe in her. If she says she can do it, she can."

Richards glanced away, then looked back at him. "You have no doubts? No reservations?"

Jack shook his head. "None. She's the rock that I cling to, my friend. If she told me the sun was going to rise in the west tomorrow, I'd believe her."

Carl's mouth turned up slightly at the corners. "That just makes you a gullible dumb-ass, Dawson." He took a deep breath. "Okay, good enough. Getting there is going to be the tough part."

"No, shit."

The two of them were standing on the rear deck of Lowmack's LAV, which would lead the other vehicles out. The column of vehicles they'd managed to salvage from the motor pool was lined up in front of the lab building at what Jack hoped was a safe distance from the blazing personnel buildings.

"Morgan's turning this into a damn circus," Carl grumbled. "He'd have brought along a Humvee for every one of us if I'd have let him."

"You should be happy. We'll need the extra vehicles."

Behind their LAV were the other four LAVs, two of them bringing up the rear of the column. In between were ten Humvees and four six-wheeled MTVR trucks. Two of the trucks were towing fuel bowsers and had their cargo beds loaded with Jerry cans full of water and cases of MRE meals. The other two were towing one hundred kilowatt generators in case the lab in Lincoln was without power, and had their cargo beds loaded with spare tires and parts for the vehicles.

Two of the Humvees near the rear of the column, sandwiched in between a pair of LAVs, carried the harvesters. Over Carl's protestations, Jack had insisted that they be armed for their protection. So they had been given four shotguns loaded with Dragons Breath ammunition. Jack figured they couldn't do too much damage with those to any of the other vehicles before the escorting LAVs blew the Humvees to bits.

Every vehicle, even those with the harvesters, carried as much ammunition as the vehicle could hold.

"I think it's about time we left, sir," Lowmack told him. "The scouts are reporting a lot of bugs heading our way."

"Roger that," Jack replied. He heard the crump of a mortar firing. Some enterprising Marines had salvaged one of the 81mm mortars from the roof of the lab building and crammed it into the back of one of the Humvees, packing the rest of the vehicle with white phosphorus and high explosive mortar rounds. Lowmack had sent the vehicle out to scout out the enemy and start raining on their parade.

"We're ready," Howard reported. He was riding in one of the Humvees toward the rear of the column.

"All right," Carl said. "I guess I better get to my ride." He stuck out his hand. "Good luck, Dawson."

"You, too."

Carl climbed down and headed for his Humvee where Renee was waiting for him.

Terje poked his head out of the LAV's troop compartment. "This should be fun."

"Don't be a smart-ass." Jack dropped down beside him, careful not to hit Naomi or Melissa with his feet.

The two cats were ensconced in boxes lined with fleecy blankets, Alexander beside Melissa, and Koshka next to Naomi. Alexander peered up at him with his green eyes, and Jack leaned down to give him a quick scratch under the chin. Naomi had sedated Koshka before splinting her leg. She gently caressed one of the sleeping cat's front paws.

Jack reached over and took her hand. "Are you ready?"

Naomi looked up and nodded, giving his hand a quick squeeze.

Hopping up to sit on the rear deck beside Terje, who handed him a rifle, Jack spoke into the radio. "This is Dawson. Let's roll."

***

Jack took them north to avoid the choked kill zone of I-80 for as long as possible. They made their way along Denton Road. He planned to keep heading east on Denton until they reached the town of Central City, then veer a bit farther north on US-30 to catch 92, which would take them across the Platte River, which was the only major natural obstacle between them and Lincoln. He hoped that route would keep them clear of the harvesters coming up from the south.

Just before they reached the intersection with Merrick Road, they passed a small cemetery on the southeast corner.

"Huh," Terje said, looking at the GPS. "It says here that this is called the Norwegian Cemetery."

"Let's try not to add any more bodies to it, shall we?"

Terje grunted. "I have no plans to die in Nebraska. It's much too flat here."

Jack laughed. "You should see some parts of Texas."

They passed endless fields, many of them edged with trees. Some of the fields were fallow, while others had early spring crops, and the leaves on the trees were only just starting to emerge from their buds. It was cool, bordering on chilly, especially sitting in the open on the LAV, and it would get colder as the sun went down, which wouldn't be long now. Cows raised their heads and twitched their ears as the convoy passed by.

"It seems odd that we haven't seen any harvesters," Terje said after a while.

"Let's count our blessings," Jack told him. "According to the last imagery I was able to dig up before we left, most of the big harvesters were due east and south of the base. I'm sure some must be around here, but I'm hoping we miss most of them."

"At least until we get closer to Lincoln."

"Yeah," Jack said, uneasy. With a population of just over a quarter of a million people, Lincoln wasn't huge, but concentrations of people also meant possible concentrations of harvesters.

Ten minutes later, Jack was doubting the wisdom of coming this way.

"Contact right!" Lowmack reported just before his gunner opened fire with the coaxial machine gun on a group of harvesters heading for the road. The tracer rounds stitched across the group of creatures, dropping some and setting others alight.

Jack saw the turrets of the LAVs in the column turn to point in the direction of the action. The gunners manning the .50 caliber machine guns in the Humvees did the same.

He keyed the radio. "Watch your sectors! I want eyeballs watching three hundred and sixty degrees around us."

The Marines in the other vehicles turned their weapons back to their assigned sectors, alternating left and right, with the last vehicle, an LAV, turning its weapon to cover the rear of the column.

Lowmack's added his top-mounted 7.62 machine gun to the firepower raking the approaching harvesters, then his gunner opened fire with the vehicle's 25mm cannon.

"Major," Lowmack said, "I think we may have a situation developing here."

More and more harvesters were streaming toward the road. Many of them had been milling around in the fields, while more had begun to appear from a line of trees about two hundred meters away.

The 25mm cannon raked the tree line.

The result was instantaneous and terrifying. A solid mass of harvesters surged forward from the trees, and more rose up from the fields to the east, beyond which lay the Platte River about three kilometers away.

One of the LAVs farther back in the column opened fire, the commander reporting, "Contact left, ten o'clock!"

Jack turned to look, and saw another mass of harvesters emerging from another line of trees behind a group of farm buildings about five hundred meters north of their position.

In only a few seconds, every vehicle in the column was firing at waves of harvesters, thousands of them, approaching from the north and east. Despite the massive casualties his people were inflicting, the harvesters were getting closer, and their numbers were still growing.

Keying his radio, Jack ordered, "Mortar crew, start laying down a barrier of Willie Pete between us and the harvesters approaching from that line of trees to the north. For everyone else, stop and turn around! Reverse the line of march and head back toward Central City! We'll cover the rear."

The only thing that saved them, Jack reflected afterward, was the furiously burning bodies of the harvesters themselves. The flames became so intense at one point before Lowmack's LAV was able to turn and follow the other vehicles that Jack and Terje had to duck down inside to avoid being scorched.

"I hope we don't run into our friends that were coming up from the south," Terje said.

"What if we do?" Melissa looked up at him with wide, frightened eyes. "What if we can't get through?"

"We will," Jack said. "I promise." He leaned over and put a hand on her shoulder, speaking loud enough that she could hear him over the firing of the LAVs Bushmaster cannon and machine guns. "We knew when we started out that this wasn't going to be easy, honey. We expected there would be lots of bugs, but we're prepared for them. We'll be okay."

She nodded, but didn't look convinced. Naomi wrapped her arm around her and pulled her close. "We'll be all right. Jack will get us there."

"Damn straight." With that, he climbed back up to sit on the rear deck where he could see better. The vehicles had stopped firing as they finally left the harvesters behind.

"I'm glad we brought a lot of ammunition," Terje said. "If this keeps up, we're going to need every round."

"If we have to fight like that all the way to Lincoln, I'm not sure it'll matter. Those bastards are determined to get at us."

As the sun went down, the LAV gunners switched to their thermal sights. Everyone else flipped down their night vision goggles, which turned the world an eerie green.

Jack could sense the anticipation building as they ran southwest along US-30, and had to clear his throat, which had become bone dry, to give his next orders to convoy. "All units, turn south on 18th Road, which should be the next intersection. Once you get to Hord Lake Road, take a left and head east. It's the first hardball road you'll come to, so you can't miss it. Whatever you do, maintain speed when you reach the bridge and *do not stop*. We're pushing across the river, no matter what."

In turn, each vehicle confirmed the order, and Jack breathed a sigh of relief as the lead LAV, which had originally been at the tail end of the column, slowed and made the turn onto the dirt road, and the other vehicles followed suit. It seemed like a simple thing, but Jack had been on more than one operation where a driver had screwed up and blown a turn and everyone else just followed along like lemmings.

"Three kilometers to Hord Lake Road," Terje told him, pointing at the GPS display.

"Lowmack, what's our speed?"

"Thirty-five miles an hour, sir."

Shaking his head, Jack keyed his radio again. "All vehicles, step on the gas and bring your speed to forty-five."

"I hope no cows get in the way," Terje said.

Jack tightened his grip on his rifle, scanning the open fields around them. "To hell with the cows. I hope forty-five is fast enough to outrun any harvesters who want to come chase us."

"Good point."

"Turning onto Hord Lake now," the commander of the first vehicle reported.

So far, so good, Jack thought.

The lead LAV commander spoke again. "Major, there's a thick band of trees about a kilometer from the intersection here. It looks clear so far...*oh, shit!*"

Jack heard a Bushmaster open up, followed by machine guns.

"Keep moving!" Jack ordered, wishing his vehicle was closer to the head of the column so he could see what was happening. "Don't stop!"

More weapons were firing now, and he could see the tree line, limned by the weapons flashes and fires that erupted as harvesters were hit with tracer and incendiary rounds.

Motioning for Terje to follow suit, Jack dropped down into the troop compartment, but kept his head up so he could see.

Vehicle commanders and drivers were reporting contact all around as the column passed through the tree line. Machine guns, assault rifles, and shotguns spewing fountains of Dragons Breath blasted away at harvesters attacking from both sides of the road.

Jack shot a harvester that was hanging onto one of the Humvees ahead of them, its arm reaching through the window for the front passenger. He wasn't sure if he hit the beast, but it didn't matter. A shotgun blast from inside the Humvee sent the monster flying backward, its body igniting from the halo of Dragons Breath that enveloped it.

One of the Humvees spun off the road and crashed into the trees. It was covered by gleaming, hideous bodies that tore at the doors and windows to get at the occupants. The Humvee following behind slowed and began to pull over to assist the besieged occupants.

"Keep moving, damn you!" Jack shouted into the radio. "*Do not stop!*" It tore at his heart to leave anyone behind, but to stop now was to die.

The Humvee veered back onto the road and sped up, the .50 caliber gunner pouring fire into the wrecked vehicle, which exploded, scattering burning harvesters like molotov cocktails.

A group of harvesters managed to reach one of the precious cargo trucks, swarming onto the trailer before leaping into the cargo bed. The gunner manning the weapon in a ring over the cab was firing at another group of harvesters and never had a chance. They tore his body from the weapon mount before crawling down after the driver. The big vehicle weaved back and forth across the road before it swerved to the left and overturned, flipping the trailer over and blocking the road just before the bridge.

Jack saw in his distorted green view of the universe that the trailer was one of the fuel bowsers.

"Shit," he said through gritted teeth as the other vehicles slammed on their brakes and the drivers spun the wheels to right or left to avoid running into the overturned trailer, the truck, and each other. One by one, most of them with harvesters clinging to them, they managed to get around the wreck.

"Lowmack," Jack ordered, "once we're past that fuel bowser, put a few cannon rounds into it."

"With pleasure, sir."

The other LAVs, trucks, and Humvees dashed across the three hundred meters of the bridge at full speed, with Lowmack's LAV close behind.

Jack looked behind them. A solid mass of harvesters was pursuing them across the bridge. "Light it up!"

The LAV's Bushmaster cannon roared, and the fuel bowser exploded in a cascade of fire that rained down on the harvesters. The gunner pumped more rounds into the harvesters leading the charge across the bridge, creating a solid wall of flame that trapped those behind.

"Burn, you bastards," Jack whispered as the column fled eastward. "Burn in hell."

ODYSSEY

The odyssey to Lincoln was a hundred miles of kill or be killed. The convoy left a trail of burning harvester corpses in its wake, but had paid in precious blood. Another truck, this one hauling one of the generators, and two Humvees were destroyed. While the crew of one of the Humvees had been saved, five Marines and three civilians had died.

As the column approached the city, Angie Boisson and her agents broke off to take Ferris to Lincoln Airport, which lay just to the northwest of the city, to find anything that would fly. Once Naomi and her harvester allies had created their weapon, Carl wanted the virus and Naomi flown to a safe location. Ferris hadn't been wild about the idea, but Carl hadn't given him any choice. "You know," Ferris had told him, "my old man always told me that learning to fly was the biggest mistake of my life. Now I know why. Pilots get all the shit jobs."

Not long after Boisson's departure, Lowmack's LAV led the way up the overpass over I-80. Both sides of the interstate, all four lanes and the shoulders, were full of cars that had been heading west out of Lincoln. Now it was a parking lot filled with the charred hulks of cars, trucks, and tractor trailers. Most were still on the blacktop, but had overturned on the median or the drainage swales that ran along either side of the blacktop.

Survivors were still fleeing on foot through the mass of cars. They waved frantically at the passing convoy and ran toward the overpass.

But the convoy didn't stop.

After making it the entire way from SEAL-2 without losing a tire to larvae on the road, three of the vehicles in the column lost at least one tire to them within a mile of crossing the interstate. Jack had been forced to call a halt to change tires when they reached a spot that had a wide kill zone all around and no immediate evidence of adult harvesters. One Marine's luck had run out when he was yanking the tire from a Humvee and a larva he hadn't seen attacked his hand. A pair of Marines held him down while Naomi cut off the limb under the glare of flashlights. When she was done with the grisly operation, one of the Marines tossed the hand and the bruised-looking gob of tissue feeding on it into the grass and set it on fire.

It had taken them nearly five hours to cover the hundred miles from SEAL-2, and everyone was ready to drop. But the real work was just about to begin.

"Everything's dark," Terje said as the LAV came to a stop at the intersection of West Rokeby Road and Southwest 12th Street, not far from the perimeter of the Lincoln Research University campus. It was much smaller than the sprawling campus of the University of Nebraska at Lincoln, for it had been created with only one true purpose, kept secret at the time: to engineer the children of the original harvesters and design a system to inflict their genes upon the Earth. He glanced at Jack. "Do you think this will work?"

Jack shrugged. "Sure. All we have to do is secure the campus, get power to the labs, and tackle about three dozen other minor problems. It'll be a piece of cake."

"I don't see anything, sir," the gunner said after scanning the campus through his thermal sights. "This place looks dead."

"Good enough." Keying his radio to the convoy frequency, Jack said, "All vehicles, follow our lead. The objective looks deserted, but stay sharp." Then, leaning down, he said to Naomi, "Okay, babe, you're up. Lead us in."

**

Terje smiled at Naomi as he dropped down into the troop compartment so she could take his place, but she caught the wistful glance he gave her as she stood up and breathed in the open air. The trip had been a jarring, vibrating, blind hell of fear and worry inside the belly of the LAV as the convoy had fought its way through to Lincoln. Jack had insisted she stay in the vehicle, but she would have been far happier sticking her head out the top hatch, rifle in hand, than trapped down below.

She glanced down at a familiar *meow* sound. While she was still a bit groggy from painkillers, Koshka had been awake for the last half of the trek.

Melissa had spent most of the trip in frightened silence as the vehicles fought their way through the harvesters. One of her hands was always reaching under her seat where Alexander had hidden after the first shots had been fired.

"Here." Terje handed Naomi his helmet, which she slipped on over her grimy hair. Then she fastened the chin strap and adjusted the microphone to her lips before dropping the night vision goggles into place. He gave her a squeeze on the shoulder, then sat down beside Melissa, carefully setting the tray holding Koshka onto his lap.

Jack looked over and gave her a tired smile. That was all she could see of his face beneath his NVGs.

"It's your show," he said.

"The main entrance to the lab complex is down the road along the fence line on your right," she told Lowmack. The entire campus was bounded by a four foot concrete wall topped with an ornate, but quite functional, wrought iron fence topped with spikes in the shape of the *fleur de lis*. "You can't miss it."

"Understood. Driver, move out."

The LAV accelerated, and the ghostly green image of the LRU campus slowly slid by. She was chilled by the sight of the place, her skin breaking out into gooseflesh. It had been a little over two years since the fateful day when Dr. Kempf had revealed, at least in part, the true nature of the work that Naomi had been doing here. Naomi still had nightmares of that day.

"You okay?"

She turned to find Jack staring at her. "Yes," she told him. "I'm fine. You just pay attention to what you're supposed to be doing, Mr. Gunslinger."

"Yes, ma'am." He smiled and turned to keep an eye on a vacant field.

"Here's the gate," Lowmack said. "Holy shit. I'm glad somebody left the thing open or we would've had to use C4 to get through it."

"LRU never encouraged visitors," Naomi told him as the big vehicle turned into the entrance, passing by the empty guard shack and over the half dozen eight inch diameter hydraulic pistons that were normally raised to their three foot height to keep out the great unwashed. "Anyone who wanted to visit the campus had to get a pass signed by the dean, which wasn't easy to get."

The main lot was empty. The three level executive parking garage that adjoined the first of the campus buildings was empty, too.

"Where to, ma'am?" Lowmack asked.

"Head to the left of the building next to the parking garage." She got up and crouched on the top of the hull, holding onto some of the gear that was strapped to the rear of the turret. Leaning forward, she pointed so Lowmack could see where she meant. "The campus lab buildings are laid out in sort of a U shape, and we're facing the top of the U. Just drive straight into it. The building we want will be at the end."

Jack came on the intercom. "How many of these buildings are we going to have to occupy?"

"Only one. The same one that Sheldon broke into to get the corn samples. Everything we should need is there, except for power, and the physical plant is just behind the main lab where we'll be."

"Thank God for small favors," Jack said.

She nodded, but didn't want to let her hopes get ahead of reality. "Let's just pray that everything hasn't been torn to pieces. Captain Lowmack, let's go."

"Aye, ma'am."

The LAV rumbled forward across the parking lot, then up over the curb, crushing what had once been meticulously maintained shrubs before the driver took them down the wide and elegant walkways that joined the campus buildings.

"I don't see any signs of fire," Jack said, "and all the windows seem to be intact. It looks like they just closed up shop."

"I don't see any bodies," Lowmack added. "I'm not sure if that's good or bad."

They passed by what served as the student union, a round building at the center of the 'U' that looked like a carousel enclosed in glass. "We should check in there to see if any non-perishable food is left," Naomi said. "Most of the food they stocked was fresh, so that's probably spoiled, but the might be some other things we can use to supplement the MREs."

"I'll have a detail check it out once we get settled in," Lowmack said, "if that's okay by you, major."

"Hell, yeah," Jack replied. "I'd kill for a pizza right now."

"This is it," Naomi said as the LAV approached a four story building, a green monolith against the black sky in her goggles.

"Captain Lowmack," Jack said, "have your men make a recon around this building and the physical plant, and make sure they take the Army engineer guy to see if he can figure out how to hook up the generator. Once they've reported back, we'll check out the inside."

"Yes, sir."

Lowmack quickly issued orders, sending one of the LAVs and a pair of Humvees around each side of the lab building while the other vehicles pulled into a defensive circle, the LAVs and the Humvees on the outside, and the two remaining trucks on the inside.

"The buildings look clear on the outside, sir," Lowmack reported a few minutes later. "The engineer says to send the truck with the generator back to the physical plant. We should have power in about twenty minutes."

"Outstanding," Jack said, and Naomi breathed a sigh of relief. Turning to her, he said, "Ready to go inside?"

"No, but let's do it before I completely lose my nerve." She ducked down into the innards of the LAV and flipped up her night vision goggles. "Melissa, honey, we're going inside. I want you to stay here where it's safe, and..."

"No!" Melissa shook her head, a look of desperation in her eyes. "I want to go with you. Nowhere is safe. Nowhere."

Beside her, Terje shrugged. "She's right, you know."

Naomi frowned, but decided to let Melissa have her way. "Fine, you can come with us. But you have to carry Alexander, all right? He's our only functioning harvester detector."

Then Naomi leaned down and stroked Koshka's face. The cat licked her fingers, then closed her eyes. "We'll come back out and get Koshka when we've got things set up inside. Okay?"

"Okay."

Terje opened the LAV's rear doors, and Naomi held out her hand to Melissa. "Come on, troublemaker, let's go."

THE LAB

The darkened campus was utterly silent except for the tic-tic-tic of cooling engines and the muffled movements of the Marines as Naomi stepped out of the LAV. The night was chilly, but she drew in a deep breath, savoring it, flooded with relief that the air didn't reek of the stench of harvesters or corpses.

"Okay," Jack said, "let's get this done."

Lowmack had left the three-man crews in the LAVs in case trouble reared its ugly head outside and, as he had at SEAL-2, had assumed command of the defensive perimeter while Jack and two squads of Marines went inside.

"We're coming, too," Renee exclaimed as Carl and Howard helped her out of the Humvee. "I'm not staying in this death trap a goddamn minute longer."

"This way," Naomi said, leading the others up the granite steps to the glass entry. Jack motioned for her to hang back as two Marines darted ahead of her. They peered inside, then slipped through the unlocked doors. More Marines followed.

Alexander made an unhappy mewling sound.

"He's not a happy kitty," Melissa whispered nervously.

"I don't think any of us are happy kitties," Terje said. By unspoken agreement, he walked beside Melissa, her personal bodyguard. He slowly swiveled his head, keeping watch on the darkness.

"Cut the chatter," Jack said quietly.

"It looks clear, sir," one of the Marines who'd gone inside reported.

"Understood. We're coming in."

They entered the atrium, which reached four floors above and encompassed the entire front of the building. The centerpiece was an ornate fountain thirty feet across with a bronze rendering of the

Winged Victory of Samothrace in the center. The fountain was still now, of course, the water in the pool around the statue forming a perfect mirror in the darkness.

"Wow," Melissa breathed, gawking at the sight.

"Nice digs," Jack agreed.

Leaning over, Naomi smelled the water in the fountain, then reached out to put her hand in the water.

Melissa stepped forward and grabbed her arm. "What if there's something in there?"

"It's okay, Melissa. If there was something bad in there, Alexander would let us know."

Other than a sigh of discomfort, or perhaps boredom, the big Siberian cat gave no indication of any nearby harvester threat, other than the ones they'd brought with them. His gaze remained fixed over Melissa's shoulder, where their seven allies remained under Marine guard.

Naomi dipped a couple fingers in the water, feeling the marble sides of the pool.

"It still smells okay," Naomi said, "and I don't feel any algae buildup. So the power can't have been off very long."

"It might not be a bad idea to see if we can make it safe to drink," Jack told her. "There's no such thing as too much potable water."

"That shouldn't be a problem," she said, wiping her hands dry on her pants. "All the chemicals we'd need for testing and purification are here, and I'm sure we can find filters somewhere." She pointed off to an elevator bank to the right. "Come on. We have to get to the third floor. The stairs are that way."

They stopped in their tracks at a series of popping sounds. Gunfire.

"It's somewhere outside, a long way off," Jack said. To the Marine on point, he said, "To the stairwell. Third floor."

"Roger," the man said, his voice tight.

The leading Marine palmed open the metal fire door to the stairwell and stepped inside to look around. "Stairwell is clear," he said.

"You'd think someone would still be here," Naomi whispered. "Somewhere."

"There still could be," Jack said. "Remember, we just got here. There could be a hundred people hiding in this building and we wouldn't know it."

"That makes me feel so much better," murmured Terje.

The staff sergeant who was in charge of the Marines said, "Should we check out the second floor, sir?"

"Not right now," Jack told him. "Post two men at the landing to cover our backs, then let's move up to the third floor." He looked at Naomi for confirmation, and she nodded.

"Roger that, sir. Mullens, Scott, cover our six."

The two Marines at the end of the line remained behind while the others went up to the third.

The lead Marine slowly pulled the fire door open and glanced out into the hall. "Looks clear."

"Go," Jack told him, and the Marines quickly stepped through into the hallway.

***

Twenty minutes later, the third floor was declared clear, the locks on the secured doors had been blown open, and the Marines were busy scouring the other floors and the basement for any signs of survivors or harvesters.

Everyone's mood lifted five minutes later, when the lights flickered on. The Marines gave out a cheer.

"Maybe that Army engineer guy isn't such a weenie after all," one of them admitted.

"There's only one problem," Terje said as he stood at the railing that looked out over the glassed in atrium from the open mezzanine walkway.

"Yeah," Jack said. "This place is going to stick out at night like a sore thumb to anyone with eyes."

"Yes, anyone or any*thing*. And we don't have enough fuel to make a flaming moat."

Turning to look through the door of one of the labs where Naomi and the handful of surviving lab workers from SEAL-2 were feverishly taking inventory of what was working, what wasn't, and what supplies they needed, Jack said, "They're just going to have to work fast."

The Marines who'd been celebrating the return of man-made illumination quieted down as more Marines herded in the harvesters, marching them up the stairwell to the third floor.

Alexander, who was sitting at Jack's feet, let out a low growl.

"Easy, boy," Jack said, his hand tightening on the leash attached to the improvised torso harness one of the Marines had rigged up. Alexander hissed and lunged at the harvesters as they filed past, and the creatures flinched away. "These are friendlies. Kind of."

Vijay ignored the cat and nodded at Jack. Then his gaze rested for a moment on Melissa. The other harvesters stared at her, too, before they were ushered into the lab. Four Marines stood guard inside the room, with four more outside.

"They scare me," Melissa whispered as the door hissed shut.

"They're the ones who should be scared," Jack told her.

"Scared of what?"

"Of you, kid."

She wasn't convinced. "If you say so."

Jack could hear Naomi's voice through the door.While she was speaking in English, he barely had a clue what she was talking about. Centrifuges, electrophoresis and FISH machines, homogenizers, incubators. The words reached his ears and bounced right off his tired brain.

"When was the last time you slept, Jack?"

He rubbed his eyes and looked at Terje. "Damned if I know. Probably about the last time you did. Last year, maybe?"

"Can we get Koshka?"

They both looked down at Melissa, who was a bit deflated now that she didn't have Alexander to care for.

"She's been out in the LAV alone since we got here."

As if reading her thoughts, Alexander whined, and after a last long growl at the harvesters in the room with Naomi, tugged on his leash, pointing toward the stairs.

"Okay, Romeo," Jack said with a last look at the lab door, "let's go get your girlfriend."

"He probably just has to pee," Melissa said.

"Or eat, more likely. He hasn't had anything in a while. Terje, would you mind keeping an eye on things here until we get back?"

"Sure." He winked at Melissa as she and Jack, led by the limping Alexander, headed toward the stairs.

"Why can't we use the elevator?" She asked.

"Their motors use a lot of power," Jack answered as he scooped up Alexander to carry him. "The main thing is that you don't want to get stuck in an elevator if something happens to the generator and we lose power."

She took hold of his wrist, and he could see the spark of fear in her eyes. "That won't happen, will it?"

"I don't think so. But we don't want to take any chances, right?"

"I guess so."

Jack smiled. "It's a shame, though. Those elevators are really cool."

The elevators, one on either side of the open atrium, were built like glass cylinders. But the designers of this building had gone one step further: the floors of the elevators were clear, too.

Jack opened the front door and they stepped out into the night. Unlike when they arrived and the night was preternaturally quiet, now they could hear the muted sounds of human activity all around them against the background hum of the generator. The entry steps to the lab building were bathed in light, which both soothed and worried Jack.

Carl stood outside the main entry with Lowmack, who had the rest of his Marines hard at work setting up the defenses.

"Where are Renee and Howard?" Jack asked as Alexander rubbed up against Carl's leg.

Carl squatted down to scratch the cat under the chin. "They're down in the basement, trying to get the computers back online." As he stood back up, Alexander head-butted Carl's leg. Looking down at him, Carl shook his head. "Sorry, buddy. I'm all out of sardines."

They're down in the basement. Those words sent a sliver of ice sliding down Jack's spine. The crime scene photographs of Sheldon Crane's murder flashed through his mind. Sheldon had been Jack's best friend and a fellow FBI agent, and a harvester had vivisected him in one of the basement service tunnels beneath this very building, looking for the corn samples Sheldon had stolen from the lab.

Melissa took Jack's hand in hers. "Are you okay?"

"Shake it off, Dawson," Carl said. "We've got enough trouble without you worrying about ghosts."

"I'm fine." Jack said the words, but they didn't echo his feelings. "Are they safe down there?"

"My men are blocking off the access tunnels," Lowmack told him. "The adult harvesters won't be able to wander in without battering through steel and setting off some fireworks, but any larvae could still be a problem."

"What about the ground-level perimeter?"

"We're stringing up a fence of triple concertina and claymores around this building and the physical plant, and we're setting some Claymore mines along choke points the things would have to take to reach us. I've also got observer teams up on the roofs who can warn us if anyone...or anything...is heading our way."

"What about the ones that look like us?" Melissa asked.

"Our night sights can tell the difference," Lowmack told her with a smile. Turning back to Jack, he said, "The LAVs and armed Humvees are our main defense. If we get mobbed by so many that the vehicles are overrun..." He shrugged.

Frowning, Carl said, "I can't escape the feeling that the bigger threat is from those seven things up there working with Naomi."

Jack glanced through the glass front of the building to the fourth floor mezzanine. "What do you mean?"

Carl squinted at Jack. "Who's to say those things aren't cooking up something to help finish what their dead creators started? What if they're sticking a little extra something into that virus to help kill us off?"

"Naomi would know."

Carl looked away, a hard expression on his face. "Naomi's the smartest person I've ever known, Dawson, and I don't claim to be a hundredth as bright as she is. But can a single human, even one as smart as her, really know everything that's going on with this stuff? She said it herself: the harvesters are naturals at all this genetic jazz, like some sort of monstrous idiot savants, except without the idiot part. There's something deeper going on here. I can feel it twisting in my gut."

"Even if that's true," Jack said, "what can we do about it? Naomi said she needs the harvesters. We don't have a choice."

"I know, and I hate it. I'm tired of feeling helpless. We've been reeling backward since day one. Just once, *just once*, I'd like to have the initiative. Shit." Carl blew out a breath and stared off into the darkness.

Changing the subject, Jack said, "Any word yet from Boisson and Ferris?"

Carl shook his head. "Not a peep. I didn't really expect them to have found Air Force One waiting for us up there, but I told Boisson I wanted hourly sit reps. It's not like her to not call in, and she hasn't answered my radio calls."

Jack looked to the north. The airport was about ten miles in that direction. Ten miles of exactly what, only Boisson, Ferris, and the agents with them could know.

"I should have sent them in one of the LAVs," Jack said quietly.

"Don't second guess yourself. We need the LAVs here. As much as it would hurt us, in the great scheme of things we can afford to lose Boisson and Ferris. We can afford to lose nearly anyone and anything except this." He jabbed a thumb over his shoulder at the building behind them.

Melissa tugged on Jack's sleeve. "Can we get Koshka now?"

"Sure, hon," he said, happy for the distraction.

Granting Alexander a moment of privacy on a patch of grass along the way to do his business, they headed for Lowmack's LAV, which was parked in front of the building, facing toward the student union and the main parking lot.

The rear doors were open, and Melissa hopped in, then stopped, dead still, staring at the seat where she'd left Naomi's cat.

Jack leaned in and looked. "Oh, shit," he breathed.

Koshka was gone.

WE NEED THIS PLANE

The ten miles from the LRU campus reminded Ferris of all the other war zones he'd seen in his life. The bodies, burned out cars and houses, the cries and pleas for help from terrified civilians were all too familiar. It was all the same, except that it was in his own country rather than somewhere else.

Hundreds of civilians flocked toward the Humvee as Ferris wove through the wrecks on the roads, which this close to Lincoln included the back country roads they'd been on since splitting from the convoy before it crossed I-80. The agent manning the vehicle's heavy machine gun had to shoot over the heads of the refugees now and again to keep them at a distance.

Then came the curses and ugly gestures, the screams of impotent rage that faded into the silence of the damned.

He felt like the world's biggest pile of dog shit.

"Fuck," he cursed, pouring every ounce of venom he could into the word, wishing he could turn it on the harvesters and fry the bastards with it.

"I hear you," Boisson said softly. She tore her eyes away from the scene outside to check the map display. "Take a right when we get to West Mathis Street. That should take us right to the western apron, about a klick and a half ahead."

"Got it."

As they neared the airport, the refugees thinned out and disappeared.

"You'd think people would be going to the airport," Ferris mused.

Boisson shrugged. "Maybe they know something we don't."

"Shit!" He spun the wheel to the left to steer the Humvee clear of a suspicious looking patch on the road. He'd seen enough of the damn larvae to be able to spot them on a smooth road surface once they were close enough. Otherwise, they would have run out of tires about a mile after they'd split off from the convoy.

A few moments later, they found themselves in a parking lot, facing the fence that bounded the old apron for what had once been Lincoln Air Force Base. One of the agents hopped out with a pair of bolt cutters and made short work of the lock on gate 44.

Once the agent was back in the Humvee, Ferris headed out onto the ramp that joined the apron with Runway 36. Once he reached the runway, he turned right and sped south. Nearly a thousand meters later, he turned again, taking them east on another ramp. "We'll see if the Army National Guard guys are home first."

They drove across to the Army facilities, which included a landing area that could take nearly three dozen helicopters. Behind that was a large hangar and various other buildings housing the Nebraska Army National Guard aviation battalion garrisoned there.

"This doesn't look so good," Boisson said.

"That's the understatement of the year," Ferris whispered as he brought the Humvee to a stop.

A pitched battle had been fought here, and lost by the human defenders. The metal carcasses of three helicopters lay on the apron, their fuselages now little more than ash silhouettes on the concrete, with the more resilient bits of machinery laying in a heap on top. The fence line that surrounded the buildings had been reinforced with concertina wire, but it was crushed and torn in half a dozen places. Overturned and burned out Humvees, some with their dead gunners still clinging to the weapons mounted on top, encircled the buildings.

Harvester corpses were stacked in enormous piles on either side of the breaches in the fence line, with hundreds, maybe thousands, in the open kill zones around the compound, and more inside. Many had been burned to ash, but just as many more weren't. Hundreds of dead soldiers also lay inside the fence line, many of them entwined with dead harvesters. Ferris could smell the scent of war in the smoke that wafted from the vehicles and buildings and the scorched marks on the ground where harvesters had been incinerated.

"Custer's last stand," he whispered. As he watched, the nearest pile of harvester bodies shifted. Larvae, large and small, were at their devil's work, eating their dead parents. "God, those things make me sick."

Boisson turned to him. "Should we check out the buildings here?"

He shook his head. "There's no point. We're looking for something that flies, and their choppers are all toast." He looked at the wrecks. "We really could've used one of those."

He heard the other agents breathe a quiet sigh of relief as Boisson said, "I'm not going to complain. We'd need steel galoshes to get through all those damned larvae."

"Yeah. Well, let's see if the Air Force can do us any better." Ferris swung the Humvee around and turned north on the ramp that led to the Nebraska Air National Guard's 155th Air Refueling Wing's facility.

The 155th's apron had room for half a dozen KC-135 tanker aircraft. The facility boasted a huge hangar that could hold one of the four-engine jets, plus a smaller one that could partially accommodate one of the planes.

Both hangars were charred wrecks. The smoking remains of a KC-135 lay in the large hangar.

"Scratch that one," Ferris said as he headed toward another of the big planes parked on the apron. While the apron could hold six planes wingtip to wingtip, only one was still here, parked right in the middle.

"It looks intact," Boisson said, a note of hope creeping into her voice.

"Look again." Ferris didn't mean to snap the words, but he couldn't help it. "The fucking tires are gone." He hammered a fist against the steering wheel in frustration.

Every one of the plane's tires was gone, and it now sat on the runway on the metal rims. Huge pools of hydraulic fluid and fuel had spilled under the plane, and around the edges of the pools were larvae as small as Ferris's fist up to the size of a horse.

"Christ," he said, "they're drinking the fuel!"

Boisson turned to him. "It's carbon based, right?"

"Yeah. God."

As he left the marooned KC-135 behind, he said, "I guess we'll have to try the commercial terminal. If we don't find something there, maybe a smaller airliner, I think we're going to be screwed. The best we'll find otherwise is a corporate jet. We won't be able to take many people anywhere in one of those."

He headed back out onto the taxiway that led north across the front of the 155th Refueling Wing's operations area, planning to follow it up and around to where the passenger terminal was. He kept his eyes on where he was going to keep from running over any larvae.

Boisson reached over and touched his arm. "Wait!" She pointed off to the right. "Look!"

He stopped the Humvee and looked where she was pointing. "Son of a bitch," he whispered.

A KC-135 was sitting off by itself on a much smaller auxiliary apron north of the main facility. The plane was facing toward the main runway, its tail not much more than a stone's throw from the road that ran along the passenger terminal on the far side.

"I'm not sure, but it looks like the tires are intact," Boisson said carefully.

"Don't jinx us, woman." Ferris spun the wheel and took the Humvee onto the asphalt access between the taxiway they'd been on and the apron where the KC-135 was parked.

"I'm sure it has tires," she said.

Ferris had to work hard to keep his eyes on the asphalt ahead of him to watch for harvesters and not pin his gaze on the plane. "Come on, gorgeous," he said. "Stay beautiful for old Al."

Boisson glanced at him. "Ferris, you have some serious female issues."

"Why the hell do you think I'm single?"

Ferris brought the Humvee to a halt just short of the aircraft's nose. Taking a deep breath, he said, "Let's check her out."

He, Boisson, and three of the agents got out, while the fourth remained on the .50 caliber machine gun. Once on the ground,

Ferris led the others, ever watchful for larvae, on a clockwise circuit around the plane. "Landing gear looks good, all the tires and hydraulic lines seem to be intact." He scanned every inch of the plane that he could see from the ground, looking for any telltale signs of problems. As he rounded the port side main gear and headed back toward the nose, he said, "I don't see any damage on her belly, and nothing's leaking that I can see." Next to the plane was a big box on wheels with an electrical cable snaking across the asphalt to where it plugged into the plane. "We've even got an APU, assuming it still works."

"Ferris," Boisson said, "I hate to ask this, but let's assume this plane is operable. Can you even fly it?"

He turned and gaped at her. "Lady, I can fly just about any goddamn thing with wings, with or without engines." He stomped over to the crew hatch, which was on the lower side of the nose on the port side. "Can I fly it? Jesus."

The hatch was closed, which didn't surprise him. What did come as a surprise was that the ladder that provided access to the main deck was on the ground.

"I take it the ladder shouldn't be there," Boisson said.

"No." He shrugged. "Whatever. Let's see what we've got." He opened the hatch slowly, peering into the darkness beyond. "Don't see anything."

Grabbing the ladder off the ground, he stuck the hooked end up into the plane and secured it. As he began to climb up, he felt Boisson's hand on his shoulder.

"No you don't, flyboy," she said. "I'll go first, then Willis. We'll make sure the coast is clear first."

"Right," Ferris said, disappointed. "Sure."

He stepped away from the ladder to make way for Boisson and Willis, who went up fast, pistols in hand.

A few moments later he heard Boisson's voice calling from above. "It's clear. Come on up."

Relieved, he climbed up the ladder. Shaking off the helping hands offered by Boisson and Willis, he got to his feet. He was standing in the cockpit, just behind the seats for the pilot and copilot and across from the navigator's station. After quickly scanning the instrument panels, which were festooned with dials, gauges, buttons, and switches, he said, "Nothing looks like anybody's taken a hammer to it or blasted it with a gun. Past that we'll have to see what happens when we start throwing switches." To Boisson, he said, "Did you see anything wrong in back?"

"No, but we were only looking for things that might eat you. You're the one who knows planes."

"Yeah, I vaguely recall saying something to that effect." Ferris reached over and flipped some switches that brought up the overhead lights. Then he headed aft through the door in the bulkhead that separated the cockpit from the cargo area. All but four of the dozen or so passenger seats, which were nothing more than red nylon webbing over a light metal frame, on each side of the compartment were folded up and stowed against the fuselage. Several pallets, mostly laden with cardboard boxes, were secured with heavy duty nylon tie-downs in the center.

Ferris made his way through the cavernous hold past the pallets and the two auxiliary power units before he came to the boom operator's station near the rear of the plane.

"Hold up," Boisson said, her voice sharp.

Ferris turned around. "What is it?"

Boisson held up a dark brown wrapper of an MRE meal packet. It was open, with the end of the spoon sticking out. "Mediterranean Chicken," she read from the side of the packet. "And it's warm." She smelled it, then stuck her finger in it and gave it a taste. "Still good and fresh." Setting the packet back down where she'd found it near the forward APU, she brought up her rifle. "We're not alone in here."

Ferris drew his Desert Eagle and turned back toward the boom operator's station, which was a recessed cubby below the main deck, partly hidden by two stacked rows of large orange oxygen tanks. "Look," he called out, "we know you're in here. We're friendlies. Just come on out so we can talk. We don't want anybody to get hurt."

All he got in return was silence. But it wasn't the silence of a completely empty plane. *Someone* was here. He could feel it.

"Please," he tried again. "Come out. We're not harvesters, if that's what you're worried about. My name is Al Ferris, and I work for, ah, the government. I'm a contractor, sort of, and a pilot. The folks with me are FBI agents. They'll come dig you out if they have to, but I'd like to avoid that, and I think you probably would, too. These people don't screw around. What do you say?"

For a moment, there was only more silence. Then a young woman's voice said from the darkness of the boom operator's pit, "What do you want?"

"We need this plane," Al said, "if it'll fly."

"I think Colonel Cox will have something to say about that," the voice said from the darkness, "when she and the others get back."

Ferris glanced at Boisson, who was slowly moving toward the dark recess in the deck where the woman was hiding. He shook his head, and Boisson stopped. "How long has your colonel been gone?"

A long pause. "Two days. She and the others went out to get some spare parts. She told me to guard the plane. She'll be back. I know she will."

Ferris shook his head. "What's your name, kid?"

"I'm Staff Sergeant Kurnow," she shot back. "And I'm no kid."

He laughed. "When you get to be as old as me, Kurnow, everybody's a damn kid." Then, serious again, he said, "If your Colonel Cox has been gone two days, she's not coming back. You know there was a hell of a battle here, right? You probably watched the fireworks through the windows."

"Yeah, I saw."

There was no easy way for Ferris to say what had to be said. "It was a slaughterhouse, Kurnow. There weren't any survivors. And the hangars and other stuff for your squadron were pretty well toasted, too."

"The 155th isn't...wasn't my squadron," Kurnow said, finally emerging onto the main deck. She was petite, Ferris saw, maybe five foot four and probably weighed all of a hundred pounds soaking wet. Her short cut blond hair was a greasy mess, and she looked like she hadn't slept in a week. She was also holding a 9mm pistol pointed at his chest, and he noticed that her hand wasn't shaking at all. "We're from the 171st Air Refueling Squadron out of Selfridge Air National Guard Base in Michigan. We were on a mission to refuel some B-52s and had to divert here after we had problems with the cabin pressurization. The ground crew had just finished testing the repairs when...when..." She bit her lip.

"When your colonel saw that things were going to shit out there and wanted to try and salvage what she could before the base was lost," Ferris finished for her.

Kurnow nodded. "She left me here to watch the plane. They were only supposed to be gone thirty minutes, maybe an hour."

"Now it's time to make sure she's not one of *them*." Boisson's voice was quiet, but her tone made it clear that it wasn't a negotiable issue. She withdrew a lighter from her pocket.

"Uh, that's not such a good idea," Ferris told her. "Remember, this plane is a huge flying gas tank. If it's fully loaded, we're sitting on around a hundred tons of fuel." He wished they had thermal imagers, but there hadn't been enough to go around and they were stuck with the regular night vision goggles.

"Then what do you suggest? We don't have a cat, and we're sure as hell not trusting her on word alone."

"Boisson!" The agent she'd left outside had climbed into the plane and was calling from the cockpit.

"What is it?"

"We've got movement out here. Looks like harvesters moving up from the main hangar area."

"It's the lights," Kurnow said. "They're drawn to them at night."

"Shit," Ferris breathed as he dashed toward the cockpit and hit the switches, throwing the plane into darkness.

"You stay here," Boisson told him as she slid past and took hold of the ladder, her night vision goggles once again in place. She pulled a Taser from the holster on her belt and handed it to him. "This is the only other way we have to test for harvesters if we can't use a lighter." If Kurnow was a harvester, she'd revert to her natural form after being shocked by the weapon. "The electrodes shouldn't arc and light off any fuel fumes if they're buried in her skin. If I'm wrong, I guess we won't be around long enough to worry about it."

She stared at him, and he felt like he was looking into the face of an alien. "And don't you dare be a sentimental sap and not do what needs to be done or I'll fucking shoot you."

Then she was gone, sliding down the ladder.

"God, what a hardass," Kurnow whispered.

"You don't know the half of it." Dropping his own night vision goggles into place, he turned to find Kurnow standing just a few feet away, looking at him, her gun lowered by her side. With a sigh, he raised the Taser and took aim at her chest. "Sorry, kid," he said softly as he squeezed the trigger.

THE HITCHHIKER

Jack and Melissa looked everywhere for Koshka. Jack crawled on his hands and knees under the LAV, walked the perimeter out to the wire, searched through the bushes and shrubs around the lab building, and asked every Marine he came across if he or she had seen Naomi's white cat.

No one had.

"Naomi's going to have your head, Dawson," Carl told him after Jack had returned empty-handed. Jack set Alexander down. He'd had to carry him most of the time during their search.

Melissa's cheeks were wet with tears. "It's my fault," she said in a hoarse voice. "I was supposed to watch after her."

"Koshka can't have just disappeared into thin air," Jack insisted.

"That doesn't leave us with very many possibilities," Lowmack, who'd been talking with Carl about the progress on their defenses, pointed out.

Carl's expression hardened. "What if someone took her?"

Jack shook his head. "Who would do that? Everyone in the convoy knows how important she and Alexander are now, especially since all the other cats are gone."

"It wasn't one of my Marines," Lowmack said. "I can guarantee you that. Even the ones who normally hate cats would never let one come to harm or let someone other than Jack or Naomi walk off with her."

"What if there's a harvester with us," Melissa said, "one that we don't know about?"

"I don't think that's one of our worries, young lady," Lowmack told her with a smile.

Jack was about to open his mouth to agree, then snapped it shut.

Carl stared at him. "What's the matter, Dawson?"

"I don't like to admit the thought," Jack said, glancing at Melissa, "but maybe we shouldn't dismiss that possibility so quickly."

"How would that even be possible?" Lowmack asked. "Except for the seven lab rats, everyone in the convoy was human when we left SEAL-2, and we didn't stop to pick up any hitchhikers."

Carl and Jack exchanged a look. "We didn't verify everyone's identity before we left," Carl said. "We were in too much of a rush and just went on the belief that there were enough of us with eyes on the others that we maintained continuity on our identities. And any reaction from the cats was already messed up because of Naomi's pets. But that's not the real problem, is it?"

"No," Jack agreed. "When the crew of that Humvee was rescued on the way here, we might have picked up a hitchhiker or an impostor."

"Bull." Lowmack shook his head. "There's no way."

Jack gave him a hard look. "How many people were in that Humvee when we left?"

"Three. The driver, a rifleman riding shotgun, and the machine gunner."

"And how many were in the Humvee that picked them up?"

"There should have been four in that one."

Carl said, "And how many people got out of that Humvee when we got here? You did the head count on every vehicle, right?"

"There were seven...no, eight. Shit." He looked sick. "But even if I fucked up on the count, the other Marines would have known they had someone who didn't belong."

"During that mess of a firefight, in the dark?" Jack shook his head. "For all we know, a harvester could have claimed it was a survivor from the other Humvee or the truck that we lost during the same battle, and could have been masquerading as one of the dead crewmen. We weren't able to stop and count up the bodies, and all they would've had to do is act panicked like everyone else trying to pile into that Humvee. Nobody would have even thought of leaving someone behind."

"And the thermal imagers might not have been much help with all the gunfire and the flames in the background," Lowmack finished, a note of anger creeping into his voice." He looked down at Melissa. "Maybe we need to put you in charge, kid. You're sure as hell smarter than we are."

She looked up at him, her eyes glowing with the reflection of the lights shining down over the entryway. "What are you going to do?"

"The only thing we can do," Lowmack said. "We're going to find the son of a bitch."

"And Koshka, too," Jack said. "If she's still alive."

***

Lowmack ordered his Marines to stay put, wherever they were. He, Jack, and Terje checked the LAV crews first, using Alexander as a harvester detector. One after another, the five three-main crews (which included Lowmack himself) were cleared.

Then they moved on to the various details that had been setting up the defenses, the observers on tops of the buildings, and the Army engineer and the handful of Marines covering him.

Man by man, woman by woman, all the Marines were cleared.

Lowmack ordered a rotation of the detail guarding the harvesters working with Naomi and the civilians and checked each Marine as he or she came outside. They didn't want any accidental false positives from Alexander by taking him closer to the harvesters in the lab.

Finally, the civilians, including Naomi, were marched out of the lab and run past Alexander, whose only reaction was intense boredom.

Last through the gauntlet was Naomi. "What's this all about?" She asked.

"We think we might have picked up a hitchhiker during that firefight when the Humvee crew was rescued." He tried to get out the rest of what needed to be said, but the words caught in his throat.

Naomi put a hand on his shoulder. "And?"

"And we think that he...it...may have taken Koshka. When Melissa and I went back to get her from the LAV, she was gone."

Pulling her hand away from his shoulder, she used it to cover her mouth. Shaking her head slowly, she whispered, "No. God, not after all this."

"I'm going to find who...what did this," Jack said, "and I'm going to find Koshka."

"*We're* going to find her," Melissa added, taking hold of Naomi's other hand. "It was my fault."

"But all the Marines and civilians are clear." Carl looked around them, beyond the lights and into the darkness that enveloped the campus. "The thing we're after could be anywhere by now. We don't have any way to track it down."

"Maybe we don't," Jack said, his eyes looking through the glass of the lab building's front to the fourth floor. "But they do."

Carl stared at him. "Have you lost your mind?"

"No, he's right," Naomi said, turning to look in the same direction. "We know they can sense other harvesters, even at great distances. If there's one who shouldn't be here, they'd know."

"Then they probably already do," Carl said. "I take it they haven't said anything to you?"

"No, and I wouldn't really expect them to. Would we tell them about an extra human we picked up?"

Carl's face twisted into a grimace. "No."

"All right, let me ask them." She turned and jogged back into the building.

A short while later, Naomi and Vijay, escorted by a pair of Marines, emerged from the building.

Vijay, as usual, wore a polite smile. "I am told you require some assistance in finding one of our kind."

"That's right." Carl looked like he'd swallowed a cigarette butt.

"Vijay's agreed to help," Naomi said, "on the condition that the harvester be taken alive."

"So there is one," Jack said.

Nodding his head side to side in the Indian fashion, Vijay said, "Yes. One joined the convoy on the way here, as you suspected. And before you ask, we said nothing because we owe you nothing more than we have already promised."

Carl tensed up, the veins on his temples standing out.

"We accept your help under the condition you stated," Jack told him.

"Fine," Carl grated. "Get it done." To Naomi, he said, "Let's go back inside. You can give me an update on the way."

With a last glance at Jack, she turned to walk beside Carl as he strode back into the building, her voice fading to silence as the door closed behind them.

"So," Jack said to Vijay, "where do we start?"

The thing's human-looking lips parted in a smile, making Jack's skin crawl. "Why, we start underground, of course."

***

Koshka had sensed it coming when she had been resting in the large box-that-moved where her human had left her to rest. Closer and closer it had come. She had cried out for her human, or the smaller female who had attended her on the way here, but none heard the warnings.

She got to her feet. She staggered at first, her leg and ribs making her cry out in pain. Then she had to escape the great metal box. What normally would have been a sedate and graceful hop to the ground became a fear- and agony-filled controlled fall onto soft grass.

The thing was approaching from her left. Following her instincts, she went right, making her way on three legs.

Humans wandered to and fro making their strange noises, but she dared not call attention to herself. The thing could move very quickly, and would be upon her before the humans could intervene.

Seeing nowhere to hide near the building that was bathed in bright light, she turned and fled into the darkness. She threaded her way through the fence the humans had built, slicing open her nose on one of the tiny blades as she leaned in close to sniff at it.

Beyond the wire, she kept moving. The thing was somewhere behind her. She could tell that it had stopped, but only for a moment. Moving again now, it was coming closer.

She needed a place to hide, but she knew nothing of this strange place. Everything was unfamiliar.

Behind her, the thing moved farther away, then nearer. That cycle repeated over and over again, as if it was crossing back and forth over her trail. But with each cycle it gained ground, coming closer, ever closer.

She reached the next building and turned the corner. *There!* A door stood propped open by a body, a dead human. Hopping over the carcass, ignoring the hunger in her stomach that had come alive at the smell of meat, she limped into the darkness.

It was a stairwell.

She mewled softly in indecision, a reflection of anticipated pain if she went forward, of fear of death if she didn't.

One set of stairs led up, while the other led down. Going up the stairs would be too difficult. Down would be easier, and would take her into the earth. There, perhaps, she could find a lair. Safety.

Her senses tingling with fear as the thing came closer, she made her way down, step by agonizing step.

GLIMMER OF HOPE

Boisson crouched down behind the Humvee beside the KC-135, watching the harvesters approaching.

One of the agents whispered, "How many of them are there, Boisson?"

She snorted. "How the hell do I know? Enough to take us down." Looking at the silhouette of the other tanker they'd passed, the one with the eaten-away tires, she said, "There are flares in the Humvee, right?"

"Yeah, I think so. Why?"

"I think we need to have ourselves a barbecue. Go dig a few out."

The machine gunner glanced down at her while the other agent rummaged around in the Humvees storage bins "Why not just blast them into burning bacon bits?"

"I don't want to draw attention anywhere near this plane. We'll open fire if we have to, but not here." She turned and looked back at their KC-135. "You two," she nodded at the two men beside her. "Take cover behind the main wheels there and guard the plane while the rest of us go for a little joyride. You," she gestured to the agent occupying the driver's seat, "move over. I'm driving."

As soon as she cranked over the Humvee's engine, the approaching harvesters paused, then began to run toward them. Boisson stomped on the accelerator and the Humvee shot forward, right toward them.

"Holy shit," the machine gunner cried, "are you crazy?"

At the last second, Boisson spun the wheel to the right and took off along the cracked and rutted concrete edge of the apron in the direction of the main taxiway. They zoomed by a big "X" on the apron, then bounced onto the asphalt joiner between the old apron and the taxiway, where Boisson pulled to a stop and looked over her shoulder.

"What the hell are you stopping for?" One of the other agents asked.

"I just wanted to make sure we didn't lose anybody," she said with a feral grin. All the harvesters were in hot pursuit, running on the ground like giant, loping cockroaches. While not a full-blown swarm, the group was bigger than she'd thought.

Just before the leading creatures reached the Humvee, she again jammed on the accelerator and turned down the main taxiway, the Humvee's tires squealing in protest as they slid on the concrete.

"Christ, Boisson!" The agent riding shotgun gasped, leaning out so he could see behind them. "They're practically on the bumper!"

"That's right where I want them!" She shouted back. It was like one of the zombie video games her young niece (now probably dead, Boisson thought sadly) used to play. She would run around in a particular pattern until she had all the zombies following behind her in a big gaggle. Then she would whirl around and hit them all with a flamethrower, toasting dozens of the virtual undead at a time.

What Boisson had in mind wasn't far different, although the penalty for getting caught in this game was a bit more serious than having to restart the level. "Flares! Both of you, get ready to throw 'em!"

"Shit," the agent beside her cursed as he handed a pair of flares up to the machine gunner, keeping another pair for himself.

Boisson slowed down ever so slightly until the agent on the machine gun began a constant stream of fear-filled invective. She wanted the harvesters close. Really close.

They passed the north end of the 155th Air Refueling Squadron's main ramp, heading south. The KC-135 with the eaten-away wheels was just to her left when she spun the wheel so hard the Humvee, even with its low center of gravity, skidded and almost tipped over.

Ignoring the curses of the two men with her, she gunned the engine, heading straight for the plane. "Light off the flares!"

The KC-135 was big, but not big enough for her to drive under the fuselage itself. So she guided the Humvee for the spot between the plane's two port-side engines and put the pedal to the metal, pulling away from the harvesters behind them. "*Do NOT throw the flares!* Not yet!"

"Goddamn!" The machine gunner ducked down as they sped under the wing. "Jesus, Boisson! The larvae are sticking to the tires!"

"I know, I know!" That was the one little problem with her plan.

Glancing back in the mirror, she saw that the pack of harvesters was stampeding right through the fuel spill, leaping over the larvae that were busy drinking it up. "*Throw!*"

Four red flares arced out and landed in the huge pool of JP-8 fuel under the plane, igniting it with a titanic *whump*. Boisson felt the heat wash across her back as the fuel lit off. In a fraction of a second, the malleable flesh of the harvesters ignited, and the plane disappeared in a roiling column of blinding bright flame.

She kept her foot on the accelerator, guiding the Humvee to relative safety behind the wreckage of the unit's smaller hangar before the KC-135 exploded, sending up a huge fireball into the night sky behind them. Flaming debris rained down across the airport in every direction, setting off even more fires where the chunks of metal set fire to more larvae. Boisson watched, praying, to make sure that none of the debris fell on the KC-135 where Ferris and the others waited.

They were lucky. None did.

"Anybody behind us?" She shouted.

"Zip. I think we toasted them all," replied the machine gunner. "And this is the last fucking time I go anywhere with you, Boisson. You're a lunatic!"

As she eased off the accelerator, one of the front tires blew out, sending the vehicle into a sharp skid to the right. "Shit," Boisson cursed as she fought to retain control, barely keeping the Humvee from rolling over.

As the vehicle slowed to a stop, a second tire blew.

"Everybody out!" She grabbed her weapon and leaped clear of the vehicle, and the other two agents did the same.

It would take more than a tire change to make the vehicle useable again. The undercarriage was completely covered in oozing blobs that were hungrily consuming everything down to bare metal.

Taking out one of the half dozen cans of hair spray she carried in her combat vest, Boisson put a lighter near the nozzle and flicked it into flame. Leaning closer to the Humvee, she squeezed the nozzle's top, and a gout of flame spat forth, enveloping one of the larvae. It sizzled and flared, burning bright and hot. Boisson fried a few more of the things until the vehicle fully caught fire.

"You really enjoy that, don't you?" One of the agents asked.

"Hell, yes," she said as the things burned. "And I hope they feel pain just as much as we do." Putting the hairspray back in her vest, she said, "Come on. Let's get back and make sure Ferris hasn't gotten himself into trouble." Staring at the burning Humvee, she realized something else. "I hope that plane has a working radio so we can contact Richards. I just fried ours, not that it was working worth a damn." She looked to the south. "God, is he going to be pissed."

***

"It is done."

Naomi gave a start at the sound of the young Iranian woman's voice. Zohreh had come up quietly behind her, and Naomi tabbed another window up on her computer to conceal the one she had been working in. The arrangement of the workstations in the LRU lab was less than ideal for maintaining any sort of privacy. But it wouldn't do for the harvesters to find out what she was doing. That would be fatal.

Gathering her wits, Naomi turned to face the harvester. Whoever Zohreh had been, she had been beautiful, and Naomi had caught more than one of the Marines eyeing her. *It.* "The code is finished, then?" She knew that it was done, because she had been working on a parallel copy of the design, but she had to pretend otherwise.

"Yes," Zohreh nodded. "The payload design is complete and ready for integration into the virion carrier. Then we can begin replication."

Naomi smiled. It was partly genuine. The harvesters had sequenced the code in a matter of hours. She felt like a child beside them.

But children can be clever. While the monsters had been working at a blinding pace recoding their species' DNA to their own ends, she had completed the work that she and Harmony had begun. Using the sequences from Melissa's DNA that were associated with the Morgellons fibers in her skin, Naomi was able to pin down their location in the harvester DNA. After comparing those sequences across a set of samples taken from mature harvesters and those transforming from the larval stage, she determined that those genes controlled the growth of the harvester skeletal structure.

While the harvesters put the finishing touches on their creation, she did the same for hers by splicing the appropriate elements of a particular mutation of the human ACVR1 gene into the harvester skeletal control sequence. That bit of information was known only by Naomi, and is what she had been working on when Zohreh crept up behind her.

"Good. That's very good, Zohreh." Naomi was relieved to be able to say something that was true. The harvesters were very adept at ferreting out lies.

Zohreh glanced at Naomi's computer screen. "I could not help but notice that you were looking at the genes associated with our skeletal growth." She cocked her head to one side, her dark eyes fixed on Naomi's. "You were able to identify them using patterns from Melissa's DNA, no doubt. But I am curious, for what purpose?"

Naomi's blood ran cold. The harvesters had never been given access to the data on Melissa's DNA. Even here, that information had been stored in a special encrypted file on the backup disks Renee had brought, and to which only Naomi had access. While the harvesters had seen Melissa after the attack on SEAL-2, no one had ever spoken about her importance, or even mentioned her name, in the harvesters' presence. Only three people among the lab crew had known about Melissa's DNA: Harmony Bates, Carly Walker, and Naomi herself. Naomi certainly hadn't mentioned anything, Carly was tight-lipped about everything around the harvesters, working on her own as much as she could, and Jack had confirmed that Harmony was dead.

And yet, somehow the harvesters knew about the use of Melissa's DNA. But did they know just how important it was?

Tell the truth, as much as you have to, but as little as you can, or she'll kill you. "She has a dreadful disease that has genetic markers that match part of your DNA," Naomi told her, looking the thing right in the eye. "Studying those gene sequences has given me some ideas about how we might be able to heal her with gene therapy derived from the viral delivery system we developed at SEAL-2."

Zohreh smiled, but her eyes were dead. "That seems to be an ill-timed endeavor in order to save a single girl, when your entire world is at stake."

Undaunted, Naomi leaned closer, spilling out some of her anger to mask her fear. "Every one of our lives has become priceless. And the technique could be adapted to cure many forms of disease. While I've worked in genetics labs for most of my career, I'm also a physician. If I can find a way to save lives in the moments I might have free while aiding you, then I will. Is that a problem?"

The harvester stared at her for a moment more. The lab had fallen silent as everyone, human and harvester alike, turned to watch the confrontation.

After a moment, Zohreh smiled. "No, it is not a problem. I hope you succeed. Doctor."

Flashing a beauty pageant smile, the creature turned away and went back to her workstation.

After watching Zohreh go, Naomi sat back down. She quietly let out a long breath before calling up her Trojan Horse. She put on the finishing touches, then sent the data to the machines that would create a new form of microbial life.

***

"You are such an asshole."

"I've been called worse." Ferris helped Kurnow to her feet, feeling like an absolute louse for having zapped her. "The good news is that Boisson won't kill you now that we're sure you're human. Assuming the crazy fool is still alive."

"What do you mean? What happened?"

He shook his head and led her to the cockpit, which was brightly lit from outside.

"Oh, my God," Kurnow breathed when she looked outside.

"Yeah." The other KC-135 that had been on the main apron was a huge flaming pile of metal, and the rising cloud of black smoke blotted out half the stars in the sky. "I hope the crazy wench made it out."

They stared at the fire for a minute before Ferris said, "Listen, how much can you tell me about this plane? You said the pressurization problem was fixed, so I assume it's airworthy, right? What about fuel?"

She nodded. "She'll fly. We were going to leave right after the pressurization checks were done, then we were going to taxi back to the main apron to fuel up for the next mission."

"So we need gas."

"Yeah. I think we've only got the mandatory fuel aboard for forward trim and enough in the wing tanks for a short flight, but that's it."

"Shit." Ferris rubbed his chin. "That complicates things. A lot."

"Can't we just taxi over to the main apron and plug into one of the fuel hydrants there?"

Shaking his head, Ferris said, "Not without clearing the taxiway of those goddamn larvae. They'd eat through the tires and that would be all she wrote."

"Then we can get a fuel truck and bring it over here. Even if the larvae ate through its tires, we could still get the fuel to the plane."

Ferris winced. "One of those R-11 trucks carries what, maybe forty thousand pounds of fuel?" He shook his head. "I'd hate to take off with any less than a hundred thousand pounds, and more would make me a lot happier. We have no idea how far we're going to have to fly to find a secure field where we can land."

She scowled at him. "You're never satisfied, are you?"

He shrugged. "What did you expect, kid? I'm a pilot."

They turned at the sound of someone coming up the ladder. It was Boisson.

"Jesus, Angie!" Ferris reached down and helped her to the deck. Her face was streaked with soot, and half of her hair had been singed. "You look like shit. What the hell happened?"

"We had a little harvester cookout. But that's not important. We've got to contact Richards. When I tried earlier, I couldn't get through. I think maybe there was something wrong with the radio in the Humvee."

"Well, did you try it again?"

She pointed to a fire behind the secondary hangar a quarter mile away. "See that little bonfire there? That's the Humvee. We picked up a few too many larvae."

"Shit." Ferris shivered at the thought of her and the other agents covering the distance from there on foot. Even with the night vision goggles, walking around in a larvae-infested area would have given him the creeps. "Well, we've got power and Kurnow here says this bird is airworthy. And one thing we aren't short on is radio gear."

Slipping into the pilot's seat, Ferris put on the headset and began flipping switches. Some of the countless buttons and gauges on the instrument panels came to life. "You got the frequencies handy?"

"Here." She pulled a card from one of her uniform pockets and gave it to him.

"We're out of line of sight for VHF, so let's give HF a try." He punched the frequency into one of the radios. "Keep your fingers crossed." Then, keying the microphone to transmit, he said, "SEAL-2, this is Big Bird, come in, over." He listened for a response.

Nothing.

He repeated the call. Still nothing.

"Keep trying," Boisson said. "They've got to…"

Ferris jumped when a female voice burst through his headphones. "Big Bird, this is SEAL-2, go ahead, over."

"Let me talk to SEAL-2 Actual," Ferris said, giving the thumbs-up to Boisson. Unable to help himself, he was smiling like a fool.

***

Down in the basement where Renee and Howard were still working on the computer systems, Carl was tilted back in one of the workstation chairs. He had finally banished enough of the demons that tormented his mind to let exhaustion take his body into much-needed sleep.

His eyelids were just drooping shut when his radio crackled to life.

"Mr. Richards!" The young Marine's voice was filled with excitement. "We've got Mr. Ferris on the radio!"

His eyes snapping open, Carl keyed his mic as adrenaline surged through his body. "I'll be right there." *So much for getting in a few winks*, he thought. He got up and leaned down to kiss Renee on the cheek before dashing out the door.

As he ran up the stairs, taking two at a time, Carl hoped and prayed the pilot had some good news. *If he doesn't*, Carl thought, *I'm going to kick his ass.*

THEY'RE COMING

"He went this way," Vijay said, pointing out into the darkness beyond the razor wire fence.

Before Jack could say anything, Vijay vaulted over the wire to land nimbly on the other side. Turning to face Jack and the others of the hunting party, he smiled and said, "Come. Quickly."

"Damn," Lowmack whispered.

Jack grimaced. "Yeah." He led Lowmack and the two Marines with him to the access point in the fence and slid through, careful not to get hung up on the razor barbs.

"God, I hate this stuff," Lowmack whispered.

"Have to agree with you there."

"I hope the harvesters hate it just as much, if any ever come this way," Lowmack told him.

Jack grunted. "I'll be happy enough if they don't."

Vijay stood waiting for them. "Come," the harvester said before turning to lead them across the open area to the next building. "I cannot smell our quarry, but I can smell the cat. She came this way, and I believe he must have followed."

"You're not sure?" Jack asked.

Vijay shrugged. "I can tell he is near, and that he is in this general direction. It makes sense that he would follow the cat. Killing her would be a worthwhile goal." He glanced at Jack. "It is what I would do, if our roles were reversed. Eliminating the cats would be the best first step toward safe assimilation into the group."

The matter-of-fact way in which Vijay spoke gave Jack the chills.

"Ah," Vijay said. "Look there." He pointed to the doorway in the back of the building adjacent to the lab. "I believe they both went that way."

Jack knelt down to examine the body that was pinned between the heavy steel door and the jamb in the wall.

"This has been here for a day or so," Vijay told him. "It is not one of yours."

Leading them through the door, Jack found himself in a hallway that adjoined an open stairwell. "Which way?"

Vijay stood for a moment, a look of concentration on his face.

He even fakes that for us, Jack thought.

"I am not certain. He is not far, but the direction now is unclear, fuzzy. I suspect he must be either above or below us." Kneeling down, he touched a finger to a dark brown spot on the floor near the steps that led down. "Ah. This is from the cat. Blood."

"Down, then," Jack said.

"I suspect so, yes." He stood up and gestured with his hand toward the stairs. "After you."

Jack motioned with the barrel of his shotgun. "No, after *you*, if you don't mind."

Vijay clucked. "Where is your sense of trust, Jack? After all we've been through." With a shrug, he headed down the steps, with Jack and the others behind him.

"Look there, sir," Lowmack said after they'd reached the bottom.

Jack saw a rectangular opening in the basement wall a dozen yards away that led into a concrete-lined tunnel. "Vijay," he said, "what do you think?"

"Yes," Vijay said, rocking his head side to side, "I believe he is in that direction. Not far ahead, but farther than he was earlier."

"Then let's get him." Jack moved forward toward the tunnel, the muzzle of his AA-12 shotgun leading the way.

"The only problem with this," Lowmack said quietly behind him, "is that if Vijay can sense our hitchhiker, the reverse is true. The hitchhiker will know someone's after him."

"I know. That's a risk we have to take. But there are four of us and one of him, so I'm hoping the odds will be better than even."

Leaning closer, hoping that Vijay couldn't hear, Lowmack whispered, "Are you sure it's just one we're up against and not two?"

"No, I'm not. But if Vijay so much as twitches the wrong way, blast his ass. Now come on, let's do this."

He and Lowmack turned into the tunnel, weapons raised. It was seven feet high and about four feet wide, with pipes and conduits along the walls and ceiling.

"He's moving farther away," Vijay whispered. "I think he is heading in the direction of the lab building."

"Great," Jack hissed as he began to move down the tunnel, as quickly and quietly as he could.

They passed alcoves at periodic intervals that sheltered electrical boxes and communications equipment. They searched them all in hopes of finding Koshka, but every time they came upon one of the dark, damp recesses, all Jack could think of was Sheldon Crane's mutilated body.

He and Lowmack were just about to round a corner in the tunnel when Jack heard something metallic bounce along the floor near his feet.

"*Grenade!*" Lowmack shouted as he shoved Jack backward down the tunnel, right into Vijay.

An automatic weapon opened up at close range, deafeningly loud in the confines of the tunnel, and Lowmack's body danced as 5.56mm slugs tore through him, his body caught in freeze frame motion by the muzzle blasts.

Jack rolled to the floor just before the grenade went off, the blast driving the air from his lungs as white hot shrapnel ricocheted off the concrete around him. Several fragments ripped into his legs and back. He screamed.

Shaking his head clear, he looked up, his ears still ringing. Lowmack's body was crumpled against the wall. Turning the other way, down the tunnel where the Marines and Vijay should be, he saw a chaotic ballet of dark shapes, then the muzzle flashes of an assault rifle as it sent tracers ricocheting through the tunnel.

Someone...something...was leaping and whirling between the two Marines.

Vijay.

One of the Marines open his mouth in a scream just before Vijay rammed his stinger down the man's throat. The second

Marine was fighting, shooting, but something held the muzzle of his weapon in an iron grip, keeping it pointed down the tunnel the way they had come. The Marine let go of his rifle and came at Vijay with his fists. Vijay snatched him and shoved the Marine upward, smashing his head against the low ceiling of the tunnel and breaking the man's neck.

Vijay dropped the lifeless body to the floor, then turned toward Jack. He took one step closer, then another.

Jack raised the muzzle of the shotgun and pulled the trigger.

A stream of Dragon's Breath blasted down the tunnel, and the Vijay-thing dodged to the left, disappearing into the nearest alcove. Before Jack could shift his aim, the harvester fled back the way they had come. Jack fired a few more rounds, but missed.

Vijay might have run away, but the hitchhiker was just around the corner.

Jack was just getting to his feet to pursue the thing when his night vision goggles failed.

***

"Sir? Captain Halvorsen?"

Terje looked up at the Marine who was standing uncertainly at the door to the lunch room off the main lobby of the lab building. It boasted a dozen tables with chairs, along with a row of working microwave ovens and four well-stocked vending machines that the Marines had pried open.

Melissa had been well on her way to beating him at another game of chess. Alexander was lying on the table. Other than knocking over Terje's queen, which Melissa had claimed was a valid move because Alexander was helping her, the big cat had taken little interest in the pieces moving around the black and white squares. Terje had been keeping an eye on him, because the cat seemed to be more tense than he had been since they'd arrived here. His gaze alternated from looking up at the ceiling, as if he could see the harvesters at work with Naomi above them, and out toward the lobby.

Terje frowned as Melissa took one of his bishops with a rook. "Yes, what is it?"

"Sir, please come with me. Right now."

Melissa looked up at Terje, her eyes round with fear.

"You know where Howard and Renee are, right?" Terje asked.

"Yeah, down in the computer center." She'd gone down there earlier to take Renee a few cans of Coke after the Marines had opened up the vending machines.

"Take Alexander and go to them. You should be safe down there. Okay?"

"Okay." She gently gathered up Alexander and followed Terje out of the lunch room. With one last look over her shoulder at him, she disappeared down the stairs to the basement.

Terje turned to the Marine. "What's happening?"

"We've got major shit heading our way, sir," the Marine explained as he quickly strode out the front entry to Lowmack's LAV. "And every which way at the same time."

"What do you mean?"

"He means," Richards said from where he stood near the rear of the LAV, "that you're no longer an active observer. I'm sorry to do this to you, Terje, but I'm going to have to ask you to take temporary command of the Marines."

Terje stared at him, shocked. "But..."

"There aren't any *buts* about it, captain. One of the observation posts up on the rooftops reported a wave of harvesters approaching the building, and we've lost contact with both Jack and Captain Lowmack. As if that wasn't enough, I just got word from Renee that she and Howard heard what might be gunfire somewhere down in the basement level, maybe in one of the service tunnels."

Terje could feel the blood draining from his face. *Melissa.* He had sent her down to the basement, right into harm's way. "What? But I've got to go back and..."

"No." Carl stepped up to him and jabbed a finger against his armored chest. "I'll go back to the basement and sort things out there. Besides sitting my ass behind a desk, that's something that my training and experience qualify me for." He gestured to the LAV and the Marines who watched them with anxious expressions. "Maybe this is a different military from your own, but this is the stuff that *you're* qualified for." He leaned closer and dropped his voice. "If Lowmack and Jack are down or even just incommunicado, you're the only officer we've got left. These people need you, so man up and take charge."

With that, Carl turned and headed toward the entrance at a fast trot. "There is some good news," he called, turning around as he held one of the front doors opened. "Ferris says he found us a plane. You'd better make sure we live long enough to reach it."

Clearing the shocked expression from his face, Terje turned to face the waiting Marines just as the first Claymore mine went off not far beyond the student union.

Behind him, the lights in the building went dark.

NETWORK DOWN

The phone on Naomi's desk rang.

It was Renee. "Carl told me to call you," she said, her words coming in a breathless rush. "Harvesters are coming, so things are about to get interesting again. And in case you wander out into the lobby area, the lights are off. Carl talked to Ferris — and that's some good news, by the way, as I guess he found a plane that might work — and he said that the things have figured out that light at night means people."

"Renee, calm down," Naomi told her. "The only surprise is that there's still a serviceable plane at the airport. We knew the harvesters would probably come sooner than later. It just happened to be sooner."

"I know, but..."

Renee paused.

"Spit it out," Naomi said.

"We've lost contact with Jack," Renee blurted. "Lowmack, too. The Marines haven't been able to raise anyone in the search party, and we heard what sounded like weapons fire somewhere down here in the basement, probably in the tunnels."

Naomi's hand clenched around the phone and she squeezed her eyes shut. "I'll be right down."

"No! No. Carl said for you to keep working. The idiot took Howard to look for Jack and the others."

"Without backup? What about the other Marines?"

"They're all on the defenses except the ones guarding you guys. And listen, they're probably out of touch because of the radios. I can't imagine they work worth crap in those tunnels."

"Sure. I'm sure you're right." Naomi sat back in her chair. She was so tired that it had become something deeper than mere exhaustion, a numbness that had consumed her. The only things keeping her on her feet were a constant stream of coffee and the elation-fueled adrenaline of the work they were doing.

"Okay. Okay," Naomi said, trying to put her worry about him into a mental box. "What about you? Are you all right?"

"Yeah, about to pee myself, but I'm okay. Melissa and Alexander are here with me. I gave the kid one of those automatic shotguns, just in case. The damn things have less recoil than these hand cannons we use."

Naomi had a hard time picturing Melissa even holding one of the AA-12s, let alone firing it. "Does she know how to use it?"

"Point the end toward a harvester and squeeze the trigger." Renee tried to laugh, but it came out as a nervous cough. "What else does she need to know?"

Naomi thought a moment. They had four Marines on guard duty up here. That was probably two more than they really needed. "I'm going to send two of the Marines on guard duty down to keep you safe until the others get back."

"But Carl said..."

"I don't care what Carl said! I'm not going to leave you two down there by yourselves, so just shut up about it." Outside, guns began to fire. "Looks like our company's here. You call me the instant you hear anything, or if you're in trouble. Understand?"

"Yes, mom," Renee said softly. "Be careful."

"You, too. Talk to you soon."

Naomi hung up the phone, then went to the door. Opening it a crack, trying to not let too much light out, she said to the nearest Marine, "Two of you are to head down to the basement and guard the computer center."

"Ma'am, we don't have orders to..."

"I just gave you new orders, Marine," she snapped. "Two civilian women are alone down there, and they need someone to protect them. That would be you. Now get moving."

The Marine licked his lips in uncertainty, then nodded his head. "Yes, ma'am. We're on it."

"Good."

Just before she closed the door, a series of explosions ripped through the darkness beyond the front of the building, shaking the glass. Bright orange flares blossomed in the darkness, and the Marines manning the defenses opened up with everything they had, the muzzle flashes of their weapons and the tracers making a beautiful fireworks display.

"I sure hope that Norwegian guy knows what he's doing," she heard the Marine say before ordering two of his men to the basement.

***

From the commander's position in Lowmack's LAV, Terje watched in horror as the people fleeing from the harvesters pursuing them ran straight into the mined approaches. The warning signs the Marines had put up had been intended to keep stragglers who wandered onto the campus away from the kill zones. No one had anticipated a panicked stampede in the dark.

One Claymore mine went off as someone in the approaching crowd stepped on the tripwire, then half a dozen more mines exploded across the forward part of the perimeter. Thousands of metal balls scythed through the people in the lead, cutting them to ribbons.

The green image in his night vision goggles flared over and over as the moving mass of people and creatures continued to press forward, setting off successive waves of mines as they entered the main kill zone.

"There was nothing you could have done, sir," the gunner said in a wooden voice. "Even if they'd made it to the fence, we couldn't have brought them inside with that pack of monsters right behind them."

Feeling like his tongue was a dead lump of flesh in his mouth, Terje keyed his mic to the unit channel and said, "Open fire."

Once again, just as they had so many times earlier on this God-forsaken night, the LAVs spat death and destruction into the darkness, raking the harvesters with machine gun and cannon fire. Marines hurled white phosphorous grenades into the midst of writhing, snarling creatures, sending up gobbets of white-hot death that rained down on the enemy.

The courtyard area was transformed into a blazing inferno. Terje cringed at the heat on his exposed face as he stood up in the commander's hatch, firing with the top-mounted 7.62mm machine gun.

He bared his teeth as his hands swept the muzzle of his weapon back and forth, sending tracers into the maelstrom. The growl that began at the back of his throat became a scream of rage.

"Sir!" He heard a voice through his headset over the hammering of the machine gun. It was the gunner, shouting at him. "*Sir!* You can stop shooting now!"

Terje was the only one still firing. He let go the trigger and his weapon fell silent.

Taking a shuddering breath, Terje keyed his mic. "All units, cease fire."

One by one, the vehicle commanders and squad leaders checked in. They hadn't suffered a single casualty.

"When the flames die down," he ordered, "I want a sweep for any possible survivors and to replace the mines. In the meantime, get your ammunition topped off so we'll be ready to send the next batch of harvesters to hell."

He collapsed down into the turret, sitting on the commander's seat to escape the raging furnace beyond the wire outside.

The gunner was grinning at him. "Fuckin'-A, sir," the Marine said. "Fuckin'-A."

***

"If anybody ever told me that I'd be hunting monsters in a dark tunnel with a billionaire," Carl muttered as he made his way forward through the service tunnel, "I would've told them they were nuts."

"And if someone ever told me that I'd be doing something as stupid as this in company with a bad-tempered senior FBI agent, I'd have fired him," Howard replied.

Carl's mouth cracked upward into a grin. He was glad he was facing away from Howard. Showing that he had the slightest sense of humor could damage his reputation.

As they approached an intersection, he knelt down.

"Which way?" Howard asked.

"Left. The smell of gunpowder's definitely stronger that way."

"March to the smell of the guns. That's a new one."

"Come on," Carl said. "And watch behind us. I don't want to get shot in the ass like Renee."

"I'm sure it would do wonders for your disposition."

"Smart ass. Let's go."

Carl led the way down the tunnel to the left, their footsteps echoing off the stark walls. His imagination was running wild now, with spectral shapes writhing and crawling in every shadow in the green world of the night vision goggles. His respiration and heart rate jumped, and he had to stop for a moment.

He jumped when he felt a hand on his shoulder.

"You okay?" Howard asked.

"Piss off. Of course I'm okay. I thought I heard something."

"You're a lousy liar."

Carl could almost hear the bemused grin in the man's voice. He mouthed an obscenity as he started moving forward again toward a bend in the tunnel to the right.

As they turned the corner, Carl saw a body, a Marine. "It's Lowmack."

"Damn," Howard whispered.

Carl swung low and fast around the corner where Lowmack's body lay, his finger tense on the trigger. A few feet away lay two more dead Marines. "Cover me."

"Go," Howard said, sweeping the tunnel with his weapon while Carl crept up beside the Marines.

"They weren't killed with weapons fire," Carl told him after a quick examination of the bodies. "These two were killed by a harvester. Stinger wounds."

"Our friendly neighborhood hitchhiker must have pulled a fast one," Howard murmured.

"Maybe. And maybe not." Standing up, he continued down the tunnel. Up ahead he could see the opening to an alcove on the left. "Now we just have to find Jack and Vijay."

"You won't find Vijay down here."

Both men stopped at the hoarse voice that came from the dark recess of the alcove. The momentary silence that followed was broken by a plaintive meow as Jack staggered out, his shotgun cradled in one arm, Koshka in the other.

"The bastard killed those two Marines, then ran," Jack told them.

"Christ, Jack!" Carl was doubly relieved that his friend was alive and that Koshka was with him. "Are you all right?"

"I took some shrapnel in my legs. It hurts like hell, but none of the fragments are very deep. What's going on topside?"

Carl grimaced. "Turning on the lights in the building foyer was like hanging out a *Come and Eat* sign. Your buddy from Norway is up there dishing out some humble pie to our bug-eyed friends. I hope."

Jack cocked his head, listening, as the three turned back toward the lab building basement. "Sounds like it." Then he stopped. "Wait. You guys didn't nail the hitchhiker, did you?"

Carl shook his head. "We didn't see anything or anyone until we found Lowmack's body. We just figured he went out that way." He pointed down the length of tunnel past the alcove where Jack had been hiding.

"No, Vijay went that way, but not the hitchhiker." Jack broke into a fast limp toward the lab building. "Shit! He was somewhere over here when we got ambushed. I holed up in the alcove back there after my night vision goggles died. But he must have doubled back this way, because he didn't come past me."

"We went left at the T-junction leading out of the lab," Howard mused. "He must have gone to the right before we got there and hid around the next corner."

"And only Renee and Melissa are in the basement," Carl said through gritted teeth.

The three men ran faster.

***

Renee glanced at the ceiling at the sound of the firing outside.

"It's okay," she heard Melissa say. The girl was sitting in the chair next to her, with Alexander in her lap. "Terje won't let them through."

"Don't tell me you've got a crush on him?"

Melissa's mouth dropped open. "I do not!"

Renee began to laugh, then cringed as a rippling series of muffled booms echoed through the rooms, followed by what sounded like raindrops the size of bowling balls hammering against a tin roof. "Thor, God of Thunder," she murmured as the firing outside rose to a fever pitch. She looked back at Melissa. "Thor. Did you know that was the name of my first networked computer?"

"How long ago was that? Did it have a color monitor, or one of those icky green ones?"

Renee scowled at her. "Don't go there, smartypants." She leaned forward on the desk, resting her chin on her folded hands. "All I want to do is sleep, but I've had so much coffee I'll be peeing for a week." She looked at the computer screen, trying to somehow divine what Naomi was doing upstairs from the information fed through the network to and from the various computers and lab equipment upstairs. But all she could really understand was that there was a hell of a lot going on. "God, I wish I was a tenth as smart as she is."

"Naomi?"

"Yeah." Renee grinned. "Talk about an overachiever."

"I wish I was as pretty as she was."

"You're beautiful, hon," Renee told her. "Don't ever let anyone tell you different. That stuff on your skin doesn't define you."

Melissa looked doubtful. "It did before. Everyone thought I was a mutated freak. And I'm only here now and not dead in Chicago because of it. Jack wouldn't have come for me, otherwise, would he?"

"I guess not. But in that case, give thanks for it. Believe it or not, sometimes crappy stuff that happens to us in life is for a good reason. We just don't know it at the time."

Before Melissa could say anything, Alexander tensed. With a deep growl in his throat, he stood up and jumped the short distance from Melissa's lap to Renee's desk, taking up a position right in front of the two monitors and blocking Renee's view.

Rather than scolding him or trying to push him out of the way, Renee reached down and picked up her shotgun. "Get your gun, kid," she said, "and go over there and duck down behind that cabinet."

"But..."

"Do it!"

As Melissa did as she was told, Renee knelt down behind the almost nonexistent cover of the open-bottomed workstation, her eyes following Alexander's rapt gaze toward the access door to the service tunnels. She pointed the shotgun in the same direction, propping the weapon's bulky magazine on the desktop.

Alexander's growl deepened, and he crouched down low.

"I'm scared," Melissa whispered.

"Just keep your head, and don't shoot unless I'm down. I don't want to get shot in the ass again."

"Okay."

Gripping the shotgun tighter, Renee focused her attention on the tunnel, trying to ignore the sound of Melissa's teeth chattering.

"Ma'am, are you okay?"

Renee spun around at the voice. Two Marines drew up short, staring down the barrel of her shotgun.

"Jesus!" She lowered the weapon. "I just about killed you, you idiots! What are you..."

"*Renee!*"

Renee spun back around to see a Marine tumble through the door from the tunnel.

He looked at her with wild eyes. "*It's right behind me!*"

The two Marines raised their weapons, taking aim at the tunnel door as their comrade staggered clear, limping badly.

Turning back around, Renee looked at the tunnel, then at Alexander. The big cat opened his mouth and hissed.

At the limping Marine.

Oh, no. That was all she had time to think before the Marine impostor whipped up his assault rifle, inhumanly fast, and opened fire.

Tracer rounds whizzed over her head and she ducked down, grabbing Alexander by one of his rear legs to pull him out of the line of fire.

Caught by surprise, the two Marines were knocked backward by the bullets that struck armor and flesh. One of them reflexively squeezed the trigger of his weapon and held it as he went down, shooting half a magazine into the racks of precious computer equipment around them.

Then the harvester turned his weapon on Renee's workstation. The computer monitor and phone were blasted into pieces. One of the tracer rounds grazed her hair, and she could smell the acrid stench of a few strands burning as she dove to the floor.

Something roared and the room was bathed in a searing white light. Then again. And again.

The harvester screeched and stopped firing.

Getting up on her knees, Renee peered out from under the workstation, through the legs, to see the harvester slumping to the floor, the malleable flesh of its face and chest burning furiously. Turning around, she saw Melissa standing behind the cabinet where Renee had told her to hide. She was holding her AA-12 shotgun, which still had smoke drifting up from the muzzle.

"Jesus Christ, kid," Renee croaked. "You can have as much dessert as you want tonight."

"Hold your fire!"

The two turned back to the tunnel, where a familiar bald head was peeking out. "It's okay, hon," Renee said to Melissa. "Put that thing down. Carl gets very upset when people shoot at him."

Nodding, Melissa did as Renee asked. Then the girl doubled over and vomited on the floor.

"My God," Howard said as he and Carl entered the room. "Are you all right?"

"A little shaken up, but past that, yeah, we're fine," Renee answered.

Tossing all decorum aside, Carl pulled her into a tight embrace and held her. He didn't say anything, just held her.

At their feet, Alexander meowed and strutted over to the third person to enter the room.

"Jack!" Melissa shouted. Then she saw the white fluffy shape Jack held to his chest. "Koshka!" Running to Jack, she threw his arms around him while burying her face in Koshka's fur.

"Annie Oakley here blasted your hitchhiker to pieces," Renee said, finally pulling away from Carl, who looked at Melissa, then at the burning body of the harvester. "We're going to send her out to do your dirty work next time, boys."

"I'm not going to complain," Howard said as he took a fire extinguisher off the wall and put out the flames. "But look at this place. What a mess."

The power lights on most of the server towers were dark. Half of the server boxes had holes in them as big as Renee's index finger, or had their cases blasted to bits. A few threw sparks and smoke into the air.

She caught Melissa's look of horror and guilt. "It wasn't you, hon," she told the girl. "The damage isn't from your shotgun. Most of it was fire from the harvester's gun, and the rest from one of the Marines who went down. You did good, understand?"

"Here," Jack said, "why don't you look after her."

Nodding vigorously, Melissa took Koshka from Jack and held her close before kneeling down to show her to Alexander, who sniffed at his companion.

Looking around at the devastated electronics, Jack leaned against one of the server racks and asked, "Any chance this can be fixed?"

Renee and Howard exchanged a look before the billionaire said, "It would take us days to fix this, even assuming we could get spares for everything."

"Then I guess we'd better pray that Naomi got what she needed from the network," Carl said grimly, tossing aside the blackened remains of a hard drive he'd picked up from the floor, "because we don't have days. We'll be lucky if we have hours before we're overwhelmed here or the harvesters find Ferris at the airport."

Jack winced and blew out a breath. "Great. Just great."

BETRAYAL

Naomi looked up from monitoring one of the dozens of items of lab equipment as the door opened and Carl stepped into the room. Two Marines came in with him, weapons at the ready.

"Naomi, a word please," Carl said.

She could tell he was tense, and his eyes flitted over the harvesters. They were, for the moment, easy to spot: Naomi had given them all blue lab coats. The humans wore white.

"Did you find Jack?" She got up and hurried over, and Carl ushered her out the door onto the landing that overlooked the now-darkened foyer. It was a disorienting experience, looking out from this high up into the darkness below. "Is he all right? And when is the network coming back up?"

"Come with me." He took her by the arm and led her to the stair well. The two Marines he'd brought with him stayed inside the lab.

"Carl, what is it?" His behavior was more than odd. He was spooking her.

He remained silent until they reached the lunch room on the ground floor. Opening the door, he quickly ushered her in before closing it behind them to minimize the light spillage.

"Jack!" Naomi exclaimed.

"Hey." He gave her a quick hug, then hissed as the Marine corpsman put some antiseptic on one of the shrapnel wounds in his legs before dressing it with gauze.

As a doctor herself, Naomi surveyed the man's work with a critical eye, nodding to herself in approval. Then, to Jack, she said, "God, what happened to you?"

"I had an argument with a grenade and lost, as usual."

"I've got good news and bad news," Carl said, interrupting. "I'm going to give you the good news first. Melissa?"

Naomi turned around to find Melissa coming over with a furry friend in her arms. "Koshka!" Naomi picked the cat up gently and held her.

Koshka meowed at the indignity of it all.

"Now I've got some bad news," Carl went on grimly. "Vijay turned on us and escaped."

"*What?*"

"We were ambushed by the hitchhiker," Jack told her, "and just as the bastard took down Lowmack, Vijay attacked the other two Marines. I'm not sure, but I think the only reason he didn't kill me is that he might have been more afraid of the other harvester. He turned and ran."

"My God. Where did he go?"

"We don't know," Carl said. "And that's what bothers me the most. He knows everything, Naomi. Where we are, what we're doing, our strengths and weaknesses. If he hooks up with another group like the one that wiped out SEAL-2 and brings them here, we're finished. The other bad news," he went on, "you already know about. The computer network is screwed. Half the servers were blasted to bits in the firefight with the hitchhiker. Renee and Howard say it would be days before they could get it back up again, and we don't have that kind of time." He stared at her with a questioning look in his eyes. "The question is, where does that leave us?"

"We don't really need it now," she said. "It would make certain things easier, but we're past the analytic and development stage. We had already programmed the equipment before the network died, and the machines can run in local mode."

Carl leaned forward slightly. "So you did it? You created the weapon?"

"We've prototyped it and are replicating it now."

"You don't sound too happy about it," Jack said. "I thought you'd be jumping for joy."

"We won't know for sure that it will work until we can test it."

Carl cocked his head. "And when will that be?"

"The first cultures should be done soon, assuming nothing goes wrong upstairs."

Jack frowned. "And how are you planning to test it?"

"On the harvesters in the lab."

"What if you need them again?" Everyone turned as Terje stepped into the room, quickly pulling the door closed behind him. Like the rest of them, he looked as if he'd aged a decade in the last twenty-four hours, and a hundred years in the last week. He collapsed into a chair and set his helmet on the table. He gave Melissa a wan smile as she handed him a cold drink from one of the vending machines.

"I don't think we will," Naomi said. "The culture that's incubating in the lab will either work or it won't. I don't think we're going to have time for another run at this."

"If their part in this is over," Carl said, "then it's time we got rid of them."

Naomi shook her head. "Carl, we should let them go after they're infected. They can help spread the virus, and it would be a perfect field test to make sure it works."

"I'm sorry, but there's no way I'm letting those things walk out of the lab alive. We've already got Vijay on the loose, and I'm not going to let any more out. I'm sure we can figure out a way to spread the virus ourselves once we get out of here." He looked at Jack. "Let's go put an end to this."

***

Zohreh smiled at the lab technician, then shyly averted her eyes. He was a middle aged man, as skilled at his craft as he was naive about women. The memories the harvester had taken from Zohreh were filled with such men. In their eyes, she was extremely attractive and highly desirable. Even in the oppressive culture of modern-day Iran, men remained men. A flutter of the eye lids, an inviting smile, a tilt of the hips or a turn of her chest to accentuate her ample breasts never failed to affect them. Men like him tended to be single, because their outward appearance and mannerisms were not highly desirable by women. To be favored with so much as a smile from a beauty such as she made such men stammer and act the fool. She saw the paradox, of course: such men knew they would never possess a beautiful woman, yet they would trip over themselves to please her just the same.

This one was no different from the others the ghost of the human woman's memories had known. He had watched her since she had arrived at SEAL-2, and she had stoked the fire of attraction while barely speaking a word to him, for she had been assigned to a different section of the human-harvester team. She had done the same with the other men. Not all were quite so foolish as this one, but it was easy for her to gain their attention. That was all that mattered.

With another smile at the man, she glanced around the room, as if wistfully looking for someone to talk to, to ease her boredom. With the computer network down and the synthesis work on the prototype virus completed, there was little for any of them to do now other than wait for the incubators to do their work, replicating the virus into a quantity that they could use.

That time had come.

Pushing back from her workstation, Zohreh stood up with a tired sigh. Looking at the two Marines, who were only a few feet away, she let the hint of a smile grace her lips as she put her hands on her hips and leaned back into a languid stretch, her breasts straining against the blouse beneath her unbuttoned blue lab coat.

With their attention firmly riveted to her chest, she pitched herself forward as the stinger exploded from her blouse, propelled by the tightly coiled umbilical in her thorax. It speared the throat of the Marine on the left side of the door, while the stinger from the harvester working beside her sank into the other Marine's left eye.

The human scientists in the room were momentarily paralyzed with shock as the Marines' twitching bodies slid to the floor.

The harvesters wasted no time. In a frenzy of thrusting stingers, the humans died.

Zohreh watched the demise of the lab technician who'd been so enamored with her. His mouth opened and closed like that of a fish, his body unable to do anything more after a stinger had severed the spine in his neck. The look in his eyes was one of hurt, of surprise. Then he lost all expression as death took him and his muscles relaxed, his gaze still fixed on her.

Turning away, Zohreh moved to one of the two Marines and began stripping him of his uniform and equipment. One of her companions did the same to the second Marine. The other three harvesters took the clothes from the bodies of the lab technicians while commanding the malleable flesh of their bodies to transform, to take on the appearance of their victims.

Quickly donning the Marine uniform over her newly transfigured body, Zohreh became Private First Class Gabriel Woodson, a young African-American male.

When finished with their transformation, they dragged away the bodies and stacked them behind some lab equipment in a corner of the room, away from direct view from the doorway.

An electronic chime sounded from the biological safety cabinet that housed the incubator that had been nurturing the first batch of the cultured virus. The thing that was now Woodson carefully removed one of the trays of culture flasks and extracted some of the liquid with a dropper.

Turning around, Woodson found his five companions standing in a row.

Without a word, Woodson went to his companions and put a drop of the clear liquid on their faux tongues, then gave himself a dose. "This will have little effect on us," he/it said, "as we have already reached maturity. But we will be able to spread the change to others of our kind."

They quickly transferred some of the virus culture from the flask to smaller vials they could carry with them. Woodson had briefly considered destroying the rest of the batch and the equipment, but in the end decided not to. More of the virus here simply meant a greater likelihood of more of her kind being reborn.

"Someone is coming," said the harvester mimicking the other Marine, who had gone to stand watch at the door.

The others took their places at the workstations nearest the door, prepared to play their part in the final act of this farcical play. Heavy footsteps could be heard outside in the hall mezzanine. They stopped just outside.

"Let them come," she said, tightening her grip on her assault rifle. "Let them come."

ESCAPE

Naomi stood outside the lab, with Jack, Terje, and six Marines behind her.

"Remember, we've got friendlies in there," Naomi warned. She reached for the door handle.

"Oh, no you don't," Jack whispered, gently moving her to the side. To the Marines, he said, "Go."

The first two Marines opened the door and stepped through, followed by Jack, Terje, and then Naomi. The other four Marines waited outside.

They found the two Marine guards still inside the door, and four lab technicians were looking up from their work stations.

She saw white lab coats, but no blue ones. *The harvesters were gone.*

Before she could shout a warning, the two harvesters dressed as Marines opened fire, killing the pair of Marines who'd come in with her. She caught a fleeting glimpse of the other harvesters leaping over their desks toward the door before a hard shove from Jack sent her tumbling backward.

"*Open fire!*" Jack's shout was lost in a cacophony of gunshots and screeching as the harvesters mobbed the door. Jack fired a burst from his weapon, then grabbed Terje by the rear of his belt and hauled him out onto the mezzanine.

Once they were clear, the Marines outside the lab opened fire, shooting through the doorway and the wall. They brought down one harvester, then another, which exploded into flame barely two feet from where Naomi was lying on the floor.

She got up on her hands and knees and tried to crawl away, hoping to find a small eddy in the chaos swirling about her, but was knocked flat by a Marine who tripped over her as he backpedaled away from the door. Still firing, he hit the wall overlooking the lobby below just as bullets struck his chest armor, blasting him backward over the railing. Naomi grabbed for his feet, but couldn't hold him. With a terrified scream, he fell.

Drawing her Desert Eagle, she got to her knees and turned back toward the fight, but in the glare of the flames she wasn't sure who was friend and who was foe.

Jack slammed to the floor beside her. His eyes were open, staring toward the ceiling, as he fought for breath.

As she reached for him, someone scooped her up from the floor. It was one of the Marines who'd been posted inside the lab. Woodson. A harvester.

"Fuck you!" She jammed the muzzle of the gun against the thing's chest, but before she could squeeze the trigger, she was weightless, falling into space.

Still clutching her in its arms, the harvester had leaped over the wall overlooking the lobby three stories below.

***

With the computer center destroyed, there was nothing left for Howard Morgan to do in the basement. The only piece of equipment they bothered trying to salvage was the storage unit Renee had brought from SEAL-2, which, for what it might be worth, hadn't been damaged in the firefight.

After escorting her and Melissa up to the lunch room, he decided to pay Naomi a visit. He'd never been a lab rat, of course, but having owned a multi-billion dollar pharmaceutical company had given him the opportunity to rattle a test tube or two. If nothing else, he could watch a display or mop up any coffee spills, or just sit there and keep an eye on the harvesters, shotgun in hand. And if Naomi shooed him out as a nuisance, he'd go stand watch with the Marines. He wasn't a military man, but he could shoot as well as any of them.

The only thing he didn't want was to do nothing. He was a man who'd always enjoyed his leisure time, but otherwise needed to feel, and be, productive, to make a contribution. That was one of the traits that had helped him to become a wealthy man, and he wasn't about to abandon that philosophy now.

He was halfway up the stairs to the second floor when he heard gunfire coming from above.

Taking the steps two at a time, he just made it to the third floor landing when the door to the mezzanine on that level burst open. A Marine with an unconscious woman slung over his shoulder charged onto the landing.

It took him a heartbeat to realize the woman was Naomi, and the Marine had to be a harvester. No one had been on this floor since the Marines had first cleared it.

As he tried to raise the shotgun, the Marine slammed into him, knocking him back against the far wall. Howard's right elbow cracked against the concrete, and he lost his grip on his weapon as the thing turned for the stairs heading down.

Ignoring the pain in his arm, he rebounded from the wall like a boxer coming off the ropes. Wrapping his arms around Naomi, he tried to wrestle her off the thing's shoulder.

It was a brief, savage tug of war before the harvester whirled around and used Howard's momentum against him, pushing him up against the wall with Naomi's body pinned between them.

Something slashed across Howard's abdomen, just below the lower edge of the body armor. He lost control of his core muscles and felt a sharp tugging sensation in his belly. His legs collapsed under him, and he slumped to the floor as a warm, wet gush flooded over his lower body.

The thing said nothing as it again tossed Naomi over its shoulder and fled down the stairwell.

Howard touched his hand to his belly and recoiled at the feel of something not unlike a string of sausages, only warm and slick, smelling of blood.

"Oh, no," he whispered as the pain finally hit.

***

Jack blinked his eyes, trying to clear them of the afterimages of one of the harvesters exploding into flame. He was on his back, gasping for air like a kid who'd fallen backwards off a swing to slam into the ground.

Terje's face appeared above him. One side of his face had second degree burns and a deep gash that ran from the temple down to his jaw. Blood was running freely down his neck. "Jack! Are you hurt?"

"No," he wheezed as Terje helped him up. "Got the wind... knocked out of me." One glance around told him what he'd most feared. Four of the six Marines were down. They'd killed two of the harvesters, but the other four escaped. "Naomi?"

"One of them grabbed her and jumped over the wall."

"Jesus." His heart in his throat, he looked down, expecting to see her and the harvester splattered against the floor.

Instead, he caught sight of a figure in a Marine uniform tearing down the third floor mezzanine, Naomi's body draped over its shoulder. The mezzanine hallways were designed like ascending terraces. The harvester had only jumped ten feet, instead of forty.

Jack shouted at the Marines downstairs, but they couldn't hear him over the shouts and screams of the harvesters pretending to be terrified lab technicians who'd just burst from the first floor stairwell. They were pointing up at the burning lab.

Pointing up at him.

"All units, all units," Jack called over his radio. "Those lab technicians are the harvesters! Shoot them!"

One of the two surviving Marines opened fire over the mezzanine wall at the lab-coated harvesters down below.

The Marines downstairs, thinking they were under attack, returned fire.

Everyone dove for the floor as bullets blasted hunks of drywall out of the mezzanine wall.

"This is Jack Dawson! Cease fire! I say again, *cease fire!*"

After a moment, the gunfire from downstairs stopped.

Carl's voice come on the radio. "Dawson! You and the others come down with your weapons in the air so we can verify you."

"Verify the goddamn lab techs and the harvester who's making off with Naomi!"

"What?"

"They're harvesters, goddammit!"

The lobby lit up with a flash as a grenade went off, then another, followed by more screams.

Jack popped his head up long enough to see that more people were down. In the darkness he couldn't tell who.

"Jack!" Terje was pointing at the lab, which was now burning fiercely from the dead harvesters. "The virus!"

"You and the Marines put out that fire! I'm going after Naomi!"

"Understood!" With a few quick instructions to the two surviving Marines, Terje led them down the hall to find fire extinguishers.

Getting to his feet, Jack ducked low in case any of the Marines downstairs were still trigger happy and ran as fast as he could for the stairwell.

He found Howard slumped against the wall of the third floor landing in a pool of his own blood. He'd been eviscerated. His intestines had slipped from a slash all the way across his abdomen, and now lay coiled, glistening, in his lap. "Medic!" Jack's shout echoed in the stairwell shaft as he knelt down beside the billionaire. "*Medic!*"

"Save...your breath," Howard rasped. "I saw...Naomi. Tried to stop...harvester." He took Jack's arm in a surprisingly powerful grip. "Save...her."

"Don't worry about that," Jack said. "Just hang on!"

The billionaire tried to smile, shaking his head slowly. Then his grip weakened and his hand fell away.

"Fuck," Jack hissed as he gently closed Howard's eyes.

Getting back to his feet, he ran the rest of the way down the stairs. As he reached the bottom, he found Carl and a team of Marines waiting for him, weapons pointed at Jack's chest.

Without a word, Jack grabbed a lighter from his pocket, flicked the flame into existence, and touched the orange tip of the flickering light to the skin of his wrist.

With a sigh of relief, Carl lowered his weapon, and the Marines followed suit.

"We've been had," Carl said. "They..."

More shouts and gunshots came from outside, followed by the sound of a Humvee starting up.

"Cease fire!" Jack shouted into his mic. "Naomi Perrault was taken hostage by the harvesters. Hold your fire, damn you! Let them go!"

The guns went silent. All Jack could hear now were moans of pain, the crackling of the fire upstairs, and the sound of the Humvee crashing through the concertina wire fence.

"They took her," Jack rasped. "Goddamn them, one of them took Naomi, and they killed Howard and the people in the lab."

"Oh, God, no." Carl put his hand on Jack's shoulder. "Dammit! I let the bastard walk right past me! I thought he was taking Naomi to safety."

"Forget it. I would have thought the same thing, and you've got other things to worry about. You need to get everyone packed up and heading to the airport." He gave Carl a hard look that brooked no argument. "I'm going after her."

"Why did they take her?"

Jack turned to find Melissa standing beside him, holding Alexander. Behind her was Renee, her face streaked with tears. She was holding Koshka. "Oh, God, Jack," she choked. "I'm so sorry. And Howard. Poor Howard."

The lights came up, and Jack saw that the floor was slick with blood. Three more Marines had died and two were badly wounded, already being tended by the corpsman and another Marine.

"I think they want her knowledge," Jack said, answering Melissa's question.

"They're going to eat her head."

"Not if I can help it. Sergeant," he called to the senior surviving Marine. "I need a driver and gunner for one of the LAVs. Now."

"Aye, sir!" He got on the radio and called two Marines, telling them to get Lowmack's old LAV cranked up and ready.

To Renee, Jack said, "You've got to get upstairs and find the virus samples, if any survived. We don't have any idea..."

"I found them." They turned to see Terje emerging from the stairwell with the two other Marines from upstairs. He held a styrofoam cooler that was big enough to fit two six-packs.

Carl lifted the lid to see six culture flasks, carefully entombed in bubble wrap.

"These were sitting on a tray near one of the machines at the back of the lab. One of them was open, and a dropper was beside it."

"That's the virus," Renee confirmed, looking into the box. "There was a dropper? They must have already dosed themselves with it. God, I hope this stuff works."

"And I hope it doesn't kill us instead of them," Carl said, warily eyeing the flasks.

"If it's harmful to us, we're already in the shitter," Renee said. "If they left one of these open up there, it's airborne. We've all been exposed."

"The LAV's ready, sir," the Marine sergeant said to Jack.

Terje grabbed Jack's arm. "I'm coming with you. Don't even try to argue about it."

Jack managed a grim smile. "I wasn't planning on it."

Melissa tugged on his sleeve. "I am, too. So is Alexander."

"No," Jack told her. "I'm sorry, honey, but there's no way. It's..."

"Too dangerous?" She looked at him with an expression that he could have sworn she learned from Naomi, who used it when Jack said something she found particularly obtuse. Alexander gave him the same sort of look, albeit in his feline way, all the time. "Nowhere and no one is safe. If we have to go out, and we all do now, I'd rather go with you. Naomi's my friend, too. Besides, you'll need Alexander, and I can take care of him in the LAV. Renee can take Koshka with the others."

"The kid's right," Carl told him. "Stop screwing around and get going. We'll meet you at the airport."

"Okay," Jack said. "Let's move."

"Good luck, Dawson," Carl called after him.

"You, too!"

As Jack, Terje, and Melissa ran for the waiting LAV, Jack radioed the Marines in the observation posts, asking if they had a visual on the escaping Humvees.

"Roger, sir," one of the observers reported. "They made a beeline through the courtyard where the mines hadn't been replaced yet and are headed for the main gate."

Jack clambered up into the commander's seat in the turret, while Terje got Melissa situated in the troop compartment before slamming the rear hatches shut.

"Secure!" Terje called.

"Driver, head for the main gate, and step on it."

"Yes, sir!"

As the big vehicle roared forward, grinding over the crumpled remains of the concertina and churning up the grass through the safe zone in the mine field, the observer reported in again. "Sir, that Humvee turned east on Rokeby Road toward US-77. We can see the intersection from here, but if they go very far north or south from there, we'll lose sight of them."

"Driver, head east on the main road."

"Will do, sir, but you know we're not going to be able to catch them in this thing, right? The Humvee's not a Lamborghini, but it's faster than an LAV."

"I'm hoping we'll make better time through all the abandoned cars," Jack said. "Now step on it!"

***

While Carl and Terje had the Marines packing up to leave, Renee busied herself with her own creation. She had rummaged around in the utility closets and managed to find a gallon pump sprayer, the kind used to spray weed or bug killer. She didn't smell any chemical odors when she opened it, and it looked brand new. After rinsing it out a few times with alcohol and flushing it with water, she filled it with distilled water and then added half the contents of one of the virus beakers. After capping the virus container and returning it to the styrofoam cooler, she put the pump cap on the sprayer and gently swirled the water around to mix it.

She had no idea if the damn thing would work or if she'd just wasted half a beaker of virus culture, but it made her feel better and had given her something to do. She hated just being excess baggage for Carl and the others. Having been shot in the ass, she couldn't even lift a box of MREs.

Pumping up the sprayer had her sweating with effort. "I'd much rather be tapping on my keyboard," she gasped.

Unfortunately, in a world where electricity had pretty much gone the way of the dodo bird, she'd become a dinosaur. *Reneeasaurus Rex*. All the things she'd taken for granted, all the things that let her express her own form of genius, were gone. Not just the big things like the Internet, but the little things like her refrigerator, which had a display that told her what today's weather would be while reassuring her that the pasta leftovers from the previous night were being maintained at a constant thirty-five degrees. Or the washer and dryer that sent a message to her smart phone when they were done so she could make Carl take out the clothes.

All that was gone now, replaced by a stupid pump sprayer filled up with a high-tech biological concoction that she didn't fully understand.

Carl poked his head into the lunch room where she'd been working. "If you're done screwing around with that thing," Carl said, "it's time for us to leave."

PURSUIT

When Naomi regained consciousness, she was on the floor of a Humvee with someone's boot on her neck. The vehicle swerved and swayed, and her head banged against the driver's seat mountings as the Humvee ran into something with a shriek of grinding metal before moving on.

Looking up as far as she could without turning her head, she saw one of the harvesters, in native form, poised in the machine gun position just above her. That explained the stench that overwhelmed the smells of oil and gunpowder residue.

She blinked and the harvester was gone. It had jumped overboard.

Two harvesters remained in the Humvee, the driver and the one holding her down.

Naomi cried out as the vehicle struck an animal or person, she couldn't see which, that bounced up over the hood and slammed into the windshield before sliding off to one side. Blood, the crimson a vivid black in the pre-dawn light, spattered over the passenger side of the glass.

"So you're awake," the voice of a young man said from above her. "Good."

Naomi struggled, trying to free herself from the boot, but the harvester pressed down harder. She screamed as the thing nearly broke her neck. "Let me go, damn you!"

The harvester lifted its foot. A hand yanked her up and shoved her into the seat beside the harvester.

When she turned to look at him, she sucked in her breath as the face and shape of the body beneath the Marine uniform transformed.

"Zohreh," Naomi whispered.

The thing smiled. "If it pleases you."

Naomi turned away, craning her head to try and get a look in the side mirror.

"No one is coming after you," Zohreh said. "We killed more of your people in the lobby of the building. And with some luck, we might even have killed Jack outside the lab."

Naomi whirled around, slamming the palm of her free hand into the harvester's face, snapping Zohreh's head back. She managed to wrench her arm free from the harvester's grip before lunging over the driver's shoulder to grab the wheel.

Zohreh sank her hands into Naomi's hair and pulled. Naomi clung to the wheel, fighting the harvester mimicking Carly Walker for control of the Humvee.

The vehicle's tires screeched as it swerved back and forth across the highway. It slammed into the side of a car. The impact sent Naomi flying into the back seat to land on top of Zohreh.

Naomi slammed her elbows into the thing, but even had it been a human, her blows would have been futile against the body armor Zohreh was wearing.

With the sound of rending metal and a shout of surprise from the driver, Naomi found herself weightless. The pre-dawn world spun around and around as the Humvee flipped over the side of the concrete barrier of the bridge that spanned a gully just south of the exit for 55W.

Tumbling about the cabin, she grappled with the harvester until the Humvee slammed into the ground below. It rolled over three times before finally coming to rest among a stand of trees.

***

Naomi came to with a start. Lying face down, her mouth was filled with dirt, dry leaves, and blood. With a cough that sent a flaming lance through the right side of her rib cage, she tried to spit it out, but only managed to send a warm, gritty ooze running down her cheek.

With a groan of pain, she tried to roll over, but gave up when more searing pain shot up her right leg. Twisting her head, she saw that the wreckage of the Humvee was resting on her calf, midway to the knee. Blood was soaking her pant leg, and she felt faint.

"I give you credit, Naomi. You're very hard to kill."

She looked up to see Zohreh standing over her. Carly was behind her, standing near the top of the slope by the highway. Scrapes and chunks of soil had been gouged into the ground where the Humvee had tumbled down. Clawing at the ground with her hands, Naomi kicked with her free leg to free herself, but gave up as a spear of agony shot up her broken leg.

"You need not worry about me biting your head off," the creature said with a smile. "We have what we need, and I am not hungry. But they are." She nodded toward the trees, where a larvae the size of a tractor trailer rig oozed its way through the trees in their direction. The woods were filled with rustling and popping sounds made by more larvae, large and small. Some were only a few yards away. "A great swarm of our kind is gathering nearby, moving northwest out of the city. They will be the first of our true progeny."

"They'll kill you."

"They will try. But our intellect gives us a great advantage." She/it shrugged. "And even if we die, we will have spread a new beginning among dozens, perhaps hundreds or thousands of them." She held out a pouch that held several vials.

"You took samples of the virus," Naomi whispered.

Zohreh nodded. "With the gift we will give them, they will rise above the chaos intended by our creators and take this world from what few of your kind may remain."

The harvester knelt down beside her, running a hand through Naomi's hair. Then the hand moved down to Naomi's neck, the fingers wrapping around it, exerting gentle pressure.

"I could give you mercy if you begged for it," Zohreh whispered.

"Go to hell," Naomi rasped.

"I expected no less from you." Zohreh stood up. "This is goodbye, then." The harvester made its way up the slope to join the Carly-thing. After shedding their human attire, they assumed their natural forms and disappeared over the ridge onto the highway.

Naomi kept her eyes on the sky, trying to focus on the beauty of the wisps of cloud, made red and gold by the rising sun as the larvae behind her drew steadily closer.

***

"There's no sight of them, sir." The gunner had just made a full three hundred and sixty degree sweep of the area with the LAV's main sights while Jack and Terje looked for the escaped Humvee with their binoculars.

Jack slammed a fist against the top of the LAV's turret. "Goddammit! They couldn't have beaten us by that much, not with so many cars blocking the lanes on 77."

They were sitting at the intersection of US-77, which the harvesters had taken north, and 55W. When the Marine observers reported that the escaped Humvee had turned north on US-77, Jack had ordered the driver to turn onto 1st Street, which ran parallel to US-77 through a set of small farms until it intersected 55W. From there, US-77 was only a quarter mile to the east. Few vehicles were abandoned along 1st Street, and the LAV made good time, the driver running flat out the entire way until they slowed to turn onto 55W.

Unfortunately, the Humvee was nowhere to be seen.

"Could they have turned off somewhere before this intersection?" The driver asked. "Maybe we missed them back there."

"I don't think so," Jack said. "The map shows only a single road connecting to 77 along this stretch, and it leads right back to the road we took."

"Jack," Terje said, tapping him on the shoulder. "Look there." He pointed to the north.

Putting binoculars to his eyes, Jack looked in the direction Terje was pointing. A herd of dark shapes loped across the highway about half a mile away, heading northwest.

"Jesus," he whispered. "There must be tens of thousands of them."

"And they're heading in the direction of the airport," Terje said.

"Damn." Jack keyed his radio. "Carl, this is Jack, come in, over."

"This is Richards. Go ahead."

"Be advised that a huge swarm of harvesters is heading in a northeasterly direction across US-77 toward the airport."

There was a long pause before Carl answered. "Understood. I'll give Ferris a heads-up. We're taking a westerly route along the county roads. The larvae are all over the place out here. We'll be lucky if every one of the vehicles isn't running on the rims by the time we reach the airport. Any luck finding Naomi?"

"No," Jack told him. "They must have got past us somehow, but if they did, I can't figure where they went. The way north is completely blocked by that herd of bugs, and I can see more coming our way down 55W, so I don't think they turned toward Lincoln."

"Do what you need to do to find her, Jack," Carl told him. "But don't wait too long. I can't risk the plane, assuming we can beat that herd to the airport and Ferris can actually get us off the ground."

"I know. We'll be there. Dawson, out."

"Jack," Terje said gently. "We can't stay here."

"I'm not giving up on her," Jack told him. "Even if I have to send you guys on to the airport and look for her on my own, I'm going to find her. But where the hell did that Humvee go?"

"When you have eliminated the impossible," he heard Melissa say through the intercom, "whatever remains, however improbable, must be the truth. Sherlock Holmes said that."

"I never would have figured you for a fan of Arthur Conan Doyle," Jack said.

"I didn't *read* it," she said with a trace of exasperation. "It was on TV."

"Right."

"So," Melissa went on, "if they didn't go north, they didn't go east, and they didn't go west, that only leaves one direction, right?"

Jack looked at Terje, who shrugged. "Nothing says they might not have doubled back. We couldn't see the highway while we were coming north on 1st Street."

"Damn," Jack said. "Driver, head south."

"Yes, sir."

The LAV swung around and headed south on US-77. Jack and Terje scanned the way ahead with their binoculars, while the gunner swept the field of view with the LAV's main sights, the turret whining as it slowly slewed right, then left, then back again.

The big vehicle shouldered its way through the cars, and Terje dropped back into the rear compartment, not wanting to be thrown from the vehicle from the repeated heavy impacts.

An ear-splitting boom announced the loss of a second tire. The LAV swerved momentarily, crushing in the side of a Volkswagen Beetle before the driver could straighten it out.

"That's two on the same side, major," he reported. "If we lose another one..."

"Keep going," Jack grated, "even if we lose them all."

***

Naomi thought at first that she was just imagining the sound, a faint, deep hum that rose above the nerve-wracking crunching and cracking of the feeding larvae.

Then she heard the unmistakable crash and squeal of metal against metal.

Holding her breath, trying to focus on the sound, which was coming from somewhere to the north, she was rewarded with more crashes and scrapes, and the hum turned into the familiar growl of an LAV.

"Jack," she whispered, tears of relief welling in her eyes.

She wanted to shout and scream, but didn't. The sound would only attract any adult harvesters that might be nearby, and Jack and the others in the LAV wouldn't be able to hear her over the sound of the engine.

A loud *boom*, the sound of a tire rupturing, startled her as the LAV drew closer.

The sound of the engine grew louder, then began to fade. It was passing by her, heading south, but she couldn't see it because the southbound side of the highway was blocked from view.

"No, no," she moaned. Despite her earlier reservations, she shouted, "Jack, I'm here! Jack! *Jack!*"

The LAV continued its way south, the sound of the engine beginning to fade.

Propping herself up on one elbow, wincing from the pain, she turned toward the trees and the horrors that lurked within. The huge larva was feasting on the trees and wasn't moving, but it could shatter into tens of thousands of larvae any second.

The greatest threat was from a larva the size of a grapefruit that had eaten its way along the ground in a bee line toward her, and was now nearly within arm's reach.

Grabbing a stick as big around as her thumb and a foot and a half long, she poked it into the larva's bruised-looking flesh. The beast eagerly enveloped the end of the stick, the malleable flesh rapidly flowing toward her hand.

With her free hand, she dug around in one of her pants pockets, closing her fingers around a disposable butane lighter. "Take this, you little bastard," she hissed as she set fire to the larva.

The creature instantly exploded into a ball of fire. Grunting with pain from her broken ribs, she cocked her arm back and flung the stick and the flaming larva as far as she could into the woods.

The effect was cataclysmic. The tree line exploded in flames as if it had been hit with napalm.

Naomi cried out and turned away from the scorching heat as more and more of the things caught fire.

***

"Jack, look!"

It was Melissa. She had popped her head up out of the rear hatch and was pointing behind them.

He turned around to see flames leaping up from the woods on the far side of the highway.

"Naomi," he said. "It's got to be! Driver, turn us around and get across the median to the northbound side! Get us as close as you can to those woods!"

"Yes, sir," the driver said. "Oh, shit," he added as he turned the vehicle and caught sight of the flames licking the sky above the trees.

"Terje, grab the fire extinguishers and have them ready."

"Already working on it," the Norwegian said as he unstrapped the fire extinguishers and set them near the rear hatch. "I think firefighting will be my new line of work when I get home."

The LAV swerved to the left and churned through the median, the driver maneuvering through the grass and more abandoned cars.

Another tire, this one on the opposite side of the two they'd already lost, blew out.

"Shit," Jack cursed. "Come on, come on!"

The driver slammed his foot down on the gas, dispensing with finesse and just using the vehicle's mass to crash through the cars that remained between it and their objective.

They crossed the overpass, beyond which lay the burning woods.

"There!" Jack saw the Humvee at the bottom of the slope near the trees. Naomi was curled up beside it. Jack's face already felt like he had a sunburn. He had to reach her fast.

"Come on, Marines," he ordered as the driver slammed the LAV to a stop.

Tossing off his helmet, Jack climbed out of the turret and dropped to the ground, followed by the loader and driver, while Terje flung open one of the rear doors and emerged bearing the vehicle's fire extinguishers.

"You wait here," Jack told Melissa, who stood at the rear door. Alexander was hiding under her seat.

Jack led Terje and the Marines at a run down the hill, careful to avoid the larvae that were everywhere. "Watch your step!"

The heat as they reached the Humvee was astonishing. Jack could hardly breath and his exposed skin felt like it was boiling.

"I've got you," he said as he reached Naomi, shielding her from the fire with his body.

"Oh, God, Jack," she cried, holding onto his hand.

Terje used the extinguishers on some burning larvae that were dangerously close, then turned back to help.

"Her leg's pinned under the Humvee," Jack said. "We've got to lift it up."

The other three men took up positions where they could get a good grip on the vehicle.

"On three," Jack told them. "One...two...*three!*"

Grunting with effort, Terje and the Marines dug in with their feet and strained to lift the vehicle. Naomi screamed as the pressure eased on her leg and Jack tried to pull her free.

"Come on!" Jack bellowed. "Lift, dammit!"

Their faces contorted with effort, the tendons standing up in their necks, the three other men strained to lift the Humvee, but it wasn't enough. The way the vehicle was sitting on the bottom of the slope was working against them.

"Please forgive me," he whispered. With his hands clasped tightly together around Naomi's chest, Jack heaved as hard as he could. She screamed in agony, then passed out as he wrestled her smashed leg out from under the wreck.

The instant her foot was clear, he shouted, "She's out!"

With relieved cries, the men let the Humvee settle back down as Jack gently put Naomi over his shoulder and threaded his way back up the hill through the larvae, the others right behind him.

"Is she all right?" Melissa asked as Jack and Terje lay Naomi down in the back of the LAV.

"She's alive," Jack said grimly. He quickly looked at her leg. She'd suffered a dreadful compound fracture in her lower leg, and he prayed the corpsman could save it.

"I'll take care of her," Terje said as he closed the rear hatch and the two Marines manned their positions. "You need to get us out of here."

"Right," Jack said, running a hand over his blistered cheeks. Naomi's face, which she'd kept turned away from the fire, looked all right, but her hands were burned and some of her hair had been scorched. Leaning down, he kissed her lightly on the lips. "I'm sorry," he whispered before he climbed into the commander's seat. "Driver," he said after hastily donning his helmet, "head west across the fields until we hit Denton Road. Let's get away from this goddamned place."

"You got it, sir."

Looking to the north and the huge mass of harvesters streaming out of Lincoln, Jack added, "You'd better step on it. I don't think we're going to have much time."

A TANKER OR TWO

Ferris tore off his headset and slammed it down over the control yoke. "Goddammit," he said.

Boisson, who had been standing between the pilot's and copilot's seats while Ferris had received their marching orders from Richards, snorted. "That's one way of putting it."

Beside him, Kurnow stared out the window, the light of the rising sun highlighting her face.

God, I'm so fucking old, Ferris thought as he looked at her. In that moment she looked like she was about ten years old, and reminded him of his own daughter just before she and his wife had been killed in a car accident while he was off fighting in one goddamn war or another. Not a day had gone by when he didn't think of them. There had been other women over the years, of course, but he never got over losing his wife and little girl. Looking at Kurnow made him miss them even more.

"So, Ferris, what's the plan?"

He turned to stare up at her. Boisson's teeth and eyes stood out against her black skin and made her look like some sort of mutant Cheshire Cat, and he wanted nothing more than to cock his arm back and punch her in the nose. All the fear that had nearly overwhelmed him during the escape from Grand Island bubbled to the surface again. He'd known gut-wrenching fear many times in combat, but he'd always managed to overwhelm it with sheer confidence. But it was hard for him to be confident in a world overrun with horrors.

Instead of punching Boisson, which he knew would have been one of his life's bigger mistakes, he said, "Plan? What plan? Old Baldy wants us to have this bird ready to fly by the time he gets here. But how the hell are we going to fuel up, taxi to the end of the runway, and then — after the rest of the partygoers arrive but just before the hordes of monsters come to eat us — take off without losing half the tires to those oozing pus balls out there? And let's not even think about what would happen if one of those little bastards comes up into the plane with the landing gear. That'd be a nice fucking surprise at thirty thousand feet."

Kurnow reached over and touched his arm. "It's okay, Mr. Ferris."

He snapped his head around to look at her. In his mind he heard, *It's okay, Daddy.* Those were the last words his daughter had spoken to him when he'd told her he had to deploy again. There had been tears in her eyes. He'd told her he loved her and that he would try to be home soon, but he hadn't come home soon enough. Biting his lip, he looked away, fighting to keep the hot tears that welled up in his eyes from pouring down his face.

"Get a grip, Ferris," Boisson snapped. "We've got a job to do and not much time to do it. You're the big airplane expert. Figure it out."

"Fine," he growled, pretending to rub something out of his eyes. Turning back to Kurnow, he said, "Fuel first. All things being equal, I'd just taxi us over to the main apron and plug into one of the hydrants there, assuming we could find a pumper truck. But that's not going to work because of all the debris from the KC-135 that our friend Boisson here blasted to pieces." He glanced at Boisson, who put her hands on her hips and glared at him. "Now we've got about a hundred thousand pound of metal just waiting to be sucked into the engines."

"I should've just let all those harvesters eat your ass," Boisson told him.

"We'll have to bring fuel to the plane," Kurnow interjected. "We need a tanker truck, like the R-11 refueler. I know you said you didn't want just a fuel truck, but we don't have any choice. The only thing is, I don't know if the 155th has...had any R-11s here. They may only have had the R-12, which just pumps fuel from the hydrants into the planes."

"We're not going to have time to look around and come up empty," Boisson said, still scowling at Ferris.

"I know where we should be able to find a tanker or two ," he said, "but you're not going to like this."

"No doubt."

"The general aviation terminal back that way," he hooked a thumb over his shoulder toward the northeast, behind the plane, "should have some. The closest ones are normally sitting toward the south end of the apron near the taxiway that leads to their main runway, assuming nobody ran off with them."

"How far?"

"Call it half a mile as the crow flies."

"I hate crows," Boisson muttered. "All right. So we go and bring back a fuel truck. While we're doing that, you should be moving this beast to where it needs to be so we can get out of here."

"I know, but that's going to be a bitch, too." He pointed out his window toward the wreckage of the KC-135. "We'd normally taxi that way onto the apron, then turn onto the main taxiway to reach either end of the runway."

"But you said we can't go that way without sucking stuff up into the engines."

"Right. That leaves going straight ahead." He pointed out the windscreen. Between the plane and the main taxiway was a short but wide taxi area with a huge yellow X painted in the middle, about where the plane would normally turn left to head back to the main apron. Beyond the section with the X was a strip of asphalt about as wide as a two lane road that joined up with the taxiway. On either side of that narrow strip was nothing but bare ground. "In case you didn't realize it, that big-ass X means *don't go this way.* The concrete and asphalt might not be able to handle our weight, and that narrow strip up there sure wasn't meant to take anything bigger than trucks. Plus we have to clear the larvae out of the way of the tires."

Boisson clapped him on the shoulder. "Al, that's your problem. Mine is to get the damn gas truck over here."

The urge to punch her returned with a vengeance, but he managed to restrain himself. "So what's *your* plan?"

"I'm going to take Kurnow with me." Before Kurnow could object, Boisson told her, "Just stow it. I don't know shit about any of this stuff. You might think you don't know much, but it's a lot more than me. I'll take one of my men and leave you with the other three, Al. They should be able to clear any of the little bugs out of the way of your precious tires and hopefully keep anything bigger off your back until Richards gets here with the circus." To Kurnow, she said, "Come on. The clock's ticking."

Al nodded at Kurnow. "Go on. And for God's sake, be careful." After a moment's reflection, he unstrapped the rig holding his Desert Eagle and handed it to her. "Put this on and give me that useless pea shooter."

"Thanks." She handed him her weapon and took his hand cannon. After strapping it on, she put on a brave face and followed Boisson down the ladder.

He could hear Boisson giving the three agents who'd be staying with him some instructions, and a moment later they started moving ahead of the plane in line with the three landing gear struts, frying any larvae they found with cans of hairspray and lighters.

Someone down below slammed the forward hatch shut, and he felt very much alone.

Looking again out the windscreen, Ferris guessed the taxiway was around eight hundred feet away across the *verboten* section of the old apron and the asphalt road.

"This should be just a barrel of monkeys," he muttered.

Returning his attention to the KC-135's instrument panel, he found a well-worn pre-flight checklist and began to bring the big plane to life.

***

"Vijay" no longer wore a human face or human clothes, but moved through the gathering dawn as he had when consciousness had first touched him. He loped along, low to the ground, his powerful body propelling him in smooth strides, his dark exoskeleton gleaming in the morning light, the malleable tissue gathered around his thorax. It rippled, waves and puckers flowing across the surface, as if anticipating the next facade required by its master.

He had originally planned to escape with the others in the lab, but the hunt for the unknown hitchhiker had presented an unforeseen opportunity to both escape and kill Jack Dawson. Unfortunately, the hitchhiker's attack in the tunnels had ruined that part of Vijay's plan. While Vijay had managed to kill the two Marines, he had decided to leave Jack to the hitchhiker. Vijay did not wish to risk a confrontation with his unknown kin, for fear it might hold the same views as those that attacked SEAL-2. Vijay could not afford to be killed. Not yet.

From LRU, he had made his way north toward the airport, avoiding the larger groups of non-sentients and the areas most heavily infested with larvae. His objective was the airport and the humans Carl Richards had sent there. None would be allowed to escape.

At last, he reached the grandly named Platte River, which was little more than a canal bounding the airport's southern and western sides. He crossed a bridge to the airport side, then ran east through the trees along the bank of the river.

He had nearly given up on finding a covered approach to the airport buildings when he came upon a small tributary just before the river passed under I-80. The tributary led him straight into the heart of the military portion of the airport. On the left side of the drainage culvert through which he made his way, dodging more and more larvae, was an Army garrison, judging by the number of destroyed vehicles. Many dead soldiers and far more dead harvesters were strewn about, a feast for the larvae.

On his right was the Air Force facility. The wreck of a plane smoldered on the huge expanse of concrete, a tremendous pall of smoke trailing into the sky.

My kin may have already completed my work for me, he thought as he surveyed the scene. But he was not one to leave things to chance.

Moving carefully along the side of a building at the south end of the facility, he spied the wreckage of a second plane inside an enormous hangar. Seeing no signs of movement other than more larvae, he dashed across the concrete to the burned out hangar and crept along the wall, moving north.

A second, smaller hangar stood across more concrete to the north. Seeing no humans about, he sprinted across the gap.

Turning the corner of the hangar, he stopped. A Humvee, mere yards away, lay burning. *The humans from the lab probably came here in this*, he thought as he crept closer. Peering into the smoking hulk of the vehicle, he found no trace of human bodies.

Moving to the northern end of the hangar, he saw another large jet sitting by itself on an apron about a thousand feet to the north.

Humans were guarding it. Lowering himself to the ground, he watched. Four humans that he recognized as the FBI agents brought by the one called Boisson stood at the compass points, watching for threats.

After a few minutes, two more humans emerged from the nose door of the aircraft. One of them was easily recognizable as Boisson. The other, also female, was unfamiliar to him and wore an Air Force uniform.

Boisson called the other agents together for a moment to speak with them. Then, when finished, she, the second female, and one of the agents turned and began jogging across the ground to the north, following the fence line that separated the airport's runways and operations areas from the passenger terminal and public access zones that ran behind the big plane.

One of the three remaining agents closed the hatch before they all took up positions near the plane's landing gear, then began to slowly walk forward.

Vijay could not understand what they were doing until one of them took out a small can. Leaning over, he aimed it at the ground and held something just in front of it. A cone of fire burst forth, and what must have been a larvae exploded into bright flames.

At the same moment, one of the plane's engines began to start, the low growl quickly becoming a high-pitched whine.

They are clearing the way for the plane. But why would they have sent Boisson and the others away?

That, he did not know. What he did know was that his chances of successfully attacking the three agents and inflicting irreparable damage on the plane were poor. There was nothing but open ground for nearly a thousand feet between him and his prey, and the FBI agents, while focusing on the runway, remained vigilant to nearby threats. All three periodically looked up and around, checking the approaches to the plane.

Vijay would never make it before they cut him down.

Boisson, then, he thought. She and the others would not have left the plane unless their mission had been of great urgency. If they were killed and their mission failed, it might be enough to doom the other humans to staying in this place long enough for the swarms to arrive.

He could not follow Boisson directly, for that would take him over the same open terrain between him and the aircraft, where he would risk being seen. But the fence line they were following bent to the right, looping around the northern end of the passenger terminal.

Making his decision, he scuttled across the concrete to the parking lot east of the hangar where he'd been making his observations. Then, keeping low, he made his way to a section of fence that he could climb without the agents being able to spot him.

Once on the other side, he ran across the street south of the main parking lot to a large warehouse-like building. From there, he vaulted over another section of fence into the civilian part of the airport.

Looking around, he could see nothing that would be of value to the humans. The main passenger terminal was empty of aircraft and vehicles. Only luggage carts and a few other odd items of ground support equipment remained.

To the northeast, across the airport's secondary runway, was a collection of hangars and other buildings, in front of which stood a handful of corporate jets and some even smaller planes.

He also spotted something else: three fuel trucks, parked in a neat row in front of one of the hangars.

Of course, he thought. *The fuel.*

Leaving caution behind, he sprinted across the intervening ground to reach the building behind the fuel trucks before Boisson and the others had a chance to spot him.

GO FASTER

"God, I thought I was in better shape," Kurnow panted as she jogged along behind Boisson, with the other agent bringing up the rear.

"Running from harvesters is great cardio," Boisson told her. "And we've had lots of practice."

"Have you killed a lot of them?"

Boisson grinned. "Not nearly as many as I'd like."

"The only ones I've seen for real were the ones that came poking around at night." She paused to draw in some air. "Even then, I couldn't see them very well. I just knew what they were."

"Consider yourself lucky. I hope you never have to see any up close and personal."

They fell silent as they crossed the passenger terminal apron, which, aside from the four jetways extending from the terminal building, was completely empty. Then they crossed the bare ground between the apron and runway 32, and the taxiway that led to the general aviation terminal.

"Ferris and his damned crows," Boisson growled. "This isn't half a mile, seems more like ten miles."

"Better than trying to climb over the barb wire fence," Kurnow huffed.

"If you say so." Boisson pointed. "Are those our trucks?"

"Yeah. God, yeah."

The taxiway led directly to where three fuel trucks were parked between yellow cross-hatched rectangles painted on the apron. Half a dozen corporate jets were still parked outside the hangars and service buildings that lined the apron, with a handful of prop planes farther to the north.

Boisson took a closer look. "Well, if we strike out here, it looks like some more trucks are up there."

"Let's hope these'll do," Kurnow said. They slowed to a fast walk as they reached the trucks. "This so gives me the creeps. It's just like everyone suddenly died. You'd think people would have tried to fly out of here."

"I'm sure some did. But most probably got caught somewhere in town. A harvester infestation doesn't develop gradually. It starts with a few, but the next thing you know, thousands are swarming all over the place."

"God," Kurnow whispered.

Boisson snorted. "God's got nothing to do with this. So what's the story on these trucks?"

"This one's carrying avgas," Kurnow said, looking at some of the markings and the control console. "We can't use it." She hurried to the next truck. "This is it! Jet-A. It's not military grade fuel, but it should work, and the tank looks like it's nearly full."

"It had better work. It's all we've got." Boisson took a close look around the vehicle. "Best of all, I don't see any larvae sticking to it."

Kurnow opened the driver's door. "No keys. They must be in the FBO office."

"FBO?"

"The fixed base operator. They own the trucks and service the planes that come here." Kurnow pointed to the building next to the trucks. "Come on."

"Angie," the other agent, Mason Juilliard, called out as he raised his rifle to his shoulder. "We've got company."

A small group of harvesters were coming toward them, bounding from open ground onto the concrete at the southern edge of the apron.

"Shit," Boisson cursed. "Kurnow, go find the keys! We'll take care of our visitors."

Kurnow paused, staring at her.

Boisson shoved her in the direction of the FBO office. "Go!"

***

Kurnow ran for the office door as Boisson and Juilliard opened fire. Glancing toward the harvesters, she saw them leap and dodge through the tracer fire, using the corporate jets for cover as they came closer.

She ran faster, slamming into the door when she lost her grip on the handle and it failed to open. For a moment, she thought it was locked. Grabbing it firmly with her shaking hand, the handle turned easily and the door opened.

Stepping through, she shut the door behind her and leaned against it for a moment, safe in the darkness, her heart hammering in her chest. Her heartbeat sounded even louder than the gunfire coming from outside.

Come on, she told herself. *You can't waste time.*

Making her way behind the main counter, she found a key box fastened to the wall. It had been left open. Glancing at the desk, she saw a box of donuts, half of which hadn't been eaten, and a half-full (or half-empty) cup of coffee. The coffeemaker had a full pot. It was off, as power to the airport had been cut off, but the switch was still on. Whoever had been here had simply left. They'd gone in such a hurry that no one had bothered to close up or shut anything off.

She returned her attention to the key box. The keys were labeled, but she wasn't sure which one went to the truck with the Jet-A. With a shrug, she took them all and stuffed them into one of the cargo pockets of her flight suit.

That's when the hairs on the back of her neck stood on end and a trickle of electric current ran down her arms to her fingertips.

With her breath catching in her throat, she turned around to find a dark shape crouching on the counter behind her.

She brought up the Desert Eagle Ferris had given her, but it was too late. Far too late.

***

"Damn it! Out!" Boisson dropped the empty magazine from her weapon and slammed in a fresh one. She only had two more. "These damn things are getting smarter."

Between them, she and Juilliard had only taken down two of the eight harvesters that had found them. Of the six that remained, two were playing hide and seek behind the corporate jets on the southern end of the apron, while the other four had disappeared to

Boisson's left around the back of the FBO buildings, no doubt hoping to flank them.

"Kurnow!" She shouted. "Hurry the fuck up!"

One of the two harvesters by the jets was transformed into a torch as the tracers from her own weapon and Juilliard's caught it in a crossfire.

The other one gave up the ghost and ran behind the building, following the others.

"*Kurnow!*"

"Coming!"

Kurnow emerged from the FBO office and ran toward her.

"About time," Boisson said. "Did you find the keys?"

"Yeah..." Kurnow patted one of the pockets of her flight suit. "Yeah, they're right here. I brought all of them."

"Good. Because we're taking two of these trucks."

"Right. Okay." Kurnow opened the door to one of the trucks and was about to climb inside.

"Why don't you take the one with the Jet-A," Boisson told her. "I've got plans for the gasoline."

"Sure. Let me find the key for it." After trying a few, the engine growled into life and Kurnow hopped down.

"Juilliard, go with her and watch our asses," Boisson said. "Now let's get the hell out of here before those things get in behind us."

The agent nodded and joined Kurnow in the cab of the truck with the Jet-A fuel as Kurnow started the engine.

Boisson climbed up into the cab of the gas truck and slammed the door closed. She'd driven heavy vehicles before in the Marines, and this one wasn't that different. Putting it into gear and releasing the brake, she jammed down on the accelerator, heading toward the taxiway that led to Runway 32 and then back to the Air Force section of the airport, careful to avoid the larvae oozing across the concrete.

Kurnow followed close behind.

***

"Okay, baby," Ferris whispered, "here we go."

With his hand firmly on the four throttle levers, he eased them forward and released the brakes. The cockpit felt absurdly lonely without a copilot. He was confident he could fly the plane alone, but he missed having an extra set of hands, eyes, and a brain to handle the plane.

The engines rose in pitch, and as the plane began to roll forward, he eased back slightly on the throttles, balancing the thrust against the plane's inertia. Except for rapid scans of the instruments, his eyes were fixed up ahead on the narrow strip of asphalt that separated him from the main taxiway.

The three agents were making their way along the taxiway to the north, flaming any larvae they found. They'd have to clear about four thousand feet of taxiway, plus nearly ten thousand feet of runway. As one of the agents bent down and blasted another larva with his makeshift hair spray flamethrower, Ferris couldn't decide if he wanted to laugh or cry. They'd never clear the runway in time.

"Shit," he cursed as he gently applied the brakes. The plane had picked up more speed than he'd intended. His sphincter puckered as the nose gear passed over the huge yellow X, and he felt like he was violating a law of nature by ignoring it.

Looking ahead, he began to sweat as he saw just how narrow the asphalt strip was. The minimum safe runway width for the plane was seventy-five feet. The connector to the main taxiway was maybe twenty.

He tightened his grip on the throttles as the nose gear thumped from the concrete apron to the asphalt connector.

Out of the corner of his eye, he saw the three agents turn to watch.

He caressed the brakes, slowing ever so slightly as the main gear moved to the connector with another set of thumps. The plane was arrow straight down the center of the asphalt strip...

The starboard side suddenly dipped down and the nose began to slew to the right. He brought up the power in the starboard engines and eased the nose wheel left. More...more...more...

With a sudden heave, the plane began to move again, and he had to quickly bring up the power in the port engines to compensate.

"Come on, baby," he whispered as the plane juddered and bounced. He knew the asphalt must be collapsing under the mains, sinking into the ground. He eased the throttles forward even more. It was a risk, but he couldn't let the plane get stuck.

The main gear began to sink even deeper, nearly bringing the plane's forward movement to a halt.

Gritting his teeth, Ferris pushed the throttles forward to the stops. It was all or nothing now.

"Come on, goddammit! Give me another hundred feet!"

As if it were fighting its way out of a mud bog, the plane moved forward slowly, ever so slowly, then finally surged forward.

Ferris pulled back on the throttles as the nose gear crossed over onto the main taxiway, then throttled back more as the mains followed. Turning the plane hard to the right, he centered the nose on the taxiway and moved up to where the agents stood waiting.

"Goddamn," he sighed, wiping his sweaty forehead with his sleeve.

Looking out the windscreen, he saw not one, but two fuel trucks racing toward him on the taxiway from the main passenger terminal area.

"There's some good news for a change." Overcoming a sudden dreadful certainty that they wouldn't start again, he shut down the engines.

A voice erupted from his headset, startling him. "Ferris, this is Richards, come in."

"Ferris here, over."

"What's your status, over?"

The truck driven by Kurnow slid past the tip of the port wing and parked close to the fuselage. "I can confirm the plane should fly. The engines work, at least. Boisson found us some fuel, which we're going to start pumping in soon. The big problem is going to be clearing the taxiway and runway of any larvae."

"What's so tough about that?"

Ferris rolled his eyes. "We're only talking about clearing maybe, oh, ten or twelve thousand feet, and I've got three feebs with cans of hairspray and lighters to do the job."

Richards was silent for a moment.

Dumb-ass, Ferris thought as Boisson, who was driving the second fuel truck, turned to face the same direction as the plane along the taxiway, bringing it to a stop about a hundred yards ahead of the plane.

"Is there any chance you'll have it cleared soon?"

"I don't see how, Carl. We can't afford to miss a single larva, and that's nearly two miles for these guys to cover..."

Boisson got out of the fuel truck and trotted off to the side of the runway. She waved to the agents and shouted something. They didn't seem to understand, and she shouted again. They dropped prone to the ground.

Then she turned to face the truck and raised her rifle.

Ferris had forgotten the mic was still open to Richards when he exclaimed, "Holy shit!"

***

Like most other people who owned a television, Boisson had seen her fair share of action shows. She'd lived one most of her adult life, first in the Marines, then in the FBI. She'd done a lot of crazy things but nothing as insane as what she was about to try.

The idea had come to her while Kurnow had been digging around for the keys to the trucks. A tanker full of gasoline was just full of lethal potential for burning the larvae clear. That was why she had decided to take it. The only problem had been how to put it to good use in clearing the runway. Just opening the valves and letting it spew out the back wouldn't work, because Ferris would need a clear path that was a good thirty or more feet wide to keep his precious landing gear clear of any oozing horrors, and the valves on the truck would just leave a track of gas behind her. At best, she'd have to make three passes along nearly two miles of taxiway and runway. Having someone try to spray fuel through the hose had the same problem.

So she came up with a more creative solution.

After reaching the edge of the runway and putting some distance between herself and the tanker, she turned to the agents who'd been clearing the way for Ferris. "Get your asses down!"

They looked at her, confused. "What?"

She raised her voice to a bellow. "Get your asses down on the ground!"

They dove for the runway when she turned and took aim with her rifle at the gasoline-filled fuel tank. She'd seen countless films and shows where cars or even tankers just like this one blew up when struck by a bullet, but she'd also read that gasoline in liquid form wouldn't burn. It was the vapor, gasoline mixed with oxygen, that was flammable. She'd loaded her weapon with the single magazine she carried that contained standard bullets, rather than tracers. They were almost useless against harvesters, but she'd been in enough spots where having something that didn't set fire to everything was handy.

One of her men shouted, "Boisson, are you insane?"

Smiling at the thought, she pulled the trigger.

She was almost disappointed when the tanker didn't explode.

Instead, the bullet lanced through the metal tank about a third of the way from the bottom on the driver's side. As she'd hoped, a stream of caramel colored liquid shot out to the side under pressure from the weight of the thousands of pounds of gasoline inside the tank.

Moving quickly to the center of the runway behind the truck, she put a hole in the rear of the tank, then one in the far side.

Nothing exploded. The streams didn't perfectly cover the tracks the KC-135's landing gear would have to take, but they came close.

"Close enough for government work," she said. Slinging her weapon, she called out to her men. "As soon as I'm a few hundred yards ahead, light this shit up!"

To the west, she heard the sound of LAV cannons and heavy machine guns firing.

She hopped into the cab and started the tanker forward, careful to keep the truck in the center of the taxiway unless she had to dodge a larva. Watching in the rear view mirror, she saw her men move forward and with visible reluctance set fire to the gas.

"Shit," she said as the gasoline trails lit and the flames raced after her. "Guess I'd better go a little faster."

BOISSON

"Holy shit!"

"What the hell's going on?" Richards demanded.

"That lunatic Boisson just fired a rifle at a tanker truck. Jesus! She shot it again. What the hell..."

Richards was just about to key his mic again when Ferris continued, "All right, Boisson is a suicidal maniac, but she's a goddamn genius. She poked some holes in the tank on the truck so it'll spray gas all over the runway. I think...yeah, she's going to drive ahead of me, letting the gas burn off any larvae that are in the way." He paused again. "Oh, my God! She just had the agents light up the streams of gas! She's a fruitcake!"

"Is it working?"

"Yeah, until the fire catches up to her and blows her sky-high. Where the hell do you find these people?"

That's a good question, Richards thought. *But thank God for them.* "How about fuel for the plane?"

"We're working on it. I'll let you know when we're ready. What about Dawson?"

"Last I heard, he should be right behind us. Just get the bird ready and let me worry about that."

"Roger. Ferris, out." To the Marine driving the Humvee, he said, "Hang a right up here at Adams. That should take us to the airport."

"Yes, sir," the Marine said.

Richards reflected on their exodus from SEAL-2. The convoy had only encountered a few small groups of harvesters here and there, and the larvae were much easier to avoid in the daylight. The worst part of the trip had been finding a way across the rail line just south of I-80. An abandoned train had blocked their way for at least three quarters of a mile. Getting around it had diverted them even farther west, and they hadn't been able to turn north again until they reached Northwest 84th Street, which had taken them over the slaughterhouse of the interstate.

"Mr. Richards, this is LAV-1."

"Richards here. Go ahead."

"Sir, we've got movement in the tree line at your ten o'clock."

Richards looked left, past the driver. Some tree tops poked up over the slope at his ten o'clock, but that was all he could see.

"What kind of movement?"

"Lots of it! Contact, ten o'clock! Harvesters in the open, moving out of the tree line. Thousands of the bastards!"

Richards saw them as the Humvee came over a small rise and the trees were fully exposed. A horde of the creatures was streaming toward them across the furrowed ground, and would cut off the convoy before the next turn. "All units, all units! Get off the road and head northeast across the fields! Follow our lead, and fire at will!" To the driver, he ordered, "Get us the hell off this road and away from those things."

The kid looked at him with eyes as big as dinner plates. "Yes, sir!"

With a spin of the steering wheel, he sent the Humvee barreling into the field off to the right. Richards clamped his mouth shut so he wouldn't bite his tongue off as the vehicle bounced and jolted across the furrows.

The other vehicles turned and left the road, the plumes of dust from their tires mixing with the smoke from the cannons and machine guns as they blasted the harvesters.

The front right tire of the last Humvee in line blew out. The driver managed to keep it under control, but the vehicle quickly fell behind the others.

One of the LAVs pulled alongside, then both vehicles slammed to a stop. The occupants of the Humvee piled out and clambered onto the LAV, which then took off at full acceleration, the tires throwing rooster tails of dirt out behind it.

"Swing north to the road!" Richards told his driver. "We've got to get out of these damn fields!" West Adams Street would take them to within a block of the airport, and from there he planned to take the route Boisson had told him she'd used to get onto the field.

The Humvee veered to the left into a drainage swale. Swerving around the solitary tree that was planted right in the middle, the Humvee reached Adams Street and headed east.

He looked at the GPS. The airport was now just three miles away.

The swarm of harvesters chasing after the convoy had spread out on either side of the road like a black tide. The convoy was gradually pulling away, but would reach the airport mere minutes before the swarm caught up to them.

Richards turned to Renee, who was sitting in the back seat, clutching the sprayer to her chest. "If you're going to use that thing, now's probably a good time," he said.

"What?" She looked sick, and he caught sight of blood soaking the seat cushion beneath her. Glancing down at the sprayer, she blurted. "Oh, Jesus. I'm such a dumb-ass."

Sticking the wand out the window, she squeezed the handle. A wide cone of fine mist jetted from the wand's tip. "Breath deep, assholes!" She shouted.

She kept squeezing the handle until the tank ran out of pressure and the flow dribbled to a stop.

**

Even with the helmet on, Jack's ears were ringing from the hammering of the LAV's guns. He'd wanted to veer more to the west and follow the path Richards and the convoy had taken to the airport, but after Richards had called and warned him about the swarm approaching from the east, he'd changed his mind. After speeding west about a mile from US-77, Jack had the driver turn north on Coddington Avenue.

"Contact!" The gunner reported. "Harvesters! Uh, more than I can count, coming from the southeast."

Jack didn't hesitate. "Open fire!"

The 25mm Bushmaster cannon roared, and Jack fired with his machine gun. The harvesters streaming into the open ground southeast of the overpass were packed so close together that they could barely move an inch in any direction other than forward.

Harvesters burst into flame from the explosions of the cannon shells and the machine gun's tracer rounds, setting fire to more harvesters around them.

They had to cease fire as the driver took the ramp down to US-77, temporarily blocking the harvesters from view. But a moment later they reappeared, running at breakneck speed under the overpass and down the ramp after the LAV.

Jack let the gunner keep the pursuers occupied while he kept watch ahead of them.

The driver shouldered his way through more abandoned and burned out cars, and their pace was slowed to a crawl as they made their way across the overpass that took them over the rail yards.

But the overpass gave them a temporary advantage. The harvesters behind them had to bunch up to get across, and the burning corpses as the gunner blasted them created an impassable wall of flame that reached up well over a hundred feet in the air.

That was the good news. The bad news was that more harvesters were charging through the rail yards below the overpass. Some were far enough out that Jack could depress the muzzle of the machine gun enough to shoot them, but the bulk of the creatures were directly below, out of sight.

"We've got to get to the other side!" He told the driver. "Gun it!"

The driver jammed down on the accelerator. If he hadn't been wearing body armor, Jack would have broken half a dozen ribs on the hatch coaming when the LAV slammed into the next car. He heard cries of pain and surprise from below as Naomi, Terje, and Melissa were thrown about, and he clenched his hands on the machine gun controls, cursing their luck.

At last, they were across, and the driver had a little more room to maneuver as he wove through cars and tried to avoid larvae.

"Sir," the driver called as they crossed over US-6, heading straight for the westbound ramp for I-80, "which way?"

"Straight ahead! Don't take the right turn onto the I-80 ramp, just go straight. The airport's dead ahead!"

"Roger that."

Jack swiveled the machine gun to the right and blasted a group of harvesters pounding toward them from a residential complex just southeast of the junction with the interstate.

The gunner had been keeping up a steady stream of fire from the Bushmaster, which fell silent with appalling suddenness. "Main gun ammo is out!" He began firing the 7.62mm coaxial machine gun. It wrought its own form of devastation on the pursuing mass, but Jack could immediately tell the difference in how many harvesters fell or began to burn.

"Dawson, this is Richards."

Jack keyed the mic while blasting another group of harvesters that appeared over a huge pile of concrete debris off to their left as the LAV zoomed down the I-80 ramp, then shot off onto the open ground to the north. "Dawson here. We're a little busy."

"What's your ETA?"

The LAV crashed through a chain link fence and darted through a thin line of trees. The airport lay just ahead, along with a bridge that would take them over the Platte river.

"We're almost there. Can't you hear us shooting?"

"We're doing a little shooting of our own, wise ass. Boisson's going to try and give you some cover. Ferris is waiting at the north end of the runway."

The LAV tore across the bridge and smashed through the boundary fence of the airport. Off to his left, a tanker truck was racing toward them from the southern end of the runway. Something about it was strange, and it took him a moment to realize that fuel was spraying out to either side, and three trails of flame were following along about a hundred yards behind it. Boisson, he saw, was at the wheel.

"What the hell is Boisson doing? She's insane!"

"No argument from me," Richards replied.

Boisson waved at him as she passed behind them. She took the truck along the fence line near the southeastern corner of the airport before wheeling it around. Following the fence line, she left a trail of gasoline along the perimeter, the flames racing along behind.

The harvesters that hadn't been gunned down by the LAV blundered right into the fiery barrier. A few had the prescience to leap over it, but most of them, pouring over the bridge and climbing the fence, didn't. In seconds, a wall of fire enveloped the southern end of the field.

The LAV sped north on a service road that joined up with the main taxiway, while Boisson took the tanker along the western side of the fence line. Up ahead, far ahead, Jack could see a big Air Force jet at the far end of the runway.

Boisson was keeping up with him, following the long taxiway that ran parallel to the main runway on the western side, the flames still chasing her. He was wondering what she was doing when he saw the LAVs and Humvees from the main convoy near the plane. The muzzles of their weapons were flashing, and he saw flames rising from an enormous concrete apron on the western side of the base, opposite the Air National Guard facilities.

A solid mass of harvesters was moving forward across the apron. Even with so many burning and being blasted apart by the cannons and machine guns of the Marine vehicles, they kept coming.

Boisson's truck arrowed straight for the heart of the advancing monsters.

"*Angie, no!*" Jack shouted.

***

Boisson had never really had an exit strategy for her chariot of fire idea. Driving north now along the western taxiway, she saw and heard the guns of the convoy open up, the tracers and cannon shells blasting at a swarm of harvesters that had appeared on her side of the field, having crossed the Platte River and jumped the fence. The gunfire from the vehicles was taking its toll, but also causing the swarm to spread out toward the buildings on the western edge of the apron. From there, they might run behind the buildings and flank the Marines, or just attack the plane as it made its takeoff run.

With a slight twist of the steering wheel, she aimed the truck at the swarm's center of mass. With her free hand, she pulled the four grenades from her combat vest. Two were high explosive frag grenades. The other two were white phosphorus. She took one of the white phosphorus grenades and pulled the pin with her teeth. *That's real John Wayne shit*, she thought with a grim smile as she spat out the ring.

Jamming down all the way on the accelerator, she slammed into the harvesters, sending them flying like bowling pins over the hood and cab of the truck. After the initial impact, she tossed out the first grenade, then grabbed one of the HE frags. Yanking the pin again with her teeth, she shoved it into the mouth of a harvester that tried to lunge through her window. Choking on the olive drab sphere, the thing fell way from the truck, which was quickly losing momentum against the horde that was surrounded her.

She pulled the pin of the second willie pete and tossed it out. As she let it fly, a harvester reached in and raked her arm into bloody ribbons.

The first white phosphorus grenade exploded somewhere behind her, sending up a plume of burning blobs that lit dozens of harvester on fire. Then the frag grenade went off with a *whump*.

She lost control of the truck as two harvesters forced their way through her window, using the steering wheel for leverage, while a dozen more hammered at the windshield, trying to get into the cab.

The tanker swerved, then rolled over onto the passenger side, crushing a bunch of harvesters and throwing the others from the cab.

The grenade bounced around, finally coming to rest on the passenger side.

With her good hand, Boisson released the seat belt and fell, smashing her face on the top of the passenger door. Dazed, she managed to take hold of the grenade as a dozen claws sank into the flesh of her legs and hauled her out of the truck.

Pulling the pin, she let the handle fly as a set of jaws opened impossibly wide and descended toward her face.

"Eat shit and die, you fuckers!"

The world ended in fire and darkness.

FIVE HUNDRED MILES

The western side of the airport was consumed in a titanic explosion that sent up a miniature mushroom cloud.

"My God," Terje whispered over the intercom. "What was that?"

"Angie Boisson just bought us some time," Jack told him. To the south, the direction from which they'd come, dark forms capered beyond the line of burning gas Angie had sprayed along the fence. "I just hope it's enough."

Up ahead, people moving around under the wings and belly of the KC-135, which was still almost three quarters of a mile away.

"Richards, this is Dawson," he called over the radio.

"Richards. Go ahead." There was no mistaking the sadness in his voice.

"I'm sorry about Angie. I wish there was something we could've done." Carl didn't answer. "It looks like she cleared out the threat on the western side. I don't see any movement there. But we've still got hostiles approaching from the south. The defensive line Angie laid down won't last long." He looked back again. The flames were already guttering out.

"Understood. Just get your asses to the plane so we can get the hell out of this God-forsaken place."

"On our way." To Terje, he said, "How's Naomi doing?"

"She's in a lot of pain, but she's holding up." He paused. "We need to get her to a doctor soon, Jack. If we don't...she might lose her leg."

"We'll find one," Jack said. "There must be one wherever we're going."

"And just where are we going? Does anyone know?"

"Not yet. Ferris said that he had tried to raise someone on the radios, but wasn't getting any joy. All he was picking up were other groups like us. He's thinking we'll have better luck once we're airborne and have longer signal range."

"I hope he's right."

The LAV finally pulled up alongside the other Marine vehicles by the plane. Jack tossed off his helmet and dropped into the guts of the big vehicle where he found Naomi. She was awake, her forehead covered in sweat. "How you doing, babe?"

"Okay." She managed a smile. Jack looked at her leg. Terje had carefully dressed the wound and applied a splint. Melissa was holding one of Naomi's hands, and he spied Alexander's green eyes peering out from under the girl's seat.

The back doors flew open to reveal Carl, Renee, and a handful of Marines.

"Oh, God, hon." Renee put her hand to her mouth and tears gleamed in her eyes when she saw Naomi.

"Let's get her out of here," Carl said. Looking at Jack, he added, "We don't have any stretchers."

That's when Jack noticed that it was awfully quiet outside. "Hasn't Ferris started up the plane?"

"Not yet." Carl's expression wavered between anger and resignation. "He doesn't want to start them until he's taken as much fuel as he can from the tanker."

Jack glanced over at the plane. A tanker truck, much like the one Boisson had been driving, was parked behind the wing. A thick hose snaked over the runway from the truck to the plane, where the end was plugged into a receptacle in one of the wheel wells. A blond woman in a flight uniform tended the tanker's controls.

"He knows we have lots more company coming from the south and east, right?"

"Yeah, I told him. I almost threatened to shoot him, but he was adamant about getting every drop he could. But he's right. We don't know how far we might have to go."

"That won't help us if we never get off the ground."

Together, the three men managed to get Naomi out of the rear compartment, and with the help of one of the Marines took her over to the forward hatch of the plane.

"Jesus, how are we going to get her up there?" Jack looked up the trunk that led to the flight deck. "We'll need a rope."

"I think I have a better idea," Terje said. He had one of the Marines bring over an LAV, and they carefully lifted her up onto the back deck. Then they backed it up to the leading edge of the port side wing. The LAV's hull was just high enough that they were able to pass her over to a pair of Marines on the wing. From there, they were able to get her through the over-wing hatch.

"Sorry about that," Jack told her as they laid her down in one of the fold-down bunks in the rear of the plane.

"It's okay," Naomi whispered. Even in the dim light, she looked deathly pale.

He leaned down and dabbed some of the sweat from her forehead with a cloth, then kissed her. "I love you," he whispered.

"I love you, too." She managed a brittle smile. "Now get us out of here, please."

"I've got her, sir." Jack looked up to see the corpsman.

"And I brought someone for you." Renee was carrying Koshka, who'd been handed up the forward ladder. Naomi reached for her injured cat, who immediately curled up between Naomi and the fuselage.

"Major Dawson." It was his LAV gunner on the radio.

"Dawson. Go ahead."

"Sir, we've got hostiles breaking through the southern perimeter and heading our way."

Jack looked at Carl. "Did you catch that."

"You're not the only one who has a radio." He looked at Jack, a sick expression on his face.

"I've got this," Jack said, a sinking feeling in his stomach.

As he headed for the nose hatch, he found that Terje and Melissa, who was holding a disgruntled-looking Alexander, were both right behind him. "And where do you think you're going?"

Terje just cocked his head and looked at him. "Do you have to ask that every time?"

"Yeah," Melissa said. "That's really dumb."

He looked at her and just shook his head. He leaned down, taking her face in his hands. Despite the disfigurement of the

Morgellons disease, he saw nothing but a strong, beautiful girl who deserved more than any of them the chance to survive. "Not this time, kiddo. You stay here and take care of Naomi, okay?"

"But I'm good luck for you."

"You sure are. But your luck stays here. This plane needs all the luck it can get. Okay?"

"What about Alexander?"

"You keep him here, too. He won't be able to help me on this one."

"Be careful." The girl's hoarse words were nearly lost as she hugged him, burying her face in his shoulder. Jack could feel Alexander squirming between them. Then she gave Terje a quick hug before turning and running aft to Naomi.

"Hey!"

They turned to see Ferris leaning out of the pilot's seat, staring at them.

"Did any of you clowns realize a bunch of bugs are coming at us down the runway?"

"Get going, Jack," Richards said. He reached out to shake Jack's hand. "Good luck."

"Come back to us, you two." Renee looked like she was about to cry.

"Yeah. Come on, Terje." He paused in the cockpit before dropping down the ladder to the runway. "We're not going to be able to hold them for long," he told Ferris.

"I know, I know! It took us forever just to get the damn pump on the truck started, but I'll save that story for later. We're taking on fuel. It'll take about five more minutes to suck the tanker dry, then I can start the engines and do the shortest pre-flight checklist I can get away with. So, figure maybe ten minutes altogether before I can get us in the air."

Jack looked out the windscreen at the mass of harvesters coming up the runway. *Ten minutes.* He swallowed hard. "You've got it."

"And Jack, you've got to make sure none of those bastards are on the runway when we roll. If one of them jumps into an engine on our takeoff run, we've had it."

"Right. No worries." Jack dropped down the ladder, Terje right behind him. "Marines, we need to buy the pilot ten minutes," he called over the common radio channel as he climbed into his LAV. "I want three Humvees guarding the plane, one on each side and one to the rear, in case we get any company from that direction. Everybody else, mount up and form up in a V formation with the point centered here on the runway and the wing vehicles out on the east and west taxiways. We'll head down the runway to the south and blast everything that moves. Any questions?"

There were none. No one bothered to ask how they would get back to the plane before it took off. Jack figured they were smart enough to answer that themselves.

As the LAVs and Humvees cranked up and took up their positions on either side and behind him, Jack was reminded of the old poem *The Charge of the Light Brigade*.

"All vehicles," he called over the radio. "Commence firing!"

***

The thing that had once been Vijay and was now masquerading as Kurnow watched from her vantage point below one of the main landing gear wells, where the main fueling port was located, as the Marine vehicles began to fire on the non-sentients moving up the runway.

Kurnow had originally planned to do anything necessary to ensure the destruction of the humans at the airport and prevent the escape of everyone who had been at the lab, but that had changed when it saw the humans load a biological sample cooler into the plane. It could only contain one thing: the virus. Spreading the virus now took precedence over killing the humans.

Until then, Kurnow had been stalling the efforts to refuel the plane, giving her non-sentient cousins a chance to draw nearer. It had gone so far as to disconnect one of the electric leads to the pump when Ferris had come down from the cockpit, furious at its feigned incompetence. Kurnow had contemplated killing him, but the FBI agents and, after Richards and the convoy arrived, the Marines, would have killed it, and there was no way to be sure no one else in the group could fly the plane.

After persuading Ferris to go back to the cockpit, Kurnow had reconnected the electrical lead and got the fuel flowing.

The sound of the pump on the tanker truck changed. Quickly moving to the controls, she saw that the tank was finally empty. She switched off the pump and shouted to one of the FBI agents guarding the nose hatch. "Tell the pilot we've got all we're going to get!" Then she ran to the wheel well, disconnected the fuel hose, and dragged it clear.

As she climbed into the truck to drive it clear of the plane, the number one engine began to turn.

***

"Hot damn, we've got gas," Ferris exclaimed. They'd taken on a hair over thirty-eight thousand pounds, which was a lot less than he'd wanted, but more than he'd hoped for. The truck could have been mostly empty, but instead had been mostly full. He hit the starter switch, keeping his eyes glued to the instruments as the inboard starboard engine began to spool up.

"How far can we go?" Richards asked.

"Like the old saying goes, it all depends." Ferris shrugged. "It's a matter of air temperature, pressure, prevailing winds, weight, and all the other technical stuff. Remember, in the old world, we'd have all that information at our fingertips and plugged in before I hit the starter switch. Now I don't know shit. Even trimming this bird is going to be a guessing game. I think I can guarantee five, maybe six hundred miles, and if we have a nice tailwind up our ass we might even make a thousand before we turn into a flying brick. But I'd stick with five hundred to be on the safe side. We could probably stretch it a few more if we absolutely had to, but I really like to walk away from landings."

Richards looked at him, shocked. "Only five hundred miles?"

"What, you were hoping for a trip to Bermuda? Come on. This plane can hold five times the amount of fuel that dinky truck pumped into the tanks." He moved the engine's throttle to the start position and breathed a sigh of relief when the fuel ignited and the engine temperature began to rise. Then he began the start procedure for number two. "We're lucky as hell we got what we did." Taking his attention from the instruments for a moment, he looked up at Richards. "When we were bailing out of SEAL-2, you suggested Denver. That didn't make sense then because we would've been eaten along the way. It makes a lot of sense now, because the bugs can't fly. Better yet, let's shoot for Colorado Springs. If we have a government left, it's probably at the NORAD bunker in Cheyenne Mountain."

Nodding, Richards said, "Then that's where we're going. If NORAD's gone, we're pretty much screwed, anyway."

THE LIGHT BRIGADE

The Bushmaster cannon on another of the LAVs went silent. One by one, they were running out of ammunition. But the machine guns kept hammering at the harvesters, continuing to pile them up in a flaming barrier around the southern end of the runway.

The harvesters were oblivious to their grievous losses, but they learned. Some vaulted impossibly high over or through the flames, while more made their way around the ends of the barrier formed by their flaming kin.

"They're flanking us," Terje said, pausing to reload the light machine gun he'd liberated from a dead Marine.

"I know." Over the radio, he said, "Watch the flanks! They're moving around behind the fire line, trying to get in behind us."

The vehicle commanders acknowledged, but one ended in a scream. The Humvee on the far right flank disappeared under a mob of harvesters that had poured over the fence from the cover of the Platte River.

The two LAVs on that side hammered the breach closed. Both of them ran out of cannon ammunition.

"Come on, Ferris," Jack said as he glanced over his shoulder at where the KC-135, looking like a toy, still sat motionless on the runway almost two miles behind him. "Get that fucking plane out of here!"

***

"What's happening?" Naomi heard the words as if someone else had spoken them. The pain from her leg came through in slow, lapping waves through the fog of the painkillers, and her thoughts were disjointed, unreal. It was hard to focus. "It feels like an earthquake."

Melissa peered down at her. "It's the engines. Mr. Ferris is getting ready to take off."

Groaning with the effort, Naomi propped herself up on her elbows and looked down the expanse of the cargo compartment toward the cockpit. The plane was frighteningly empty. She could see Carl. Renee. A few FBI agents and civilians. Everyone but Carl was strapped into the red fold-down seats along the sides of the fuselage.

No Jack. No Terje. No Marines. The only one in uniform was the Navy corpsman, who was tending one of the civilians.

"Where's everyone else?"

"Mr. Richards said...he said we had to go. Jack knew..." The tears came then. "He and Terje knew they wouldn't be coming back."

Naomi shook her head. "No. No. Come on. Help me."

Sitting up, she felt like she was going to vomit.

"You shouldn't get up!"

Naomi got to her feet, hanging onto the edge of the upper bunk that was still folded against the fuselage. "Help me or get out of my way."

Melissa slipped an arm around Naomi's waist, helping to support the side with the injured leg, and Naomi began a tortured stagger toward the cockpit.

Behind her, Koshka stayed on the bunk, watching with eyes dilated wide and her ears laid back. Alexander was a dark shadow on the floor underneath.

The corpsman saw her and got to his feet, rushing to her side. "Ma'am, you can't..."

"I can and I will." She shoved him away and kept moving. The cockpit seemed like it was a mile away and slowly rotating to the left. She nearly fell, but Melissa managed to keep her up.

"Naomi!"

She looked over to see Renee, who also got up and limped over.

"Don't try to stop me."

"I'm not." Renee put Naomi's other arm over her shoulder and wrapped her own arm around Naomi's waist to help Melissa. Melissa had managed to hold back her tears, but Renee was making up for her. "This whole thing is insane, but I don't know what else we can do."

They finally made it to the cockpit, giving Carl, who was standing between the pilot and copilot's seats, a scare when Naomi reached out and touched his arm.

"What the hell are you doing up?" He demanded. "I was just going to call up the Marines from our guard detail. You need to strap back in. We're taking off."

"No, we're not. We're not leaving the rest of them behind."

Behind him, through the windscreen, she could see flames licking the sky near the end of the runway and the threads of the tracers the Marines were firing into the dark, undulating mass of monsters that were trying to slip by them. "They're buying time with their lives so we can get the virus out of here," Carl told her. "That's the only thing that's important now, Naomi. The virus. All of us are expendable."

"No, we're not!" She wanted to slap him, but was afraid she'd fall. "With every one of those things that's spawned, every human life becomes more precious. Every single one, Carl. We've left enough people behind. I'm not leaving anyone else." She remembered all the people they passed by on their way to Lincoln from SEAL-2. They couldn't have taken many into the convoy, but they could have taken some. There were empty seats in the Humvees, the trucks, and the LAVs. They didn't stop because it might have endangered the mission. But if their mission didn't include saving people, especially their own, then what was the point? "I'm not leaving without them. If you want to go, that's fine. But I'm staying here."

"Jesus, Naomi, don't you dare pin that guilt trip on me! You know what's at stake here. We've got the entire world riding on our backs."

"I hate to break up the debate," Ferris interjected, "but every second you two stand there pissing on each other is that much more fuel we've burned. Make up your goddamn minds!"

"Naomi..."

She turned away. Shaking off Renee and Melissa, she staggered toward the trunk that led to the nose hatch. Her leg gave out, and she would have fallen had Carl not grabbed her.

"Goddamn you, woman," he muttered, helping her into the empty navigator's seat. "Ferris, get Dawson on the radio."

***

Jack was reloading his machine gun with the last box of ammunition when Carl's voice came over his helmet earphones.

"Dawson, do you read me?"

Jack glanced behind him at the gray shape at the far end of the runway. "Why the hell haven't you taken off, yet?"

"There's been a change in plans. Pack your bags and get your asses back here. You're coming along after all."

Holding back a bitter laugh, Jack told him, "Thanks for the offer, but there's no way. If we try to break contact and hightail it back to you, the bugs will follow right on our heels and the plane'll be overrun." There was no reply. "Richards, did you copy?"

Another voice came on the radio. "We're not leaving you and the others behind, Jack."

"Naomi, listen to me! There's no other choice!"

"Yes, there is. Just hold on. We're coming to get you."

"Naomi...Naomi?" He slammed the receiver on the machine gun closed, pulled the charging handle back, and squeezed the trigger just in time to blast a pair of harvesters about to hop into the Humvee to his left. "Naomi, did you hear me? Don't do this! Just take off and get out of here!"

There was no answer. Glancing back to the north end of the runway, he thought he saw the big jet move.

***

Ferris shook his head. "I don't have enough curse words to use for this level of stupidity. You idiots are going to get all of us killed."

"Just shut up and do your job," Richards told him.

"Yeah, I can do my fucking job, Richards," Ferris replied angrily. "You want me to taxi down to the south end of the runway, pick up our gang, and then just turn around and take off. But what you don't understand is that we may not be able to make that damn turn. This pig with wings doesn't have thrust reversers."

"Meaning what?"

"Meaning that the runway isn't wide enough for us to make a normal turn. Without thrust reversers, I can't make a partial turn, back up, then turn us the rest of the way. One of the landing gears could get stuck in the ground and then we'd be kaput."

"I saw a pushback at the 155th Squadron base."

Richards looked down to see the Air Force girl, Kurnow, sticking her head up through the hole in the floor that led to the nose hatch. "What the hell is a pushback?"

"It's a tractor to move planes around," she told him. "I can head over there in the tanker and get it, then meet you at the south end of the runway."

Richards looked at Ferris, who, after a moment, nodded.

"Jacobs! Coleman!" Richards called to two of the FBI agents in the cargo area. "Get over here!"

The two men unstrapped and hurried over.

"You two provide cover for her," he nodded to Kurnow. Kneeling down, Carl said, "Good luck."

She nodded, then disappeared back down the trunk.

To the two agents, Richards said, "Go! Tell the Marines in the Humvees we're moving down the runway and to follow along."

They quickly climbed down after Kurnow.

"Okay, here we go," Ferris said. He released the brakes and eased the throttles forward.

Over the roar of the engines coming up through the trunk to the nose hatch, Richards heard him say, "And I thought for a while there that we might actually survive this."

***

"Tango Two, Tango Two," Jack called out over the radio, "watch behind you! *Behind you!*"

It was too late. A group of dodging, twisting harvesters broke from behind a flaming heap of their kin and leaped aboard the LAV just to Jack's left. One of the Marines who'd been firing from the passenger compartment in the rear was thrown from the vehicle and pounced upon by two of the things, while the other creatures dove through the hatch to slaughter the other crewmen. The vehicle rocked from side to side until a plume of flame and smoke erupted from the hatches at the rear and the body of the commander, minus his lower half, was blasted from the turret to land on the far side of the now-burning vehicle.

"We're not going to be able to hold much longer," Terje said in between bursts from his machine gun.

They'd been gradually retreating to the north, forced to give up precious yards of runway to keep the harvesters from flanking them. No matter how many they killed, more appeared. The only thing that had saved the Marines was the brutal flammability of their enemy. Pyres of the dead acted as fortifications against the living.

But while the harvesters burned with wanton fury, they didn't burn for long. Their malleable flesh was like rocket fuel, blazing fast and furious. As the fires waned, more harvesters leaped over to start the cycle anew, with every new pile of smoldering dead coming closer and closer.

The end of the runway was shrouded in a pall of oily smoke from the guns and burning harvesters. Jack's eyes burned as much as his throat from having to breathe in the stinking mixture.

"Jack, look!"

He turned around and saw the nose of the KC-135 emerge from the smoke as it taxied toward them down the runway.

"Goddammit!" He fired a burst at a small group of harvesters that dashed toward the plane.

He missed, but the trio of Humvees escorting the plane made quick work of the attackers with their heavy machine guns.

That's when he noticed how fast the plane was moving. It wasn't anywhere near takeoff speed, but it wasn't poking along like a taxiing airliner, either.

Ferris brought the plane to a smooth halt as he reached two wide white lines painted on the runway, just past where an antenna mast rose from the field on the western side.

A squat tractor-like vehicle buzzed down the main taxiway, then turned onto a small access road of cracked and broken concrete that joined with the main runway.

Jack keyed his radio. "Pull back toward the plane, but don't let any of those bastards through!" Most of the machine guns had run out of ammunition, and half the men and women left to his tiny command were shooting the harvesters with shotguns and assault rifles.

The three Humvees added a welcome weight of fire, but it was going to be a close thing.

The tractor backed up to the nose gear of the plane. The blond airman whom he'd seen fueling the jet jumped out of the vehicle's cab and ran back behind it to connect the tow bar.

A group of three harvesters broke through and ran straight for her. None of the Marines dared fire a shot for fear of hitting the plane.

"*Watch out!*"

As if she had heard him, which was impossible over the din of the engines, she whirled around. Drawing a pistol from a shoulder holster, she aimed with cold precision and fired three times. All three harvesters went down.

"Christ," Jack said as the woman jumped into the tractor and got the plane turned around, pointing north on Runway 36.

Finished, she unhitched the tow bar and drove the tractor off the runway far enough for the engines to clear it before she ran back to the plane.

"Dawson," Richards called. "It's now or never!"

"Marines," Jack called over the unit common channel, "retreat to the plane, but watch your backs!"

Pulling up as close as they could without getting in the way of the plane's wings or behind the engine exhausts, the Marines abandoned their vehicles and made a fighting retreat.

The oncoming horde of harvesters pressed closer.

"Get aboard!" Jack ordered.

One by one, they climbed up through the nose hatch. Only ten Marines had survived.

"Ferris!"

"I'm here, Jack," the pilot said.

"Get off the brakes and get this bird moving or they're going to be crawling all over you."

"Shit."

The plane began to move. The Marines pushed and shoved one another up the ladder to the flight deck like their comrades were rounds of ammunition in a breech loading cannon.

Then Jack, Terje, and the airman were left, along with an army of harvesters charging toward them.

Jack grabbed the woman and shoved her toward the ladder. "Get up there!"

"No! You go first!" She raised her pistol and shot another harvester that had strayed too close.

"I'll go," Terje said. "I'm out." He tossed his now useless weapon to the ground and disappeared up the ladder.

"Go!" She fired twice more, and two more harvesters went down.

Jack took down a third before he said, "Bloody stubborn woman."

They were both running now to keep up with the plane. Jack grabbed the ladder and hauled himself up.

The airman was right behind him. He reached down and grabbed one of her hands and hauled her up into the cockpit, just as a dark appendage reached for her leg.

She fired another round from the Desert Eagle, and the arm was severed in a spray of ichor. Having fired the last round in the magazine, she dropped the pistol to the concrete that rushed by below them.

Jack dumped out the ladder as the plane suddenly accelerated, the turbofan engines rising to a deep, whining roar as Ferris pushed the throttles to the stops.

Bracing himself, Jack held onto the young woman's legs as she leaned down and grabbed the hatch handle. With a grunt of effort, she managed to slam it shut and latch it before he hauled her back up to the cockpit.

Collapsing into one another's arms, both heaving with exhaustion, Jack gave a whoop of joy as he felt the nose of the plane rotate, the nose gear coming up off the ground.

A moment later the main wheels left the runway with a bump, and the KC-135 and its passengers were in the air, with the earth and all its horrors falling away behind them.

AT WHAT COST

Jack lay against the cold metal of the floor, sensing the increased sense of gravity as Ferris pulled the plane's nose up into a climb. He heard shouts and cheers from the cargo compartment aft, and the Marines broke out in a round of applause. Someone started a chant of "Air Force! Air Force! More than a *Chair Force!*" Ferris shot back with some particularly colorful epithets, and everyone broke out laughing.

"That's for you as much as Ferris," Jack said to Kurnow, who was curled up against him.

She smiled. "I just did what I had to."

"And it's a damn good thing," Carl added. "Come on, you two," he said. "Get out here where you can be properly celebrated."

"You first, major," Kurnow said. "The best can wait for last."

"As you wish, staff sergeant," Jack said. As soon as he stepped through the doorway to the cargo compartment, he found himself in Naomi's arms, her lips on his. "Naomi," he said when their lips finally parted, "you should be in bed." Her skin was deathly pale, and her eyes, one brown and one blue, were terribly bloodshot. Glancing down, he saw that the bandages over the wound in her leg were red with blood.

"Don't you wish," she whispered in his ear. "You can take me back to my cot in a minute. But I need this. I think we all do."

"We made it!"

Jack looked down to see Melissa, clutching Alexander to her chest. She pressed up against Jack, and he reached down and gave her a hug, then rubbed the big cat's head.

Alexander lashed out with one paw and opened his mouth in a hiss.

"Chill out, cat," Jack said.

"I don't know what's wrong with him," Melissa said. "He scratched me, too."

Jack was just wishing they had some beer or champagne when one of the Marines pressed a metal flask into his hands.

"Drink up, sir," the man said with a wide grin.

Jack raised the flask in a toast. "To the Corps!" Then he tossed his head back and took a deep swig, hoping it wasn't filled with spit from chewing tobacco. A trail of liquid fire ran down his throat to his stomach, and he began to cough.

The Marines had a good laugh at his expense, then they cheered again as Kurnow appeared through the doorway, with Richards behind her.

Grinning at Kurnow, Jack was just about to hand her the flask and offer up another cheer for the Air Force when everything went to hell.

***

Alexander could sense the enemy falling away from the strange metal box in which he, his feline companion, and the humans were now encased. It was loud and foul-smelling, the strong scent of frightened, unwashed humans intermingled with noxious smells from man-made things and the lingering stench of the enemy. But now, at last, the fear began to leave him.

Except...a single threat signal emerged as the background sensory noise faded. It was clear and constant. It was *here*.

His companion felt it, too. She sat on the bunk above him, staring toward the end of the great metal box where the humans had gathered and were making noise.

Then the girl came and picked him up. He growled at her to signal his displeasure, but she either did not hear him or, as humans often tended to do, ignored his warnings.

He squirmed, but the girl held him firmly while making soothing noises. He clawed her as a warning, but did nothing more as she carried him toward the gathered humans, toward *it*.

His own human hugged the girl and reached down to stroke his head. He batted the human's hand away and opened his jaws to hiss a warning, a challenge.

The *thing* was close now. So very close.

Then *it* appeared, stepping through the doorway.

The enemy saw him, and its gaze locked with his for just an instant before Alexander attacked.

***

The Kurnow-thing's attention was focused on the big cat in the girl's arms, and so the harvester had no warning before the other beast, Koshka, dashed through the legs of the humans clustered around Kurnow to sink her teeth and claws into the malleable flesh of Kurnow's leg.

As Kurnow tried to kick Koshka away, Alexander sprang from the girl's arms, the partially undone pink bandages streaming behind him like war banners. His fangs bit deep into her throat.

Kurnow screeched in pain as she flailed at the cats with her hands and spun like a top, her arms smashing into the humans around her.

***

The force of Alexander's leap shoved Melissa backward into Renee, who instinctively pushed her forward again toward the monster. Kurnow — *the harvester* — tried to grab Alexander, but Terje was there, holding onto its wrist while a female Marine tried to grab the other one. Both were sent tumbling into the close-packed group of well-wishers, half of whom were knocked to the ground like bowling pins. Several of the Marines who still had weapons raised them, taking aim at Kurnow, when Jack shouted, "*Guns down! Hold your fire!*"

Mr. Richards tried to grab the thing from behind, but it slammed an elbow into his face, knocking him back into the cockpit.

The stinger on its cord, which looked like a long, skinny, slimy worm, shot out of Kurnow's chest to strike another Marine in the face. The man screamed and went down. The hand-length stinger, now dripping with lethal venom, pulled free and whipsawed through the air like it had a mind of its own, and everyone scrambled out of its reach.

Everyone, that is, except Melissa. Darting under the questing needle while Kurnow was preoccupied with Alexander, Melissa grabbed Koshka and yanked her clear of the harvester's leg. Koshka raked the back of Melissa's arm before Melissa half threw and half shoved the cat away.

Meanwhile, Alexander was moving with blinding speed, clawing, biting, and shifting position to attack again, just a hair's breadth ahead of the human-looking hands that were trying to kill him. The big cat shifted position to the harvester's back, sinking his teeth into her spine between the shoulders, right where Kurnow couldn't reach him. The harvester whirled around and let out a long shriek as Alexander bit into something more substantial than malleable tissue.

That's when Melissa grabbed him. Wrapping both arms around his chest, she yanked him loose, then turned around and sent him flying into the gawking group of terrified onlookers.

Both cats, their flight reflex overcoming that of fight, beat a hasty retreat to the rear of the plane.

Until then, Melissa's only thought had been to save the cats. She hadn't given any consideration to getting away herself.

In the blink of an eye, Kurnow had her by the throat and had pulled her close.

The stinger was hovering about half an inch from Melissa's eyeball, and she could feel the umbilical against the back of her head, pulsing and undulating where it emerged from Kurnow's chest. It made Melissa want to throw up.

"Stop," Kurnow said. "Put your weapons down or I'll kill her."

Then she brought up her other hand, which held a grenade. Bringing it to her mouth, she pulled the pin with her teeth and spat the metal ring out on the deck.

***

Naomi lay on the deck where she had landed after a Marine had bowled her over. She now watched with horrified eyes as the harvester, Kurnow, held Melissa, the damnable stinger pointing right at one of the girl's eyes.

"Stop," the monster said. "Put your weapons down or I'll kill her. Try to kill me," it gestured with the hand holding the grenade, "and you all die."

Everyone lowered their weapons.

Naomi managed to get to her feet with the help of Terje and one of the Marines.

The thing looked at her. "Naomi," it said, just before its face began to morph, the features losing their clarity as the malleable tissue reformed into a likeness of Vijay.

"*You,*" Jack hissed.

"Yes," it said in Vijay's voice. It was his face and his head, absurdly out of proportion atop Kurnow's petite frame.

"What do you want?" Naomi asked.

"I should think that was obvious enough," the thing said. "I want to live. I want to continue helping you. There is much yet that we can accomplish together."

Naomi laughed. "So you can what, slaughter the rest of us like you and your friends did to the technicians and Marines back at the lab?" She shook her head. "Please. We're fallible and don't always make the best choices, but we're certainly not that stupid."

"There's nothing you can offer us for your life," Jack said. "It's not worth shit."

"And hers?" The stinger drew a lazy pattern through the air, just above Melissa's skin.

Naomi hobbled forward a step, raising her hand in protest. "Don't! Don't hurt her. She's done you no harm."

"Listen to me, Naomi," it said. "We acted out of self-preservation." It turned to Jack. "Tell me that you were simply going to let us go, that we were going to be allowed to live."

"Actually, I did want to let you go," Naomi said. "The others didn't, but I wanted to set you free."

"You're telling the truth," it said. "Interesting." It glanced at the biological sample cooler beneath Renee's seat. Renee, seeing where the thing was looking, moved to block the thing's view. "You have the virus?"

"Yes. We took the other flasks from the incubator that your friends left behind."

"As proof of my good faith, I will tell you something you might wish to know, something that Kurnow knew. Something that will help spread the virus."

"And that is?"

Vijay smiled. "This plane. This flying gas truck. Did you know that this particular variant has two separate fuel delivery systems? One could be used to hold the plane's fuel, while the other could perhaps be sanitized and filled with a viral slurry."

"And then what?"

The thing's smile widened. "Then you could fly over infested areas, dumping the slurry from the boom, just as the pilots would sometimes jettison excess fuel before landing."

"Jesus," Jack said, turning to look at Naomi. "It'd be like a king size crop duster."

"Quite correct, Jack. It would not, perhaps, be optimal, for a large percentage of the virus would be killed off during dispersal. But much would survive to infect the target hosts." It looked at Jack. "Just think of the potential applications. In a single sortie, you could create a manageable harvester population over the area of a small city!"

Jack and Naomi exchanged a glance. *My God*, she thought. That could help solve one of their biggest problems, dispersal of the virus. One plane couldn't cleanse the world, but it could spread the virus far faster and farther than host to host transfer. If more of this particular aircraft type had survived, the possibilities were staggering. A plane like this could dispense thousands of gallons in a single flight.

"You could cover the globe in a matter of months," Vijay went on, "rather than decades."

"All right, so you've told us something that we probably could have figured out on our own." She wasn't going to give the harvester an inch, other than to pay out the figurative rope she hoped to strangle the thing with. "What else do you have to offer?"

"You know the challenges you will face from the legacy of my creators will be far from over, even after the virus sweeps across the globe to make my kind more...manageable. There will be mutations, possibly even hybridization. Things you cannot now foresee. Even with your genius, Naomi, you will not be able to conquer all these things alone, especially with so few scientists of your caliber left in the world. You will need my help."

"Naomi..." Jack said uneasily as she stood there in silence.

But he, like the harvester, misunderstood the reason she was silent. She was not considering its proposal. She was thinking furiously about how to free Melissa.

Then she had it. The idea wasn't foolproof by any means, but might work if Melissa and Renee could read her mind. Cocking her head to the side, she said, "You were never infected with the virus, were you?"

The Vijay-thing shook its head. "No. That, perhaps, is my one regret. I would have liked to pass on the gift to others of my kind."

"Maybe we can accommodate that wish," Naomi said.

"Here you go, you sorry bastard!"

The thing whipped its head around just as Renee lunged forward, raising the wand of the sprayer and squeezing the handle. While there had still been plenty of the virus-containing liquid in the tank, she'd used up all the pressure and hadn't had time or the need to pump it back up. But the cabin pressurization was far lower than at ground level, and served the same purpose. A cone of mist hit the harvester right in the face.

The harvester began to laugh.

***

Melissa recognized the spray for what it was: a diversion. As the harvester began to laugh in the weird man's voice, she grabbed the wavering stinger with her free hand. It was warm and slimy, and she wanted to puke as she touched it. Wrapping her fingers around the base of the pulsating venom sac, she shoved it upward, past her right ear, as hard as she could, right up into the harvester's fake human-looking lower jaw.

The laugh turned to a strangled screech as the thing let her go to clutch at its own throat.

Terje grabbed her and pulled her away as Jack charged forward past her, his body slamming into the thing and driving it backward into the cockpit.

***

Richards had kept quiet after the thing had sent him sprawling into the cockpit, staying out of sight behind what looked like a huge box of circuit breakers that went from floor to ceiling in the rear of the cockpit near the door to the cargo area. Being out of sight and out of mind of the harvester might yield an opportunity.

That opportunity came when Jack sent the thing flying into the cockpit, the grenade still clutched in one of its hands.

Come to daddy, Richards thought as Jack and the harvester slammed to the deck at his feet. The harvester was already transforming into its natural state, the clawed appendages emerging from the malleable tissue while the stinger whipped back and forth.

Ferris screamed.

Richards fell on the creature, ramming his knee into its head as he wrestled it for the grenade. Jack grunted with pain as the thing clawed him, and the wavy-bladed cutting appendage sliced through Kurnow's flight uniform, nearly cutting Richards' leg off.

The harvester twisted and bucked, slashed and jabbed. The stinger caught Richards in the chest, but was deflected by his body armor. He couldn't grab it, because it took all the strength he had in both hands to hang onto the grenade. The harvester's grip was too tight for him to pry it away, but he dared not let go.

Jack cried out as the harvester slashed his face just below his eyes. He lost his grip and rolled away from the fight.

While still clinging to the beast's hand that held the grenade, Richards twisted his body and caught the harvester's head between his thighs in a move he'd learned while wrestling in high school. Locking his lower legs together, he squeezed as hard as he could and twisted.

That's when the stinger found him. It stabbed him in the thigh, the tip driving deep into his femur.

The creature tried to whipsaw its body back and forth, trying to break away. Richards rolled with the motion and twisted, bringing the thing next to the opening to the hatch trunk. "Dawson! Push! *Push, damn you!*"

Bracing himself against the navigator's position, Jack kicked at the thing with his legs, driving it across the deck.

Richards rolled into the opening, dragging the creature with him.

The two of them slammed against the hatch at the bottom, and the harvester finally threw him off.

As the thing stood up, reaching for Jack and the flight deck with the grenade still clutched in its hand, Richards grabbed it in a half nelson hold and dragged it back down.

"Jack!" he cried. "Close the grate! *Close the goddamn grate!*"

* * *

Jack looked at the two heavy, bright yellow safety grates that covered the hatch trunk during flight to keep the crew from accidentally falling in. They were still flipped up, out of the way.

Richards screamed again. *"Close it! I can't hold on much longer!"*

The harvester reached up toward Jack with the hand that held the grenade.

It let the handle fly.

Jack's heart felt like a huge, cold stone in his chest as he reached up and flipped the forward grate down.

He cursed as the thing tried to force the grate open again, and he had to put all his weight on it to hold it. The stinger lanced up at him through one of the gate's openings, barely missing his neck.

He met Carl's gaze for just an instant. "Carl, no!"

* * *

Richards' body was on fire from the harvester venom, with more pain radiating from the bruises and broken bones the thing was dishing out as it writhed in a frenzy, trying to break his grip. But what he felt now didn't seem that much worse than some of the torturous beatings his father had given him as boy. Very few people had seen the scars on his body, and the only person other than his dead mother who knew the truth of them was Renee.

Renee. The thought of her was what had kept him going. That and his own stubborn refusal to yield. While he didn't always win, he'd never given in or given up on anything in his life, and he didn't intend to go out as a whimpering loser. His only true regret was that he hadn't had time to tell Renee goodbye.

He let go of the harvester with one hand long enough to find the hatch handle. For a brief moment, he wasn't sure he had the strength to pull it open. Then he remembered who he was.

The FBI's number one asshole.

His lips twisting into a bloody grin at his own joke, he yanked the lever and opened the hatch.

***

One second the harvester was there, inches away from Jack below the floor grate. The next it was gone, blasted through the hatch with Carl as the plane hemorrhaged its air in explosive decompression.

The grenade, too, was carried away to explode somewhere behind the plane.

Jack's ears felt like someone had rammed ice picks through them as the pressure dropped. Automated alarms were going off in the cockpit, blaring over the tornado of air that rushed past him and pinned him against the grate. Ferris was shouting, and the plane's nose pitched over into a dive. Jack was pelted by everything that had been floating around loose in the cockpit and cargo area, blown toward the hatch by the escaping air.

Someone grabbed his combat harness and hauled him back. Terje. He, too, was prone on the deck, a pair of Marines holding his legs.

In a moment, it was over. The hatch was still open, but the pressure from the slipstream flowing past the plane's nose kept it banging open and shut, but mostly shut.

They were alive. The harvester was gone.

And so was Carl Richards.

Jack stayed like that, sprawled on the deck, until Ferris leveled the plane at an altitude where they could breathe.

"You've got to get that hatch closed," Ferris shouted. "We won't make it halfway to grandma's house with the fuel burn rate at this altitude."

With a weary sigh, Jack nodded to Terje and the Marines. He pushed aside all the debris that had been trapped by the floor grate, then opened the grates themselves. With the Marines holding his legs, he dangled upside down just like the Kurnow-thing had done after they took off. After five tries, he managed to grab the handle and dog the hatch shut.

The Marines pulled him back up, and after flipping the grates back down, Terje helped him to his feet.

"Fly us the hell away from here, Mr. Wizard," Jack told Ferris.

"Right," the pilot said quietly. Tears glistened on the man's cheeks.

There's going to be plenty more of that soon, Jack thought grimly as he made his way back to the cargo hold. Naomi, who was so weak she could barely stand, hugged him, as did Melissa.

Then he turned to Renee.

She stood there, still clutching her garden sprayer, looking so alone and forlorn. She was trying so hard to be brave, to confront Fate with quiet dignity, but the facade crumbled as soon as he wrapped his arms around her.

"The goddamn moron," she sobbed against his chest as he held her tight. "Why did he have to leave me?"

"It was the only way he could save us," Jack whispered. "He knew it was the only way we had a chance to live."

AFTERMATH

Aside from the droning of the four engines, it was a quiet three hour flight to Colorado Springs. Ferris managed to make contact with NORAD, and everyone aboard was relieved to find out that the president and most of the cabinet had survived, and the airport was still secure, if overcrowded.

They were joined an hour out by a pair of F-16s that escorted them to Peterson Field, where Ferris made a smooth landing. Following an armed Humvee, that met them at the far end of the runway, he taxied to an open spot on the apron, right next to another KC-135.

A welcoming party of heavily armed airmen, half a dozen armored Humvees, two ambulances, and an Air Force blue bus was waiting for them.

"That was good timing," Ferris said as he shut down the engines. "We might've had enough fuel left to make it halfway to Denver before we crashed."

"All I want is to get off this fucking plane," Jack said. Kneeling down, he flipped up the yellow grates, trying his best to ignore the smears and spatters of blood, the blood of his dead friend, on the walls of the access trunk.

The hatch opened, and he was greeted by the muzzle of a shotgun held by a heavily armed airman.

Jack was not amused. "Put that thing away unless you want me to ram it up your ass."

"Sorry, sir. It's our procedure. If you'll come down one at a time, unarmed, I'd appreciate it."

"We've got wounded aboard. I'd like to get them out first."

"We'll get to them, major, but we have to clear the plane first."

"How about a couple crates for our cats, unless you want me to just toss them down to you?"

The young man squinted at him, then he spoke over his radio. "Will do, sir. We'll have some here in a minute."

Under the watchful eye of the shotgun-toting airman, a ground crewman poked a ladder up through the trunk, and Jack locked it in place. He stood up and turned to face aft, where everyone was lined up. "One at a time, no weapons. Let's go."

One by one, they disappeared down the ladder. *So few*, Jack thought bitterly. *So few of us are left.*

"Come on, Al," he said after the last of those who could move under their own power had left the plane. "Out you go."

Ferris looked around the cockpit. "I feel like the captain abandoning his ship."

"Don't worry. I have a feeling you'll be seeing this plane again."

The older man looked at him, and Jack was surprised how much he seemed to have aged since they left Lincoln. Ferris had barely known Kurnow, but her death had hit him really hard. "That's all I have left," he said quietly before he climbed down the hatch.

"Sir?"

Jack glanced down to see the airman and his shotgun pointing up at him. "If you'll come down, please."

"No, I won't come down, please." He scooped up Alexander, who had come to the cockpit, sniffing after the mountain air coming in through the hatch. "Here, see this? This is a cat. He's my cat, and the only thing he's upset about right now is that there's nothing in this plane for him to eat." Alexander looked at the airman and meowed. Jack went on, "I'm not a harvester. Neither is anyone else on this plane. Now get the medics up here so they can help our injured, including the woman whose work is going to save our asses, or so help me God I'm going to blow your head off. That's *my* procedure."

***

"I assure you, Mr. President," Naomi told President Lynch and the others gathered around the conference room table, "the virus will work."

Despite the protestations of Jack and the medical personnel who'd taken a look at Naomi's leg, Lynch had insisted that she be brought straight to one of the conference rooms of the underground NORAD complex after their plane landed. She hadn't wanted to leave Renee alone, either, but at least Terje and Melissa, along with the two cats, were with her. What had happened to the others, she didn't know.

But when she saw Lynch, she couldn't help but be overwhelmed. The man's hair had turned completely gray, he'd lost at least twenty pounds, and his eyes had deep circles under them that made him look like he'd gone ten rounds with a heavyweight prize fighter. His skin was paler than hers, and he had a persistent tic in his left eye. The stress of watching his country, his world, being torn apart was killing him.

"But how do you know? How do you really know without any kind of testing that the virus will kill the damn things, and that they didn't do some sort of bait and switch, targeting us, instead?"

"First of all, sir, they didn't need to target us with a virus. We'd already lost this war." The Chairman of the Joint Chiefs opened his mouth to say something, an angry look on his face, but Lynch cut him off with a gesture of his hand so she could continue. "I know what you're thinking: things would have been different if President Miller had bombed Los Angeles." The general rewarded her with a curt nod. "That only would have delayed the inevitable, and not by very long, not with outbreaks in half a dozen other countries. No. We lost this war as soon as that one bag of seed was stolen from New Horizons. There was no other possible outcome once the first seeds were planted or eaten. The genie was already out of the bottle."

She looked at the display that took up most of the wall at the end of the room. On it was a map of the world showing the estimated harvester infestations. Every country had widening swathes of red, and some had been entirely consumed by it. "Second, as I tried to explain to you earlier, the critical element, creating a strain of virus that would rapidly infect harvesters, was tested at SEAL-2 before the facility was destroyed. We know it worked, and worked very well, but it was effectively inert and unable to replicate a new set of genetic instructions. The harvester team gave us the keys we needed to fully enable the virus, and with the genetic information we derived from Melissa Wellington, I was also able to add in a kill gene to the viral Trojan Horse." She looked at the clock on the wall. "Even as we speak, the first harvesters exposed to the virus, the ones who escaped from the lab in Lincoln, will be experiencing what, for them, are the first very mild symptoms: a modest increase in body temperature coupled with glandular swelling and aching in the joints as the virus begins to take hold. I'll be surprised if they really even notice it at first onset." She looked back at Lynch. "Every one of them will be highly contagious, and we know they took samples of the virus with them to help spread it, thinking it was going to lift their species out of its lethal reproductive cycle and produce nothing but sentient harvesters that can replace us as the only sentient species on the planet." She smiled. "The virus will, in fact, do just as they intended." Her smile faded. "But about seventy-two hours after exposure, over ninety-nine percent of them will be dead."

"And how are they going to die?" The Chairman of the Joint Chiefs asked.

She stared at him. "Slowly and horribly."

"How," the president snapped.

"The disease infecting Melissa helped me pinpoint the gene sequences in the harvester DNA that control their skeletal growth," she explained, "and by comparing the genetic data from adult harvesters with immature creatures transitioning from the larval stage, I was able to identify the gene switch that shuts off their skeletal growth when they reach adulthood. The code I added to the virus both turns that switch back on and adds in a failsafe in the form of a sequence from a mutation in the human ACVR1 gene that causes a rare disease known as *Fibrodysplasia ossificans progressiva*, or FOP. In humans, FOP causes fibrous tissue like muscles and tendons to spontaneously ossify, literally turning those tissues into bone and causing spontaneous bone growth at the site of any injuries." She stared at the president. "The infected harvesters will be entombed in their own skeletons."

***

The harvester that had masqueraded as Zohreh, that had kidnapped Naomi from the lab in Lincoln when the harvesters had escaped, could no longer move its limbs. It had known, of course, that the virus would produce uncomfortable symptoms for a time. That was to be expected as her body's DNA was transformed.

But the discomfort had become something more ominous near the forty-eight hour mark after exposure. The ache in its joints had become acute, and after a few more hours had become so painful that it could no longer walk. Soon after that, every joint was engulfed in fiery pain, even when Zohreh lay completely still.

After about sixty hours, the harvester guessed, it could not move its limbs at all, as if they had been fused in place and filled with molten metal.

Then the true pain began, literally in every bone in the thing's body. It could feel itself slowly reshaping, and realized that its bones were growing again, just as they had when its body transitioned from the larval to adult stage. The bone growth of its species during that phase was phenomenally fast, the malleable flesh of the larva condensing into the adult form, the carbon fiber-like bones forming in little over twelve hours.

The Zohreh-thing understood then that something in the viral payload had switched the genetic signal for bone growth back on, and its skeletal structure was growing out of control. The bones were expanding in a completely random fashion, causing unbearable agony. Some of the bones, starting with the rough equivalent of the left femur, snapped under the pressure exerted by the frantically growing bones on the other end of the knee joint. The bones in the thorax bent and cracked as the ribs and segments of the spine elongated and twisted out of shape. Its claws extended and curled inward, the sharp nails at the end spearing the wrist joints. The plates of the skull thickened, slowly crushing the brain. The pain was excruciating...and inescapable.

Near the end, even the malleable tissue began to transform itself into a thick, hard carapace of twisted bone tissue that encased the thorax, and random bone spurs grew inward, slowly skewering the internal organs.

It was almost a relief when Zohreh was found by a larva on its random quest for food .

***

"It's a miracle."

"I'll take that as a compliment, Mr. President," Naomi said with a smile. Lynch still looked like a shell of what he had been before he'd assumed the presidency, but hope and determination had replaced weariness and despair.

"It was intended as one, Dr. Perrault. Please continue."

Naomi gestured to the map display behind her showing the status of the harvester infection across the globe. Instead of showing the unstoppable spread of harvesters, it showed the success of the ongoing containment operations. "Today marks the end of the sixth week since the virus was released," Naomi went on, "and multiple streams of intelligence reporting are showing clear and unambiguous signs..."

"Now that doesn't happen very often," the Chairman of the Joint Chiefs said quietly with a wink to Naomi. Several of the military officers, none of whom wore anything less than a single star on their rank insignia, chuckled. Jack was among them as a newly minted brigadier general by direct order of the president.

"...that the harvesters are being wiped out in the infected zones," Naomi went on. "Fifteen major population centers have been recategorized from red to yellow status." Red, of course, meant that the area was overrun with harvesters. Yellow indicated that the harvester population was largely destroyed. "I'm also very pleased to report that Phoenix has been added to the cities on the green list." Areas on the green list were safe zones that could be resettled. "That's the first city with a pre-war population of over a million that's been placed on the list, and I believe we'll see San Antonio and the entire island of Oahu added next."

That earned her a round of applause, led by Lynch, and she bowed her head and tried not to blush.

When the applause died down, she went on. "We have eight virus production centers now, up from six a week ago. Centers in Norway, Russia, China, India, and Argentina will be opening within the next two weeks." She gestured to the map. "As you can see, our main problem now is distribution. As you know, we began the mass clearing operations using the surviving KC-135T aircraft from the 171st Air Refueling Squadron, converted to carry a viral slurry in their fuselage tanks. The first missions established a cordon here, around Cheyenne Mountain, and other surviving critical facilities and population centers. Since then, we've been trying to put every potential asset from crop dusters to hand hand-held sprayers into service." She paused. "While it's a bit of a gloomy fact to mention, in about six months nearly every human being on the planet will be an asymptomatic carrier of the virus."

An admiral who was new to Naomi's weekly briefings looked at her quizzically. "And what exactly does that mean, doctor?"

"It means that we don't suffer from the disease, but our bodies harbor the virus."

"In other words, sir," Jack clarified, "an adult harvester can catch the virus from an infected human. If they so much as breathe the same air, they'll catch it. Or if they eat one of us."

The admiral *humphed*. "Nice. I guess that should put the fear of God into any of the impostors, then, shouldn't it?"

Naomi nodded. "Four were inside this very complex, having somehow avoided the cat patrols. But they didn't escape the virus every one of us now carries."

The president leaned forward. "So what does the future look like in your crystal ball, Naomi?"

"We have a long haul ahead of us, sir," she told him grimly. "We're gaining ground quickly, of course, but the virus isn't one hundred percent lethal, and the harvester population is still growing at an exponential rate in areas that haven't yet been inoculated." She paused. "If my estimates are correct, we could lose as many as five hundred million to a billion more people over the next three years."

The room fell deathly silent. "How can the harvesters kill so many more of us when we're wiping them out left and right?" Lynch spoke the words in a whisper.

"Most of those deaths won't be from direct harvester attacks, sir," she told him. "We knew early on that even if we were able to contain the harvesters, we'd still suffer dreadful casualties from starvation, followed by disease. Remember, most of the world's grain and rice producing regions have been devastated, with either the population eliminated or the land itself laid waste. And the widespread destruction of the transportation infrastructure means we often won't be able to get food and other essentials from where they're produced to where they're needed."

"Please tell me you're working on a plan to deal with this," Lynch said, looking at the Secretary for Agriculture.

"Yes, sir, we are," the secretary said, "but until we have reliable communications again, it's hard to find anyone in a position of authority beyond the military bases and the green zones." She frowned. "It's the Wild West out there right now, but we'll deal with it."

"Another longer term issue," Naomi said when Lynch turned back to her, "is that we don't know how much of the infected grain may still be out in the biosphere. As best we know, it was never planted here, and whatever was in Russia was most likely destroyed by their nuclear strikes. But we have no way to know how much might have been planted in the other countries that received samples of the original seeds. We could have recurring outbreaks until we can track down and destroy the last of it. That also assumes that it doesn't naturally hybridize — crossbreed, if you will — with other varieties of corn. If that happens, it could take years or decades, perhaps longer, to completely neutralize the threat. Any resulting harvesters shouldn't last long after being exposed to the virus, but there's always the possibility that they'll develop an immunity or adapt to the virus. I think that's unlikely in the short term, but it's something we can't allow ourselves to forget."

"I don't think that'll happen, doctor," Lynch told her as he eyed the map. "I don't think we'll be forgetting any of this for a very long time."

***

Jack rapped on the door of the small conference room. After the second knock, Melissa opened the door.

"Jack!" She stood up on tiptoe to kiss his cheek, then wrapped her arms around him to give him a hug.

"Hey, kid! Take it easy or you'll break my ribs!"

"Pansy," she said with a smile as she let him go and stepped back as Alexander and Koshka moved past her into the room, their tails in the air.

"Oh, my Lord," he whispered as he took a closer look at the girl's face. He hadn't seen her in the two weeks since he left on his most recent deployment, and the ugly lesions and tiny fibers that had covered most of her face and head were nearly gone. Turning to Naomi, who stood beside him on crutches, her broken leg still encased in a cast. "You did this?"

Naomi nodded, a very happy and proud expression on her face. "Yes. I told her the gene therapy was risky, but she insisted on trying it. The one positive legacy from the harvester disaster is that we might be able to cure many diseases. She was our test case."

"I'm not hideous anymore," the girl said, touching her face with her hands. "I may not be great-looking, but I don't feel like a monster."

"You've always been beautiful," Jack told her. "Anyone who ever thought any different was an idiot."

"Oh, you smooth talker, you." Renee came to the door. "Get your asses in here before anybody else smells what I'm cooking and crashes the party."

She ushered them in, giving Jack a hug before she hung a sign on the outside of the door and closed it. "Those Air Force guys are worse than bloodhounds. They can smell my cooking a mile away and come begging like Oliver Twist."

Naomi burst out laughing. "What did that sign that you put on the door say?"

"Emergency Executive Meeting. Stay The Hell Out."

"You did not," Jack said as he moved over to the table that Renee had turned into an ad-hoc kitchen with two hot plates heating a skillet and sauce pan, a crock pot, and a toaster oven. He found himself salivating at the aromas of garlic and basil from whatever she was cooking.

She gave him an evil smile. "I did. Come on, sit down and let's eat. I haven't seen you in ages, and you look like you've lost weight. I can fix that."

Jack and Naomi sat down while Renee and Melissa served up the food. "Bruschetta with sautéed mushrooms, *tortelli di patata*, and stuffed *agnolotti*."

"Just don't ask what they're stuffed with," Melissa whispered. Her lips twisted up in a smirk.

"Shut up, smart ass, or you'll be back to eating those God-awful MREs for the rest of your life." She poured the girl a glass of wine. Melissa gave her a shocked look. "If you're old enough to fight harvesters," Renee said, "you're old enough to have a glass of wine."

Naomi looked at the food Renee was serving. "Where did you get the ingredients for this? Even the president doesn't eat this well."

Renee laughed. "Why do you think Jack keeps going on all his little junkets? He's not killing harvesters, he's doing my shopping. Now shut up and eat."

Naomi turned to Jack. "Is that true?"

He chuckled. "Sort of. Now eat." To Renee, he said, "How are you holding up?"

"Okay, I guess. I still miss the Bald Bastard. I guess I always will, but what can you do?" She wiped her eyes with the back of her hand. "At least I've got Melissa. I'm working on corrupting her properly. That's become my life's work."

"Yes, I heard," Naomi said as she wiped her mouth with a napkin. "Someone's been putting shaving cream on the ear pieces of the phones in the congressional staff spaces." She looked at Melissa with narrowed eyes.

"I have no idea what you're talking about," Melissa said with complete innocence.

Renee guffawed. "Hey, somebody has to brighten this place up. You should have seen General Reynolds. He laughed his butt off about that. In private, of course."

"Well, just keep your pranks out of the operations areas, okay?" Jack gave the girl The Look, just like his dad used to give him.

"I know," she complained. "I'm not stupid."

"No, you're not," Renee told her. "She's been a huge help to us in rebuilding what's left of the Internet. She might even be as good as me, someday." After another sip of wine, she said, "So what's the story with you two?"

"We're leaving for Norway tomorrow," Naomi told her. "I've got a round of meetings with the Scandinavian and Russian scientific advisors, and Jack's going to go talk to the military people."

"That's going to be fun," Jack tossed back what was left in his wine glass, and Renee poured him some more. "We're trying to sort out the mess in northern Russia. Half their population seems to think the grass would be greener in Finland or the Baltic countries, with the people up in the far north clamoring to get into Norway. Harvesters are still running loose, because large-scale sanitization operations have only just started in most places outside the States. But we want to defuse that powder keg before we have another war on our hands." He smiled. "So we'll get to spend a week on an all-expenses paid vacation to Tromsø in Norway."

"God," Renee said. "I hope you remember to take your heated undies. Why are they holding it there?"

Jack shrugged. "Security. The city is on a small island. They've sprayed every inch of the place with the virus, and the Norwegian Navy has locked it down and put a ring of troops around it. The Norwegians are involved in the issue, but not nearly so much as the Finns and the Baltic countries, which have already had some battles with Russian forces, on top of the harvesters. No one could agree on any other place to hold the talks."

"Will you see Terje?" Melissa asked.

"Yeah, he's on the Norwegian delegation, along with another officer they call The Troll. You'd love him, and he has a cool cat named Lurva, too." He gave Melissa a thoughtful look. "Tell you what. How would you like to go?"

Her mouth fell open. "Could I? Really?"

Shrugging, Jack said, "I don't see why not. As a matter of fact, we'll need a cat-herder while we're in the sessions. Cats will be allowed in the rooms, of course, but we're supposed to take someone to keep them out of trouble while we're working. I thought you might be interested."

"Will Uncle Al be flying us?"

Al Ferris had been an emotional basket case after the escape from Lincoln, and Melissa had taken it upon herself to cheer him up. It had taken her a while, but she had finally cracked through his outer shell. He'd returned to his irascible normal self, and had even begun teaching her to fly.

"He's on the return side of a long range sanitization sortie," Jack told her, "which is why he couldn't make dinner tonight. But yeah, he'll be flying us out in the morning in one of the corporate jets."

"But before you decide for sure," Naomi added, "you need to know that this is actually the first part of a much larger trip. After Norway, I've got meetings scheduled in China, Japan, and India, and we might have to stop at some other places, too. Lots of people need our help out there, so you probably won't be back here for a while. You'll be stuck with us and the cats in all sorts of interesting, exotic places."

Melissa's face lit up with delight until she remembered something. "What about Renee? Are we leaving her behind?"

Renee wrapped an arm around her shoulders. "I'm staying right here, kid. No more planes for me. Not ever, if I can help it." She smiled, but Jack saw the sadness in her eyes. "So you have to promise to call me every night on the satcom and report on how many phones you rigged with shaving cream."

They all laughed. It was a sound that warmed Jack's heart. It was the sound of a loving family, bound together by fate, if not by blood.

More than that, it was the sound of hope.

WANT TO GET AN EMAIL ABOUT NEW RELEASES?

If you'd like to get a heads-up on upcoming releases, sales, or giveaways, head on over to my site at AuthorMichaelHicks.com and join my mailing list!

DISCOVER OTHER BOOKS BY MICHAEL R. HICKS

In Her Name: The Last War Trilogy
First Contact
Legend Of The Sword
Dead Soul

In Her Name: Redemption Trilogy
Empire
Confederation
Final Battle

In Her Name: The First Empress Trilogy
From Chaos Born
Forged In Flame
Mistress Of The Ages (Coming Soon)

***In Her Name* Trilogy Collections**
In Her Name: Redemption
In Her Name: The Last War

Harvest Trilogy
Season Of The Harvest
Bitter Harvest
Reaping The Harvest

ABOUT THE AUTHOR

Born in 1963, Michael Hicks grew up in the age of the Apollo program and spent his youth glued to the television watching the original Star Trek series and other science fiction movies, which continues to be a source of entertainment and inspiration. Having spent the majority of his life as a voracious reader, he has been heavily influenced by writers ranging from Robert Heinlein to Jerry Pournelle and Larry Niven, and David Weber to S.M. Stirling. Living in Florida with his beautiful wife, two wonderful stepsons and two mischievous Siberian cats, he's now living his dream of writing novels full-time.

CPSIA information can be obtained at www.ICGtesting.com
Printed in the USA
BVOW07s0640060214

344020BV00001B/298/P

9 780988 932159